A CAUSE I

MICHAEL HOLLIN

For my mother Sue; the eternal maternal goddess.

'The furies are at home in the mirror; it is their address. Even the clearest water, if deep enough can drown. Never think to surprise them. Your face approaching ever so friendly is the white flag they ignore. There is no truce with the furies. A mirror's temperature is always at zero. It is ice in the veins. Its camera is an x-ray. It is a chalice held out to you in silent communion, where gaspingly you partake of a shifting identity never your own.'

Reflections, by R. S Thomas
(From 'No Truce with the Furies')

Prologue

Liptovský Mikuláš, Slovakia

A secret's power is self-fulfilling. The moment it is revealed to the world it loses its defining characteristic. It is no longer a secret. But hopefully by then its power has already been applied to its full effect, its intentions realised.

The view from the cottage set deep into the forest looked out on a set of two mountain ranges; the High and Low Tatras. August had brought scorching thirty degree heat. At ground level the air had a sweet, sticky viscosity. Up in the Tatras there were swirls of fog and moisture, guarding the peaks like a warm blanket of particles, preserving the secret of their beauty, keeping them pure and untainted.

The cottage was essentially a log cabin with modifications. There were two storeys to the structure. The attic at the top served as sleeping quarters for six men. It was littered with sleeping bags and self-inflating mattresses and it was supported by four wooden beams. The ground floor comprised of one room after partitions had been knocked through, offering a combined living and kitchen area. In back there was a small bathroom.

The living room was decked out with old communist furniture. The colour scheme betrayed its history; greys and browns predominated, dull and repressive. Strewn across the sofa were piles of waterproof clothing; textile armour worn in battle against the savage ravage of the Slovak mountain elements. A small black and white television mounted on brackets played back a muted

1

documentary from the corner of the den. It showed several men inside a cave studying stalagmites. There were dirty dishes in the sink; bright red crockery covered the white ceramic surface.

The place accommodated six men; six scientists, to be accurate. Unity-Six, they were called. All through the day they had laboured diligently to keep their secret exactly that – a secret. Medical journals and pharmaceutical text books were strewn haphazardly throughout the den.

Beakers and funnels sat on shelves in the kitchen. The experiment had been a success, so much so that six lives were now in immediate danger. They had to pack up and be ready to leave in twenty four hours. The cabin had to be left in a state that denied they had ever been there. Tomorrow their transportation would arrive and they would be out of the country, flown away to a safe place of hiding.

For the remainder of the day they quietly worked. They did not say a word to each other, for nothing needed to be said. They were all petrified, but there was no point in dwelling on fear, each one of them realised. So they kept themselves busy, distracted; detached from small talk and focused on the task in hand.

They cleaned up the den, cooked, ate and washed the dishes. They packed up their belongings, cleared the attic, and finally they dusted the whole place down. Their fingerprints were a bane on the mission, so they removed every trace of their habitation in the cottage.

When night fell, the air cooled. A sudden burst of sound marked the beginning of a thunderstorm. At intermittent intervals, potent blasts of blue light lit up the brush around them. Nature is impressive when man is protected by a fortress of construction from its involuntary mood swings. They bunked down in wooden chairs on the porch, under the shelter of the sloped cabin roof, sleeping in their clothes.

There was a rustic smell of smoked flesh in the air; the cinders of a barbecue dwindled on a deathbed of charcoal. Soon they would be gone forever, their kinetic energy transformed into another source to fuel the planetary routine. With the next new light of dawn the men of science would have to be ready. They would have to abandon their own routine; there would be no time for it. The men of science would have to simultaneously become men of faith.

As the hours of the early morning encroached, the storm died, and the Tatras were at peace. Sound was reduced to the whistling of the wind through the forest trees. The six men dozed but could not properly relax; they could not shut down fully. They stayed half-alert, wary, afraid.

Their experiment would change the world. It would eradicate a bitter enemy that had plagued humankind for decades; an evil force that hit without warning or remorse, just like nature's involuntary mood swings. It would be the ultimate panacea.

They were still in the first throes of processing; the test product, the concept. Now it had to be marketed, mass produced and sold, but only on the black market, the only place that could offer it a home. The only market it would be safe in. The only market where it could prosper and take full effect, to begin with.

The porch was stocked with Winchesters; high calibre .300 single shot hunting rifles with an adjustable trigger and a modifiable scope. They were loaded with Barnes X bullets. Each weighed just over three kilos and had been purchased in Scotland.

The scientists had survived for weeks on roe and fallow deer. The small arsenal of weaponry were a mild comfort to the scientists, who were not military nor field trained, but required some kind of protection nonetheless, not least from angry black bears stalking the Slavic wilderness. They preyed that their location had been kept a secret.

An hour passed. It was pitch black. The men dozed in rapid succession on the porch, positioned in a neat line like pieces on a backgammon board. They tossed and turned, trying to find a comfortable position inside their sleeping bags, their heads resting on pillows made of concrete. The sleeping bags were well equipped for the outdoors, covering temperatures down to -12 degrees, so the scientists would not freeze to death.

It was well into the early hours and nocturnal creatures disturbed the night with their mating calls. Slovakia has a diverse ecosystem, and the woodlands surrounding the cabin are home to the praying mantis, tree snakes, eagles and dormice, amongst thousands of other creatures offering their own contribution to biodiversity.

Then something happened to the third scientist from the right. There was a loud booming sound that disturbed the tranquillity of the nocturnal landscape. The man's head suddenly exploded in a hiss of muscle, bone and sinew, like an egg being beaten out of its shell. Bright crimson seeped forth in a mist.

He had been shot in the head, the blast coming from a high powered rifle; perhaps another Winchester, perhaps something more solid like a Ruger. It did not make much difference. He was dead the moment the bullet entered his skull, spewing out lead and mercury into his brain.

The five men with heartbeats lurched up. They did not have long to process what had happened or act accordingly. They grabbed for their torches tucked in pouches inside their sleeping bags. Each took a Winchester, fully loaded, and prepared to use it for the first time on meat from their own kind. By the time they stood they had become four. A second blast hit the fifth man in the back of the neck. Gravity pulled the body's two hundred pounds to the ground with effortless efficiency.

'Get inside!' one scientist screamed. The four men burst open the cabin door and dived inward for cover. Three men successfully entered the den. The fourth turned back to catch a glimpse of their attackers. He saw nothing in the darkness but felt two explosions of pain in his chest and knew the inevitable. Internal haemorrhaging wasn't good. Then he bled to death.

Already their group had been halved. Whoever their assailants were, they were expert marksmen. The three men took up positions by the cabin window, switched the rifles to night mode and glared through their telescopic sights. They tried to pinpoint the enemy through a spectrum of green neon light covering the trees and the brush.

One of the group's men spotted three distinct human silhouettes running toward them four hundred yards up ahead. They all carried rifles. The man by the left window strained his eyes and lightly touched the trigger with his right hand. He began to squeeze it softly then took aim. He lifted up his head a fraction to get a better view. It was the last thing on Earth he did.

Another explosion arrived to disturb the woodland with sound and light. Another mangled mess of human skull fragments splattered on the concrete façade of the cabin, giving it a fresh new lick of paint. Some of them hit the two men remaining. They screamed out in fear and disgust.

'How do they know our location?' one said to the other.

'Inside job. We've been compromised. No other possibility.' He was the leader, the point man. He was in his early fifties. His blonde hair had receded back a way, and was slowly turning grey. He had an ugly scar on his left cheek; the product of a long-forgotten, backfired experiment.

The younger scientist turned back to the window, watching the hostiles advance closer. Two hundred yards and closing. He was in his thirties and had long brown hair worn in a fashionable ponytail. He took aim and fired his rifle. Three booms, three shots, all misses. Splinters of bark flew up in front of them. The hostiles took cover in the underbrush.

'What the hell are we going to do?' the younger man screamed helplessly. His name was Stewart Banks.

'Die' the leader stated coldly. 'We're out of options, outnumbered, outflanked. We're pinned down in here.' His name was Paul Murphy.

Banks reloaded and fired again. Both men waited, surveying the landscape in front of them. Nothing stirred. They would not find what they wanted out front. The three hostiles had split up in wide positions and snuck around to the back of the cabin like sly pythons. And now they were ready to move in.

5

Suddenly a crashing sound came from behind the two scientists, as shattered glass fell down the stairs and landed by their boots. They had lost. The three hostiles burst down the stairs and stopped dead in front of them. The scientists whirled around to face them, taking off their night vision goggles in resignation.

The first of the three hostiles took out a radio with his free hand and spoke into it. 'This is Chaplin. We found them, killed four, two prisoners. Confirm action, over.'

A voice garbled a reply at the other end. It was not clear what was said from where the scientists were knelt, but they had understood the command; they had heard it in the tone of the man's voice, felt the cold menace of inevitable doom grip them like snake venom.

'Understood, over.' The man calling himself Chaplin replaced the radio on his belt clip and peered down at his captives. They were a nervous wreck. 'Gentlemen, I apologise profusely, but I have my orders. And what is a soldier without his orders? He is only half a man.' He grinned as he squeezed the trigger.

Paul Murphy was splattered with bullets. The porch was shattered with the glass from the front door and windows. But Chaplin had misjudged his last target, having failed to notice him reach into his pocket and bring out a small device; missed him flicking a lever and activating the small button. But he did not miss the ensuing explosion, the devastating effect of C4.

The other two hostiles hit the deck and Chaplin rocketed forward with the force of the blast. He sustained minor injuries, but he had been too close to the blast for anything more terminal. The shrapnel hadn't had time to pick up momentum at such a short distance.

Low speed, little gravitational effect and a minimal mass at ten yards meant it did little damage. It was a common misconception – it seemed obvious to anyone that the closer you were to the epicentre of a bomb-blast, the greater damage you would incur. But often the opposite was the case. Lieutenant Corporal Matthew Croucher found that out the hard way in 2008, when he jumped on a

6

grenade to save his comrades from oblivion during an operation in Afghanistan.

Croucher escaped with minor bruising and was awarded the George Cross by the Queen, one of only twenty living people to covet the award, and the first since the Second World War. One hero in a million.

The blast had propelled Banks through the shattered window and out onto the porch. He hadn't looked back; he had simply vaulted at full speed into the forest. Chaplin's accomplices were incapacitated, but Chaplin gave chase, sprinting after him.

Banks was the last one left; he was on his own. His escape was treacherous in the dark, without rifle or flashlight. He stumbled through the trees, sweating and panting, adrenaline feeding him like a mother to a baby. He knew if he made it another mile, there was a road to the east that would take him back to the village. He would have more options there. To his west was a rocky outcrop that jutted down into Žiarska valley below.

Another boom penetrated the silent night. Another rifle shot sprang up like a rattlesnake, the venomous bullet ripping into his left calf, and he hit the deck. He writhed in pain, clutching at the wound. He started to crawl forward.

'Stop right there Mr Banks.' Chaplin had been through rigorous training routines. He'd had to run flat out for miles while officers incited him with their degradations, all the while taking tabs on his times. Now he caught up with the scientist. He was barely out of breath. 'I'm here to put an end to this, to your experiment, to you.'

'Please' Banks begged. 'This isn't about your orders. This is about making the world a better place, about saving millions of lives. You cannot get in the way of that.'

Chaplin took a step forward. 'I can, and I will.' Before he could shoot Banks he was pushed to the ground. A deep growl had penetrated the silence. Not a gunshot, but a primal, natural roar, echoing nature's frustration at human trespass.

Banks glanced back and saw Chaplin wrestling with a large brown bear. They were not uncommon in this part of Slovakia. They were an endangered species hunted as a profitable business venture. They had been known to attack tourists before.

And now, provoked by this intruder, trespassing on his habitat, this one was going to work on Chaplin. It mauled him and dug its claws into his flesh. Chaplin screamed.

Banks sensed an opportunity for survival, so he ran like crazy. But he was heading in the wrong direction; not east, to the road, he was heading west, to the rocky outcrop. And then he reached it, glaring down into the abyss at the bottom.

He heard water gushing; a waterfall. It was a long, hard drop to the valley at the bottom. He glanced back and saw the unbelievable; saw Chaplin limping towards him. Somehow he had taken care of the bear. The species was threatened even further by the dwindling of its numbers; although Chaplin had not killed for profit, he had done so for survival first and foremost, and for sport thereafter.

And now he wanted to finish his task and reduce the number of his fellow species, so that he could report a mission accomplished status back to his superior.

Banks made a decision. He had worked hard for the cause, a cause he truly believed in. What their experiment would achieve would make the world a better place. It would save millions of lives, and dollars. He had not exaggerated. And desperate times called for desperate measures.

Without a second thought, or an intervention from Chaplin, he jumped, rocketing downward into a black void which took no hesitation or displeasure in swallowing him up. Chaplin heard a distinct thud at the bottom and smiled; it was over. He was relieved.

He took out the radio and called his boss. 'It's Chaplin. They're dead; all of them. Unity-Six are no more. We need medical supplies; my men sustained minor injuries. Now get me the hell out of here.'

A distant voice garbled a reply. 'I'll send the chopper.'

Chapter One

Chester, England. Monday 20th February. 2:30 p.m.

Six months later.

The man moved like he had never moved before. Puddles of sweat dripped down his face. His eyes were wide in concentration, and determination. He was bent forward, his triceps bulging with the effort. He was running out of time. The digital readout in front of him counted down; red glowing numbers glaring back at him. Reminding him.

He had to beat it. He couldn't fail. His pride was too strong. Twenty seconds. The other man was stood next to him. He shouted. 'Come on! You're not going to make it at this rate!' He smiled devilishly, as if he was enjoying watching the other man strain his entire body in effort.

Fifteen seconds. It was going to be a close call. Both men felt the adrenaline and the testosterone fuel their eagerness. Ten seconds, then five. The final countdown. Three. Two. One. Both men braced. Then there was a bleeping sound. It was over.

*

James Loxbridge stopped pedalling. He breathed out in relief and saw the clock on the bike stuck at zero. Then the other man hit him on the back. 'You made it! You beat your old time! James, I have to hand it to you, you're impressive!'

James swivelled off the bike like a bench gymnast at the Olympic Games, and sucked on a water bottle, feeling the cooling sensation of hydration. His heart was hammering like a metronome set to a fast jamming rhythm.

He checked his pulse by placing two fingers to his wrist, counting the beats for twenty seconds. He calculated his heart rate; one seventy. Nearly three times the norm. Then it began to slow down. The thudding within subsided. His twenty nine year old body was in good shape.

'What's the final count Matt?' he managed between deep breaths. He dried his forehead with a towel.

'Two thousand metres, three minutes thirty eight seconds. Three seconds up on your old time. I'll adjust the board.'

'Team effort, Matt. You make one hell of a training programme.'

'And you're one hell of a student.'

The gym, like most tenements in the neighbourhood, was a structure steeped in history. It stood in a secluded spot up on Eastgate Row. You'd have to have walked past it to know it was there. It was a cosy place to work out, especially in winter.

The warmth of the mint green paint lick on the walls was complemented by small decorative evergreens caressed with fairy lights draped across them, spilling out a sickly moon-white glow. They were akin to a lingering Christmas decoration that some festive desperado had forgotten to take down.

It was a small place with just two rooms; one held the bikes, the rowing machines and the squat balls, the other was for the cardiovascular machinery and the weights. James had a generic programme intended to build stamina, muscle tone and strength.

He loved to work out and he loved Dutch Houses gym. He would come on a Saturday afternoon, just before closing time when it was dead. He'd chat to Amber on the desk and then he'd have the whole place to himself, like his very own personal gym; a home five minutes away from home.

James hit the showers, changed into casual fatigues then headed home. Chester was now home; a nice town, one of the original Roman ramparts that had blossomed into an impressive city. It was still walled. Remnants of the old amphitheatre lay on Little St John Street, near the County Court.

The city was a tourist attraction all year round. It was the only city in England that had The Rows; a two-tier platform of shops. Shops at ground level, different shops up top. And most buildings on Foregate Street, the main commercial front, were clad in the traditional black and white latticework, a Tudor influence.

It boasted pubs established in the seventeenth century. Its racecourse brought in the rich and decadent on race days; guys dressed in suits, women in glamorous dresses and high strappy sandals; the kind that caused car crashes. It had Grosvenor Park. It was a place for the kids, a place to raise a family.

It could be a little intimidating at night, when the bar-hoppers and weekenders came out to debauch. But generally it was a safe, prosperous place. The sprawling countryside and coastal resorts of North Wales hung just the other side of the border. Liverpool, Capital of Culture 2008, was a forty minute train journey away. You could reach Manchester, the London of the North, in a little over an hour. It was pretty. James liked it.

He'd taken a job teaching Acquisitions at the College of Law in the nearby village of Christleton. He was on forty grand a year, but most of that stayed in the bank. He wasn't materialistic, never had been.

He lived in a quaint terraced house on Albion Place, five minutes walk from the city centre. It had a view of the River Dee the other side of the city walls. It was tucked away in a quiet spot. A perfect spot.

He had interesting neighbours. Next door to the left was a thirty-something Australian couple from Brisbane with a newly born baby. They'd migrated all across the world because of his job as an IT project specialist, installing bespoke software for a cluster of his company's clients.

Their daughter, baby Annabella, had a small cleft of ginger hair and wore a permanently cemented smile of wonder on her brand new lineaments, as she processed her strange new surroundings on the other side of the hemisphere.

Next door to the right was a young guy who'd worked like a dog in the hospitality trade since graduating from high school. He'd done well for himself. He now owned four pub-restaurants in the Chester area, and drove a convertible Beemer.

His girlfriend came by in a sporty Mazda roadster. She was in the same line of work, work that had yielded a veritable fruit salad of prosperity. A Spanish family had just moved in further down the street.

James walked down Foregate Street and cut right onto St John Street. He passed the new Cruise bar on his right, following it round and crossing the street. He contemplated the easy money the proprietors made week after week, fuelling people's magnetism towards alcohol with special deals like 'get two for one on all bottles', or, 'free shot with every drink after midnight'.

He walked up Park Street, tracing the city walls as if in the shadow of a Roman ancestor, turning right at the end onto Albion Place. He marched up to number sixteen, put his key in the lock of the turquoise door after showing next door's cat how affectionate he could be, and felt the door struggle to open; felt the obstruction of mail on the other side.

He went inside and bent to retrieve some bills and a newspaper from the doormat. He sliced each item open in turn with his thumb. Another letter invited him to the annual Junior Lawyers' Division masquerade ball. He'd have to decline on this occasion. Besides, who would he go with? Since his separation from his wife Radka Rosická, which had not yet been finalised by the courts, he hadn't been with a woman. Six months, no action.

The invitation reminded him of the law college balls he used to take the Czech to. Ancient history now, it seemed. Romantic occasions when she would put on a glad rag and some heels, he a bib and tucker, and they'd dance the night away. Not this time. James threw the invite away and turned his attention to the newspaper.

He left the bills – they were just direct debit notifications anyway. They would take his money automatically. How easy twenty-first century living was. How easy one was robbed of his hard earned currency by the system.

The front page of the Chester Chronicle displayed an article about billionaire entrepreneur and philanthropist Casino Collins. He'd just donated another hefty wad to NASA for their next trip to the moon. He wanted to leave a keepsake up there. He wanted first dibs on lunar real estate. He certainly had the green to make it happen.

The headline read 'Space-ious Accommodation You Can't Afford!' like a mockery of an estate agent's ad. James read the front page article. NASA had teamed up with construction giant Caterpillar to set in motion the idea of creating civilised communities on the moon, kick starting Neil Armstrong's legacy forty years after his giant leap for mankind and his first steps into a brave new world.

Collins was all over the project like a rash, no doubt throwing piles of money into a bottomless pit, just so he could be the first. And, thereafter, a quote from the man himself. He spoke of it as his lifelong ambition, ever since watching Armstrong with bated breath, as so many millions had that hot summer day on July 20th 1969, walk on the surface of the moon.

James continued to read the article, enthralled by the lightning speed that scientific innovation bettered itself through the eyes and hands of human endeavour. The article explained how the moon, very much like the Earth, has a North and South Pole. Because of the lunar orbit around the Earth, and the Earth's orbit around the Sun, the South Pole basked in daylight most of the time. It saw very little darkness. So it was the perfect spot to lay down foundations. The clever people at NASA had figured it all out, right down to the infrastructure, down to the launch and landing pads required, to the irrigation of roads, to water and sanitation systems. It was the next giant leap for mankind. Armstrong would have been proud.

Collins' keepsake was to be an suburban-American style mailbox stuck in the grey sand alongside the US flagpole already erected, labelled *Collins*, marking his territory, establishing him as the very first lunar citizen. James sniggered as he read that part. A little superficial, but cute nonetheless.

James slipped off his tanned loafers in the porch and walked through his living room to the kitchen. The newspaper was thrown down onto the pine table. He took off his North Face bomber jacket and boiled the kettle. Opening a cupboard above his head revealed an inviting concoction of aromas and at least four varieties of alternative tea – green, black, white, herbal.

He selected fennel and liquorice, ripped the bag out of its sachet and threw it into a mug. He poured boiling water over it and headed upstairs, but not before grabbing a bag of dried apricots from the cupboard. He'd picked them up from a health store in town.

Apparently apricots were particularly beneficial in warding off potential health risks. James took his health seriously – he didn't drink nor smoke. His workout regime at the gym was tireless, and so whenever he felt peckish he reached for the apricots and nibbled on them. They helped him concentrate when he was marking assignments – he did not know why.

He had not heard from Radka in the six months since they had parted ways like estuaries of a sea, although he presumed Radka would be in the Czech Republic visiting her family. He should have been there with her. They had spent Christmas together in Brno the last three years. James loved Brno – it had been his second home, and a place of escapism for him, like his very own parallel universe.

The colourful facades of the *panelaky*, high-rise flats stretching up from the metropolis on the outskirts, guarding the populace within, were akin to composites from a fairy tale. Not to worry – he had plenty to do to help him take his mind off the pain. His class had just taken their mid-term examinations, and he had a hefty wad of papers to sift through.

He had to separate the competent from the not-yet-competent. He hoped most would be competent, not least for the sake of not being in the same boat in the summer, marking the re-sits when he should be kicking back in the heat.

He hated being in the house alone. With Radka gone the house was no longer a home. He missed falling asleep with her snuggled up to him. He missed waking up to being snuggled up to her. Somehow they swapped positions overnight, neither knew how.

He missed her soft murmurs in her sleep, like a distant dolphin calling out to him from a faraway ocean. He missed the scent of her perfume, the smell of her skin, her hair. He missed the shimmering glint of beauty in her green eyes in the dark.

He missed watching her sat up in bed wearing headphones, catching up on rumours and gossip from her homeland on Seznam, a Czech news website. He missed how her toes would peek out of the duvet at the bottom of the bed, painted red or pink or purple, and wriggle as if to be playful. He missed the intimacy of spending every waking hour with his wife.

James went through to his makeshift office, the room where he had sweated out many long nights of assignment writing and revision during his studies at the College he now taught at. It was a tiny cupboard of a room; a cubby-hole, a mere elbow-space of area. It housed a computer desk which held his Dell laptop, a state of the art monolith of processing power and circuitry.

The only other notable item inside the office was a chair that opened out into a bed for guests. James had slept on it himself for a straight week, during his quarter-life crisis half a year earlier which had culminated in him making the hardest decision of his life.

Cracks in the relationship had transpired before the crisis, but James had fought to make it work. They had been in a new honeymoon period of rediscovery. But in spite of both their efforts, the flames of passion had dwindled to smoke dust, and the memories of what he'd done still lingered like a gremlin inside his head, punishing him for being human.

One of the principal reasons for their relationship irretrievably breaking down amounted to sex. Some people believe sex is the number one factor in relationship issues, the prime constant where all other problems are variable factors that come and go as they please.

A close friend of James' had once told him that she didn't believe in the concept of monogamous relationships, and never wanted to be in one. That deep down we have not evolved beyond our primal legacy of self-sustainability through reproduction. That ultimately we are still animals whose only purpose is to find a mate and dance the horizontal dance of love.

His friend had told him of her theory of the three-year itch; how after three years most relationships break down due to impassion and boredom, when it becomes time to discover fresh meat for furthering one's heritage.

Of course he had never believed her. He valued the importance of other factors in a relationship over sex; love, companionship, trust, togetherness, a unity of souls with the eventual aim of parenting their young. Yet in spite of his own marital misgivings, it made him wonder whether the girl had had a point.

No! He refused to believe it even now. Love had to eclipse the other factors. It just had to be with the right person. Statistically two-thirds of all marriages fail; but who makes up these statistics anyway? Every human being possesses an individualised construct, so how can generalisations be therefore made? A lifelong romance had to be possible, in theory. But getting over Radka was hard to do.

James switched on the Dell and launched the internet using his Firefox browser. He checked his emails but found an empty inbox bereft of unread correspondence. Then he went to his blog. He still had Casino Collins on his mind as he checked for new posts. He definitely agreed on one thing; Casino Collins was an extraordinary man. His appreciation for just how extraordinary Collins was got a fresh lease of life in the next moment, because Casino Collins had just left him an urgent message:

TO: JAMES LOXBRIDGE
FROM: CASINO COLLINS
SUBJECT: URGENT!

JAMES, YOU NEED TO GET OFF THE WALL.
THERE'LL BE NO TIME FOR QUESTIONS AT
QUESTION TIME!

Chapter Two

Bratislava, Slovakia. 2:45 p.m.

The man called Chaplin was blindfolded and led through a corridor by two other men. He couldn't see the men, but he could tell they were tough guys. He could tell by the way their powerful arms rested on his shoulders, by the way their claw-like hands dug into his blades. He hadn't complained when he'd been asked to put the blindfold on. He certainly wasn't going to complain now it was affixed to his head. He was on his way to see the boss, and he intended to do that with all his limbs intact.

He was led into a pitch dark room. If he hadn't been wearing the blindfold, he still wouldn't have been able to see anything. But his unit were careful. They weren't risk takers. Not with stakes and monetary figures so high. The two men carrying him left the room and closed the door behind them. They immediately locked it. Chaplin shuddered at the noise. It had caught him off guard.

'Sit.' The voice came from in front of him; that much Chaplin could ascertain. It was the voice of age, deep and worn, like sandpaper. It came from a body that had lived many years, from vocal chords that were overworked and due for retirement. Their hollow, tinny twang sounded like electric guitar strings that had seen one too many rock concerts, and needed replacing.

Chaplin hesitated. Then the voice spoke once again. Sound travels fast, and it only had a journey of a few metres. So Chaplin heard it instantaneously. 'In the exact spot where you stand there is a chair perfectly positioned. It is an ordinary

19

chair, non-descript really. And if you lower yourself down, you will find it.'

Chaplin didn't hesitate a second time, didn't want to anger the powerful man the voice belonged to. So he lowered himself down awkwardly. He hadn't been lied to. The chair was there. It was even comfortable.

'There. Good. Wasn't difficult, was it?'

'No, it wasn't' Chaplin said.

'So, down to our affairs. Your work in Slovakia was a great success. A great success indeed. Unity Six, wiped out. Extinct. Gone.' As he said 'gone' he threw out his right arm, as if he'd just swatted a fly, not that Chaplin could see.

'Thank you' Chaplin remarked.

'But think of it as the first stepping stone in your career. Because there is more. Much more.'

'I'm listening.'

'I have reviewed the papers you retrieved from the cabin. There appears to be some discrepancies.'

Chaplin shuffled in his seat and felt the clammy onslaught of sweat on his brow, brought on by the stress of his circumstances, in spite of the damp conditions inside the room. He cursed himself for being intimidated by this antique relic who should have retired decades ago. 'What kind of discrepancies, may I ask?'

The old timer smiled. As he did, the lumps of fat on his cheeks wobbled in a sinister fashion. 'The background theorising and the research are all accounted for, along with insightful explanatory notes. But, there is no specific formula. The ingredients may have already been sourced and production could be occurring as we speak. They'll be doing it underground. We need to find out where, and put a stop to it. It's the first time anyone's got this far with it. We are walking a tightrope across the danger zone with this. It must be elsewhere.'

Chaplin sucked in what little air the room had to offer. Blindfolded, and in a dark room, he was totally debilitated. He jumped at intermittent rustling clamours as the old gent refolded his arms or scratched at his face, sending out sudden echoes in the dark. 'Elsewhere?'

'Elsewhere. Tell me Chaplin, the reports from your mission detail five dead bodies. What of the sixth member of the Unity? Can you be certain you have not fallen prey to an act of misdirection?'

Chaplin felt his voice tremble as he advocated his side of events. 'He jumped into the abyss, Sir. Only certain death can await the man who takes such a course. The three hundred metre descent to craggy rocks at the bottom can testify to that.'

'I hope you are right, for all our sakes. Are you alright Chaplin? You sound a little tense.'

Inside, Chaplin winced. *Of course I'm not alright, you fossil! Would you be alright under the circumstances?* The frustration brought a new inkling of courage. 'I fail to see why a blindfold is necessary in an already darkened room.'

The old man grunted in amusement, a subtle laugh which quickly turned into a cough. It was too much exertion for his frail carcass. His bones were already beginning to disintegrate. 'I wanted you to understand the brevity of our position, and I wanted you to be prepared.'

'I don't follow?'

'It's quite ironic really, Chaplin. You see, if this thing comes to light, there can be only darkness for our kind. I wanted you to fully admonish the darkness that will fill our souls if this thing gets on the market. That is why we are sat today in this darkened room, and that is why you are wearing that blindfold today.'

Suddenly his voice changed tone and the baritone became one of sheer bitter anger as he raised it to decibels off the chart. 'You have to grow accustomed to the darkness, for that is what we will all experience if we fail! So do not question me again, young man! Do you hear me straight? Over five decades I built an empire, a legacy, a veritable smorgasbord of care that helps millions of people every single God damn day. You do not question me, of all people!'

Christ Almighty, Chaplin thought to himself in the eerie backdrop of nowhere. This ageing veteran is a kook! But a kook who paid generously. And for that, Chaplin could tolerate the old bugger. Who didn't want to kill their boss? But this was different. This boss was throwing enough green at Chaplin to make him ill. And in that respect he was a masochist. So he played along. 'My apologies. What do you want me to do?'

The old boss relaxed a little, his voice returning to its previous baritone stability. How his outburst had not prompted a cardiac arrest was a small miracle that he enjoyed profusely. At his age, every extra second breathing in oxygen was a metaphorical two's up to the Almighty. He was playing with God, and he was winning.

'We need to know where the missing documents are. Our intelligence service is working that detail. In the meantime, I want you to dig deeper into the Unity-Six endeavour. Find me their base of operations. Begin by running surveillance on our illustrious man in the spotlight; our spaceman! I swear he is behind this. He is the key. I know you have the skills necessary to monitor his activities in a discreet fashion.'

'I understand.'

'I hope you do. On your way out you will be given full instructions. You will also be given a new cell phone. It is on this and this alone you will keep me updated on your progress.'

'Fine.'

Paul Ross must have signalled to somebody in the darkness that the meeting was adjourned, because Chaplin heard the rustling of keys and then the door grinding open. Chaplin understood the immediate objective, but in the grander scheme of things was none the wiser about what his boss was plotting so lecherously. He was in the dark, literally and metaphorically.

But he never questioned orders. He was a soldier, and soldiers follow their orders without question. It was a code, a way of life, a religion in itself. He was escorted back out of the room and walked back up the corridor with the same two bruisers who had taken him there. He was driven twenty four miles, then he was asked to leave the car. It sped away and Chaplin removed the blindfold.

The sudden smack of light coming from all directions jolted him into submission. Then his cell phone bleeped, and he read the message. His instructions had arrived; an influential man, to be followed and watched from a distance. He shrugged, pocketing the cell. If that's what was wanted, that's what would happen. Of course he was prepared to do more if required. If there was to be a simple contract killing, then so be it. He would be paid, and then he would move on.

Chaplin was a man of few credentials, but many convictions. Still, he had a shrewd business sense. And in a perverted sort of way, he looked to Paul Ross as a father figure, a role missing from the man who had filled those biological shoes.

Sure, he could be aggressive and give the guy a hard time, but he always looked out for his people. And he had looked out for Chaplin for the entire eight years they had known each other. If it were not for Paul Ross, Chaplin would have still been rotting inside that Eastern European prison, serving out a life sentence for trafficking girls, some as young as thirteen, back to the UK where they could be bought and abused. So Chaplin had to be grateful, when all was said and done.

With that warm breeze of nostalgia warming his mind like a radiator, and the memories of those girls stirring his loins with a rekindled fire, Chaplin found a quiet place in the wilderness to absorb the details of his next job, and to get the jittery feeling of pleasure out of his system. As he reached his climax, picturing little Crystyna in that skirt and those boots, he roared like the bear he had killed in the mountains of Liptovský Mikuláš six months earlier.

Chapter Three

3:30 p.m. Chester. Still Monday.

James had never spoken to Casino Collins before. He knew only of the man's entrepreneurial brilliance. He was a minor celebrity in Britain, marvelled and adored in the business world, shunned and despised by certain idealistic sectors of public society, hailed as the next Richard Branson by many. And now, this enigmatic force of human genius had thought it upon himself to post a message on the blog of a humble, twenty-nine-year-old law tutor, whose usual threads rambled on about the effect of the credit crunch on future acquisitions, or the pros and cons of the conglomerate merger.

Collins' apocryphal bulletin seemed out of place amongst the other topic threads posted on the forum. No doubt it would soon attract replies of inquisition from the blogger population, amongst them a few die hard fans of James' academic musings on his homepage, the rest a general public of interested readers free to offer their opinions on the internet, the ultimate democratic conference room. 'How is this relevant to the current financial climate?' they would ask from their connection points all around the world, represented by cute little avatars in the corner of the screen.

James felt their frustrations echo his own, as he read the message once more.

JAMES, YOU NEED TO GET OFF THE WALL.
THERE'LL BE NO TIME FOR QUESTIONS AT
QUESTION TIME!

As a lawyer he had been trained to be a problem solver, an analyst. But he hadn't practised as an SRA-regulated solicitor for two years. To say he was rusty was an understatement of epic proportions. He figured he would need a notebook, a biro and some room on his desk in order to crack this little puzzle.

He had learned from past experience not to waste time being philosophical about it, to question the message's origin, its purpose, and its intended recipient.

No, best to focus on the solution. That much from practice he did remember, for in those shoes he had billed by the hour, so time was of the essence, otherwise the client would be biting at his ankles for failing to observe the economic concept of opportunity cost. Although, Casino Collins could hardly be considered a client of his, not least because he had hung up his advocacy cloak in the closet, not least because he hardly knew the guy.

So, James cleared away the intimidating pile of student mock exams waiting to be judged by tucking them into a desk drawer. He'd meet the Law Society's deadline, one way or another. He took a pad and pen and slipped his cognition into first gear. *You need to get off the wall!* What the hell did that mean? What wall was he on? The only one that sprang to mind was the City Walls, a stone's throw from his house.

He used to get up early and get on them to view the River Dee slowly gesticulating under a pale sunrise, watched over by pigeon vultures, the gentle surf carrying the swans to and fro, the dawn sky a pale pastel patchwork. He used to walk along the Walls to reach the city centre, pausing at the watchtower to gaze down like a Roman sentry at the mechanics of the city in full swing, driving the engine of routine. It looked like a giant Mexican Wave, or a domino slam, as the traffic slowly traversed out of the deadlocked centre and to the business parks on the outskirts.

He would walk further and soak up the aroma of Chinese food drifting up from the yard below him; the back of the buffet joint where the garbage was thrown out; the leftovers of human greed, of eyes too big for their stomachs. Then he'd cross the bridge by the golden clock, donated to Chester in 1897 by some long-forgotten aristocrat, and he knew he'd hit the hustle and bustle of the city centre.

And still, as James sat at the desk in his office, thinking back to his short residency as a Chester citizen, he could not think of any other significant walls. He only hoped Collins was talking physically, literally, and not metaphorically or philosophically. If the latter were true, the puzzle would be a great deal more difficult to crack.

The best metaphysical reasoning James mustered up was to think of walls as mental barriers. So did that mean he had to look at the problem laterally, by bringing down the barriers in his mind and being more open to the solution? Or did it mean he was too impartial, sat on the fence, and had to choose a side one way or the other? He did not consider himself a narrow-minded person, so he was almost insulted by the musing.

He gazed out the window for inspiration. A new wave of winter had hit overnight some weeks ago, springing up out of nowhere. You would think people would have got used to it by now, but every year at this time it would suddenly change seasons in the blink of an eye. Pipes would rattle as central heating systems were activated for the first time in months, the warmer coats were dug out from the back of the wardrobe, cars were filled up with antifreeze and de-iced, severe weather warnings would be given out on commercial radio, warning commuters about black ice. And all this trouble for temperate Britain, the stable island who never witnessed tropical storms or forces of nature so powerful as to claim mass loss of life, like the tsunami of Boxing Day 2004.

Regardless of the fact, the mystic movements of the weather over Blighty were to be marvelled. The unpredictability of the heavens over England never ceased to amaze tourists and frustrate the natives; Mother Nature's great mood swing, forever changing her mind. Today it had snowed, only to be washed away by succeeding rainfall, then to fall again as hailstones, and again to be taken by the rainfall. This repeating pattern of precipitation had turned the streets into a grey mush of sleet and sludge, littering the pavements like a dirty virus.

James ventured out to buy groceries. With Radka history for the immediate future, and perhaps for good, he was cooking for one, which was a tricky and lonely proposition. Supermarket portions never catered for one.

He took the same route he had made home from the gym, reversing the direction. He thought about nothing but the message on the way there, and nothing but the message on the way back.

As he once again passed the Cruise nightclub on Little St John Street and neared the Amphitheatre, he suddenly stopped dead in his tracks. An elderly woman had to perform an evasive manoeuvre to sidestep around him without crashing straight into him. She muttered an utterance of irritation under her breath and he mouthed his apology. The poor old lady was no doubt suffering more from the sub-zero temperatures than he was.

He remained where he was stood, three shopping bags in each hand, gazing further down the street, grinning like a madman. Radka and he had lived here for a little over a year; they had savoured the city's diverse range of watering hole, from the trendy wine bars for the elite and pretentious, to the traditional establishments with bar-propping regulars giving the stranger the dark stare as he enters, like a scene from a spaghetti western. *There's a stranger in town.*

Case in point being The Albion Inn, around the corner from his house on Albion Street, whose welcoming sign outside the premises explained *'No children, no dogs, family hostile, no poofs' or tarts' alcopop drinks, traditional ales only'* – a brave move in today's obsession with political correctness, James thought to himself.

But one place he had promised to take Radka, which ultimately had never transpired, much to her disapproval, was the place on the corner of Little St John Street, the place he now gazed at with muted mirth. The pub that he had walked past a thousand times but had never been inside.

Off The Wall, it was called. *James, you need to get off the wall.* What Collins had literally meant was *you need to get to Off The Wall.* The pub was to be a meeting place. But who was he supposed to meet, and why? Again he chastised himself for being philosophical. He had solved the first half of the message. All that remained was *There'll be no time for questions at question time!* He had no idea what that meant.

So, he was going to see what the place looked like inside, even if it was under unexpected circumstances. James made the journey back to his house, unpacked the groceries, changed into casual evening wear and cooked himself a hearty meal – fish stew with prawns, rice and spinach. He nibbled on more dried apricots for dessert.

By the time he had washed and cleared the dishes it was seven. He had no idea of the timeframe – nothing in the message had offered any clue as to that. At seven fifteen he ventured back out into the freezing wrath of the outside realm and acknowledged the two bouncers stationed outside Off The Wall as he entered. They gave him a robotic nodding gesture in response. They blew out clouds of cold air and tapped their feet to keep warm.

Off The Wall's interior was like an American sports bar. On the immediate left wall a row of flat-screen high-definition screens depicted the vivid green of a football pitch, switched on to Setanta Live, broadcasting the Liverpool-Everton game. It was the ultimate Merseyside derby, as the Reds and the Blues went head-to-head for the league cup. James rooted for the blue underdogs.

The place was decked out in chestnut, from the bar to the tables to the stools. Comfy sofa-chairs, their chic fabric finished in the same colour scheme, offered a relaxing vantage point from which to watch the game. In the background a barman busied himself with the pumps; he poured a draft Guinness for a thirsty punter, extra cold.

James approached the bar and acknowledged the barman. He was just a kid – probably a student trying to earn his keep whilst funding his studies, cramming in as many hours as he could between lectures, just to keep adrift of the red. James sympathised – he had done the same thing just half a decade prior.

'What can I get you?'

'Single brandy and coke.'

29

'It's Janeau; that alright?'

'I'm easy like Sunday morning.' He would have preferred a finer malt, like a Camus, but he couldn't expect to find that in a bog-standard establishment like Off The Wall. And he lacked the patience to kick up a stink over a lousy beverage.

The young barkeep made the drink and placed it down on the counter two minutes later. 'Two fifty, mate.'

James handed him a five pound note. 'Much obliged.'

The kid gave him his change. 'Say, what's upstairs?'

'A room full of pool tables, mate.'

'Do you play?' James whirled around at the voice. A man stood behind him. He looked like a happy-go-lucky type, like nothing irritated him, as if life was peachy all the time. The notion immediately infuriated James, who was going through a tremulous time in his personal life.

The man the voice belonged to was short but slim, with short black hair spiked up with gel. He was a regular shaver and his thick stubble clung to his features like glue. It was cut fashionably into a template, as neat tramlines met with his sideburns and ran all the way around his chin in a neat square, like a blueprint for his face. He was dressed in jeans and a casual brown sweater.

'Mine's a Becks' the stranger said to the student. The kid flicked out a bottle opener from his trouser pocket, tossed it in the air, caught it with his other hand behind his back and snapped off the top in one quick fluid motion. Then he slammed the bottle down on the counter. 'One-ninety, mate.'

The stranger paid up and gestured at James with a shake of the Becks bottle in his direction. 'Chin chin.'

James drank from his glass without returning the pleasantry, feeling a judder as the brandy hit his central nervous system. 'Who are you?'

The guy gulped down a fifth of the bottle. 'Me? I'm just a guy in a bar who wants to shoot some pool.'

James grunted. 'Aren't we all?!'

'After you then?'

'You're not some sort of hustler are you? Out to shark me for every penny I've got?!'

The man grinned. 'Please. I don't play for money, I play for fun.'

James paid the deposit for the cues, grabbed a cube of chalk from the end of the bar, and the two men headed upstairs. The décor on the first floor was identical to the ground, save for some framed shots of Fifties celebrities on the wall; Elvis, The Rat Pack, Clint Eastwood, Gary Cooper, the cast of High Society, amongst others. The law tutor slipped a pound coin into the slot and racked up. 'Who breaks?'

The stranger shrugged. 'Flip you for it?'

James took another pound coin from his pocket. 'Call it.'

'Dogs.'

'Dogs?'

'Yeah, they have heads and tails right?! I can't lose!'

James smiled. 'Looks like we have ourselves a comedian. Call again.'

'Tails', the man declared. 'Tails never fails.'

James flipped. The coin landed on the table, Queen's head up. 'Well they did for you tonight, friend. I'll break.'

James lined up the white and slid the cue smoothly through his fingers. Physics and geometry took over from there. The cue-ball careened into the pack with high velocity, splitting the triangle wide open. He sank a red and a yellow. He elected yellow as his chosen side and took aim. 'So what's your name, friend?'

'Murgatroyd.'

James abandoned his shot and stood firm. 'You're giving me a surname? What, are we in high school?'

The man laughed. 'It's Joel. Most people call me Murgatroyd though.'

'Whatever for?'

'I have no idea. I guess we're still in high school.'

James took the shot and sank a long yellow by rolling it down the cushion. 'Yes!'

'Nice shot.' Murgatroyd encouraged his opponent with gracious appreciation. They played for two more hours. James drank three more brandy-cokes, Murgatroyd stuck to his one bottle of Becks beer. The amateur tournament went down to a seventh frame decider after a three-all deadlock. Then it went down to the wire as only the black ball remained. James nailed it with a cross-double to the centre pocket. 'And that's how it's done, Murgatroyd. That's how it's done.'

'Fair play. You beat me fair and square.'

James suddenly remembered his reason for being inside the bar. The brandies had relaxed him to a point of comfort and he had forgotten all about the message. But now it came back to him.

'Listen, it was good shooting pool with you, but I'm actually waiting for someone tonight, so without sounding rude, I think you should make tracks, friend.' With that he grabbed the chalk and the cues and made for the stairs back down to the bar.

Murgatroyd feigned a look of hurt, then smiled. 'Time to be quiet, Mr Loxbridge. There'll be no time for questions at question time.'

James stopped dead in his tracks. As he heard the harrowing words from behind him, he glanced up at the row of TV screens, now to his right. The game had finished; another victory for the Liverpudian favourites over the blue Evertonian underdogs. James grunted. *That figures.*

The channel had been switched to the BBC. David Dimbleby was sat on his plush velvet couch, chairing a meeting live from Scotland between key members of government, from the legislature, the executive and the judiciary. The debate – should the UK have a written constitution? The obvious conclusion was – no, we don't need one. The nations who have written codified documents do so because of a fundamental change in their makeup that required such a formal representation. The French have their Code Napoleon, after their Industrial Revolution of 1789 that changed everything for them. The Americans have theirs because of their independence from Britain. But the fundamental makeup of the former British Empire has remained unchanged since 1066 – there has always been a monarchy ruling over the kingdom. But James lacked the time and the concentration to formulate those arguments in his head. Things were changing for him in this very moment.

He glanced at his watch and it all fell into place. It was ten-thirty, and Question Time had aired. The programme had become an institution in Britain, a kind of constitutional element in its own right. And it was the source of the second half of the message left cryptically by Casino Collins. *There'll be no time for questions at question time.*

James turned back to face Murgatroyd, whose smile had been replaced with a sombre solemnity. The short man pointed to an empty booth in the corner of the bar and James slid into a seat. Then he followed suit.

'We need to talk, James. Correction; I need to talk, you need to listen.'

Chapter Four

10:45 p.m.

As the two men faced each other with equal measures of weariness, in the ultimate standoff, the jukebox kicked in. Apparently someone had good taste. Pearl Jam's classic Evenflow broke the awkward silence, and James felt comforted. He listened to the deep sultry vocals of Eddie Vedder, complemented by Cameron's nano-second-perfect-timing percussion, Ament's haunting basslines that reverberated through his soul, Gossard's groovy rhythm licks and, probably most impressive of all, the preternatural sonic wizardry of lead guitarist McCready.

McCready's fingers found their way around the fret board with effortless accuracy, making his 1959 Fender Stratocaster sing like Pavarotti. It was as if him and his guitar were connected symbiotically; neither one able to survive without the other. James owned all ten of their studio albums and a concert DVD live in New York. His dream of being at one of their concerts, as close to the stage as was physically possible, had not yet been realised. *One day* he thought to himself.

Then the pressing reality confronting him from the other side of the table in Off The Wall shook him out of his fantasy.

'So talk. I'm listening.' James reached into his inside jacket pocket as he spoke, rummaged for a few seconds, then brought a tissue out and blew his nose. Then he replaced it back in the jacket pocket.

Murgatroyd leaned forward in his seat. 'I think we both know who I represent.'

James followed suit so that there was mere headspace between them. 'Casino Collins.'

Murgatroyd nodded. 'Right. That's a nice easy starter to warm you in gently. I'm an associate of his.'

James relaxed a little, withdrawing back to a postured position. 'What business does Mr Collins want with me?'

'He needs your help, James, with a matter of great urgency and importance.'

'Aren't they all? What matter precisely?'

Murgatroyd reached into his inside jacket pocket and took out a small white envelope. He threw it down on the table. James permitted one placid glance at it; then his gaze returned to the man who had done the throwing.

'It's all written down for me, is it?' There was a tone of flippancy in James' response. Murgatroyd's lips pursed into an attempt at a smile.

'It's all written down for you.'

James nodded. 'So if it's all written down, why, prey tell, are you needed here? Not that I didn't enjoy our little pool tournament, but why not just post it to me? If you've made this much effort, I doubt finding my residential abode wasn't too much of a stretch, not to somebody with Collins' finances anyway.'

Murgatroyd shuffled in his seat. He showed no signs of impatience just yet. 'Because some of it needs explaining.'

'What am I, an idiot?'

'Far from it, James, far from it. That's precisely why he came to you.'

James smiled. 'I was just about to get to that part. Why me?'

Again, Murgatroyd leaned forward, after glancing around the place to ensure nobody could overhear his words. There was no need to worry on that front – Vedder was still taking care of matters musical. A die-hard fan had obviously used several credits on the band – now Jeremy burst out of the speakers, as if being given a fresh lease of confidence, like the bullied-child subject of the song reaching adulthood. Then Murgatroyd spoke again.

'Aequitol.'

Something stirred in James' soul. His heart skipped a beat, his spine tingled with a tickling cold chill and his forehead clammed up with perspiration. A blast from the past, returning to haunt him? *But how, and why?* Now James scanned the immediate vicinity for imposing eavesdroppers. There were none – they had their privacy.

'What of it?'

'For the past four months, Mr Collins has poured vast amounts of his personal funds into research to find the perfect candidate for the difficult task ahead.'

'What difficult task?'

'I'll get to that in a moment. Collins' insatiable appetite for the truth has led him to pump further private finance into unmasking the world's conspiracies to discover the secrets they claim to reveal. One of our sources, who will remain anonymous for his own protection, has discovered something fascinating about the encounter that took place on that yacht two years ago. More specifically, about the people onboard.'

James instinctively gripped the table edge with his right hand and squeezed at the mahogany until it creaked with the effort. The skin on his inner palm became abrasive as the splintered surface dug into him.

'Firstly, what the hell does a two year old scandal have to do with me? And secondly, how does that relate to Casino Collins, this envelope and you?'

Murgatroyd grinned, like he knew the punch line of an inside joke that had escaped his acquaintance. 'James, you don't need to play dumb, it's not necessary! We know you were on that yacht on that day; that you were somehow involved. In fact we know a great deal about your clandestine efforts to stop those Chinese agents. You are quite the hero, albeit the great unknown.'

James' background prompted his first line of defence to be on legal grounds. 'Anything you have ascertained about my involvement in the Aequitol fiasco contravenes many Human Rights Act articles, including right to privacy, and the Data Protection Act. I would be very careful about your next moves, Mr Murgatroyd.'

The man scoffed. 'Oh please James, if that's all you can come up with then I'm disappointed! Like everything, you need evidence to prove any misdemeanour. And all you have here my friend is hearsay, inadmissible commentary from a third party. Now, if you had my written confession in a document, then maybe you'd have some ammunition against me. But this conversation is off the radar and off the record my friend. So let's cut the crap and get down to the nitty-gritty, shall we? Open the envelope.'

James did not appear deterred or dismayed by the man's blowback. Once again he reached into his jacket pocket, took out a tissue, blew his nose, and then replaced it, smiling all the while. Murgatroyd picked up on the repeated gesture.

'Catching a cold? You'll need to be fit for the mission we have planned for you.'

James reached over, took the envelope and tore through the seal with his forefinger. Inside was a single sheet of paper. It read:

James,

I wish I could tell you more at this stage. But unfortunately I cannot, for the safety of our plight. So, you'll just have to trust me. You're in capable hands with Murgatroyd. Do not throw this away, as for safety's sake it is the only copy – there are no electronic backups, for they are always prey to the vigilant observers. Turn over the page, and your journey begins. The very best of luck. I look forward to meeting you on the other side. God speed. Remember James, nobody's perfect!

Casino Collins.

James turned over the A4 sheet. It was blank on the other side – nothing, not a word, not a smidgen of ink to be seen.

'I don't understand?'

'All I can offer you is a clue, James. This is for everybody's own good, trust me on that accord. Are you a musical man?'

Of course he was a musical man. Jeremy had finished, segueing into Rear View Mirror.

'Yes, Mr Murgatroyd, I am a musical man. Can you be more specific?'

'Of course. There are words on the other side of that paper; you're just not looking hard enough!'

'What the hell? That's not a clue!'

'Everything you need is on that piece of paper.'

'And what makes you think for one minute I am going to help you? What makes a rational human being of sound mind believe that a random stranger, who has a shitload of papers to mark before next week, and what ultimately amounts to a normal life, is going to help you with a secret mission, that I know nothing about, from a person I have never met before, whose only guidance appears in the form of a written message on a piece of paper and some cryptic clue? Would you, in my position? Or would you think you were some kind of deranged loon?'

It was Murgatroyd's turn to reach into his inside jacket pocket. He pulled out a microscopic device, black and about three millimetres in diameter, circular in shape. He held it between the tip of his thumb and forefinger like a fly waiting to be squished to death. Then he placed it carefully on the table. James followed the movement with great curiosity.

'What the hell is that?'

'It's a recording device, James. Although for tonight's purpose it is simply a playback device. There's a message on there for you. Once you have heard it, I am pretty self assured that you will leap at the chance to help us. Go ahead – put it in your ear and squeeze it gently. The message will begin once you do so.'

James complied and waited for the message. He had to strain his ears over the speakers connected to the jukebox. Rear View Mirror had lapsed, its departing silence replaced with Alive. As the voice became one he recognised, he shuddered with concern and confusion simultaneously. Then, as he processed the words, the shock and the fear became a crude metamorphosis into a cold, unabridged slow burn pique of testosterone, fuelled by deep-seeded anger.

James lurched across the table and crashed his fist into Murgatroyd's face. The man was caught off-guard and stumbled off his stool and onto the floor. James dived on him, winding him with a blow to the stomach. 'You bastard, what have you done?'

The kid working the pumps behind the bar waved at the bouncers outside and they rushed inside. James was about to knock his victim unconscious with another vicious blow to the head but was suddenly jerked back and upward. The bouncers scooped him up and heaved him towards the front entrance. Then they threw him out onto the street.

He landed on the concrete of the kerb with a thud. A moment later his victim was hurled out too. Then one of the bouncers approached them. 'You're both barred, indefinitely. I see either of your faces in here again, I will knock you to kingdom come. Do we understand each other?'

James responded with a groan. Murgatroyd answered the meathead's threat with reassurance. 'Don't worry Sir, it won't happen again, I promise. There is no problem here.'

'Goodnight lads. Get lost.'

Murgatroyd helped James to his feet. The law tutor tried to lash out again but the man's surprising show of strength held his arms at bay, an inch or two out of range.

'Hey, whoa, just calm down now James, you hear? I am just the messenger. We need your help – this was the only way we could ensure that we have your full consideration and co-operation. Things will be better once you're on your way. Here, you forgot to take this.'

He handed James the envelope with the cryptic instructions. 'Oh, and before I forget, James, you are going to need this.' He handed James a brand new cell phone. 'Use this to communicate with us. Once you read the instructions on the other side of that paper, you will have a starting point, you'll know where it is you have to go. Best of luck, James. There's a lot riding on this, but you're the best man for the job, we are all confident of that fact. It's the only thing we know for sure!'

Murgatroyd took off into the darkness. He ran towards the city centre; then he was gone. James stared out towards the Amphitheatre with a jarring sense of consternation. He was in turmoil. He stared at the objects in his hand – the cell phone in one, the envelope with printed instructions in the other – like he had no idea how they had gotten there. He was still wearing the earpiece that had played back that frightening message.

It was happening again. He was being drawn into something big, with minimal information. And he was on his own. What was he to do? In light of the recorded message he had listened to, he could hardly refuse to co-operate.

But how was he to interpret the written instructions, which didn't really contain any instructions at all?! What had Murgatroyd meant by looking harder at the blank page on the back? James thought back to precisely the last words he had used before he had attacked him. *Are you a musical man, James?* So the clue was themed on music. It was all in the details. But it was hardly a revelation – it was far too generic.

Then James felt a small vibration in his hand and heard a tinny metallic noise. The cell phone was vibrating. *One new message received, from: Murgatroyd.* He'd already programmed his name into the phone's address book. The message read:

> *Who do we think we are?*
> *Perfect strangers live in London!*
> *The battle rages on the house of blue light made in Japan.*
> *Abandon slaves and masters.*

Chapter Five

Tuesday 21st February – Prague, Czech Republic.

9:05 a.m.

The land that housed the decadent conference centre on Freyova Street had seen many changes over more than a millennium of civilised, and arguably uncivilised, history. Its memory jilted back through passages of time like chapters in an epic novel to tribal beginnings.

It first experienced human incursion in the ninth century when the Premyslid dynasty first established itself in the region, and Prague Castle was completed, circa 880. Christianity was brought here by Cyril and Methodius, the apostles of the Slavs. It witnessed the founding of the bishopric in 973. It saw the first Czech king come to power, Vratislav II, in 1085, equally recognising with wisdom his subordination to the Holy Roman Empire and the German monarch.

It had acquiesced to the building of the first stone bridge over the river Vltava in 1172; Judith Bridge. It had not neglected to acknowledge the establishment of the Old Town, *Stare mesto*, in 1231. It had seen first-hand the Golden Age of the fourteenth century, the Hussite Wars of the fifteenth, the second Golden Age in the renaissance era of the sixteenth, the Protestant uprising and subsequent Dark Ages of the seventeenth, the industrial revolution of the nineteenth, the devastation of the Second World War upon Czechoslovakia as Hitler took the Sudetenland in 1936, an area containing three million German

43

inhabitants, and the split down the middle in 1993 creating two independent states, the Czech Republic and the Slovak Republic, of which the land in Prague became the capital of the former.

And now, in twenty-first century Bohemia, the land housed the decadent conference centre on Freyova Street. It was a transition of monolithic proportions; a mitochondria blasting through the course of evolution like a comet hurtling through space.

Inside the conference centre, in the grand function room known as the Meridian, a large audience of two and a half thousand delegates were sat on the edge of their seats, waiting in readiness for the commencement of the event.

The Meridian was a vast auditorium, a colossal space spanning more than six thousand square feet of plush interior design. The lick of paint on the walls and ceiling was as fresh as a spring morning. The regal blue colour scheme extending to the velvet curtains confirmed the centre's prestige like evidence backing up a legal case, reinforcing the image of decadence and perfection like a Roman feat of engineering. Like the wheel itself.

The catering on the day was top notch, served up by a well-renowned French chef with enough Michelin stars to make a galaxy.

Even the carpet was exquisite; a vast cloak of canvas over mezzanine, an artistic masterpiece blown up to an incomprehensible scale. Rumour had it that the next G20 summit would be held here. It would send quakes of commerce through the Czech economy, bolstering their technical superiority in Eastern Europe, and serve as a playground for the bullies of the new age; the Franco-German alliance and the Anglo-American power duo.

As nine-thirty approached, the delegates sipped from china containing the finest ground coffee beans and munched quaintly on strudels and zavin cake filled with quark and poppy seeds; small delicacies from the region.

There was much chatter and the resonance reverberated effortlessly around the auditorium, carrying with it a sense of urgency. A hero of the pharmaceutical arena was about to descend upon

44

them like a chariot of fire to preach his gospel, the gospel of science and technology, to this choir of investors, entrepreneurs and corporate bandwagoners. It was his kind of audience and he was their kind of guy. It was poised to be a great success.

At a little past nine forty the melee quietened to a hush; a cluster of whispers, as if a small zephyr had crept inside the hall and was carrying their message like a burden on its back. The anticipation rose to unprecedented heights and finally he emerged from the left side of the stage, stepping out onto the platform to a standing ovation.

He was elderly; a man who had lived a lifetime. He appeared physically frail, yet simultaneously strong in his convictions. His eyes pierced the audience like the pincers of a scorpion. His smile and his gaze filled their hearts with instant radiation. His charisma, his demeanour, his whole unabridged aura seemed to give him the presence of a deity. And then his voice penetrated the frenzied silence; a hollow boom that transcended the sonic barrier and filled the air inside the room as if it were a mere balloon.

'Friends, associates, loyal disciples of science, thank you for your attendance this morning. I stand before you today first and foremost to thank you for your continued contributions. Your efforts make our research considerably more efficient and our goals infinitely more attainable as a result. A round of applause, for you guys. Please, I insist.'

His fragile hands began to bang together, battered lumps of vein and cartilage joining forces like old allies reuniting. The audience soon followed suit, most of the delegates nodding and smiling for extra emphasis. When the applause diffused into quiet the elderly man centre stage continued his monologue.

'You are all heroes, because your contributions save lives on a daily basis, and they reduce the pain and suffering of millions. But what of the future? What more can you do, can I do, can we do? Let me paint you a picture of the next generation of product lines to be supplied to the marketplace. Alice?'

He gestured to an unseen assistant beyond the curtain and an overhead projector was activated, lighting up a portion of the back wall with a rectangular glow. The screen was at first out of focus. An adjustment was made and the contrast of the image sharpened to a resolution kinder on the eyes. Each PowerPoint slide took the audience through its respective product line in turn, and the elderly gent pointed to bulleted lines of text with a cane as he explained each one in more detail. He was giving the seminar, the lecture; he was in total control. The audience listened like a bunch of enthralled freshmen students.

'Sutent is a drug that treats advanced breast cancer. It has proven to be more successful than its predecessor Capecitabine, better known as Xeloda. It also targets kidney and gastrointestinal cancer. It attacks a protein and blood vessels that allow tumours to grow. It is much more positive than chemotherapy, which targets cancerous but also healthy cells.' There was more applause as the delegates acknowledged the progress. Alice flipped the slideshow presentation to the next slide and the old relic continued.

'Next is Cilengitide. This little beauty has been in the experimental phase of its development for too long. Finally, at long last, I can announce it will be on the shelf within the next twelve months. I can practically guarantee it. Cilengitide is a type of angiogenesis inhibitor, a substance that inhibits the growth of new blood vessels.

'It is particularly effective with sufferers of non-small-cell lung cancer, and head and neck cancer. In addition, people with brain tumours respond to high doses of the substance.

'Angiogenesis inhibitors are designed to stop tumours growing by cutting off their blood supply. Cilengitide inhibits integrin molecules called □□□5 and □□□3, which are partly responsible for regulation of angiogenesis – the growth of blood vessels.

'They also act directly on the tumours. A lot of mice have died to get us to this stage, but we made it!' Another round of applause filled the conference hall; a wave of energy pulsating around its internal façade.

'Which brings us, dear supporters, to abiraterone.' Once again the dutiful Alice used her clicker and the slide disintegrated into the next. 'Abiraterone adds years of life to sufferers of aggressive prostate cancer. It shrinks tumours and blocks the generation of hormones in the testes and elsewhere in the body, including the generation of hormones in the cancer itself. It also reduces antigen levels in the blood.'

There was more praise for the octogenarian talking passionately about his field of expertise. 'It is able to help patients whose cancer had spread to the bones, liver, even lungs. A number of test patients have been able to stop taking morphine for the relief of bone pain, and they soon had their quality of life back. In the wider context we eventually aim to make chemotherapy obsolete.'

The seminar continued in this vein for another two hours. In that time the ageing legend of pharmaceutical development informed the delegates about upgraded versions of Avastin, Herceptin, Afinitor, Dichloroacetate, and several other new products hot off the lab bench and destined for the shelves.

By lunchtime his work was well and truly nipped in the bud. A resounding triumph of oration. The donations would be coming in thick and fast; cheques would be written fast but cashed even faster. Later on the air inside the room would become contaminated with the ugly stench of money.

'Ladies and gentlemen, I thank you for your time, your patience, your understanding and your continued financial support. You are a Godsend, every single one of you. I would like to make one last insistence. I ask that you applaud one last time, but not for me. For yourselves. Let me remind you once again, you are all of you heroes. So join me in a toast of celebration, and say with me, Hallelujah! Hallelujah!'

The crowd, like an arsenal of nuclear missiles on course for a predetermined target, heated up and went ballistic. 'Hallelujah', they roared, like a pride of lions. 'Hallelujah.' And the raucous clapping ascended new heights of sonic grandeur.

'We are winning', the elder exclaimed. 'We are beating the evil that seeps through our race, through our flesh and blood. It is a bitter war, and the enemy is relentless, but we will win, even if we have to take it a battle at a time. We will prevail. Godspeed ladies and gentlemen. I now adjourn for lunch. Enjoy the sublime catering on offer. Adieu. Ciao. Adios. Auf Wiedersehen. Ahoj. Dasve danye. Sayanara. Goodbye!'

The grandfather of cancer research descended from the stage and, like a winged superhero after saving an innocent citizen from an arch-nemesis, swooped out of sight. All that remained was the floating curtain, swishing back and forth. The great legend had vacated the arena but his energy lingered like overbearing cologne. The applause continued to drown out all other sound for a good few minutes.

Backstage Paul Ross took a seat on a leather couch and sipped from a glass of water. A grimace formed on his ancient lineaments. His vocal chords were beaten to a pulp. They felt like mere horsehairs, or long-dead guitar strings. The presentation had really taken it out of him. But he had prevailed once again over the masses. The green would continue to flood in. In the meantime the mission could go on as envisaged. He reached inside his jacked pocket and retrieved a small clamshell cell phone. He hit speed dial 4 and waited to be connected.

'Hello?'

'Chaplin. It's me. Just to give you an update; the talk was a success, as always. It's over to you now. Did you receive all the information I sent you about the mission objectives?'

'Affirmative, Sir. It's all here. I'm just prepping myself. I should be ready to initiate within twenty four hours.'

'Fabulous. Keep me posted.'

'You got it.'

Both men hung up simultaneously. Time was running out for Paul Ross. Soon he would be but a blot on the underground; a pile of disintegrated bones in the dirt. But not before the mission had been seen out to its full and finite conclusion. That was his final legacy to the pharmaceutical world. He was not about to let his life's work be nullified by a bunch of hippy scientists and their *natural* answer.

Chapter Six

Chester, England. Still Tuesday. 7:35 p.m.

It had taken him most of the day to figure it out, but he had figured it out. He was enthralled by the ingenuity of it. He was almost in awe of it; looking up to it like one might gaze at the apex of a gothic cathedral and ponder the lifetimes of labour that had been selflessly dedicated to its construction. Engineers and builders who had perished before its completion, never witnessing their efforts brought through to an accomplished conclusion.

He had started his deft analysis of the message by reading it over and over, as if the repetition would somehow bring out the answer for him. Not a lateral approach, but thorough nonetheless.

> *Who do we think we are?*
> *Perfect strangers live in London!*
> *The battle rages on the house of blue light made in Japan.*
> *Abandon slaves and masters.*

James had thought early on that morning that he recognised some of the words and phrases in the message, but from where he could not place. And yet they were supposed to be a clue, presumably an explanation as to how a blank piece of paper was to point him in the right direction. That's what Casino Collins had written in the message that Murgatroyd had passed on to him in Off The Wall. *Turn over the page and your journey begins* Collins had declared matter-of-factly. But the page was blank. So what did this four-line stanza mean?

James had loaded himself up with coffee and carbohydrates; a brunch of scrambled eggs smothered on a buttered baguette, and pressed his cognition to explain to him why there was recognition.

The first line was an apparently rhetorical question, simultaneously a statement of self-reflection, or self-criticism. *Who do we think we are?* The second read like a sweeping statement offering no meaning in isolation. *Perfect strangers live in London!* The exclamation mark seemed to offer an extra dimension to it. What was so dramatic about such a statement? Yes, it was true, but there are perfect strangers in every city, not least in every town, village, or hamlet for that matter.

The third was nonsensical – *the battle rages on the house of blue light made in Japan*. The last three words struck out at James instantly. It was the name of a song by über-German rock outfit Guano Apes. Radka had owned their greatest hits LP. It was no longer in the house – it had been removed along with every other possession of hers when she had left him. The house reeked of his former love and his past life.

He would never forget the way they had parted for presumably the last time, six months earlier. He had come back for the last of his things when she was still living there. She had kindly arranged them on the living room floor, so he would not have to go to the trouble of searching each room of the house for every last item. He had loaded them up into bin liners, called a taxi and awkwardly waited.

They had sat precociously through a final cup of tea together, and endured a brief chat at the kitchen table about what had happened. When the honk of the waiting car outside broke the dreadful silence, they embraced, and she uttered three last words to him before he clambered inside the cab: those three words that are said too much but are not enough. Out of natural habit he had uttered them back to her, and even at that point, after all that they had been through, he had meant them.

And then, like a dramatic scene from a tearjerker movie, the cab had reversed down the tiny street and he had watched her through the windshield, staring back at him from the doorstep, her frame getting smaller and smaller as the taxi moved further away, an artist's perspective diminishing, and she stole the last glimpse back at the car before heading back into the house, as the taxi rounded the corner and took him away to his temporary new lodgings. Then weeks later she moved out and he moved back in.

In that moment he had felt like he was being stabbed over and over again. The memory ended, like the conclusion of a story, and he was jabbed back into the present. A pang of loneliness pricked at him like a needle, and his heart winced.

Back in the land of the living, James had postulated mentally over the fourth line, which was more like an order or instruction. *Abandon slaves and masters.* So that was it – a question, a statement of fact, a statement of nonsense and an instruction of some kind. How utterly bizarre.

It was after another cup of Costa Rican coffee and a nibble on a few dried apricots that James remembered another salient detail. *All I can offer you is a clue, James. This is for everybody's own good, trust me on that accord. Are you a music man?* The words of Murgatroyd in Off The Wall, shortly before introducing James to Collins' message and the recording device which had housed Radka's voice, explaining calmly how she had been kidnapped by some men who refused to tell her their identity or their motive, but that they worked for Casino Collins and that her ex-hubbie had to pay attention and follow some orders for her sake. That's what had caused James to attempt to beat the living daylights out of Murgatroyd before the bouncers had intervened.

So Casino Collins, entrepreneur, had branched out into kidnapping and blackmail! The very man who had appeared on the front of a newspaper delivered to James' door was now in a position to deliver Radka back to him in any way he saw fit. In pieces? Would tomorrow's headline read: *Czech woman found dead in England, murdered. Ex-husband possible suspect.*

The thought made James shiver. Then he remembered how Collins had signed off his message. *Remember James, nobody's perfect.* Nobody's perfect? What a ridiculous notion. These were not the words of a hardened criminal, practically asking the victim for empathy. It was a very odd turn of events that had chilled the lawyer cum tutor to the bone.

James had thought of Murgatroyd's subtle nuance to him. *Are you a music man?* This had prompted him to seek a new line of enquiry over the message now sat in front of him in the den of Albion Place, which had transformed from a loving matrimonial haven into a crumbling bachelor hellhole, at least metaphorically if not literally.

James launched the Google search engine and typed in the first line of the message, then hit search. *Results for who do we think we are: displaying 1-10 of about 201,000,000.* James frowned. Hardly a Googlewhack. The thought made him smile. It had been a game on the internet years ago, loved by academics, geeks and the terminally bored. The Google search engine was, like any other encyclopaedia, prone to reveal a vast microcosm of information generated by any search using key words. That's because it brought back anything which contained any of those words, regardless of the relevance.

It was not, after all, an artificially intelligent symbiotic being which could think for itself. That was for the future; the next big thing. For now it was a slave to its master; the human who commanded it with key search terms. So, ninety-nine percent of Google searches would generate millions of results.

The Googlewhack was a competition – if you could think of just two single words to enter in a Google search, and that Google search brought back just one single result, then that was a Googlewhack. It was virtually impossible. James, in his infinite youthful wisdom, had played around with what he thought were the most complicated or rare pieces of vocabulary, but the best he had ever done was generated a search that had yielded forty-one results. Nowhere near up to par.

Now he studied the first result, which seemed irrelevant to any mystery surrounding Radka, Casino Collins or himself. He clicked on the link for the first URL. *Who do we think we are? Exploring identity, diversity and citizenship in the UK.* It made for interesting reading, but it wasn't what he was looking for.

But the second link of two hundred and one million did spark some electricity in James' core, and he felt a new wave of energy seep into him. It was a link to Wikipedia, the online encyclopaedia. *Who Do We Think We Are is the seventh studio album by the English rock band Deep Purple.*

James had made a connection. Murgatroyd had told him through a coded question that the answer lay in music, one of the biggest constants in James' life, one of the most wonderful inventions ever concocted by mankind, a therapy to billions, an academic discipline that had been used by ancient civilisations to teach other academic disciplines, such as mathematics through rhythmic counting. And now, the first line of the message, *Who do we think we are*, was also the name of an album by rock legends Deep Purple.

James read on. It was recorded in Rome in July 1972 and Frankfurt in October 1972 using the Rolling Stones Mobile Studio. It was Deep Purple's last album with the Mark II line-up of the group until Perfect Strangers (1984). Instantly a throb of excitement immersed him in its vice. It was the last two words he had read that had caused it. *Perfect Strangers, the name of another Deep Purple album.* James looked again at the second line of the message. *Perfect strangers live in London!*

Were all of the elements of the message Deep Purple album titles? It was James' inclination to believe so. He went back to his Google search and started a new one. This time he searched using the terms *Deep Purple Discography* and waited for the results. Only 206,000 this time. He was much closer to his Googlewhack, but that thought stayed at the back of his mind in respectful silence.

He clicked on the first link that offered him what he wanted and began to browse the text. It was a long list – Deep Purple had had an illustrious career, it seemed. The first on the list he recognised, sixth from the top, was *Who Do We Think We Are?* But he already knew about that one. *Come on!* He urged the information to be kind and offer itself like a sacrifice to a tribe.

Next came *Perfect Strangers*. And then, to complete the sentence of the second line of the message, another album name: *Live in London*. James smiled – very clever. A simple trick, but nonetheless one of the most effective.

The English language was a rarity – hardly any other language boasted words that are spelt identically but with different meanings - homonyms. No, the English language was a dextrous beast. It could be stretched or bent to one's advantage. It wasn't a complete sentence: *Perfect strangers live in London*. *Live* was used in the context of a concert performance not recorded in a studio, as opposed to the verb pertaining to habitation or existence.

James was now certain he would find the other parts of the poem on this very website, all displayed as album names. Next came *Big In Japan*. His earlier recognition had been well-founded. Yes, the Guano Apes had it as one of their hits on their compilation album, but it was a cover, James now realised. The original material had been written by Deep Purple. His father would have known that already, he did not doubt. Two more lit up on screen and lit up the fire in his eyes. *Slaves and Masters*. *House of Blue Light*. Eventually James found them all. *Abandon*. *The Battle Rages On*.

Through a process of elimination, and to double-check he had not neglected anything, James re-wrote Murgatroyd's text message onto a piece of paper, and then the list of albums below it. It appeared complete, and partially deciphered.

The message read:

> *Who do we think we are?*
> *Perfect strangers live in London!*
> *The battle rages on the house of blue light made in Japan.*
> *Abandon slaves and masters.*

The album titles were:

54

Who do we think we are?
Perfect Strangers
Live in London
The Battle Rages On
The House of Blue Light
Made In Japan
Abandon
Slaves and Masters

As James' eye flitted back to the screen, the presence of another album title stole the entirety of his attention. *Nobody's Perfect*. That's why Collins had signed off his message in such a way. *Remember James, nobody's perfect*. It was not a delusional plea for empathy by a madman after all; it was another clue, a compass point to put James on the map and in the right direction. It only confirmed everything else that went before it.

Late into the afternoon, once lunch had been taken care of and washed down with yet more coffee and more dried apricots, James realised he was only halfway to the final solution. So, the message was a list of Deep Purple albums, therefore the ultimate clue was Deep Purple. But that hardly explained anything. What about Deep Purple? James had to admit that a kindling of frustration and impatience had crept into his usually austere aura.

He spent two hours meticulously researching the life and times of the band, following their ride through stardom spanning three decades. It was a happier tale than for many of rock n roll's countless victims of drugs and self-perpetuated superstardom, victims of their own success, their own worst enemies. But it offered no clue to James.

He began to think laterally. Maybe the theme of music, and the band itself, was only the beginning. Maybe Deep Purple had an altogether separate interpretation. The only way he could narrow it down, and it was not so much a narrowing as a one step closer to a Googlewhack from 201,000,000 results, a needle in a haystack, was to remember, to realise, that these two words explained how to interpret a blank piece of paper. Casino Collins had instructed James to turn over the page on which he had written his message. A blank page.

So, fuelled by the lunchtime sustenance and a fresh cup of coffee, James pushed the boundaries of his mind to reveal what Deep Purple could mean in the context of a blank piece of paper. He was going nowhere fast, so he decided to take a break.

He checked his emails and made himself a coffee. It was an exquisitely buttery Puerto Rican blend. He returned to his computer and navigated the cursor over the cross icon to quit the browser page. As he did, something flashing onscreen caught his eye and prevented him from doing so.

It was one of many random advertisements that plagued internet browsing; another reminder of the chatterbox that is money: *www.maxmax.com. UV invisible inks, pens and pads. Invisible Ink uses special High-Brightness Ultraviolet (UV) Blacklight Viewable compounds. The Invisible Ink glows a bright blue under our UV or Blacklight products, including our special UV flashlight. Under normal light this ink is completely invisible. This ink can only be seen when illuminated by a UV or Blacklight emitting in the 350mm-385mm light range. The ink is permanent and can be applied to paper, plastic, skin, wood and almost any substance. The ink does not wash off, but will eventually wear off if applied to skin. Depending on the light used, this ink will appear either blue or white.*

It did not take James long to process what he was reading, and once he had, the rest of the puzzle slipped into place like the shoe on Cinderella's foot. It fits! *Indeed it does,* thought James. *It all fits perfectly.* Deep Purple was another way to express, quite ingeniously, Ultra Violet. Deep and Ultra went together as being adjectives on a scale of degree. Both words were high on the spectrum and could be used interchangeably. If something was *very*, it was deep, or ultra. And, of course, violet was a shade of the colour purple.

So the piece of paper used by Collins to construct his message to James was not blank at all. It had been written in invisible ink, the kind only viewable in ultraviolet light. James had to find a place where there was ultraviolet light. And he knew of such a place. A place very close to home.

Chapter Seven

Brno, Czech Republic. 8:12 p.m.

Brno, the second largest city in the Czech Republic and cultural melting pot of Moravia, was basking in the glow of magnanimous grandeur, which, incidentally, was the only warmth to an otherwise bitterly cold winter chill that enveloped the streets with a biting potency. To outsiders it was best known for its World Superbikes tournament track, but to educated Europeans it offered everything.

The city was littered with gothic architecture from the Baroque era, which delighted and indulged the fantasies of its countless art history students. The small metropolis was guarded in the suburbs by the *panelaky*, a series of brightly coloured apartment blocks and high-rise flats which sprung out of the icy ground and clung to dizzy heights; aged remnants of Communist Czechoslovakia that had survived the transitional journey to enlightened progress in the Nineties, springing forth an age of technical superiority in the former Soviet bloc. It was companies like automobile manufacturer Škoda that had set the proverbial ball rolling.

Brno was not particularly touristy; certainly not in a league with Prague, who welcomed with open arms brash American sightseers and drunken English jocks on stag parties and drunken weekenders. No, it was a cultural fountain. To see it for the first time was remarkable, and yet to go back for more was another pleasure altogether.

It was as if every citizen was an artist. Every house, café, restaurant, bar, museum, shop, every nook and cranny, had uniqueness to its design, individuality to its décor, independence to its purpose. There were no franchises here; no global chains of commerce. It resembled the ultimate fairy-tale land for the foreign visitor, yet existence inside it for the native was very real. A heavily controlled state economy maintained its presence there.

You could walk into a Brno bookshop and find the latest bestsellers in a plethora of languages. Czechs were bohemian but ultimately cosmopolitan, and although only twenty percent of school-leavers earned a chance to further their academic standpoints with a place at university, they were a well educated race.

In the heart of the Lišen district, near the market square, the Air Café stood proud like a statue. It was an eatery within a museum complex; a dedication to the Czech pilots who fought bravely against the Germans in the Second World War. Many of them died, but they did not surrender, unlike their Slovak counterparts, who succumbed to the whims of the Third Reich through fear and oppression. And so Air Café is a fitting name for this iconic historic bastion.

The interior was typically bohemian, a purely semantic contradiction in Czechia, for this region was Moravia; Bohemia lay to the West. Oak panelling served as the core of the structure. The walls were patterned with photographs of Czech pilots and pieces of memorabilia from the bygone wartime era. The bar was modestly tucked away in the far corner, and the waiter that manned it like a sentry guard wasn't merely a student working for tips and to fund his higher education (which was state-funded here; no need for tuition fees and ridiculous bank loans). No, this waiter, like most waiters and waitresses in the city, had been schooled in the art of waiting and was therefore a professional in hospitality.

Most of the tables and chairs were occupied with local regulars. Cigarette smoke hung in the air like a dust-cloud; the anti-smoking legislation had not yet crossed the borderlands of Western Europe. The room was filled with casual chatter. Long lost

58

friends caught up over a non-alcoholic cocktail. Elderly gents sipped from tankards of Czech lager; Starobrno, the local and famed barley and hops. Touchy-feely chic girls from the numerous universities of Brno laughed and reminisced and checked their handbags for fresh smokes.

Seated at a corner booth opposite the bar was a couple. An ordinary looking couple, at first glance. A non-descript couple, engaging in adult banter. Her heritage was Slavic, there was no doubt. Her green eyes pierced the space between them and her auburn hair hung motionless from her head to her bronzed shoulders. Another native regular.

But he was a different story, a Kafka or a Dostoevsky or a Tolstoy; more difficult to read. His chapters were long and philosophical, not succinct and to the point. His skin was of a paler pigmentation, and his complexion was ruddy and pink with the tramlines of middle age gorging across his lineaments, giving his face the cornucopia of an over-ripened peach. His genetic makeup was distinctly Anglo-Saxon, not Slavic.

The woman sipped from her apricot juice and dabbed at the stickiness of her lips with a napkin, removing the surplus fruit curdle. Finally, after great reflection and sizing up of the man sat before her, her lips parted and she spoke.

'You are keeping me here against my will?' It could have been a statement, but the rising intonation towards the sentence's unfettered conclusion turned it into a question.

The main huffed in response, his shoulders gesticulating outwards in a brief spasmodic episode. Then he smiled and stared into her eyes, but he did not respond vocally.

'For how long do you intend to keep me here?'

The man repeated his shoulder action, grunted, and then retreated backwards into a more comfortable posture. It was his turn to use a napkin, and once he had finished wiping his mouth, he offered her a response.

'Am I not treating you satisfactorily, Radka?'

'Impeccably, Mr Collins, but that's hardly the point now is it? Casino Collins. Is that really your name?' She snorted.

His smile eclipsed her frown. 'I thought I had chosen the best place. This is, after all, your home.' He gestured with an outstretched arm, pointing out the window to the view of the terrace and the rear of the museum.

'I am touched. But your answers are sketchy and vague. I am disconcerted. What is your business and why does it have to involve me, or my ex-husband for that matter?' He noticed that she did not refer to him by name.

It was a question that required careful deliberation before a response could be provided. Collins pursed his lips and blew air out of his mouth, his cheeks bulging. He made a repetitive clicking sound with his teeth, like a parakeet calling for a mate. Finally he breathed out deep, as if a weight had been lifted. His eyes had never left Radka's during the whole display. 'How about another drink? Or, are you hungry?'

Radka looked away. She was highly frustrated, but she hid it well. Her female intuition told her to keep cool and resolute; he would break eventually, it would just take time, patience, and a well-placed piece of flattery or a perfectly timed provocation. He was just a man, after all, and eventually he would buckle and trip himself up. 'I'll eat later', she responded dispassionately.

'How do I ask for the key to the bathroom?' Casino asked. The facilities were in the museum complex and were therefore locked at all times, lest some inconsiderate tourist disrespected the sanctity and sacred duplicity of the place by desecrating it with graffiti or other sabotage.

'Maš clič na toalety?' As she provided the phrase he needed, the waiter overheard and brought the key from the bar to their table. Radka smiled sardonically. 'Diky' she thanked the waiter. Collins pushed back his chair with minimal fuss.

'Excuse me. Please don't run off. My associates are outside – it would only serve as an embarrassment for you.' He patted her on the shoulder as he walked round the outside of her and eased out of the bar, heading down the museum corridor to the gents. She flinched and seethed at the gesture, but again was steadfast in her resolve to conceal her bitter rage.

When he returned he seemed more willing to reveal explanations. 'Your ex-husband is assisting me with a very important matter. Not by his own choice, I grant you that, but for his own and the greater good, I assure you. Treat this as an admonishment, not a threat.

'You are being used as an insurance policy, indemnifying yours truly for any loss caused as a result of your ex-husband's lack of faith. I need to be assured that he will complete the work I have given him. Once this has been accomplished you have my word and my good graces that you will be returned to the freedom of your own life without so much as a scratch or an inconvenience upon your person.

'I cannot give you a timeline for this, for the task requires your ex-husband to embark on a degree of travel, and it is something that cannot be rushed.'

'What on Earth are you making him do?'

'Oh, nothing heretic, you can be guaranteed. I have him on a little treasure hunt; there are certain things I need him to find, and unfortunately for everyone, they are not all in once place. Once he finds them, you are both free to go.'

'What kind of things?'

'Ah, dear Radka, I am afraid I have already divulged far more than my deepest suspicions suggest is wise.'

Radka pondered that for a second. He had clearly sidestepped the issue. 'Why can't you look for these things yourself? Why does he have to do it?'

'Because Radka, there is a bounty on my head. If I go running out into the big wide world, I'll get it blown off. You see, my dear, I am as much of a prisoner as you are.'

Radka was unconvinced, and remained aloof. Collins broke the brief silence with more dialogue. 'I think it's time to go. Shall we?'

'Where? Back to the apartment where you have me incarcerated?'

'Yes Radka, back to the apartment. I'm done talking.'

He smiled again, erudite and with a firm belief in his convictions; a smile of confidence and control, the smile one makes when one knows one has the upper hand. If he was pragmatic, then she was sanguine, but was her sanguinity just a façade? And for how long would Casino Collins hold this accolade against the Czech? Only time could narrate that chronicle.

*

He watched the man and the woman leave the Air Café to liaise with two other men by the market square. The four of them clambered into a black Škoda coupe and took off.

He started the engine of his own vehicle, a rented hatchback import made in Korea, and began to follow them. He wore an earpiece and his hands-free phone setup was functioning properly. He placed a call. An ancient raspy voice answered.

'Sir, it's me. He left the café and is moving east out of the centre.'

'Ok, tail them and find out where they are holed up. Analyse their surroundings Chaplin, and determine whether the information we seek is on-site.'

'Affirmative. Also, he is with a woman. I don't know who she is, but he arrived and left with her in tow. What shall I do if I can identify the information?'

'Get it and then kill him.'

'And the woman? What do you suggest?'

There was a long pause. 'What do you mean what do I suggest? Isn't it obvious to you Chaplin? Missions like this always create collateral damage. There are always casualties of war. The primary target is him. But if she gets caught in the crossfire, then so be it.'

'I understand, Mr Ross. So you're saying her death would be acceptable?'

'That is what I am saying, yes. Stake it out tonight and give me an update in the morning.'

'Roger that, Sir. Out.'

Chaplin ended the call. He was most thrilled. He would have to have his fun with her before he killed her. She was older than his usual type; she was over the legal age of consent after all. That kind of took the fun out of it. But he would make an exception

62

for her; she was beautiful, after all. The thought of it gave him an erection.

Chapter Eight

Chester, England. 9:23 p.m.

James retrieved the printout containing Collins'
communiqué from the den and set out on foot from
the house. There was an egregious spring in his
step, fuelled by an intermingled mess of panic,
anger, frustration and wonder. His primary concern
was the safety of his ex-wife, who at this very
moment was no doubt in the clutches of some
sleazy henchman of Casino Collins. This is what
fired his cylinders the most. But, as incensed as he
was, he was also determined in his desire to
penetrate through the intricate layers of the
conundrum standing in the way of his life.

He once again passed The Albion Inn public
house and threaded down Park Street. At the corner
he admired the grand pianos in the front facing
window of the music shop juxtaposed against the
Roman Gardens and crossed Pepper Street, heading
towards the Amphitheatre.

He passed Off The Wall on his left and cursed
the memory of the night that had set everything in
motion. He continued up Little St John Street until
he hit Foregate Street. The grand golden clock
shimmered in the stinging frost like a beguiled
apparition up on the walls to his left.

James turned away from it and headed down
Foregate Street in the direction of the train station.
The route was painful, serving as a reminder of his
past life in the city with Radka. He dug his hands
deep into the pockets of his jeans and shivered,
walking briskly, breathing out pockets of glacial air.

His iPod provided a stirring theme tune to his misery, playing back Pearl Jam's *Black* through the headphones lodged snugly inside his ears.

It was funny how song lyrics could never fail to find a connection with the experiences of their audience, how the song seemed to be speaking directly to the listener. How the words accurately described what the audience was going through, personally. James' life had been full of anamorphic colour during his marriage to Radka. In her absence his heart was filled with a blackness that transcended any physical spectrum.

And as he walked the city streets, every facet of his surroundings reminded him of her. Every restaurant he passed provoked a memory from the past; a special occasion, a romantic table for two, holding hands over candlelight, soaking up the ambience. No small talk; instead, a meaningful conversation.

The street lights only heightened his loneliness. Street musicians performing timeless classics circumvented his soul and taunted it. The lacklustre beams of red and white steaming off vehicles danced around him like tormented souls, their flickering omnipotence harsh and menacing.

He glanced inside the window of the wedding shop he and Radka had passed countless times before, each occasion providing her with a pretext to indulge him with her fantasies of a soon-to-be engagement followed by marriage in the foreseeable future. But he hadn't been ready. It wasn't a phobia of commitment, or monogamy, for these were things that James firmly believed in. No, it was something more. The time wasn't right for him, and for some reason his heart had not been into it. In fact his heart had not been into it for some months; some powerful entity had wrenched the passion out of him, he did not know why, but it had occurred nonetheless.

He had changed. He had no idea why, but it was something he hadn't been able to dismiss as a phase or a whim. It was a permanent heartfelt transition. He had lost his ability to be intimate with her, through a lack of desire. Sex had become an issue for him. His appetite for it had dwindled to a near-loss of virility. His libido had been sucked dry. With each rejection Radka had died a small death inside. Her tears would flow like the floodgates had been opened, and to see this hurt, this rejection, this total lack of desire on his part causing her severe heartbreak, meant that he then died a small death too.

From his point of view they had become seasoned companions who shared a communal living space. How had this happened? How had his desire and his passion and his unabridged love for her fizzled out like a firework disappearing from the infinite sky?

In the beginning they had made love three or four times a day, to a point of physical exertion. The thought of being intimate with another woman had managed to evade his psyche completely. They had been all over Europe together, and much of England. James had seen parts of his homeland he hadn't known had existed. But it went beyond that; it was a spiritual fulfilment that seemed insatiable, that it would go on forever. Their relationship was a religion in its own right; it was the type where ones partner is also ones best friend.

In some aspects it had been like a veteran marriage. There were no taboos. No restrictions. No uncomfortable pontificating or awkward silences. No need for caution – the boundaries had been learnt. The understanding went to the core of their souls. It was the most natural coming together of two people on Earth.

But nothing lasts forever. All good things must come to an end. It was just that James had thought that fate and the Gods were going to make an exception for them; a payment in kind for their unity, which set a shining example for humankind. But alas they had failed to do so.

James headed down a flight of concrete steps and entered the subway tunnel. Once inside he zigzagged around to the left, heading for City Road. It stank of urine and its walls were infested with bad graffiti. A homeless beggar perched near the exit, a hand extended. 'Can you spare any change please Sir?' James removed a pound coin from his jeans pocket and placed it in the grimy palm. 'God bless you Sir' the tramp mumbled. James nodded politely and turned right, heading through the exit and up the stairs.

He had made this journey many times before. Usually it was to meet Radka after work; her day job at the bank installing antivirus and spyware software and performing systems maintenance required unsociable shift patterns, and after dark he would walk up to the redbrick complex and wait inside reception for her to finish. Then he'd walk her home. There was no way he was going to allow her to walk home alone in the dark, especially not through the subway tunnel. He'd never seen any trouble down there, but he didn't want to tempt karma.

He headed up City Road, passing the banks of the canal to his right, and the Thai and Teppan Yaki place he had taken her for their last anniversary. Their satay peanut sauce was divine. He glanced in at the ornate golden décor, bringing a nuance of the Orient into the fray.

The icy canal waters twinkled under the moonlight. The moon was full and visible grey craters appeared to form in the shape of a face. James caught the warm basking glow of white and thought for a minute that the face in the moon was smiling at him; mocking him. A sinister feeling crept over him and he looked away. The train station was looming on the horizon.

He preyed for Radka's safety. He thought about the Czech Republic and how it had served as his second home for so long. He vowed to go back there and bring Radka back to safety.

He entered the train station and headed left, away from the ticket counter, and towards the portaloo cabins outside. The station itself was deserted. The coffee kiosk was manned by a sole vendor. There was one single customer, a youngish man in a corduroy suit sipping coffee from a Styrofoam cup.

James did not notice him, but if he had he would have remembered him. The man was covered head to toe in white medical dressing; there was a pot on his arm and a bandage around his waist. He appeared to be in a bad way; sat in a wheelchair with his right leg suspended, animated, elevated outwards at forty-five degrees. He appeared to have been in a terrible accident, and had probably sustained multiple injuries.

James entered the nearest portaloo and closed the door behind him. Once inside, he smiled. His hunch had paid off. Somebody at the Council had years ago come up with a most ingenious idea to a vastly escalating problem. Public toilets in city centres were breeding grounds for junkies and dealers. The simple yet effective answer had been to fill them with ultraviolet light. The UV beams ensconce the veins on your body so that injection is altogether impossible.

He pulled the note out of his inside jacket pocket and held it up in the centre of the small chamber. He was basking in an eerie blue hue; it was neither debilitating nor enchanting; it was strange but seemed to represent a middle ground, a nothing, like purgatory. He turned the paper over to reveal the blank side.

Nothing appeared to be happening. James was dismayed. His frustrations were suddenly interrupted by an eruption of resonant sound that came from behind. Somebody was banging on the portaloo door. 'Hey! You nearly finished? I'm bursting out here!'

'Hang on, just a minute pal!' James turned back around and stared at the blankness of the white A4 sheet. He had no idea how the science of the process worked. *Did it just take time?*

The banging returned. Sharp impatient blasts of noise. 'Jesus, use another one!' James blurted back indignantly. He glanced back to the paper, about to hurl a fresh new round of abuse at this irate customer, when he jumped and caught his tongue. The page was no longer blank. Instead handwritten lettering, as black as the night sky and printed in the same style as before, spoke to him with inky clarity.

F R 4 1 8 5 M 2 C D G 3 2 3 0 2 1 4 1 5

James reached into his jacket pocket and smiled in relief. He withdrew a crumpled old bus ticket from yesteryear and rewrote the alphanumeric message on the back. He was about to leave the portaloo when he froze. It was a ridiculous notion, but instinct told him to check the small cabin for any further clues. If somebody was clever enough to go this far, then they were more than capable of stashing something small inside this cramped loo, something only discoverable if one looked specifically for it.

He knelt down, making sure not to touch the dirty floor with his jeans. The loos were no doubt cleaned on a regular basis, but the general public had some pretty peculiar habits when it came to public lavatories and personal hygiene. He had even seen it inside the gents at the law college; strands of tissue strewn across the floor, taps left running, puddles of water in places where puddles of water should not be. And these were educated twenty-something law students. He had lodged numerous complaints with administration services, but to no avail. Now he was in a train station, a place notorious for its colourfully odd clientele.

Begrudgingly he placed a hand on the underside of the basin and poked around, grimacing as he did. God only knew what diseases he could leave the station with after this dire task was completed. But it did pay off. Sure enough, a small plastic object was sellotaped there. He ripped it off and took it in his hand. It was a small die-cast model of an aeroplane, the kind British Airways would sell in their in-flight brochure, or a trinket in a museum gift shop sold as a keyring. Surely its presence was no coincidence, but a clue left behind by an associate of Casino Collins; another Murgatroyd, or maybe even the entrepreneur himself, though surely he'd sooner die than get his hands dirty.

James stepped out of the portaloo and was nearly pushed to the ground by the dishevelled looking man desperate to get in. The poor guy had been patient enough. The other cabins were labelled with signs that tacitly stated *Out of order!* James now realised. He walked back through into the main waiting lounge and passed the Costa Coffee kiosk.

The bandaged man was still there, still sipping his coffee, minding his own business.

James had a hunch about what the coded set of letters and numbers represented, but he had to make doubly sure. To do that would require a computer and an internet connection. He was certain that the train station would have wireless network points for customers to tap into. There didn't appear to be any cybercafés in the immediate vicinity, so the former would have to do.

James glanced to his right and saw a businessman hunched over three metal chairs plumbed into the concrete ground, his head resting on a black leather satchel. It looked like a laptop bag. It was a laptop bag.

He approached the man and sat down on a chair two away from the guy's feet. James decided to try out a tactic he thought would work. Falsely he suddenly yawned loudly, stretching out his arms for good measure. The man stirred and raised his head, a frown of displeasure and confusion written on his face; that just-woken-up look.

'Oh sorry, did I wake you?' the law tutor offered with fake compassion.

The man sat up and rubbed at his temples. Another city slicker on his return from an intercontinental business trip. No doubt he had secured a million-dollar deal. Probably a banker. 'What time is it friend?'

'A quarter to ten, mate.' *Mate* usually sealed the deal. A friendly introduction warmed a person, putting them on your side. 'I don't suppose I could borrow your laptop, could I mate?'

The man sized James up. He didn't seem like a random thief or a kid trying to trick him. He didn't look like a junkie searching for a quick sale to make an even quicker purchase for a fast fix. His bullshit detector tuned out. He reached into the satchel and pulled out a black Sony Vaio. 'Be my guest.'

'You're a legend!' James smiled warmly and took the notebook from the stranger. He put the bus ticket with the scribbled message on the smooth metal surface below the keyboard and loaded the Google homepage. Without the toy aeroplane it could have pertained to be anything. A needle in a haystack James had not the time or inclination to search for. Radka needed him, regardless of whether they were on speaking terms or not. But with the little clue left for him, it was hardly rocket science.

James keyed into the search box the first six characters from the message. F R 4 1 8 5. Only six hundred and thirty five results – James was surprised. Still no Googlewhack though. The first link made him grin devilishly. *www.flightstats.com* was the URL, and it even carried with it the logo of a miniature aircraft, much like the one he had found in the portaloo. He hit the link. *Flight FR4185 on schedule, departing from Manchester International (Terminal 2) 23rd February 14:15, arrives at Paris Charles de Gaulle Terminal 3 16:45.*

He cross-referenced this against the coded message and made the deductions. His hunch had been perfectly accurate. *F R 4 1 8 5 M 2 C D G 3 2 3 0 2 1 4 1 5. F R 4 1 8 5* was the flight number. *M 2* clearly stood for Manchester, terminal 2. *C D G* was an abbreviation for Charles de Gaulle, the airport in Paris named after the former French President who led the Free French Forces during World War Two. *3* was the denominator for terminal 3. *2 3 0 2* was the date of the flight, 23rd February, tomorrow, and *1 4 1 5* the departure time – 14:15. So that was it – James was expected to get on a flight to Paris without asking any further questions! He would do it; for Radka.

'Why so happy? Your team win or something?' The stranger who had lent him the laptop was now trying to strike up a conversation. James handed him back the computer. 'Not quite, mate, not quite. Thanks for the loan.'

'No worries friend. Hey, put this in the trash on the way out, would you?' The stranger handed James an empty coffee cup. The law tutor frowned, but found himself taking the cup anyway, out of politeness. *Why can't you throw out your own damn trash?*

James got out of the chair and headed for the exit. He would need a good few hours of sleep if he was to come back tomorrow morning and get on a train to Manchester Airport. He'd need to arrive two hours before his scheduled departure, therefore no later than 12:15. The train ride from Chester to

Manchester International took about an hour. He didn't have that much time.

He looked inside the empty cup he was about to toss into a trash receptacle by the exit to the station and instantly froze. His feet remained rooted to the ground for several overbearing seconds. There was something inside.

He dipped into the cup, which had clearly never housed a hot liquid, for it was perfectly clean and dry, and removed a sheet of card. It was a plane ticket. His, evidently. The thought of how he was to fund such a trip and acquire a ticket at such short notice had never occurred to him. Grimacing, he turned around and darted back into the arrivals lounge. The chairs were empty; the suit was gone. James scanned the vicinity but could not make a positive sighting of the stranger with the notebook computer.

He turned and made for the exit a second time. By now it was freezing, and he shuddered as he left the warmth of the station and returned to the morose chill of the winter night. He retraced his steps and headed home, walking back down City Road, passing the canal now to his left, slipping under the subway tunnel, emerging at the tail end of Foregate Street, heading towards the clock.

He hung a left down Little St John Street towards the Amphitheatre, crossed Pepper Street, walked briskly down Park Street and cut a right onto Albion Place. The moon was still full and still shining down with great intensity. The face had vanished; all that sustained was a bright white plate in the teeming vastness of the blanket of noir enveloping the modest Roman metropolis.

James had been offered three opportunities to acknowledge the bandaged man who sat patiently at the coffee kiosk, drinking his coffee, minding his own business, and had failed to do so on all three occasions. But that was a trivial thing. What was important was that the bandaged man had noticed him. And once he had made the positive identification, he was certain that the plan was progressing swimmingly.

The bandaged man appeared to be in great pain. Nevertheless, after much wriggling about and an awkward protraction of his damaged limbs, he was able to retrieve a thin black cellular phone from a pocket and hit a speed dial key to make the call.

'Allo?' A woman answered in French.

'Tiffanny? C'est moi. Comment vas-tu?' *Tiffanny, it's me. How are you?* The conversation unfolded in French.

'I'm good. Are you safe?'

'Yes, don't you worry. He's on his way to Paris tomorrow.'

'So it's working then?'

'Apparently. But I can't fly like this, it's too painful, and I'm sure it would invalidate my insurance if I tried. So, Tiffanny, you'll have to be his chaperone.'

'Fine.'

'Where are you now?'

'Still in Strasbourg. But I have a car. I will drive to Paris. Is the rendezvous point as we discussed?'

'Yes, there has been no change. I'll leave him in your capable hands. Merci beaucoup Tiff.' *Thanks a lot Tiff.*

'De rien Stewart. Au revoir.' *You're welcome Stewart. See you later.*

'Salut.' *Bye.*

Stewart Banks, who had partially recovered from his ordeal in Slovakia six months earlier, ended the call and placed the cell phone on the table. His work was done. For now.

Chapter Nine

Wednesday 23rd February. 2:20 p.m.

The flight from Manchester to Paris was a short snapshot of aeronautical routine. The journey took approximately forty five minutes, which was shorter than the average sojourn taken from the ticket-holder's home to get to the airport. Life is full of small ironies like this. Airtime was a little over twenty minutes; the rest comprised of takeoff and landing.

James gazed out of the window for the whole stretch. Despite having always been a frequent flyer, he still marvelled at the ingenuity behind the physics of it. It seemed simple, yet in reality it was so sophisticated that it blew the mind. The wings were shaped in such a way as to ensure that the air travelling underneath them travelled faster than its counterpart on the topside. This effectively created a sucking motion that kept the aircraft sky-borne.

But it was the exhilaration of takeoff that thrilled him the most. That he never tired of. It was the combination of forces; the aircraft's mass, the aircraft's speed, and the force of gravity, all making it possible to lift several thousand tonnes of aluminium alloy and keep it suspended in flight, aided by the jet engine's fuel combusting with oxygen.

He felt a small twist of excitement convulse inside him. He had always found it fascinating how England and France could be such a world apart, considering their geographical proximity.

The law tutor made a note of the aerial view of the scenery as they cruised over Manchester, following the redbrick architecture as it gave way to a majestic polka dot patchwork quilt of blue and white. Fluffy white cumulus clouds clustered the bright azure sky like the brash smatterings of an abstract painting; a Giacometti or a Gustave Klimt.

He followed the contours of the warped sky, comprising of sheets of blue that became darker as it spanned up to the heavenly mystique of space; cyan became regal blue became royal blue became petrol blue became gunmetal blue became indigo became navy, heading to the inevitable noir of the final frontier. He imagined breaching the threshold of the Earth's atmosphere.

He'd once read about a service the Russians offered to the rich. For 12,000 US dollars, a Russian fighter pilot would take you up in a MiG-29 Foxbat to what was deemed the *edge of space* on the tip of the Earth's atmosphere eighty thousand feet above ground.

It was the highest a jet engine could go; beyond that lay the oxygen-less vacuum of space, and a jet engine cannot combust without oxygen. But it was close enough for most people that could afford the trip – from there you can see the Earth, the Sun, the Moon and the stars. You also get to break three G's on the return journey back to terra firma. They also provide a tour of Moscow Museum of Aircraft and Cosmonautics, which had been a secret until the Americans exposed its potential in the aftermath of the Cold War. And in typical slapdash Russian gumption, the health and safety check was ultimately a pilot's cursory glance up and down your body to ensure you weren't riddled with leprosy or some other ludicrous contagion.

James looked on. In a few minutes, when the pilot would bring the august bird down onto Parisian soil, he knew his surroundings would be transformed from the drab regimented industria of England's North-West into the teeming, vibrant metamorphosis of renaissance construction, a ride through the veins of history, a hark back to the various Louis' of the French monarchy who provided painstaking dedication to their kingdom's grandeur. *Paris je t'aime.*

He would soon return to that glorious strip of land that housed mainland Europe, a world apart from the island he had inhabited for the last thirty years. He would hear the soothing beauty of the Gallic tongue. He would sample culinary delights such as *escargots*; snails oozing in garlic sauce. He would smack his lips after savouring the finest vin rouge in the bistros.

He would take a stroll down the Champs-Élysées, mount Gustave Eiffel's phallic tower and gaze down on the white-stone citadel, a metropolic paradise, noting the Arc du Triomphe lambasting out like a champion to be remembered. He would visit the Louvre in the courtyard fronting la Pyramide Inversée. He would enter and be lost amongst tens of thousands of paintings. He would stroll down the Denon Wing and imagine the Da Vinci Code story unfolding before his very eyes. He would wait eagerly amongst the throng of tourists jostling for breathing space as they perched by the Mona Lisa, housed inside a small glass chamber, much smaller than most people realise; she fitted on an A3 canvas.

He would. If this was an ordinary trip. But it wasn't. He had been pushed onto the seat of a plane by an entrepreneur holding his wife hostage. And when he disembarked at his destination, then what? He had no luggage, just his ticket, passport and the clothes on his back. What was he supposed to do when he arrived? Would he be picked up? Would there be another cryptic message awaiting his attention? Would he have to find another ultraviolet viewing point lest the new message be written in invisible ink like the last?

Where could he be expected to find such a specific place in all the arrondissements of a big city like Paris? All these questions were brought into the fray, and yet the clouds he gazed at out of the plane window were twinned with the clouds in his own thoughts preventing him from knowing what to do next.

There was no time for a meal on the plane, not that any of the low-budget airlines offered. They had revolutionised the frequent flyer market. Everything was cheap and cheerful. Business theorists have identified five core objectives from which to pave their way to success; cost, speed, flexibility, dependability and quality. Focusing on one meant sacrificing the others. It wasn't possible to achieve more than one simultaneously. It was the ultimate opportunity cost.

The British Airways' and the Monarch Airlines' of the old had passed the floor to the newcomers; the Jet2s, the Ryanairs and the BMI Babies. Flying was no longer for the well to do. The bourgeoisie had to journey alongside the riff-raff, heaven forbid. James was provided with a complementary bag of peanuts, which he found unduly odd as no other passenger seemed to have been afforded the same luxury. He didn't feel like a snack, so he pocketed the nuts for later consumption.

By 4:30 James had landed, disembarked, entered the airport and was now trying to orientate himself. Once out of the arrivals lounge there was no need to collect any baggage from the carousel – he had none, just a travel bag he had taken onboard as hand luggage, containing a change of clothes, underwear and basic toiletries.

Instead he walked straight towards the exit. He glanced at the people with placards waiting to intercept specific passengers. The first two names failed to grab his attention; *M. Sharma, East India Tech., Shelley Fuller*. The third, held by a pretty twenty-something woman, made him stop in his tracks. *James Loxbridge.*

The woman was quintessentially French. Her Gallic features were reminiscent of her ancestors the Gauls, a tribe of warriors that had nearly laid waste to Ancient Rome during one unforgettable siege. Her skin pigmentation matched that of an olive.

Her hair was chestnut brown and hung delicately down her shoulders in wisped curls. Her eyes were enchanting; brown orbs piercing through her field of vision and into his. She was dressed in blue jeans, black trainers and a white top. Her smile radiated warm energy, like a sonar panel. Ironically it sent a chilling tingle down James' spine.

Even if she had not held up a sign bearing his name, he would have still stopped to gawk at her. She was immensely beautiful, like a thousand sunsets rolled into one beam. As they made eye contact James returned the smile with as much warmth and sincerity as he could muster under the confusing circumstances.

'Allo' she said, in that sexy way French people speak English, their musical accent a pleasant undertone to any conversation with them. 'I am Tiffanny. Tiffanny Tourneux.' She extended a hand.

James looked at the bronzed feminine hand and felt an intense desire to grab it, kiss it, and draw the rest of her body into his. He resisted and instead shook it delicately.

'Hello. I'm James Loxbridge. Of course, you already know that. It's written on your sign.'

Tiffanny laughed and then led him to the exit. 'You have a good flight?'

James felt another tingle. He had one each time she opened her mouth; every time her lips parted and that music released itself from her lungs.

'Yeah it was fine.' He walked in line with her, matching her petite, feminine steps by deliberately taking smaller ones of his own.

'Did you receive the key?'

James frowned, puzzled. 'Key?'

'Oui. You should have been provided with a key on the plane. Maybe it was done underhandedly. You checked your pockets since you landed?'

James instinctively reached inside his jeans pocket and rummaged around. He felt the familiar shapes of his wallet and the cell phone Murgatroyd had given him. Then he found the small bag of peanuts and pulled them out. 'I did get these, much to my amazement.' He showed them to the Frenchwoman.

'Ah yes, neat trick. Open it.'

'Huh?'

'Just open it' Tiffanny urged. 'And don't worry if you don't find anything edible in there. I'm taking you to dinner tonight.' She grinned like she had an evil plan up her sleeve.

With his teeth, James tore at the plastic shell and pulled off one of the corner edges. He ripped open the rest with his fingers and emptied the contents out into his palm. Not peanuts, not food at all. Instead, there was a small ceramic box. Inside the box was a small gold key.

'What does it open?' he asked the Frenchwoman.

'A safe deposit box' Tiffanny explained. 'Not far from here. Come on, time is of the essence, as you Anglaises say.'

'But how did I manage to get through the metal detectors with this?'

'It was given to you mid-flight. You are examined by the metal detectors at the departure point before your inbound journey. Belts, shoes, jackets, everything with any metal on it is removed. But think James; you do not go through the same process when arriving at the destination airport. You just flash your passport and you're through.'

James had never given it a second thought, but she was right of course. Terrorists would be able to take advantage of that if they had someone on the inside during the flight that could slip them something like a weapon or components for a bomb. It was a flaw in the security system that needed correcting.

Tiffanny led James out of Charles de Gaulle and down a side street. They continued for a few hundred yards before the Frenchwoman hung a sharp right and onto a small industrial estate. She opened a gate and snuck through an alley. At the end it emerged onto a forecourt. In the corner were a set of metal lockers. She motioned for James to approach them.

'It's number thirty-eight' the Frenchwoman stated excitedly. 'Don't hesitate – we have to leave soon' she added tersely.

'What is this place?' the tutor asked.

'It's still part of Charles de Gaulle. It's for the most highly regarded employees, like a gold card.'

'So how come we have one?' He used *we* as if somehow he could convince himself that they were an item, sharing a locker like couples share everything. Next he'd be inventing a whole new life for them both.

Tiffanny smiled in response to his question; the kind that infers *it's need to know and you don't need to.* James retrieved the small gold key once again and plunged it into the hole of locker thirty-eight. He shook his head as he did so. *What was he getting himself involved in?!*

Inside was a large brown padded jiffy bag. James pulled it out and ran his fingers over the edges. He studied the front and then flipped it over and checked out the back. Both sides were bereft of any writing.

'Open it' Tiffanny instructed politely, smiling at him as she did with those warm chestnut eyes that swallowed James up in their grandeur.

The lawyer cum tutor complied, peeling off the folded flap and slicing through the glue with his thumb. He emptied the contents out into his hands. Tiffanny glanced around to check that they weren't being monitored. They weren't. No prying eyes, no security cameras. The place was secluded. James studied the items; a receipt for a reservation at L'Hotel Magenta in the name of James Loxbridge, single room, and a wad of Euro bills fastened together with an elastic band.

'Good, it's all there'. Tiffanny appeared pleased with the contents of the jiffy bag. James nodded and put everything back inside. 'You do know my wife has been kidnapped?'

Tiffanny smiled, this time from polite nervousness. 'I thought you were separated?'

James smiled, but his was from the satisfaction of seeing her fall for his little trap. 'So you know quite a lot about me then, I'm guessing?'

Tiffanny pouted. 'I read your file. At least, the parts that interested me.'

James scorned incredulously. 'I have a file?'

'Oops, guilty again! You have a file.'

'Interesting. So what happens now? I'll save myself the trouble of asking you any questions about my wife or why I'm here; I have no doubt you'll think of some excuse not to give me any information. So let's just get on with it.'

'There's no need to be curt, James. I have nothing to hide. I am here to help you. I assure you of that. Help me, and I'll return the favour. I am a friend, an ally, whatever you want to call it. We are on the same side.'

'And what side is that?'

'The correct one.'

'So what happens now?' James repeated the question.

'You see you have a reservation at the Hotel Magenta. Go check in, freshen up, get changed into some nice smart evening wear, which you will find in your room, and meet me at Café Kleber at 7:30. It's opposite the Eiffel Tower, you can't miss it.'

James looked at the beautiful Frenchwoman. 'Ok, I'll take the metro to Trocadéro and walk from there. Should only take ten minutes max.'

'Ah, it sounds like you know Paris pretty well James!'

'I've been here before on several occasions. Café Kleber, 7:30, smart wear, you got it. Question is, what will you wear?'

'Oh, I'm sure you won't be disappointed. I will tell you everything you need to know, tonight. Until then, a plus tard.' *See you later.*

'A plus, Tiffanny.'

The Frenchwoman set off back towards the airport. She headed back down the alleyway. Before she disappeared around the corner, she glanced back to look at James and smiled. He felt the shivers again but returned the gesture all the same. She'd had quite an effect on him.

James went back towards the entrance to Charles de Gaulle, where a row of bored taxi drivers chatted, their vehicles idle. He motioned to one of them and clambered inside a teal coloured Renault Espace people carrier.

The driver asked where he was headed and James told him to take him to L'Hotel Magenta on the boulevard it shared its name with. The journey took twenty minutes. Charles de Gaulle airport is situated at the very north end of Paris, out of the city limits. The driver headed south, passing the Stade de France in the Saint-Denis suburb on their right. The stadium had been the venue for the 1998 World Cup final that saw the French team beat the Brazilian favourites 3-0 to claim the trophy and the ultimate accolade.

The driver continued on what was essentially the highway; the French called it the Principaux Itineraires – the main traffic artery. Eventually he came off it by the Cité de la Musique, just before the Porte de Pantin, and converged onto the Avenue Jean Jaures. After a few miles it became the Rue La Fayette, one of the most famous streets in central Paris.

The driver navigated through moderate afternoon traffic as James glanced out the window at the mobile metropolic scenery. They passed the Place de la Bataille de Stalingrad on their right. The driver was listening to the radio. This facet amused and comforted James – for him it represented the starting point of any trip abroad. After landing, leaving the airport and finding transport to the accommodation, the first subtle reminder that you were in a foreign country was hearing a radio blaring, the show's presenter spewing out rapid-fire foreign language like it was going out of fashion. The French did seem to speak very quickly in their native tongue, it was true. James strained to pick up the gist of the dialogue; some advertisement, by the sound of the excited voiceover. Something about soap.

After passing the Gare du Nord metro station, the driver reached the intersection crisscrossing the Rue Magenta. He smoothly navigated the Renault down Boulevard Magenta, passing the Gare de L'est, and pulled up outside the Hotel Magenta on the left, near the Place de la République. James paid the man with a twenty-Euro note and disembarked. The driver sped away towards his next fare. James entered the hotel and checked in. He reminded himself once again of his elation at the thought of being back in Paris. And once again, he only wished it was under happier circumstances.

Chapter Ten

Paris, France. 6:45 p.m.

The Hotel Magenta lay at the heart of the historical Le Marais district, a stone's throw from Place de la République. It had recently been renovated, and the exterior façade was basking in a fresh lick of purple overcoat. Directly above, the petite verandas of the corresponding rooms protruded, their lattice-clad awnings set back against sculptured stonework; a contrast of black and beige. A consortium of European flags hung from slender poles secured to the frontage. The cloud-devoid dusk sky was a fusion of indigo-noir, adding an extra layer of mystique and romance to the sycamore-lined street. A soft, gentle zephyr whisked through them, stirring the branches bereft of bloom in the winter solstice into an enchanting dance.

Through the foyer and into the lobby area, evidence of refurbishment was substantiated. The traditional oak panelling, beech fixtures and renaissance watercolour portraits of old had made way for a grand metamorphosis to chic modernity. The colour scheme was ultimately metallic; an amalgamation of dusty pink, gunmetal blue and industry-standard silver, coalescing into each other and the environs of the room. It was an almost sickly look. Gazing around the room and taking in the rich ambience was like over-indulging on a highly processed dessert, and regretting it afterwards.

The glass fronted reception desk was manned by a pretty mademoiselle operating an Apple Mac. Her nametag read *Camille*. Her smooth chestnut hair floated down to her shoulders. Her cheeks were prominent – they must have been a pleasure to kiss. Her chocolate eyes penetrated the details on her computer with the intensity of a professional. They radiated intelligence.

She was dressed smartly in a white blouse, black skirt and pointed boat shoes with just enough of a heel to be heard, and small ribbon bows front-side. The tops of her feet appeared smooth and luxurious under the soft ample lighting of the room. Her lips were thin; her hands petite and well looked after. Her nails were manicured. Her right ear was partially concealed beneath a tuft of hair.

The antechamber leading to the accommodations led the spectrum of colour a shade deeper and into a violet-purple courtyard of decadence. Magnificent marble pillars, some finished in two-tone cyan and plum, others given an art-nouveau zebra skin décor, were mounted from ceiling to floor. They elevated the grandeur of the hall and gave it a courtyard feel, complemented by a tiled mezzanine reminiscent of those seem in the cathedrals of the West. A large, wall-mounted watercolour painting projected a picturesque meadow setting on a framed silver canvas. Below it, comfy four-piece settees provided a resting place for the über-chic clientele.

Upstairs on the third floor, in room 316, a man was preparing in a room that continued the theme of stylish elegance. Loxbridge had been given a single, an *economie individuelle*, which was more than suitable for him, considering he'd had little choice in the matter. The walls were terracotta, the carpet a pale magenta in keeping with the hotel's identity. The ceiling and door were as white as a swan's plumage.

James had showered and changed into new clothing that had been neatly stashed into a wardrobe at Tiffanny's arrangement. It comprised of beige slacks, a blue flannel shirt and soft, comfortable loafers. He would have preferred to stick with the jeans and t-shirt he had travelled in, and he would have felt self-conscious in the new outfit at home.

But he was in France, the land of the stylish and the understatedly elegant. He remembered the classic adage *When in Rome, do as the Romans do.* Besides, he was attending a date of sorts. Although being sent on some clandestine mission for a maniacal entrepreneur philanthropist, in exchange for the safe return of a woman he used to call his wife, his life and soul, went some way in removing any romance from the proceedings. After all, it was all contrived.

Splayed out on the bed were the items he currently had at his disposal; his passport, a rolled-up wad of Euro bills, a gold key to an airport locker encased in ceramic, and two pieces of paper – the first with the original set of instructions from Collins, the second the coded printout which had been stuffed inside a Styrofoam coffee cup and discreetly put about his person by a random suit on a train station bench, who'd turned out to be quite the opposite, which, when decrypted, had him jumping on a plane and leaving the country.

A little over forty-eight hours ago, the law tutor had been contentedly basking in relative mediocrity; happily swirling in the cauldron of routine. He was working out, he had papers to mark; he was getting by. There was great irony in the situation, James realised. He wanted this charade to be over so he could get back to grieving a lost love. However, that very love was the subject of the charade. He did not appreciate to what extent, but Radka was being used as a bargaining chip for something. The items on the bed represented the jumbled pieces of James' resolve; the discombobulated pages of his life chronicle.

He pocketed the items and left the room. He threaded his way down the corridor, smoothly cast in a warm, gentle lighting subdued in pale cerise, and made his way through the antechamber, past the zebra-skin pillars, down the hallway and meandered out through reception. Camille was still there. James gave her a smile that epitomised warmth as he checked out, and she returned the gesture.

He had a choice of two stations nearby with which to jump on the metro – Gare de L'est to the North, and Place de la République to the South. He elected for the former and exited the hotel, turning right and marching briskly up Boulevard Magenta. The earlier breeze had subsided and the air was still, as were the sycamores lining the central causeway; a neat cluster planted in tiny allotments crevassed into the paving stones.

At the end of the boulevard he hung a right onto Rue du Saint Martin. He reached a small park adjacent to the canal adopted by the same saint. The canal snaked east towards the Place de la Bataille de Stalingrad. The park was deserted in the chill of February, its neglected accompaniments and water features patiently waiting for the tourist rush that would bring a stampede of foreigners inside in the summer months.

The Gare de L'est came into view up ahead. James sauntered through the entrance, beaded his way around a throng of journey-makers and found the *guichet* – ticket office. He preyed his French, although rusty, would be of a high enough standard to be understood. Actually, speaking French was the easy part. The difficulty lay in being able to pick up the rapid-fire response. Sometimes it was easy enough to blag a counter-response with a sweeping statement that prevented the conversation from becoming nonsensical. But there was always a risk of making a faux-pas and consequently looking the fool. And the French see right through it. They know if your lingo is natural native or rehearsed tourist.

James bought a weekly pass for twenty-six Euros with the money from the lockup at Charles de Gaulle. He asked in French whether the ticket covered the whole of the city, or was based on specific zones. He was told it was for *le tous de Paris* – all of Paris – and felt that thrilling sensation of communicating in a foreign tongue and being totally comprehended.

He checked the wall chart for the right train, using the colour-coded route planner as a guide. There was one change on the journey. He rode the M5 to Oberkampf, and from there the M9 all the way west to Trocadéro. The ride lasted thirty minutes. During the rickety shunt through the underground tracks, his mind wandered back to the intrigue beginning to ensnare him. He thought about Tiffanny. He thought about Radka. He thought about Casino Collins. He felt confused, like his feelings were out of alignment, as if his mind had not been configured properly.

He re-read the original instructions from Collins, which he'd scribbled in biro in case he could not find another ultraviolet hub, and the one-line code he had found in the portaloo at Chester train station, also rewritten with visible ink.

He willed his head to discover something previously unseen. Perhaps he had overlooked something. The hunger pangs cascading out from the pit of his stomach and the after-effects of travel had made him weak and weary. He learnt nothing new from the text, so he placed the papers back in his pocket. He made a silent prayer for Radka, hoping she was safe and being well looked after.

James disembarked at Trocadéro and converged through more crowds of Parisians until he made it out of the station. He climbed the stairs to the waiting cityscape. He found himself in Passy – the sixteenth arrondissement. To get to Café Kléber he would need to cross over into the seventh – Invalides.

He gazed around at the new landscape. To the southeast of his location, the Palais de Chaillot peaked out of the metropolis, morose and grandiose in the impending twilight. Beyond that, the opulent teal shimmer of the river Seine snaked around the capital with a genteel but proud impunity, like a moat protecting a castle. The Eiffel Tower loomed on the opposite bank, a grey-steel monolith basking in a fervent amber hue. The rooftop searchlight panned the city in a three-sixty-degree angle, throwing out a milk-white wash of light overhead.

The lawman walked towards it, then performed a double-take and as he faced northwest his eye caught the neon blue lettering of Café Kléber's façade beckoning him forth. He felt a rush of cold energy traverse down his spine, causing him to shiver. It was not from the temperate winter solstice, with its cold winds carried to Europe on the North Atlantic Drift from America, but from the excitement of again meeting the Frenchwoman.

He crossed over onto Avenue Kléber and made his way to the street-front brasserie. His eyes danced across the few folk offering their custom and finally settled in the far corner, on a lone woman sat sipping a *kyr* – red wine with Crème de Cassis – at a small round table. It was her! It was the

Frenchwoman. As if in confirmation, she smiled at him, and he returned the pleasantry with a wave of his hand. She stood up and stepped forward to greet him. He kissed her twice, once on each cheek, in the way French companions do.

'Salut!' Comment vas-tu? *Hi! How are you?'*

'You look beautiful' James found himself uttering, like a teenager on his first ever date. Inside he silently cursed himself for behaving like a blundering idiot. It was true – she did. She was sporting a glamorous plum coloured halter dress over low Italian heels. The curly locks of her hair were tied upward in a fancy bun at the back. They accentuated her beauty a million fold.

'How beautiful?' she remarked playfully. James blushed.

'Tu es plus belle que mille couchers de soleil.' *You are more beautiful than a thousand sunsets.* He hoped it hadn't come across as pathetically as it had sounded bouncing off his lips. He searched her eyes for their reaction. They were unwavering in their gratitude. She smiled and grunted nervously.

'Merci beaucoup!' *Thanks a lot!*

'De rien.' *You're welcome.*

A waiter approached and asked for their order. Tiffanny recommended an aperitif and asked for an extra glass and a kyr for James, which the lawyer concurred with. Then the Frenchwoman ordered l'escargots for her entrée, and again James followed suit. The snails, oozing in garlic sauce, were a delightful delicacy to behold, and the trip to Paris would not have been complete without them. They each had six, feeling that twelve would have been overbearing. The specialist cutlery came with the dish – a clamp to hold the shell and a tiny pitchfork to prise the snails out. Bread was served on the side to mop up the succulent garlic juices oozing from the shells.

In between bites of snail and bread, James tried to strike up a conversation. 'So, where do you fit into all of this, Tiffanny?'

'All of what? Je ne comprend pas.' *I don't understand.*

'That's a good question! Well, whatever it is that Casino Collins is up to, which required the kidnap of my wife and which is why I am sat here talking to you now.'

'Oh that!' Her sarcastic mocking tone was of feigned ignorance. She had clearly amused herself. James held her gaze with relative seriousness. If she was to become slack-jawed, he had to play it cool. 'Well, I am a scientist. Actually, to be accurate, I am a pharmacologist, just like Radka.' When she used that name James flinched momentarily. Tiffanny did not appear to notice.

'Where are you from?'

'Strasbourg.'

'Do you work for Casino Collins?'

'Indirectly, yes.'

'What does that mean exactly?'

'It means exactly that I managed a team of scientists called Unity Six. They invented a product that Collins was particularly interested in. So, he facilitated the production process, in return for exclusivity. So in that respect, he is ultimately the person I currently answer to, at least until the product safely reaches the market. But I work for nobody.'

James placed the improvised forceps down on his plate and chewed on the last of the snails. Dabbing his mouth with a napkin, he pondered what the Frenchwoman had revealed. A gust of wind blew across the terrace, and he felt it zip through his hair, caressing his head with a gentle massage. In the impromptu silence between deliberations, Tiffanny seized the chance to flip a tuft of her hair behind her ear. James noticed the gesture and silently murmured a sigh of desire. Then he returned to the moment. Tiffanny's preliminary explanation had sparked more questions than answers.

'What is the product? Why would it not safely reach the market? You said you managed the scientists, past tense. Why don't you still manage them? Why is Radka involved? And why me?'

It took a moment for Tiffanny to process all those questions. She did not seem phased by his amateur Spanish Inquisition. 'The nature of the product, I am afraid, is off limits for discussion. But let me tell you, it is precisely why you are here now. Your job is to find it. I can no longer manage the scientists because they are all dead. Radka was a sure way to get you involved, obviously, and you were chosen because of your circumstances. I believe you call it leverage.'

'What circumstances? What leverage?'

'You have proven yourself to be an underground hero. You are responsible for the meagre state of peace the world enjoys today, as opposed to total annihilation, and only a select few individuals are aware of that. To most, you are just another man, a cry on the wind, a drop in the ocean, a needle in a haystack.

'But Mr Collins knows about what happened on that yacht in London. So for that, you are totally expendable. You are likely to succeed, because of your talents, and if you fail, your death can be covered up as another tragic accident overseas. Perhaps it would be a sudden illness, perhaps a traffic accident, or murdered by terrorists. Who cares, non?'

James took a breath. 'Well, nobody could say you aren't forthcoming! That was very straight up.'

'I am French, we do not sugar-coat things.'

'Ok, tell you what; I'll do some guesswork, and you tell me how hot I am. Alright?'

'Sure.'

'So, my thinking is, this product must either be very dangerous, or very special, because it sounds like your scientists have been killed in an attempt to prevent it from being manufactured. So, somebody does not want that product out there. It sounds like Casino Collins does want it out there, so he must have enemies who want to stop him.

'If we disregard the fact that he has kidnapped my wife for a moment, Collins is an entrepreneur well-regarded. That makes me think the product is something beneficial to society. If you're a pharmacologist, the product is presumably a drug of some kind. So, it must be a cure for something. And if it's so special that six scientists are dead because of it, it must be unique; a panacea.

'It must be a new development, never seen before; an innovation of massive potential. Which would make Collins' enemy a rival entrepreneur? No, that wouldn't make sense. Somebody who does not desire the cure is somebody who profits greatly from the suffering the cure would prevent. So what's the product?'

'I don't know, James. They kept it a secret from even me, to protect me. The plans and the formulas were perfected about six months ago, last summer, in the mountains of Slovakia. Unity Six managed to get the documents out before they were killed.

'Since that time, an associate of mine has arranged for the production process to begin. The location of that process is also a secret, but the process is nearing completion. Soon the drug will be ready to distribute covertly.'

'But you don't know what it is?'

'Like I said, there is a great deal of risk and money involved. I was chosen for my skills, as were you. The fewer people know about this, the safer the operation will be.'

'Or perhaps you do know but you just don't want to tell me.'

Tiffanny smiled curtly. 'Let's not be pedantic James. I need your help, and I have given you all the information I have. You have my word on that.'

'Is it a replacement for Tamiflu? A preventative measure against the next influenza pandemic? Is it a cure for the common cold?'

'Please James, I care little for small talk.'

'So this is Collins' next big enterprise? How will you eventually get it through mainstream distribution? How will you stop the pharmaceutical companies from sabotaging it?'

'With your help, naturally! That is why you are here! This associate of mine, his name is Stewart Banks. His associates are very secretive, but they have disseminated clues as to the plant's location across various cities. My job is to find them. I will receive coded briefs from Collins himself. Each one will help me decide where to look.'

'So what's my take in this?'

'You are here to protect me.'

'Protect you from whom?'

'A man called Paul Ross.'

'Who is he?'

'Ross is the majority shareholder in a conglomerate of pharmaceutical organisations. He is responsible for 95% of the current drugs on the market. It's a monopoly, and yet any potential competitor is still considered a threat. We do not know for certain, but our best intel suggests it was his organisation that organised the death of Unity Six.

'Perhaps they even carried out the cowardly murders themselves. So they have picked up a scent. They know that we are trying to bring in a new product under the radar. It's just a matter of time before they sniff out exactly what's going on and where.'

'So I'm to play bodyguard?'

'Precisely that, James. And until we have facilitated the safe production of the drug, your wife will remain in our custody. I'm sorry that it has to be like that. But we had to ensure you were on board.

James pondered that. 'What's this drug of yours called?'

'B17.'

'How does it work?'

'It's not up for discussion James.'

'When will I see Radka again?'

'As soon as you have finished your job, I guarantee it personally.'

'I want intermittent confirmations that she is alive and well.'

'Absolutely. We are not savages, James. This is a peaceful operation, from our point of view. But do be warned – it's going to get ugly.'

'When do I begin?'

Before Tiffanny could answer, the waiter returned to collect their plates. They ordered mains; James selected *canard a l'orange* – duck in orange sauce – and Tiffanny opted for grilled swordfish. The food was delicious, and the wine was a pleasant accompaniment. They were too full to manage desserts, so James called the waiter over once more and asked 'L'addition, s'il vous plait' and the bill was brought. He paid using more of the rolled-up bills from the lockup.

They thanked the proprietor and walked up the terrace and onto Rue de Longchamp. It was now pitch black. The time had reached ten. James offered Tiffanny his blazer-jacket but she politely refused. They walked slowly to digest the meal.

'Do you like Paris?' she suddenly asked.

'Of course, it's beautiful.'

Tiffanny laughed. 'I hate it. But I understand why you like it.'

'Why do you hate it?'

'I hate the illusion, the misconception it brings. I hate the fact that any ignorant tourist considers it the city of love and light; the romantic capital of the West.

'But tourists only see the epicentre; the protected zones where everything is about capitalism and money and profit. But the true Paris is a dark tunnel. There are racial tensions with the Muslims who came from Algeria, which leads to rioting and public outrage.

'Most of them are honest and hardworking, but the police are brutal with prejudice. You leave the city, and pretty quickly you'll see the slums begin to appear on the horizon. You'll see the communities that society forgot, that the Government ignore. And, if you are really lucky, you might even bump into the varied terrorist organisations operating here.'

'It's a fair point you raise, Tiffanny, but surely most capital cities are like this. London has its Madame Toussards and Shepherds Bush and Canary Wharf and a great many wonderful cultural facets. It also has stabbings and shootings by the minute. Everywhere, all is not what it seems. But yes, I agree, I myself am guilty of falling into the tourist trap, although I do like to keep it authentic where I can. But let's not make generalisations.'

'You know something James? You are alright!'

He bowed in mock appreciation. 'And you, my dear, are positively stunning.'

Again she blushed, but her smile hid her deepest thoughts and fantasies. Only her eyes gave an inkling of her reaction; they twinkled in the shimmer of downtown Paris au soir.

'So, how do we do this? What happens next?'

Tiffanny reached into her handbag and picked out a thin brown envelope. 'My first instructions came in here. We begin tomorrow morning. Take this back to your hotel room and debrief yourself. I have my own copy so I'll be working on the decryptions tonight too. We'll reconvene to discuss, as I said, come the morning.'

'Where are you staying?'

The Frenchwoman bore a mischievous grin that told him not to pry. 'Not far away from you. I'll drop by the Magenta first thing. Lets meet in the lobby, say, 9:30?'

'You still didn't tell me exactly what leverage Collins has' James stated tersely.

'That's true James; I didn't.'

'So?'

'Like I said James, it all happened on a yacht in London three years ago.'

'I don't know what you are talking about.'

'Yes you do. You know precisely to what I refer. Aequitol.'

James grunted. 'You know nothing.'

'No, that's incorrect James. Like I said, Collins has a vast array of resources to hand. He has done his research. He is compiling a report as we speak.'

'A report? About what? The government issued a White Paper inquiry about the whole mess two years ago. Everything was exposed then.'

'Not quite everything, James. There is the small matter of an Egyptian man called Damian Husarz and a USB stick he possesses. We know that he has gone into hiding, that he has had several operations of plastic surgery and that he has started a new life for himself somewhere. But, see James, the thing about a person that never changes is his DNA, his genetic makeup, his fingerprint. So it's only a matter of time before we find him. And when we do, there will be many people who want to know the truth about Aequitol, and especially what is on that USB stick.'

James bit his lip. A wave of shock pulsated through him as if his organs were faultlines. *How could they know all of that? It was impossible! Yet they did.* Suddenly he felt an immense inkling of anger towards Tiffanny and her sudden provocation. He inhaled a deep breath and regained composure. 'So what are you saying exactly?'

'Well, complete this task for Mr Collins without any teething problems, and not only will Radka be released, the report will be destroyed. You have my word. There is only one copy, on Mr Collins' laptop. It's an insurance policy, just like Radka. That's our leverage. You can admit or deny whatever you want to me, but now you know what we know and what we are willing to do should you decide to be a dissident.'

'Fine. Fais de beaux reves.' *Sweet dreams.* James resigned to his dependency on co-operating with Collins and the Frenchwoman. They kissed twice on the cheek and then parted company. She took off north and James went back to the metro station at Trocadéro, armed with the envelope. He reversed his earlier journey – M9 to Oberkampf, M5 to Gare de L'est – and walked back up Boulevard Magenta to his hotel, eager to get on the instructions and see how he could take a step closer to Radka.

*

At ten-thirty, the waiter who had served them at Café Kléber hung up his apron at the conclusion of his shift. In the kitchen area at the back of the restaurant, he took out a shiny black clamshell cell phone and hit speed dial key 2. The line dialled three times before an ancient, raspy voice answered.

'Yeah, what is it?'

'Monsieur Ross? It's Fabien. I think I might have found something.'

'Are you in Paris?'

'Oui.'

'Go on.'

'A man and a woman dined at the restaurant tonight. I overheard them mention Casino Collins and something about a drug. A big secret, she was saying. I thought you'd want to know.'

A long pause preceded the inevitable reply. 'That is excellent news Fabien. You have done me proud. I can't tell you how deeply you have assisted me with this information. You will be rewarded earnestly.'

'Merci Monsieur Ross, you are most kind. How shall I proceed?'

'Fabien, you have done plenty already. Hang up your hat and go home; get a good night's sleep. I'll send Chaplin over to find out more. All I ask is that you keep it under your belt, ok?'

'Absolutely Monsieur Ross. It dies with me.'

'Au revoir Fabien.'
'A bientot Monsieur Ross.'

Several thousand miles east of Paris, in Prague, Czech Republic, Ross reached Chaplin in Brno and filled him in. The pervert had been told to assemble and send a team to monitor the movements of the Czech woman and British entrepreneur holding her prisoner. He himself was to hop on the next flight to the French capital. He was debriefed over a secure line and told to proceed with caution. The man and woman in Paris were to be watched until they provided verbal confirmation. Their abodes were to be bugged, their communication devices tapped. And, once they led him to the final destination, they were to be eliminated.

Chaplin boarded an early-hours flight which would have him land at Charles de Gaulle a little after six-thirty. All he had to do then was pinpoint their location and begin his surveillance. He hoped the woman in Paris would be as arousing as the one in Brno had been. A new spate of blood pumped down to his sexual organ at the mere prospect of fresh meat.

Chapter Eleven

Paris, France. 11:30 p.m.

James returned to his room on the third floor of the Hotel Magenta and opened the balcony doors. The envelope lay in waiting on his freshly made bed. He stepped out onto the veranda and gazed down at the lifeless street below. A light drizzle began to fall from the heavens. The droplets of precipitation fell on James' face; they were brisk and refreshing. The balcony offered a direct view of the Eiffel Tower several miles in the distance. Its amber hue, and the milk-white beam from its searchlight, was the only light as far as the eye could see across the noir horizon. It looked like a tiny sun in a space bereft of other stars.

As James watched the majestic tower, his thoughts returned to the evening with Tiffanny. He thought of her intense smile, emanating from eyes akin to bright planets. They had a hypnotic, tractor-beam quality. Then his cognition began to wonder further afield, and Polaroid snapshots of Radka began to snatch up into his mind's eye, as if they were being dispensed violently from a processing booth. Two women needed his help, in different ways respectively. One was a former love, the other a total stranger.

James began to shudder. He realised the dropping temperature of the February evening and felt the cold peck at him. It shook him from his thoughts and into the present realm. He went back indoors and closed the shutters on the balcony. He went into the bathroom to splash cold water on his face.

He was beginning to feel exhausted. The last forty-eight hours had been unexpectedly eventful. The relative mediocrity of a teacher's life in cosmopolitan Chester was starting to become a memory from the distant past, or a parallel universe. He desperately wanted to sleep, but he knew he couldn't. He had to work on whatever was in the envelope. Then he'd be able to afford himself a few hours of downtime under the covers, and hopefully he'd have a head's start come the morning. And a head's start meant a step closer to Casino Collins and Radka Rosická.

Back inside the small den of the room, James opened the envelope and stared amusedly at the sheet of white A4 paper. It was a very ordinary product – probably 250gsm, with a standard matt finish, probably sold as inkjet printer paper. James red the single sentence, which for once was written in ordinary visible ink.

Visit Christ with outstretched arms.

Visit Christ with outstretched arms. James read the five words over and over. Nothing particularly coherent immediately struck out at him. It had to be some kind of metaphor. He wondered if it would turn out to be a red herring. If he had to visit somewhere then he needed a map of Paris; that much was clear.

He left the room and snuck down to reception. It was almost midnight. The counter was deserted – no Camille, although the scent of her perfume hung in the air; lingering particles of lavender and coconut.

He wondered where the night concierge could be. Probably he had taken a bathroom break. Although his walk back had aided his digestion and left him comfortably satisfied, he could still taste the richness of the snails in the back of his throat, mixed with vin rouge, and he could still see Tiffanny's vibrant lineaments.

James looked to the left of the reception counter and found what he was looking for. There was a small, makeshift gift shop in the corner. There was a cornucopia of gimmicky stationery for children; all items carried the Hotel Magenta logo. There were surplus toiletry products for the client who felt he had been inadequately provided for. And, of course, hung on tiny metal rafters, were a variety of street maps in different languages; English, German, French, Spanish and Japanese.

James took an English one from the rack. It cost two Euros and when fully unravelled offered a bird's eye view of the whole city on an A2 sheet. It was ideal. The concierge was nowhere to be found, so James placed two Euros from the airport locker roll-up on the counter beside the Apple computer, with a brief note giving his room number and explaining what he had done. He had to bend right over the counter to do so, and the strength of Camille's scent was ever more potent near the computer. James drew a deep breath to take it in, then retreated back to his room.

He spent an hour deliberating over the disconcertingly vague clue. *How the hell would it take him a step closer to Radka?* He studied the map conscientiously for matching landmarks or places of interest he could cross-reference. Certain aspects struck a chord, but nothing concrete came from his machinations. All he felt were brick and mortar inklings. He wondered if Tiffanny was making better progress.

He felt like he was stonewalling, so he took a break and went for a brisk walk in the bitter chill of French wintertime. He was wearing a thin denim jacket, which was inadequate considering the climate. But packing a suitcase full of handpicked garments was a luxury he had not been afforded with.

Some giant force had picked him up and literally dumped him in the deep end. That force was a single human man – Casino Collins. The far-reaching magnitude of his influence was unfathomable. Again he thought of Radka. He silently chastised the entrepreneur. *She'd better be safe and well.*

He contemplated taking a midnight ride underground back to Café Kleber, but he knew the metro ceased operations at 1am until the early dawn shift, so he'd be stuck there until morning. Outside the hotel the boulevard was fast asleep. There was no trace of cellular life. He walked up and down the length of it for twenty minutes then went back to his room.

He took a shower, opening the fancy miniature bottles of shampoo and conditioner. His skin was pale but supple. He thought of Tiffanny's olive-brown complexion. Suddenly he pictured her in the shower with him, the soap suds slowly sliding down her perfect body. He shook the desire away and cut the power at the faucet. He dried himself and then brushed his teeth. Naked, he clambered into the double size bed and downshifted his cognition to a relaxed stillness. It was a comfortable bed; firm yet soft. The duvet was thick and the pillows were deep and spongy. He slipped off into a comatose that was bereft of dreams.

*

The mademoiselle named Camille returned to her station and began to plug numbers into a company spreadsheet. A flicker of red light momentarily distracted her. She glanced to her right and her eye caught sight of the blinking diode on the interface of her phone. She hit a button and picked up the receiver. She spoke in melodic French, suggesting her heritage to be southern; Marseille perhaps.

'Oui?'

'Is that the Hotel Magenta?'

'Oui.'

'Can you check a name for me?'

'A guest?'

'Bien sur.'

'Who is this? Do you have authority?'

'Camille, c'est moi, Fabien, from Café Kleber.'

'Oh. Je suis desole Fabien, I didn't recognise your voice. Certainly, what is the name?'

'Surname is Loxbridge, forename is James.'

'Bear with me.' Camille plucked away at the keyboard, her long slender fingers caressing the keys with proficient accuracy.

'Yes, we have a guest by that name.'

'Which room?'

There was a pause as Camille drew breath. She began to twirl the coil of connection cable with her thumb. Then she pouted. 'Will I get into trouble for telling you?'

'Mais non! Nobody will ever know! Do not worry yourself Camille. I must deliver an urgent message to this guest. S'il vous plait?'

'D'accord' the receptionist replied begrudgingly. She was a goody-two-shoes with a solid reputation for integrity at the Hotel Magenta. 'But you owe me one for this.'

'Oui naturellement, I understand.'

'C'est 306.'

'Merci Camille. You are a beautiful precious gem, you know that?'

'Whatever. You're a pervert. Is that all?'

'Oui, c'est tout. Au revoir Camille, a bientot.'

'Salut.'

Chapter Twelve

Thursday 24th February. 9:00 a.m.

Tiffanny was already in the reception suite waiting for him when he emerged from the antechamber. She was sat on one of the comfy sofa-chairs opposite the reception counter, elegantly cross-legged, the pointed tip of her silver high heeled court shoe looking up at him as he approached her. She wore them over tight black trousers and a red and white top with floral patterns. James was dressed in the same garments from the previous day. Yesterday they were stiff with the starch of newness. Today they had moulded themselves around his body and the creases gave them a more natural look.

He felt a stirring in his loins as he reached her side and could afford the pleasure of enjoying her up close and personal. Again he coercively brushed the feeling aside and greeted the Frenchwoman.

'How were the facilities?' she asked tenderly.

'More than agreeable' he informed her pleasantly.

'Good.' She said *good* like a teacher pleased that her student had provided her with the correct answer. It was not however patronising or condescending. James basked in its warmth; it made him beam, which in turn made her beam. Being a tutor himself, it was rare for him the experience the flip side of the coin.

She indulged his fantasy for a few more seconds, then, with that power that all women possess, quickly took it away and moved on from matters of the heart to the banal reality of their current business.

'You have the envelope?'

'Yes, and I bought a map.' He showed her the fold-out he had purchased from reception the previous night.

'Good' she said again, in that sweet melody she orchestrated. 'Moi aussi!' *Me too!* She revealed her own brown envelope. 'Alors, lets go to breakfast and we can discuss it.'

James grabbed a free copy of Le Figaro and tucked the newspaper under his arm as he followed Tiffanny out of the hotel. Camille looked up from her post and watched them exit. The Frenchwoman clicked her heels down the boulevard and James matched her small, feminine steps with steady strides of his own. She led him to a small bistro further down the boulevard, just a few doors from the hotel. It had a burgundy façade with white calligraphic lettering that had long since begun its fading decline.

They both ordered coffee and croque-monsieurs, the breakfast of champions. The elderly proprietor, a distinctly Gallic looking madame who had probably run the establishment as a family business all her life, passed down from several generations, brought the platters of toasted bread with melted brie, ham, egg, and a large salad, all drizzled with olive oil. The tramlines on her weathered cheeks were like lunar craters; the signs of a heavy smoker. The sultry tone in her voice confirmed it as she bothered herself with rearranging the condiments on the table and said 'Voila, bon appetit.'

Tiffanny was the first to break the silence, in between bites of the divine cuisine. 'Did you make, how do you English say it, head or tail of it then?' There was electricity in her smile, and her eyes lit up like orbs that had been summoned by an unseen sorcerer.

James laughed. 'Not really Tiffanny, but I guess that's your job.'

The Frenchwoman nodded. 'Oui, but I like to keep my bodyguard in the loop! After all, the safety of your wife is your priority, just as the safety of B17 is mine. But each is mutually vital. Anything interesting in today's news?' She pointed at the newspaper James had placed by the side of his plate.

'I haven't read it yet. Here, take a look for yourself.' He handed her the paper.

She took it from him and viewed the front page. In an instant she gasped, and her face became a canvas of graphic horror.

'What is it? What's wrong?' James saw the terror in her eyes and his own face registered concern. She read on for two minutes then handed the paper back to him. He studied the headline on the front page.

His French was sub-standard to comprehend every single word, but he soon got the gist of the story. A waiter had been murdered in the early hours of the morning, just hours before. Two words immediately stabbed out at him, making him jolt with fear and panic – Café Kleber. It was when he processed the image of the dead man that he fully discerned Tiffanny's petrified reaction.

It was the waiter that had served them yesterday, when they had ate a succulent meal and Tiffanny had enlightened him as to the nature of the task at hand. The very provider of that hospitable service was now in the throes of rigor mortis. He had been strangled. The deceased man was named as a Fabien Andre. He was thirty-one and originally from the city of Troyes to the southeast. He was unmarried and without offspring. He had been well respected in the community. He had worked for Café Kleber for seven years.

Tiffanny wiped a tear from her cheek and James immediately jumped up to comfort her. He held her in his arms and she nestled her head firmly in the pit of his chest. He squeezed her and stroked the back of her head. The warmth had dissipated from her. Her face became cold and hard. The light in her eyes fused out, replaced by an opaque blackness.

'This cannot be a coincidence' she stated blankly. 'They had to know we were there last night, and who we are.'

'Who are they?' the law tutor asked.

'I don't know who they are. But they exist, that much is apparent now.'

'We are not safe here' he declared solemnly. 'We need to get this job done quickly and then get out of Paris.'

'Oui.'

The elderly patron returned and saw the stress in Tiffanny's gaze. They spoke softly in rapid-fire French for five minutes. The lady offered her consolation. As they chatted, a wave of paranoia swept over James. He got out of the chair and angled it to face the exit, which was about fifty feet away.

The bistro was a long, narrow corridor from the street that eventually opened out into the eatery at back. They were seated at a booth in the far corner. James now had a clear view of the door that led out onto the street out front. The women continued to talk about the murder. James glanced behind him and noticed another door, half ajar, projecting darkness beyond. He could not tell what was back there; it may have been just a pantry or closet for the woman's cleaning apparatus. Or it may have been a back door out of there.

The woman finished and took their plates. She moved off towards the kitchen, and Tiffanny read the story once again. 'I can't believe it.'

'Did you know him?'

'Not really. I knew of him. I eat at Café Kleber regularly. I like to sit and watch the tourists milling around the Eiffel Tower. I like to indulge in their fantasy of this idyllic, romantic capital. But, as you now see for yourself, it is not necessarily a realistic depiction of Paris.' She threw the newspaper onto the table.

'Tiffanny, don't blame yourself for what happened to Fabien. We know nothing yet. It may be unrelated to our cause. Coincidences are rare but they do nevertheless occur from time to time.'

'Oui, c'est vrai, but it doesn't make me feel any better.'

'Tell me about the message' James instructed. He knew that doing something productive would help her to remove the manmade guilt fostering in her conscience.

'D'accord. Open the envelope.' James did so, glancing up at the street. He repeated this scrutiny every thirty seconds or so.

'It seemed altogether ambiguous to me' he explained. She quickly composed herself, the strong, independent scientist that she was, and nodded in preparation for her grand explanation.

'It seems non-specific, doesn't it?' she began. *Visit Christ with outstretched arms*. It's like going to church as a loyal Christian or Catholic, depending on your derivation. But which church? I can think of the twenty grandest ones off the top of my head, and then there are many more less well known monuments in smaller districts. It would be the proverbial needle in a haysack.'

'Haystack' James corrected the Frenchwoman politely. She laughed, which in turn set him off.

'Haystack' she demurred. 'Anyway, the clue is quite clever in the way that it is written. As is often the case with lingual matters, it is the correct position of the comma that gives the sentence's meaning away.'

James nodded his agreement. It was very true. As a lawyer he had studied many a contract between companies for the sale of goods, where a meagre misplaced comma could, and irrevocably did, alter the meaning of the clause to the detriment of one of the parties and the benefit of the other. Commas were powerful tools in the world of lexis and should not be underestimated.

'You see', the Frenchwoman continued, 'initially our brain reads the sentence and automatically puts an imaginary comma after the word Christ. Visit Christ, with outstretched arms. Make sure you have outstretched arms when you visit Christ. Surrender fully to the love of the Lord. Do it with your heart. You understand? Mais, if we take out the comma and place quotation marks around the last four words, we read: Visit 'Christ with outstretched arms.

'Still with me? Now, there is a very special church in the central-northern part of the city, which houses one of the largest mosaics in Europe. And, in addition, there is a depiction of Christ with outstretched arms. It is quite famous.'

James leaned forward. He'd still been glancing at the exit door as she was saying her piece. 'Fascinating. And which church is that?'

'When translated from French to English it means Sacred Heart. Do you know the one I speak of?'

James did. 'The Sacre Coeur. So that's where we're headed?'

'Oui, bon. We should get going.'

'And what happens when we get there?'

'This I am unsure of. We'll have to work it out when we get there.'

'Come on then' James insisted. 'Let's jump on the metro.'

Tiffanny laughed. 'No need. J'ai une voiture.'

'You have a car, here, in Paris?'

'Mais oui!'

'Rather you than me! The French are crazy behind the wheel! Especially in Paris! No offence!'

'None taken' the mademoiselle laughed. 'All part of our charm.'

As they stood to leave James glanced up towards the exit and froze. A blue flicker of probing light made him blink. It was the silent siren mounted on top of a police town car; the familiar vehicle of the Police Nationale. Two uniformed officers disembarked and entered the bistro. The lead man, a Sous-brigadier judging by the three white inverted v stripes on his shirt, indicating more than twelve years of loyal service, confronted the madame and interrogated her in a firm but composed fashion.

His partner looked around the bistro whilst his superior did the talking, surveying the interior landscape. His shirt had two inverted v stripes stitched into the starched indigo fabric by his breastplate. He was a Gardien de la paix – a keeper of the peace. As the only clientele offering their custom to the bistro, it was obvious that his roving eyes would soon meet theirs.

The officer interrogating the madame showed her a paper printout. She looked at it inquisitively, then shrugged an *I've never seen him before* grimace un-cooperatively. The officer nodded, retreating back a step. For the first time he glanced at Tiffanny and James himself, then spoke to his partner.

A noise from behind startled James. A young man had come through the partially ajar door, which now had artificial light streaming through it. His smart dress confirmed his place as a waiter – possibly the only waiter along with the madame in this small establishment. He was probably her son. He approached the table and acknowledged James. Leaning over in a feigned attempt to collect something from the table, he whispered into the law tutor's ear.

'I think you should pay up quickly and get out of here' he said in a calm, patient tone.

'What's going on?' Tiffanny whispered back. James unfolded enough bills to cover the breakfast, factored in a generous tip, and studied the man cautiously.

'I overheard their conversation from the garbage alley out back. The police are looking for a man and a woman in connection with yesterday's murder of the waiter in Trocadéro. A French woman and an English man, they said. Their descriptions are quite similar to your appearances, if I may be so bold. Now, we don't want any trouble here. We need all the business we can get. So you need to be out of here.'

'We didn't kill...'

The waiter cut James off. 'I don't care what you did or did not do. My concern is for the welfare of my mother and I, and our livelihood. You can use this back door. Now leave. No questions.' He pointed to the partly open door, which, he had explained earlier, led to a trash alley. James glanced back at the more junior officer of the two. His partner came back in from his car and they began a slow walk towards them. The waiter headed back to the kitchen and threaded past them, acknowledging the officers as he did.

'Excusé-moi? Monsieur? Mademoiselle? J'ai un question! J'ai un question!' *Excuse me Sir, Miss. I have a question!*

It all happened with light-speed spontaneity. James grabbed Tiffanny by the arm and dragged her to the door. It took the policemen a few seconds to process that two potential suspects, matching their description, suddenly fleeing from the scene of questioning, was too suspicious to pass up. Then they gave chase.

In single file motion, with James leading, the pair sprinted down the alley. The numerous bags of waste disposal strewn haphazardly across their path at regular intervals, like chevrons on a motorway, impeded their escape. They had to swerve around them or jump over the top. The path was narrow and dirty. They were surrounded on either side by thick walls of sandstone and granite, scorched grey by the elements and infested with artistic graffiti. James heard voices from behind. 'Arretez! Arretez!' It was the police commanding them to stop.

In disobedience they continued down the guinnel and emerged onto the street running parallel with Boulevard Magenta. James reached for his map in between gasps for air. The sudden order for exercise had shocked his body initially, but the adrenaline soon worked its magic and propelled him forward effortlessly, working like morphine to numb the pain of sudden exertion. They had emerged onto the Rue des Recollets, heading towards the Canal de L'ourco, an arcing blue waterway that slithered northeast back towards Charles de Gaulle airport.

'Where's your car?' James inquired.

'It's parked in a lockup not far from here. Just follow me.' Tiffanny took the lead and James latched on by holding her hand. They ran as fast as they could. Tiffanny was in good shape too, matching his pace without much of a strain. They turned left onto Quai de Valmy then made another left onto Rue Varlin, passing the Chateau Landon. They came around the back of Gare de L'est, and James realised their location.

'My car is on Rue Lafayette' Tiffanny announced. 'Just two more minutes.' James glanced around in a three sixty degree sweep but saw none of the authorities giving chase. Those two cops would not be far away, and he knew it. They both knew it. They threaded across the side streets and hooked onto the main thoroughfare.

Three hundred yards west down Rue Lafayette, Tiffanny stopped running. James followed suit. They marched briskly and crossed over to the east side of the road. Tiffanny took a key from her pocket and passed several small street-front facades – the offices of small enterprises – and paused by a set of metal shutters. She unlocked them and James helped her lift the corrugated sheet metal skyward to reveal a single, tiny car bay. Sat inside was a small white Renault hatchback.

They clambered inside, Tiffanny at the wheel, James her passenger, and she reversed the motor carefully out onto the thoroughfare. Then they sped north towards the Sacre Coeur. Tiffanny drove fast, which slightly unnerved James, but she appeared to be in solid control of the car. It was clearly her car and she clearly relished taking it out for a spin; that much James found evident in the way she masterfully engineered the French runaround through the tight Parisian streets.

She knew just how it handled; how it accelerated, how it cornered, the braking distance required, everything. It was a manual, and each time the Frenchwoman shifted gear it was a smooth segue into greater speed. She teased the throttle and gave the clutch just enough bite for maximum leverage.

James took the map and spread it across his knees. 'The Sacre Coeur doesn't look too far away by car' he stated tersely. 'We should be there in twenty minutes.'

'I'll have us there in fifteen' Tiffanny offered proudly. 'Just keep your head down. I know the way.' She shot up the great winding Boulevard de la Chapelle, which subsequently became the Boulevard de Rochechouart. They left the main road by hanging a right up Rue D'Orsal and Tiffanny swung the hatchback into a gravelled path that led to a parkland area. She parked up and killed the engine.

They disembarked. Up ahead, a thousand yards in the distance, the Basilique du Sacre Coeur loomed ominously. It sat at the apex of a tree-lined hill, rising out of the crest like a majestic bird. Its peak boasted to be the highest point of the city, in the arrondissement of Montmartre. Its renaissance grandeur reinforced its Roman Catholic heritage. Its marble-white façade reneged on the grey sky. Its domes and minarets showed perfect symmetry; a celebration of Neo-Byzantine and Neo-Romanesque vision.

It stood two hundred and seventy one feet tall and the Savoyarde Bell alone weighed nineteen tonnes. Its foundations had been laid in 1875. Architected by Paul Abadie, it took a further nineteen years for its consecration. It was fully completed in 1914, just as World War erupted across the tramlines of Europe. Five years later, a full year after that war was concluded, it was given the accolade of Basilica status.

Tiffanny and James jogged up the patchwork quilt of grass to its entrance point. Then they snuck inside.

*

Amongst the beaded throng of anxious and intrigued onlookers in downtown Paris, a convoy of Police Nationale town cars had filed up in a neat row. The officers chatted frantically in small huddled groups. Many carried the same computer printout containing the photofit of the suspects.

Officer Aurelien Dupuy-Mornet glanced around whilst his compatriots attempted to calm the inquisitive citizens. There was growing unrest. His eyes caught those of another man across the street. The man began to walk toward him, lighting a cigarette as he did. He crossed the road and approached Aurelien. When it appeared the man wished to pass him by, the officer stepped into his path and began to speak to him in staccato Francais.

'Excuse-moi Monsieur, can you please take a look at this?'

The man conformed and took the sheet from Aurelien. He had a deep scar cut across his right cheek. It looked to Aurelien to be the victim of a knife wound. He had seen it many a time before, especially in the fishing communities of his native Marseille, in the local bars where there was frequent rough and tumble which often became brutal and usually involved an arsenal of home-made weaponry.

The man studied the paper for a good few minutes, scrutinising everything. This made Aurelien hopeful. However, the man then shook his head and handed the sheet back to the policeman. 'I'm sorry', he said, 'I cannot help you.'

'Are you sure?' Aurelien pressed.

'Oui, quite sure. My apologies.' Aurelien stepped aside to let the man pass. The man bowed his head in appreciation and continued on his way.

Chapter Thirteen

10:45 a.m.

Many people claim to belong to one of the family of well-recognised faiths shaping the global religious landscape. Some are Christian or Catholic, some are Muslim, others are Jewish or Hindu or Sikh, or Buddhist. Others consider themselves agnostic – they simply haven't made up their mind yet. Perhaps for them there is no compromise agreement in the negotiation between Darwin and the Big Bang versus Creationism. The point is that it does occupy their thoughts. Some are atheist and dismiss the mere possibility of a divine deity overlooking the world from above. A select few have committed themselves to the controversial Church of Scientology.

But whatever a man's faith, one aspect remains constant and transcends religious preferences – the architecture constructed in the name of belief is a labour of love whose finished product never fails to deliver an awesome splendour. The Sacre Coeur was no different. As James entered, the agnostic in him was jostling for reassurance, for clarification, for answers.

Inside the entrance, first impressions of the Sacre Coeur are of gloom; sombre and stern mortifications intent on instilling fear and repression. Dim lighting protrudes from overhead lamps in the first instance. Then, as you step further into the brink of the hall, glowing golden mosaics radiate a warm, amber-coated glare from the apse; a semicircular recess carved into the stoned wall, uplifting your frame of mind. The mosaics were designed by Luc-Oliver Merson in 1922, and are the largest in the world.

115

They depict Christ in Majesty and The Sacred Heart worshipped by the Virgin Mary, Joan of Arc and Saint Michael the Archangel.

The Frenchwoman led James through the antechamber and into the grandeur of the main hall. He gazed down at his feet and noticed the floor plan to be an equal-armed Greek cross. Then he looked skyward and noticed that they were guarded from above by a domed roof which lay directly over the crossing.

It was high – James guessed it to be a hundred feet above his own head. It had been painted with a regal splattering of blue and gold. The centrepiece gave the clue away – a large depiction of Jesus Christ, dressed in white linen, his arms outstretched, with angels beside him, the ancient citadel of Jerusalem in the background, where a crowd had gathered. *Visit Christ with outstretched arms.*

'It's beautiful' James said, without taking his eyes off the ceiling. He stood still for a moment and soaked up the sacrosanct ambience of the holy arena. It was cold yet it was peacefully quiet; other footsteps across the hall and additional clamours such as a rustling of keys or the odd cough seemed like distant echoes from his past. Whatever his beliefs, it was hard not to feel something; some presence did linger in the vast chamber. It breathed through the walls and resonated through the organ pipes. It communicated through the pulpit and the stained-glass windows. It sang a song of communion from the domed roof to the Greek cross mezzanine.

'Are you Catholic?' Tiffanny asked.

'Agnostic' he replied. 'Never gave it a thought until I was twenty-two. I read a book that turned my life upside down.'

'What was it?'

'The Hitchiker's Guide to the Galaxy.'

'You're kidding, n'est pas?'

'Nope.'

'Isn't that science fiction comedy?'

'Yes, but the ironic thing was, all that intricate surmising over the incomprehensible magnitude of the cosmos, and, as Adams called it, life, the universe and everything, shook me out of the

116

bubble I had cocooned myself in all my life. It revolutionised the very way I looked at the world. That's the beauty of good comedy – behind it lies a serious message; a deep and meaningful expression. It's just that humans, by our very nature, respond to the things we do not understand with laughter and mockery.'

Tiffanny smiled as she listened to him. 'Actually, I read that book myself, at université. It had a profound effect on me too. Especially when I discovered the answer to the ultimate question – the meaning of life, the universe and everything – was forty-two. That was quite a revelation.'

James laughed. 'Well, there he is – Christ, with outstretched arms. Here we are visiting him. What now? Are we expected to get up there?!' He pointed incredulously at the domed roof.

'I doubt it. Actually, Christ with outstretched arms appears twice in this church. Up there on the roof, and as a statue in the crypt.'

'So let's go down there' the lawman intimated.

'Ok, but it will cost us five Euros.'

'That's hardly going to break the bank.' He leafed out a bill from the wad in his pocket in readiness for the donation. They threaded their way around the luxurious pews, covered in red leather awning, and walked towards the vaulted chamber at the back of the hall; where Christ with outstretched arms awaited them.

The barrelled vault was supported by eleven arches, all basking in a translucent amber hue. The altar had a bronzed complexion, and was actually a replica of another – that of the Cluny Abbey in Burgundy. The depiction of Christ with outstretched arms was known as the Blessed Sacrament. It had been there since 1885.

'If you have any questions about what you see, just ask' Tiffanny stipulated warmly. 'I made a great deal of research on this for a paper I wrote during my studies. I became rather familiar with all the salient details.'

'Ok.' James decided to test her knowledge. 'How high up is that?' He pointed to the Blessed Sacrament then quickly withdrew his hand. Something inside had told him it was a bad omen to point rudely at the Saviour.

'Eighty-three metres' the mademoiselle confirmed. James had plumped for an even hundred. It wasn't a bad guess. 'And, once you climb to the very top, you are two hundred and seventy one feet above Montmartre. Apart from the Eiffel Tower, there is nowhere higher than this to gain a vantage point over the whole city in a three hundred and sixty degree oscillation. The dome is supported by eighty columns, each one of which is topped with a different capital.'

'You sound just like a tour guide' James quipped, nudging her playfully in the rib. She reached out with her hand to push his away instinctively, and when for that brief moment they connected, a jolt of electricity spiralled up his arm and made him shudder pleasantly. He could feel the power of the Almighty, and he could feel hers. Both were forces to be reckoned with. If she felt anything, she hid it well.

James handed five Euros to an employee of the great house and Tiffanny led him down a flight of stone stairs to the crypt. The sounds of their footsteps echoed around the dank chamber, eventually becoming absorbed by the dampness of the thick columned walls.

Inside the small crypt the amber reached a new height and bleated out a furiously potent orange beam which highly contrasted the honey-brown subtlety of the main hall. In the corner a small marble statue depicted Christ with outstretched arms. He looked less grand here than on the high-domed ceiling as the Blessed Sacrament. He was almost humble; a servant of God, just like the rest of us. Nevertheless, the relic was believed to be the sacred heart of Christ.

Tiffanny and James studied the statue diligently. 'What are we looking for exactly?' he asked.

'Your guess is as good as mine' the Frenchwoman explained. 'Any significant markings or gestures.'

'This place is very well kept' James remarked. 'I don't foresee us finding any significant markings down here. I thought it would be more specific than this.'

'If it was easy it wouldn't remain a secret for very long' Tiffanny rebutted.

'Point taken' James returned. In relative privacy they studied the room and the statue itself thoroughly for thirty minutes. There were other statues of saints in the crypt too. They went over everything with a fine toothcomb. But they were looking for a needle in a haystack.

'How about you take us up to the top?' James finally offered. 'Technically, Christ with open arms is up there too. The platform we stand on up there must be the other side of the dome, where the Blessed Sacrament is. Perhaps whoever wrote the message wants us to ascend to dizzy heights?'

Tiffany nodded at the revelation. 'C'est possible. Oui, on y va!' They headed back up the staircase and out into the rear of the hall near the altar.

'Is there anything outside at this end?' James asked.

'Oui, un jardin et une rotonde.'

'A garden and a fountain?'

'Oui.'

'That's all?'

'Oui, c'est tout.'

'No Christ with outstretched arms out there?'

'Non.'

'Ok, upwards we go.'

They coiled up around the staircase in small concentric circles, heading around the inside of the dome. It offered a bird's eye view of the hall from above. Eventually they emerged on the narrow ledge at the top of the chamber. James paused to draw breath. The air was different at this altitude. The cold wind blew into his face with great ferocity, but his breaths were raspy and short. Eventually he adjusted and joined Tiffany on the balcony to admire the cityscape from nearly three hundred feet above ground.

The aerial panorama struck James with its intense pulchritude. The subterranean beiges and whites of Paris' many architectural delights chalked the horizon as far as his eye could see; a patchwork quilt of littered renaissance. Tiffany's delicate features were silhouetted against this backdrop, and a work of art began to form in James' vision. We wished he had a camera, or an easel and some watercolours. The brownness of her skin and hair complemented the brilliant white of the French capital and gave the whole picture a sublime juxtaposition.

James had to tear himself away from the reality his mind was creating – a romantic expedition with a beautiful mademoiselle which had culminated in a breathtaking view – and remind himself of the task at hand. Further to the East, Radka was trapped in a tower of sorts, and he was the white knight tasked with rescuing her.

He found the chivalrous analogy amusing; Radka was an extremely competent and independent woman. Whatever trouble she was in, she'd probably break herself free of it before he got to her. That thought was a comforting blanket around James' resolve. He imagined her captors and how they would be coping with her. She could be quite a handful when she wanted to be.

'Let's get down to business.' They walked the three sixty degree perimeter until they met back up with each other in the epicentre.

'Find anything, Tiff?'

'No, James.'

'We need to take a closer look.' Then James had a thought. He glanced down at the ground of the walkway and tried to picture the position of Christ as the Blessed Sacrament directly below them. 'I think we need to stand at the points where Christ's arms are fully outstretched. It would be symbolic, and the messenger appears to be that kind of fellow.'

'Interesting hypothesis' the Frenchwoman offered. 'Stand over there.' She pointed to a spot several metres away. James backed into the spot. Tiffanny walked away in the opposite direction and stood in a place equidistant to the centre. They stood in perfect symmetry. James moved forward and ran his hands over the smooth stone pillar. As he looked closer, he saw that something had been etched into the surface. *And fames with triumphant calm.* It was written in calligraphic lettering. It must have been there some time, because the elements had scorched it black.

'I have something here Tiff' he shouted over the wind to make himself heard.

'Moi aussi!' she exclaimed excitedly. 'Read yours out' she added.

'And fames with triumphant calm' he bellowed. What does yours say?'

'Come here and see for yourself!'

James walked over to her. She was pointing to a section of the adjacent pillar directly in front of her. Again, James leaned in. The writing was very small and so hard to see, but eventually he found it. It was etched into the stone in the same lettering – the exact same. *Pass through victory history.*

'Which part comes first?' James uttered bewilderingly.

'Mine comes before yours' she responded.

'How do you know?'

'Ladies first, right?' She giggled, and so did he.

'Seriously?'

'The sentence is: *Pass through victory history and fames with triumphant calm*' she explained. 'And I know exactly what it is referring to.'

'Do tell.'

Before she could, the silence was penetrated by a sudden fit of wailing. Several screeching sounds, multilayered over the other, began to cry out infuriatingly. The noise was emanating from several hundred feet below them. Glancing over the edge of the balcony, they both saw immediately the source of the noise. There were several Police Nationale town cars parked in a haphazard arc, their sirens blaring at intermittent intervals. Their timings were different but melodic, as if a conductor was orchestrating them from an unseen stage. A throng of tourists were being redirected away from the church as they exited. Two officers began to rope off the entrance area with red and white ticker tape. More officers disembarked from their vehicles and entered the church directly below them.

'This is about Fabien's murder!' Tiffany uttered with dread. 'How we'd escaped those cops when we left the bistro. They must think we did it. It looks like the whole precinct is out to catch us! What will be next, the gendarmerie! Then the foreign legion! We have to get out of here!'

'How the hell can we escape now? We're trapped!' James dictated the obvious to a woman rapidly becoming more distraught. Then he grabbed her by the arms and willed her to relax. 'If we are looking down at the entrance from here, where is your car parked?'

She led him around the circular walkway a few metres until they emerged on the south side. They gazed over the railing and Tiffanny pinpointed a small white square specked against a larger green square. 'There. In the parkland.'

James followed the gait of her fingertip until he too saw the Renault parked up and waiting for them. 'We're going to have to risk it. We have some time. They will check the downstairs area thoroughly before coming up here. Perhaps we can sneak into the crypt and hide there until they come up here?'

'I don't like it James. Can't we go down and reason with them? We did not kill Fabien – we can tell the police that. Offer our full co-operation.'

'But Tiffanny, if we do that, we'll be in their custody until further notice. And we need to be out in the city, deciphering clues and finding documents for Casino. I'm no good to Radka if I'm incarcerated in a prison cell.'

'Oui, vrai. *True.* Ok, after you then.'

James led them back down the spindly staircase. It wasn't any speedier descending than it had been ascending because of how narrow the steps were. There was little space and no handrail. It wouldn't take a great deal of effort to stumble and fall. In the circumstances though, with several armed policemen on their posterior, they had to throw caution to the wind to an extent and hope for the best. Hope for the best, plan for the worst.

The steps seemed to be never-ending, and each revolution around the circular pillar brought an identical view into being. It was as if they were stuck in a time loop. Eventually they descended the last of them and they found themselves back in the main hall. The police officers had disseminated themselves throughout the chamber and were searching warily but thoroughly for their suspects.

Tiffanny and James snuck into the crypt. There wasn't a great deal of space in which to become concealed. Tiffanny put her back to the statue of Christ with open arms, and James strafed towards one of the saint statues in the corner, positioning himself out of view. They waited breathlessly for several painful minutes, willing their senses to blend into the background. They had become statues themselves. They had joined the ranks of the saints. They preyed it would save them from detection.

James heard footsteps approach, and then a shadow appeared on the wall beside him. There was great contrast in the amber backdrop of the crypt and the black silhouette of the approaching police officer; like treacle and honey. The officer paused, his eyes panning the length of the room with significant scrutiny. His eyes settled on something in the far corner. He removed a two-way radio from his belt and prepared to give a new status report to the other units in his brigade.

James saw the silhouette of his hand lifting the walkie talkie, and froze in terror, fearing the worst. But the officer hesitated. Then he stepped forward into the crypt and advanced towards the statue of Christ with open arms. Perhaps he did not appreciate that cruel twist of fate, for initially he had the advantage. But now, by bringing himself closer to his suspects, he had offered James a lifeline. And as he crept even further towards the statue, presumably to confirm his earlier suspicions, James knew exactly what he had to do.

Chapter Fourteen

12:00 noon

It was a combination of factors that had cemented the frantic act in James' cognition as the best way forward; a de facto concoction of ingredients swirling in a soup of desperation. Primarily, he was anxious to get to Radka. In subordination to that, Tiffanny's and his own survival was paramount for the continuance of the escapade. If the mysterious drug B17 was such a panacea then the mission became a plight for his heart and his conscience, more than mere obedience to Casino Collins. If he could become a hero to society then he wanted a foot in the door.

But his decision was also brought on by a pinch of adrenaline that fills the central nervous system as a defence mechanism at the first sign of hostility, and just a hint of male bravado – after all, he was the alpha male by default, and he wanted to impress upon the Frenchwoman a cornerstone of bravery.

Unfortunately for James his opponent was a highly trained and well-disciplined servant of the law, the product of a country that was tough on crime and the criminals who brought its malevolence to the forefront. A man who wielded a weapon he was more than willing to use if the need arose.

James snatched out his leg in a frantic gesticulation, hoping to trip the policeman and gain the upper hand. In the split seconds before James' foot had fully uncurled and made contact with the officer's leg, the Police Nationale extraordinaire had found the time, in one fluid movement, to release his firearm from its holster on his belt and slam the butt of it down hard and fast into James' temple. The law tutor slumped to the deck in a nauseating huddle. The gremlins in his subconscious summoned him into the unconscious with untarnished hands. He was out for the count.

When James awoke his blurry eyes found a locum to focus on and pinpointed the spot on the wall in front of him. The wall was unfamiliar. He had missed the preceding moments after the officer had dispatched with his brief attempt at insurgency inside the crypt.

The officer had handcuffed him and the mademoiselle and had stashed both of them roughly in the back seat of his town car. The officer had then sat in the front passenger seat whilst his partner careened the sedan at hair-raising speeds halfway across the city, heading south towards the sixth arrondissement Stade de Police Nationale behind Boulevard Raspaii, near the Jardin du Luxembourg. At the station the officers had emptied their pockets and then bundled them into adjacent cells for processing.

James was sat on a dusty floor. A dull ache resonated through his skull like a metronome. He winced and then levitated upwards into a standing position, using the weight of his back to slide up the wall. He grunted in discomfort as his joints took to work. He shook the fatigue off by rotating his ankles in tight, concentric circles.

As he fully came to, he remembered being in the crypt, silently waiting for the officer to approach so that he could utilise the element of surprise. It had backfired, if the lump on the back of his head was testament to anything. The cell was twenty feet long and fifteen feet wide, he guessed. He ran his hand along the wall and felt the biting chill that stone emits. He walked towards the bars at the front of the chamber and checked his vantage point. He couldn't see anything past the adjacent corridor.

'Tiffanny' he whispered. 'Can you hear me?' Nothing. 'Tiffanny' he repeated, with slightly enhanced volume.

'James' the Frenchwoman responded in a hushed panic. 'Are you alright? Your head?'

'Yeah, it hurts like hell, and I feel a little groggy, but I'm still here. Did they hurt you?'

'Non, je vais bien. *No, I'm doing fine.* But we have to find a way to escape. We are under a strict time constraint.'

'Je sais. *I know.* Are the police usually so brutal?'

'Only when they are dealing with murderers'.

'I see. And from their point of view, that's precisely what we are.'

'Exactement.'

'Who could have tipped the police off? Who would want to drop us in it? Nobody knows who I am. I haven't been in the country forty-eight hours!'

'I have no idea James. Vraiment. *Really.* Shush, I think somebody is coming.'

Footsteps approached, and then stopped. A rustling of keys, then a clanging of metal against metal. A male voice, then a female's. A shadow appeared by James' cell. As it came into focus, James recognised the figure instantly. It was the officer from the crypt.

'Je suis desole' the officer barked from the corridor. Then he unlocked the door and stepped into the cell. Tiffanny appeared out on the corridor – she had been let out of her captivity.

'I am sorry' the officer repeated. 'I am sorry for hitting you on the head. It was a mistake. This whole thing is a mistake. We know it wasn't you who killed the waiter.'

'What? Why?' James shouldn't have cared – his freedom should have been sufficient information to please him. But his curiosity got the better of him. The officer ignored the question and stood aside with a gesturing wave of his arm to allow the lawyer to leave his incarceration.

James approached Tiffanny in the corridor. The mademoiselle shrugged an *I don't know what's going on either* at him. He placed a hand of comfort on her shoulder and looked her right in the eye. 'Are you ok? Unharmed?'

She smiled warmly, pleased by his concern. 'I am fine James, but thank you for caring.'

'How long was I in there for?'

'About an hour, before you spoke to me.' An hour of his life, unaccounted for. He'd want that back at some point.

The officer marched them through into the foyer. It branched out into an open plan office space where deskbound employees pushed pencils and grinded the wheels of administration; bureaucracy in motion.

The captain of the Paris Prefecture de Police came around a desk made of fibreglass and extended a hand towards James. He was a short, paunchy Gaul with a pug nose and a brow full of tramlines under a thick cleft of copper hair tinged with silver. His appearance was a tool of misdirection, for he was a fit guy with plenty of fight in him.

He looked to be in his fifties, and the inevitable greying signs of matter's slow and beautiful decline were not inconspicuous. His skin was hard and his features rugged, but he was in good shape. His lineaments were striking in that they painted him to be humble and yet correspondingly a man who commanded respect, even honesty. James took his hand reluctantly.

'My name is Lacroix. I apologise on behalf of this precinct for the mistreatment of my staff towards you. We were acting on misinformation. I would appreciate it, Mr Loxbridge, if you did not press charges. As you can see, we are already swimming in paperwork. This would drown us in madness, and we have to be on the ball in order to serve and protect the great city of Paris. Vous comprendez, n'est pas?' *You understand, don't you?* Lacroix handed James a business card, which he politely took and placed it inside his jacket pocket.

'Yes I understand' James exhorted. 'What new information did you unravel?'

'The details are unimportant' the capitaine responded reluctantly. 'But, alors, you are free to go. Enjoy your stay in Paris, Monsieur.'

'Could you tell us anyway, please, this new information?' Tiffanny asked the question, in polite formal French.

'About fifteen minutes ago, when you were in your cells here, there was another murder. Same modus operandi – the victim was strangled. And the fingerprints on her body match those taken from the late Fabien Andre. The fingerprint is not in our database, so we have no leads on the killer. The one conclusion we are able to make is that you are in the clear. D'accord, I am sorry to have wasted your time. Au revoir.'

'Who was she?' James demanded. Tiffanny gasped in shock and disgust then dashed outside for some air. James stood his ground.

'Why does it concern you, Mr Loxbridge?'

'I want to be of assistance; that's all.'

'You want to be a Good Samaritan? Heh, you have already assisted by eliminating yourselves from our enquiries. In any case, you will have the details in a few days in Le Figaro or Le Monde. Now, s'il vous plait, I am a busy man. I bid you farewell and bonne journee. Adieu.'

'Just tell me who it was and I will be out of your hair permanently' James pressed.

'Merde! Putain! C'est une abomination! Mais, the poor girl was called Camille Pougalan. She was a receptionist at the Hotel Magenta. Some files were taken from her computer. It is a mystery. Two murders in my city is a terrible atrocity. Maintenant, on y va!'

James ran out to find Tiffanny. 'This gets worse.' He filled her in. Her reaction was unequivocally the pinnacle of lamentation. His own fervour showed little sign of differentiation. He had acknowledged Camille on several occasions during his tenancy in the hotel on Bouelvard Magenta. And now she was another past tense. And all because of him. There were no coincidences in matters so serious. 'Whoever is doing this', he mused, 'is on to us, and our operation. There is no alternative explanation.' Tiffanny merely nodded her concurrence.

'Which means we have to act fast. We need to get back to your car, near the Sacre Coeur.'

Tiffanny shook her head in defiance. 'It's too far James, and I don't trust it. If we are being monitored, and our footprints traced, then who knows what they could have done to my car. It might just be a bug, or it might be a bomb. Let's take the metro. There is greater safety in numbers, and we can blend in amongst the commuters. Besides which, our next location is closer to our current location.'

'Oh yes I forgot, you'd already figured it out. So where are we headed?'

'The Arc de Triomphe' the Frenchwoman clarified. 'And you do realise that we can never go back to the Hotel Magenta now? Once the police get a hold of the logbook and discover that you're a customer there, their suspicions of you will be rekindled and we'll be pursued by the authorities again.'

'I know. I don't think we need to worry just yet on that score. The police captain said those records were missing. Whoever killed Camille took the logbook with them.' Suddenly James remembered the note he'd left her on a post-it that first night after meeting Tiffanny, when he'd bought a map but had to leave the money behind the unmanned counter. He wondered if the killer had taken that too. If not, the police had written confirmation of his lodging.

He cursed himself. If only the desk had been unmanned when the killer came to tie up his loose ends. Perhaps, if so, Camille Pougalan would still have a heartbeat. He was being sucked into a vacuum of murder and deception. It chilled him to the bone. He had to keep perspective – protect Tiffanny, solve the clues, and get back to Radka, hopefully resolving their relationship in the process. If it was already dead in the water, he needed closure. But he wasn't giving up on her without a fight with his own conscience. Her safety was paramount over all the deep and meaningful ramifications right then.

'Did you leave anything important in your hotel room?' Tiffanny demanded.

'I don't think so.'

'You don't think so, or you didn't?' she spat testily. The murders of Fabien Andre and Camille Pougalan had clearly taken their toll on the scientist from Strasbourg.

'Just some dirty laundry. Everything else I have with me – the money is the main thing. Oh shit.'

'What is it?'

'My passport! It's in the hotel safe. It's hospitality policy. They hang on to it until the day you depart the country. I have to get that. Otherwise I'm really screwed.'

'What about the key to the lockup at CDG airport?'

'Oh, I left that too, but that's not important, right?'

'Well, it is important, because that key to that particular locker connects me to this whole affair, as it is mine!' The Frenchwoman's demeanour and tone had become as sour as a lemon basking in a vat of acid. 'Merde!' she hissed. 'C'est tres tres grave. C'est affreux!' *This is really really bad! This is disgusting!'*

'Look on the bright side' the lawyer retorted, 'If this operation remains Trans-European, the Shenzen Treaty in the EU means no borders! I can still cross into other states. I have my driving licence. It's photo ID so it's just as adequate as a passport in Europe.'

Tiffanny pondered the optimistic remark. Then she nodded dispassionately. 'Mais, you better prey then that this operation does not become trans-continental!'

James ignored the comment. 'Come on; let's go to the Arc de Triomphe.' He took the folded map from his inner jacket pocket and pinpointed the nearest Metro station. 'Actually, we are just as far from the Arc as we would have been at the Sacre Coeur, just in the opposite direction. The three locations almost make an equilateral triangle.' He traced the shape with his finger. Tiffanny wasn't listening – she was far away in another universe altogether. The light had fused out of her eyes, giving their usual warmth a sub-zero glaze. Her smile had waned to a flat protrusion of her lips, like a wave crashing on the shoreline.

'The nearest Metro is St Germain des Prés, directly north from our current locale. We have to pass St Sulpice and the Musée Eugène Delacroix. It should only take us twenty minutes.' He could not tell if Tiffanny had heard him or not, so he grabbed her hand and they walked north together.

James used his map from the Hotel Magenta and the station's travel chart to construct a route to the Arc de Triomphe. They rode the M4 to Les Halles in five minutes. A hobo came into the carriage behind them and started chanting in rapid-fire French. His attempt at seriousness whilst blatantly inebriated beyond sobriety was an amusing picture of hypocrisy, lost on the native commuters who simply wanted to get home to loved ones without incident.

James could not understand his dialect and he spoke too quickly, but the lawyer knew exactly what the delusional old tramp was preaching, because men just like him could be found in most big cities, and the underground transportation systems were their territory, because of the warmth generated by the people and the power conduits and the thick stone.

It was one of those apocalyptic chants; *the end of the world is nigh! Repent all of your sins, for judgement day is upon us!* If Tiffanny could hear him, her senses showed no indications. The shock of the murders had pulled her mind into a catatonic entrapment that only her own willpower and steadfast resolve could free her from.

James placed an arm around her and gave her a tight squeeze. She murmured but did not reward him with eye contact. At Les Halles they disembarked and rode the remainder of the journey on the second train.

'I know just what will cheer you up' James chided. 'I have a great story to tell you, from my first time in Paris.' The Frenchwoman turned her head to look at him. The smile came back to her lips and the warmth to her eyes. It was like watching a supernova in glorious high definition.

'A true story?'

'Bien sur!' *Of course!*

'Does it have a happy ending?' she asked. 'I like happy endings.'

'Not really, but it will amuse you greatly, and laughter is just the medicine you need right now.'

She nodded. 'D'accord, tell me.' As the train whizzed and zipped through the sub-metropolis, James told her the anecdote.

'I was twenty-one; young, naïve, inexperienced. It was my first time in Paris. I came here with my brother for a week's getaway. We had our cameras and some cash, it was all we needed. It was a male bonding exercise over good food, coffee and sightseeing.

'So, one day during les vacances, it was a hot, sunny afternoon. We had been inside the Louvre, seen the Denon Wing, seen the Mona Lisa, done the tourist thing. When we came out we fancied a coffee so we began to scout the vicinity for a nice café. After not much walking we stumbled upon a place called La Fumois.

'This was a really classy establishment. I mean, we're talking waiters in dickie bows, polished silverware and crystal chandeliers, jazz music breezing through the background ambience, and coffee at eight Euros a pop. This was a real treat, on holiday, away from home; it was all part of the experience.

'As we entered this place, I glanced to my left and in the corner booth a beautiful girl was sat smiling right at me. I didn't know where to put myself, and my knees were trembling, but I managed to smile back with enough passion as I could muster. She was typically French in her appearance, and beautiful, much like yourself.' Tiffanny caught herself blushing.

'She was dressed in that understatedly elegant way only French women know how; very classy. Her skin was as sumptuously brown as warm chestnuts roasting on an open fire. Her hair was a silky velvet of brunette brilliance. She took my breath away, much like you did when I first encountered you.

'So my brother and I, we approach the bar and I order Café Crèmes for the both of us and for a moment I forget about the girl. We sit at the bar on high-backed stools, and I have my back to the girl. After about ten minutes, my brother excuses himself to visit the facilities. I continue to sip at my luxurious eight-Euro coffee.

'Next thing you know, there's a tap on my shoulder.'

Tiffanny interjected. 'The girl?'

'Naturellement! And she starts talking to me in rapid-fire French, and I hardly pick up a word. I was younger, and my confidence was minimal in encounters with beautiful foreign women. I had to stop her and tell her, in English bien sur, that I was sorry but that could we please talk in English.

'She apologised and, in broken English, explained that she was there on a blind date, waiting for her mystery guy to arrive, and she thought it would be me.

'Well, you have to try and appreciate the magnitude of this, from a male point of view. I had low self-esteem, considered myself a bit of a nerd, a misfit, and you see this beautiful girl thinks I am her date!

'But the real magic of this situation is that, as she is there on a blind date, there is no way she could possibly know I wasn't her guy. And if I jumped in and said *Oui, it's me*, and then the real guy comes in, he won't know the difference either – he'll be looking for a girl sat on her own, like this girl was, so if I jumped in, we'd already look like a couple and we'd blend into the background.

'So ultimately it is a win-win situation for me, a healthy, heterosexual twenty-one year old male on holiday. It would only be a white lie. All I have to say is *Yes, it's me*. Three little words, like *I love you*. Easy peasy lemon squeezy.

'But alas, no, non, nada, niet, nein. What did I say? What the hell did this buffoon blurt out in a nervous panic? *No dear, I'm sorry, it's not me.* The beautiful mademoiselle politely excused herself and returned to her seat, just as a guy walked in and introduced himself. *The real blind date.* I went back to my stool and found my brother perched on his stool, smiling back at me. When I told him what had unfolded, he nearly fell off his stool with laughter.

'He consequently chastised me for the rest of the trip, and long into our return home. He still teases me about it now, years on. *You idiot!* he would say. *Imbecile!* A golden opportunity, in the city of romance and light, gone. He used to tease me that we should go back to that restaurant and find the girl, as she has probably been going back there every night to wait for me. I will never forget that encounter.'

Tiffanny was laughing again. He had succeeded in bringing her back from the brink. 'Merci James, for this beautiful story. It has a poignant ending, from the point of view of a healthy heterosexual male on holiday, I mean!'

'Are you teasing me about it now?!' James laughed with her.

They disembarked once again at Place de Charles de Gaulle Étoile, and made their way on foot towards the Arc de Triomphe, which loomed over the tenements a hundred yards or so overhead.

*

The man continued down the Champs Élysées until a metallic vibrating in his pocket took his concentration away from the street ahead and on the task ahead. He knew it would be his boss. He answered the call.

'Yes?'

'Update me.'

'The police were after the targets the waiter identified. One of their officers stopped me in the street with their photos on a sheet of paper and asked me if I recognised them. Naturally I said I did not. But it is definitely them – the man and woman the waiter described.'

'So what are you doing about it?'

'I've already been tying up loose ends, naturally. You know what that involved, don't you?'

'Of course. Just as long as you made it clean. Like a local domestic or gang related, whatever. Just keep it clean Chaplin.'

'Absolutely. It can't be traced back to us.'

'Keep fatalities to a minimum. The French police are a tough bunch; we don't want an international incident here. That would bring Interpol into the fray.'

'Naturally, Mr Ross.'

'Where are they now?'

'My best guess would be the morgue.'

'No, the targets you're monitoring, you dumbass!'

Chaplin maintained his composure. *Remember the green. I'll be filthy rich.* 'The man and the woman? I'm not certain. I found the hotel the man was staying at – he won't be back. The woman drives a white hatchback, which I have bugged and am tracking as we speak.

'It's currently stationary, parked near the Sacre Coeur, so I guess they're still inside the church. I have managed to divert the police's attention away from them. I'll keep an eye on their activities, and keep you posted. If the ultimate target is here in Paris, we'll soon know about it.'

'Ok Chaplin. Just keep surveillance on them. And no more killing unless it's absolutely necessary. Am I understood?'

'Clear as a bell, Sir.'

'Good work Chaplin. Out.'

Chaplin hung up the phone and yawned. He despised these surveillance missions. All watching and no killing; it was such an anticlimax. Granted, he had snacked twice on that thrill already in the short time he had been in the city. But he began to feel hunger pangs. It could be hours, even days before his next kill. Who knew when these targets would lead him to the ultimate target. It could take days, even weeks.

Chaplin wasn't sure he could survive for so long on surveillance detail. He had enjoyed the forced intercourse with the hotel receptionist before squeezing the life out of her. At least that had given him a fulfilling release, literally. He wondered if he'd get to play with the Frenchwoman he was currently surveying in the same way, eventually. Perhaps as an extra thrill he'd make the man watch before he finished him off too. It was a thrilling prospect, and Chaplin began to daze into his fantasy.

Without delay he hopped on the Metro at Place de la Concorde and rode to the Sacre Coeur. He needed to check on that stationary vehicle. Perhaps it would offer a clue as to their whereabouts and their future movements. He became momentarily distracted again, but he willed the blood in his penis to subside as he sat amongst the Parisian commuters like any other and rode the tube to the Gare de Nord.

Chapter Fifteen

3:25 p.m.

The ethereal sun was vying for attention behind a formidable patchwork quilt of thick white cumulus cloud. A biting zephyr conspired with a light patter of rain to bring winter misery to the fore. They were back on Avenue Kléber, not far from the café where Tiffanny had indulged James over a candlelit dinner about vitamin B17 whilst a pleasant faced waiter busied himself with his best hospitality. A waiter who was now lying in a sub-zero storage freezer in the city morgue.

James said, 'So how did you know this was the place?'

Tiffanny said, 'I came up here as a child to draw the Arc for a school project. I became very much acquainted with the markings on the stone. As soon as I read it – *pass through victory history and fames* - I understood the reference. Come on.'

They picked up pace and marched against the brisk chill of February's solstice until they reached the busiest roundabout in Paris. James heard the furious wailing of car horns a good few hundred metres back; they were like frantic bird calls in an unravelling nightmare. Parisians were notoriously hot-headed behind the wheel.

The roundabout upon which the Arc de Triomphe proudly stood guided the great Avenue Foch east from the Porte Dauphine – Dolphin Port – and connected the great Champs Élysées. In fact, the Arc was an intersection that funnelled a total of twelve streets out into the cityscape at various bearings on the compass. It was like a complex star pulsating rays of light out into the universe.

The build up of traffic in the centre of the road acted in their favour. Whilst the erratic locals honked and cajoled their compatriots, the Frenchwoman and the lawman skittered and flittered between the stationary vehicles and threaded through to the opposite pavement.

After dodging the cross-town traffic they approached the Arc front-on, from the Neuilly side. It was a colossus of grand design. It stood one hundred and sixty-four feet high, one hundred and forty-eight feet long and seventy-two feet wide. Seen from the top of the Eiffel Tower, it stood over most other landmarks in the city. It made Tiffanny smile – it seemed that this was a special place from her childhood, and it was a powerful tool in warding off the darkness instilled in her from the double-homicide they had become embroiled in.

She reached out to caress the surface. For the most part the stone was smooth. The original veneer had been a deep oaky colour, but the harsh elements had weathered it in places to a scorched charcoal grey-black. Then there were the markings that the mademoiselle had mentioned. 'These were sculpted by Etex' she explained, running her hands over the shaped stone on the left side. 'This one is called *Peace,* and it is my favourite. I am a great believer of peace.'

James looked on, his hands in his pockets to fight off the chill. 'Aren't we all?' he quipped rhetorically.

'No, not all of us. If we were all believers of peace, then why are there currently over fifty wars taking place across the world as we speak?'

Her question did not feel rhetorical; her tone was intonated towards the end as if to incite a heated debate. When James failed to take the bait by keeping schtum, she continued the history lesson. 'You'll see that the man is putting away his sword, and the peasants are working hard. The man is protected by Minerva. Do you know who Minerva is, James?'

'The Roman goddess of wisdom' he replied. He'd only known because an American pen-friend he had emailed as a teen had used it as her email address and avatar name; in fact it had been her whole identity. Minerva122@yahoo.com.

'Tres bien James! Yeah, that's correct.'

138

'What's going on at the right face?' he asked, pointing to it.

'That one is *Resistance*' the Frenchwoman explained. 'The soldier is defending his family.'

'But he's naked' James chided. 'Why isn't he dressed?'

'It's an artistic expression James! It's beautiful! Open your eyes and your heart.'

'So you could say this is the *Peace de la Resistance!*' the lawman joked.

Tiffanny ignored the play on words that was undoubtedly lost in translation. 'You may also be interested to know that if you look up higher you see the rectangular bas reliefs on the arch itself?'

James looked up. 'Yeah, I see them.'

'Well, these depict the capture of Alexandria and Kléber. Kléber was a military General and hero. This battle was in the Napoleonic war with Austria. So now you know why the avenue and the café where we had dinner are both called Kléber.'

'Aha. Fascinating.'

'Fabien was a big military history enthusiast. He taught me about the bas reliefs after I showed him that I had drawn them.'

James raised an eyebrow. 'I thought you said you drew the Arc when you were a teen?'

'That's right. We were childhood friends, Fabien and I.'

James appeared aghast. 'You knew him, and knew him well? I thought you said you just knew of him because you ate there often and he served you often?'

'I lied. I was very upset about his death; I became confused. I'm sorry.'

James let the moment pass. He wasn't angry about the irrelevant misdemeanour. He moved close to comfort her. He reached out but she pushed his arm aside. 'Not now. We must focus.' Tiffanny led James around to the opposite section – the Champs Élysées side.

'So the clue was: *pass through victory history and fames with triumphant calm.* Now let's look at these markings a little closer.' Tiffanny tugged at James' arm and drew him into her headspace. She was smiling as she spoke. She pointed to the left face of the Arc as they now looked at it. 'This is the *Triumph of Napoleon* by Cortot.' Then she pointed to the right face of the Arc. 'Over there is *The Departure of the Volunteers of 1792* by Francois Rude, also known as *La Marseillaise*. But that is less important to us.'

She moved her finger back to the left; to the Triumph of Napoleon. 'Now James, look at these figures, and look at them closely. There are four in total, right? The figure in the centre is Napoleon himself. He is dressed in a toga. The other three are assistants. One is crowning Napoleon with a laurel wreath. The other is inscribing the names of the battles won on a stone tablet. The third is blowing a trumpet. The detail at the bottom represents a town surrendering at Napoleon's feet. The three assistants are known respectively as Victory, History and Fames.'

'Aha. *Pass through Victory, History and Fames with triumphant calm.* An arch, or Arc, is to be passed through. And we would pass through it with triumphant calm because it is the Arc de Triomphe – the Arc of Triumph, literally!' James had made the appropriate deductions.

'So the next clue has to be very close by' Tiffanny decided. 'Search the stone.' They combed the façade with due diligence, but found nothing except for dust and dirt. James glanced up to the top panel of the Arc, beside the roof guttering. There was an inscription, which he asked Tiffanny to translate for him: *This monument was begun in 1806 to honour the great army, was left unfinished for many years, was continued in 1823 with a new purpose, and was completed in 1836 in the reign of King Louis-Philippe I who dedicated it to the glory of France's armed forces. G. A. Blouet, architect.* 'But it doesn't really help us find the next clue' she stated tersely.

Just then James became distracted by a vibration in his pocket. He dug deep and retrieved the silver Nokia flip-phone that Murgatroyd had thrust upon him in Chester. That seemed like ancient history now, much like the Napoleonic chronicles that the walls of the Arc de Triomphe depicted. He glanced at the interface of the small LCD. It lit up green and said *Private Number*. He flipped open the clamshell and listened. 'Hello' he then uttered, cautiously.

A voice, heavily masked by distortion software, spoke to him. 'How are you progressing James?'

The lawyer gave Tiffanny a look that said *this is really important.* She nodded and continued to monitor the stone behemoth for the whereabouts of their next clue. 'What's the voice distortion in aid of? I know it's either Casino Collins or one of his cohorts. Put Radka on, now.'

'Tell me how you are progressing' the voice repeated. It was difficult to detect any emotion in the robotic ping of the resonance.

'We're doing just fine. Two people are dead because of us, but aside from that minor detail, everything is a bed of peaches and roses.'

'Don't get cute with me, or you will never see your wife again. Ever.'

'Put her on, now.'

'Are you still in Paris?'

'Yes, but there is still work to do.'

'I want confirmation from you the moment you uncover anything.'

'Put Radka on, for God's sake.'

There was a clicking sound and then heavy breathing and afterward total silence. Then a voice came on the line. 'James?'

'Radka! Are you ok? Are you hurt? How are they treating you?'

'I'm fine. Not hurt. I'm being treated well. It's more an inconvenience than anything else. And the company leaves little to be desired.'

James smiled at her whimsical outlook on the situation. It was a vivid display of her bravery. 'Where are you being held?'

'I can't tell you James, you know that. Say hello to Charlie for me, if you're downtown.'

'What? Who's Charlie?'

'Got to go, James. I'm alive and well. Keep up the good work. Take care.' Then she was gone. The distorted voice of her oppressor had returned to the line.

'I told you, she's fine. So there is no need for unpleasantness. All we need is your compliance. Keep me posted.' Then the line went dead.

James put the phone back in his pocket and kicked at the stone in frustration. Then he looked up as Tiffany emerged and threw an object at him. Instinctively he reached out with his hands and caught it.

'Good reactions' she said. 'How is your wife?'

'She seems fine. What's this?' James was staring at a small black cylindrical tube. It was a plastic case that thirty-five millimetre camera rolls were stored in, before the film was developed. Those old-school exposures had to be kept out of direct sunlight, else they'd be ruined. They had been replaced by the digital age, but were still used by die hard enthusiasts and retro collectors.

'It was taped to the roof. I had to throw a loose stone at it to dislodge it' the Frenchwoman explained.

James nodded. 'I've not seen one of these in time! Another relic from my childhood, and the pre-digital age.'

'Well, judging from the colour disfigurement, I guess it's been up there since your childhood' Tiffanny remarked. She was right. The plastic casing had worn down to a brown polymer undercoat. It appeared to be years, if not decades, old. James popped off the cap and pulled out a small sheet of paper. It too was old – it looked like ancient papyrus.

'What does it say?' the mademoiselle beckoned.

James studied the calligraphic lettering.

Take a thousand and sixty-three feet and view the city.

Chapter Sixteen

4:00 p.m.

Before Chaplin even reached the white Renault, he knew it was abandoned. His animal senses were on red alert, and he couldn't detect any meat. So he knew there were no people nearby. It was an odd sensation, even for his twisted psyche, but it was if wrestling the bear in the Slovak mountains had instilled some of the creature's prowess in him. He was wild and untamed, ready to maim, happy to kill.

He walked with a lumbering, primal saunter up to the car. He peered in through the passenger-side window. The Sacre Coeur loomed behind him, casting its shimmering reflection through the glass and onto the seat's upholstery. The Renault looked like it had recently undergone a valet. It was impeccably clean. The leather was soft and luxurious; the floor mats were bereft of dirt. The compartments were empty. It was useless to break in, Chaplin surmised, as the inhabitants had not left behind any evidence of their subsequent movements.

Chaplin looked back from the reflection to study the image of its master – the real Sacre Coeur. Suddenly, on a hunch or in the whiff of a fresh new lead, he marched towards it. The area was deserted, but the police had roped off the entrance with ticker tape.

Chaplin did not want to risk an international incident, so he refrained from attempting entry. Instead he monitored the external façade with great care and attention. Some words, inscribed on the stonework, caught his eye. He found more at the opposite side. *Pass through victory, history and fames with triumphant calm* is what he read when he put the two sections together. He had no clue what they meant.

He copied the text into his cell phone as a draft text message and strolled back towards the parkland where the Renault remained, cast aside like a disused toy. He glanced around for passers by. His sweeping eyes caught sight of a young woman with a little girl, playing on a swing. He limped towards them, his movements impeded by an enlarging of his genitals. He smiled at them as he approached. The mother smiled back then returned her attention to pushing her daughter on the swing.

'Excuse me' he asked, humbly, 'Do you speak English?'

'A little bit' the woman responded in musical French.

'Do these words mean anything to you?' He thrust the cell phone towards her. She leaned forward to read the text. *Pass through victory, history and fames with triumphant calm.* Whilst she read, her daughter got off the swing and stood watching the strange man smiling right at her. She pouted shyly then began to stamp her feet on the ground. Chaplin waved, and the child returned the gesture. 'You have a beautiful daughter' he remarked, wiping his forehead with the sleeve of his forearm.

'Thanks' the woman spoke, again in heavily accented French.

'So, can you help me?'

'I think so. This is a reference to the Arc de Triomphe.'

Chaplin beamed then took the phone back from the woman. 'Thank you so much, you have been very helpful.' His smile had not dissipated throughout the exchange.

'You're welcome. Goodbye.'

'Goodbye.' Again he waved at the little girl then walked away. The woman spoke to her child in soft, accentuated gestures, and the infant responded to her melodic guidance by hopping back on the swing. Then the woman began to push her again.

Chaplin glanced back before he crossed the street. He felt an urge to go back. *Stop it* he chastised himself. *Not here, not now. Focus. There will be other*

144

opportunities. He reached inside his trousers to touch his desire. The blood was flowing like wine. A shiver of excitement bamboozled its way down his spine from his shoulders. He forced himself to calm down. His breathing became laboured. He reached into a pocket and took out a small plastic cup. He opened the cup and took out a capsule. Inside the capsule was a pill. He swallowed the pill and sat down on a bench.

A dull ache protruded from the back of his head. The killing part he found easy; the murderous act without a strain on his will; a pleasure, even. It was the after-effects that screwed with him. For him it was a sensation similar to masturbation – the act itself brought great pleasure, but the feeling afterwards was one of shame, or guilt, or silliness; almost embarrassment. Still, the drugs kept him on the straight and narrow. But they brought with them painful headaches. If only he could find a way to stop the headaches. Then he would be indispensable, unstoppable, invincible.

His attention was diverted by a metallic buzz emanating from his trouser pocket. His erection began to wane. He answered the call.

'Chaplin.'

'Yes, Sir. Their vehicle is definitely abandoned. They are on foot.'

'I don't know for certain, but I have a lead, Sir.'

'The Arc de Triomphe. It's where they went next. I'm heading there now, Sir.'

'I understand, Sir.'

'Yes. I will. Bye.'

He replaced the cell phone in his trouser pocket and took out a map of the city. The Arc de Triomphe was southwest of his current location, and quite a damn distance. Still, now he had the upper hand. If they were on foot, they'd be slow. And even if they took the Metro, they'd be delayed by stops and indirect drop-off points. Yes, he definitely had the upper hand. It looked like he would need the Renault after all.

*

'Even I know the answer to this one!' They were heading back to the Metro station at Place Charles de Gaulle Étoile. This time they only had a short distance to travel – a one-stop two-minute sojourn back to Trocadéro. 'It was in some promotional literature in my hotel room' James continued his explanation. 'At the apex it is 1,063 feet tall. *Take a thousand and sixty-three feet and view the city.*'

Ignoring the question, Tiffanny asked, 'So how's Radka?'

'She seemed fine, although she was trying to tell me something important, in code. She said *Say hi to Charlie for me, if you're downtown.* I think she was trying to tell me where she is being held. Do you know where she is being held?'

'Of course not' the Frenchwoman intimated. 'I am not privy to such intelligence.'

'I get the feeling intelligence is not something you have a problem with.'

'Trying to get me into your bed, James?'

The lawman blushed as the train pulled into the station. They disembarked and headed southeast, crossing Palais de Chaillot and the opulent waters of the Seine. It mirrored the journey he himself had taken to meet her at Café Kléber on that fateful evening two days ago. 'There are three tiers to the structure. Where do you think we will find the next clue?'

'It could be anywhere James. We'll have to be thorough.'

If the Eiffel Tower is approached from the south the visitor is rewarded with the Parc du Champ de Mars, a triumph of horticulture; a botanical bastion that stretches all the way from the Ecole Militaire. From the north the intrepid tourist is confronted by a bohemian courtyard offering fast food and an unrivalled vantage point of the tower from directly beneath it. From there you can see every rivet of reinforced steel making up the tripod base, of which there are two and a half million in total.

Tiffanny and James came in from the north and found themselves in the courtyard. He left her standing to soak up the immediate environs and approached the rapidly growing throng of tourists queuing by the ticket counter. When his turn came he shelled out a total of thirty Euros for four tickets, two each required; one for the initial entrance fee and access to the first and second tiers, and another for the final elevator ride to the top. When he returned she had bought crêpes and sodas for the both of them. It was the first food they had eaten that day, and they both welcomed the surge of energy brought on by the intake of carbohydrates.

While they ate, James analysed the situation. 'As the clue requires us to take a thousand and sixty-three feet and view the city, the next instruction must be somewhere at the very top. I guess that means we don't need to waste time studying every last corner of the lower tiers of the tower, despite you wanting to be thorough.'

'I guess you're right James. It must be at the apex; somewhere on the open platform at the very peak.'

The winter sun was slowly making its inevitable decline in the west. Soon darkness would fall and the tower would be transformed into a glowing beacon of golden amber, from sunset until 1:00 a.m. A total of three hundred and thirty five spotlights are used in the display. Since the new millennium an additional ten-minute glittering light show is provided for the first five minutes of every new hour, powered by no less than twenty thousand light bulbs. Finally, a searchlight fixed atop the lighthouse section of the tower pans the cityscape in a three-sixty-degree sweep, sending out white beams as far as eighty kilometres.

Gustave's phallic tower required a taskforce of three hundred and a timescale of two years to complete. It was finished in 1889 to mark the centenary of the French Revolution. It required forty tonnes of paint to coat and, elevators notwithstanding, one thousand six hundred and fifty two steps to mount from ground to apex.

It originally existed as an observation tower, as Gustave envisaged, to monitor wind speeds. After facilitating several high-profile scientific experiments, such as Foucault's giant pendulum, its potential as a radio transmitter was realised. The modern day concept of aerodynamics, now studied and adopted by the military and commercial aviators, and indeed by NASA in their rocket technology, derives from Gustave's initial use of the tower for testing wind and air resistance. The tower consumes seven and a half million kilowatt hours of electricity every year and two tonnes of paper goes into the production of tickets annually.

Their tickets were checked and stubbed and then Tiffanny led a reluctant James towards the primary staircase. 'We should hurry James. Time is scarce and we have a great many steps to ascend.' He looked uneasy as he approached the staircase. A few impatient tourists barged past him and mounted the stairs, cameras out and eager, carefree faces gazing at the sheer scale ahead. He hesitated on the first step and gripped the handrail tight in a clenched palm. 'What's the matter?' the Frenchwoman asked inquisitively.

'I'm acrophobic.'

'You have a fear of heights?'

'Yes.'

'You neglected to mention that James.'

'Yes, I thought I'd put on a brave face about it.'

'Are you trying to impress me?'

James produced a wry smile. 'It's embarrassing.'

'Don't be silly James. We all have our vices and our fears. Me, for example, I don't like spiders. I have arachnophobia! You probably think that is irrational – such a tiny, insignificant little creature. But I suffered a traumatic experience with one as a child. I think this is where most fears come from.'

'Yeah, absolutely. When I was a baby my father took me to the top of Blackpool Tower. It isn't a patch on the Eiffel. He used to carry me on his shoulders. Nevertheless he thought it would be amusing to dangle me over the edge and pretend to drop me, catching me again in the vital last moment. I was convinced I was going to fall – I was very distraught. Consequently, flying on aeroplanes does not concern me in the slightest, for I am protected by the aircraft's interior. It's the open spaces and free-moving platforms on skyscrapers that perturb me. But I must overcome it. Mind over matter. Like you with the spider, it's totally irrational.'

'If you like, stay here and I will go up to find the next clue.'

'No, that's counterproductive. Two pairs of eyes are better than one. I'm useless if I'm stuck here.'

'Yes, but, as much as I empathise with your condition James, we aren't going to get very far if you have to take it one step at a time. If you squeeze that handrail any tighter, you'll cut off your circulation!'

James thought about her proposal. It was hardly the chivalrous thing to do, yet he had to remind himself that he was dealing with a strong, independent woman who knew the territory better than he did. And they were a team, working together to reach the same overall objective. TEAM – Together Everyone Achieves More. There's no I in team. 'I suppose I could stay here and run point. I have a good angle of vantage for surveillance. I'll watch our backs.'

'Fantastique. Ok James, I'm going to the top. Wish me luck!'

'Bonne chance. Hurry back.'

The mademoiselle leaped and bounded up the metal staircase with minimal effort, her lean figure propelling her skyward with an elegant progress, leaving in her wake a small cloud of perfumed air. She was agile and light on her petite feet. James admired her trim features until she was out of sight. James moved off the staircase and drew in thick bountiful rasps of air. The prospect of mounting the tower had sent his heart into a palpitating panic. His acrophobic weakness was a barrier he longed to break down; he just did not know how. Tiffanny had been firm but fair in having him stay behind.

He eyed the busy throng of sightseers whilst thinking about Radka and her cryptic hint as to her whereabouts. *Say hi to Charlie for me if you're downtown.* The words were somehow familiar, but we could not place them into a coherent diction.

His eyes shifted towards the faint movement of three military patrolmen crossing the courtyard up ahead. They wore desert sand fatigues and carried M16 automatic rifles across their belts. They were tasked with protecting the sanctity of their prolific capital city, which welcomed in millions of holidaymakers and housed a similar number of natives. They were big guys and they looked intimidating, which reassured James, for surely that was their purpose – to deter malevolence.

As they passed and meandered on through the gathered crowd, their disappearance from his line of sight was instantaneously replaced by a lone figure. It was a man he thought he had seen before, although exactly where he could not place. It could have been a random coincidence, if such a thing was to be believed. Paris was no small city, yet James could have seen this man elsewhere in the seventy-two hours he had been there.

The man was looking in his direction, apparently scrutinizing him openly, although that was surely a product of the optical illusion caused by the distance between them, James soon realised. The man was probably admiring some French beauty in James' general direction, or possibly just watching the tourists beginning their climb to the top of the tower.

But James' curiosity was nonetheless piqued. In the most casual manner he could fashion, and content at moving away from the staircase and the phobia that it represented, he sauntered closer to the courtyard to take in a better view of the man.

There was something about the man's image. He stood out from the crowd. His clothes were essentially nondescript and he appeared to bare no distinguishing features discernible at such a long distance, yet his demeanour exuberated a confidence that suggested a specific purpose. Tourists and holidaymakers have no such purpose; they saunter and they dawdle and they loiter, because they are in relax mode. This guy was no tourist. He was either a native who worked in the city, waiting for somebody, or he was waiting for something to happen. Or, more worryingly for James, he was watching somebody; watching somebody because he wanted to delve into the facets of whatever this somebody was doing. He could have been an off-duty policeman, or a plain clothes officer; a detective or inspector.

They'd already had a brush with the law, but they had been released without conviction of any wrongdoing. The Police Nationale had been adamant that they had made a mistake, and yet here was this man, paying James a great amount of visual attention. James walked further towards the man.

And as James glanced down at the man's tanned leather jacket, he noticed that a slip of paper was hanging precariously from the edge of his left side pocket. And when just for an instant the sun reappeared for one final showdown before its pivotal decline, it flashed across that sheet of paper, revealing its contents to James; a photograph of himself, alongside a similar mugshot of Tiffanny.

*

Tiffanny clambered up the metal staircase three steps at a time. She dodged and weaved past her slower compatriots, who paused for breath and gawped out at the city view below them, gradually becoming smaller and further away with each vertical incline. The cogs of the underground hydraulic elevator machinery whirred underneath her.

On the first tier she passed Bourdelle's 1929 sculpted bust of Gustave Eiffel and bypassed the souvenir shops and snack bars. She found the second staircase and continued her ascent to the second tier. Once there she was confronted with several more tourist attractions. She saw the original hydraulic pump which had supplied water to the old elevator machinery in a simpler, more civilised age. She slithered past the small model of an observatory tower that used a laser beam to monitor wind and temperature effects on the tower's oscillation; another revolutionary invention from the great mind of Gustave Eiffel.

The only way from the second to the third and final tier was by elevator. The Frenchwoman squashed her way inside behind a group of Japanese tourists, each one the proud owner of the best digital camera money could buy, strewn around their necks on long nylon straps. The lift transported them one hundred and eighty metres skyward and provided a bird's eye view of the Parc du Champ de Mars below. Fountains, rotundas and spraying water features phalanxed the gravelled path like proud militia. The elevator stopped and Tiffanny disembarked at dizzy heights.

At the apex the sightseer was confronted with two options. He or she could enter the internal viewing chamber, which offered a three-sixty-degree panorama of the entire cityscape, or they could brave it out on the open balcony, which also ran the circumference of the tower, offering a complete picture of aerial Paris. Tiffanny plumped for the latter and shredded her way past ignorant tourists who seemed infuriated by her quick pace. There were several plaques mounted on canvas boards, offering information about the views and more of the tower's history. It was information she knew better than the back of her hand, so she paid it little heed. She was looking for something more specific – she was looking for the next clue.

She studied the plaques and the metalwork itself on the steel rivets at the top of the tower. She found no messages etched into it. She felt downhearted, but refused the initial pang of negativity. She made her way back through the exit and into the internal viewing chamber. It too, like the veranda, was packed to the rafters with gawking tourists. She patiently slithered around the circumference like a lost ghoul, her feet sliding inches forward at a time. After one complete revolution she had read yet more historical information but found nothing referencing their plight.

Undeterred, she went back around for a second time. Again, she saw nothing useful. On the third time around she paid more attention. Two thirds of the way around from her start position, she happened to glance down at the bottom section of one of the plaques.

The plaque was a whimsical map which pointed out directions and distances to other places. *Milan 645km, Victoria 2,839 km.* Upon closer inspection she realised that the bottom section was loose. Where the top section was screwed in to the feature permanently, the bottom plinth had become a chattel.

Causing great irritation to the people behind her, Tiffanny prised away the board with her fingernails and bent down to see what was underneath. She heard their cries of bewilderment and mockery but dismissed them as unimportant. Burnt into the steel, in the same calligraphic font, was a short sentence of words:

Fly fast to the obelisk that stands so pretty.

The Frenchwoman applied pressure to the bottom plinth in an attempt to preserve the covert secrecy of the message. She smiled apologetically at the impatient crowd behind her, mumbling something about dropping her keys underneath the plaque with humble impropriety. She removed her cell phone, a metallic pink razor-thin device of modernity, and typed the words into a draft message so that their essence could be preserved. It was a long way back down to the courtyard, and she didn't want to have to commit it to memory hence she inadvertently changed one of the words, thereby masking the true meaning of the clue. Just as she finished typing the sentence her phone buzzed furiously. It made her jump and she murmured in brief annoyance. Then she answered the call.

'Oui?'

'Aha. Yes. I know. It's fine, don't worry. The Eiffel Tower. Aha. Yes. No, he doesn't suspect a thing. I know what I'm doing. Au revoir.'

The Frenchwoman replaced the phone in her jeans pocket and took the elevator back down to the second tier. Once there she began her descent back to ground level, where he would be waiting for her.

Chapter Seventeen

5:00 p.m.

James saw her vaulting down the metal staircase and stood to engage. 'Well?'

'I have it! I stored it in my phone. It's in the drafts folder, here.' She handed him her cell. He read out the message. 'Fly fast to the obelisk that stands so pretty. Tiffanny we have a problem. I think we've been made.'

'What do you mean, *made?*'

'I think someone is watching us. Don't look now because it will arouse his suspicions, but there is a man with a photograph of us; the same one the police had before they arrested us.'

'Merde! Putain! C'est trés grave. This is bad, James. Are you sure this is what you saw?'

'Absolutely. Allow yourself a passing glance in the direction of the courtyard. Tanned leather jacket, black hair. You'll see the paper peeking out of his pocket.'

'I don't see anybody like that James.'

James turned around to face the courtyard. The man had vanished. 'He was there a moment ago. I know what I saw, Tiffanny.'

'It's ok, I believe you. We'll have to be more vigilant.'

'Of course, I've got it!'

'James?'

'Say hi to Charlie for me if you're downtown. Oh my God. She's in Brno.'

'How do you know that?'

'It's such a subtle little nuance, it's beautiful. Whenever we returned to her home city of Brno to visit her parents, we would arrive in the city centre and then we would take the number eight tram to her house in Lišen. At the bottom of her street is a little hardware store. Actually it's a national franchise – they are everywhere. The company is called Charlie Centrum. That's what she meant when she told me to say hi to Charlie if I was downtown. Centrum is the Czech way of expressing downtown. She wanted me to know she was back home. So she is being held somewhere in Brno. That's a start.'

'Congratulations James. You must be relieved. You will be back with her in no time, I do not doubt.'

'Yeah, well it's not really progress. If I go after her Collins will know about it. At least she will feel relatively safe in her home territory. I'm surprised Casino has made that move. Usually the kidnapped are taken to unfamiliar places because it makes them debilitated and vulnerable. That doesn't make any sense.'

'Perhaps Casino Collins is more compassionate than you give him credit for' the Frenchwoman insisted.

'What makes you say that?'

'I'm just asking you to keep an open mind about the whole affair. Let's stay with the task here in Paris. The sooner it is finished, the sooner you can go back to your wife, ex-wife, whatever she is to you.'

James sensed a strain in the mademoiselle's voice, but he did not wish to fuel her dissident fires. He needed her onboard if he was to get Radka back. And she needed him to protect her from an unseen foe. It was a relationship of mutual obligations, a marriage of sorts; except there was no sex involved. So in fact it was just like a marriage. Tiffanny broke the silence.

'Place de la Concorde is the next destination.'

'What makes you so sure?'

'Because the clue says to fly fast, and the Concorde is the most synergistic analogy to that action. And the Place de la Concorde is an obelisk.'

James retrieved his city map. 'We head east but it's a fair walk. You want to take the metro? I think we'd be safer amongst greater numbers.'

'Sure. We can get on at Trocadéro. It will just be a few stops.' They rode in silence from Trocadéro to Charles de Gaulle-Etoile on the M6, changing there for the M1 to Place de la Concorde. The whole journey, including changeovers, took just fifteen minutes.

James sensed that something was plaguing Tiffany's mind. He wondered if chemical feelings were interfering with the task at hand. At both stations and on both carriages James scrutinised the passengers, searching for the man in the tanned jacket. Something about the man had unnerved him. Some of the commuters returned his inquisitive gesture as if his attention had made him paranoid. This in turn made him paranoid. He could not shake the disconcerting feeling that they were being followed; being watched. The man had a photograph of the pair of them.

'Something on your mind, James?'

'I'm just thinking about the man I saw. I want to know who he is and the nature and extent of his involvement. Does he not worry you?'

'No, because I didn't see him; you did!'

'What is that supposed to mean? You think I'm making it up?'

'What I think is that we are both exhausted and under a great deal of pressure. What I think is that in such circumstances the human senses are able to play tricks on us.'

'I know what I saw' James stated tersely for the second time. The Frenchwoman smiled wanly but did not offer anything verbal by way of response. When they disembarked Tiffany shunted on in silence. James brought up the rear and glanced around to check the passengers leaving the other carriages.

Then he saw it; a blur of tanned leather. The man with the jacket was right on their tail. Without further ado James grabbed Tiffany firmly by the arm and looped her around a one-eighty-degree arc and they headed for the east exit. He dragged her up one flight of stairs and around a stone corridor at Place de la Concorde.

'What are you…'

'Shush. It's him. Just keep moving.' They rounded a corner and reached a connecting chamber that took them to a bay of ticket machines on the left and the exit to the right.

Without really thinking about the consequences, James marched her over to the ticket machines and he pushed her up against the back wall and he kissed her, hard and firm, on the lips. He held her head with his right hand and stroked her cheek with his left. Then he held her chin and softly slipped his tongue into her mouth and then out again. It was a wet, passionate kiss that had taken her completely off guard.

They looked just like any other pair of star crossed lovers in Paris, the city of romance and light. And that was just the disguise he was going for. But he had killed two birds with one stone. He had been aching to kiss her since the moment he had first laid eyes upon her in Charles de Gaulle airport nearly two days ago.

He glanced up and witnessed the success in his grand scheme. The tanned jacket skipped past them with quickening pace, carried along by the bustling crowd of commuters rushing home from the daily grindstone like a shifting Mexican wave. Once the man was out of range James grabbed Tiffanny's hand and they headed back in the direction they had come, running down the flight of steps and heading for the west exit. 'I think I just bought us some time. Take us to the obelisk.'

Tiffanny was speechless after her mouth had been violated in such an unprovoked manner. James knew that no matter what lengths she took to rebut it, her genuine opinion of the matter was favourable. He could tell as much from the way her tongue had returned the gesture and how she had softly murmured with desire and pleasure. She had not pulled away, which would have been her primary instinct had she been displeased. One thing was certain – he had certainly smashed any remaining ice between them.

They made it out of the metro station just as twilight had peaked and the sky had become a myriad of twinkling silver stars penetrating an indigo canvas. The moon was low and crescent-shaped. A biting chill enveloped them in its embrace.

The obelisk stood at the conclusion of the morose and grandiose Champs Élysées. Beyond it stood the impressive botanical thoroughfare that is the Jardin des Tuileries, which during daylight hours presented a luxurious park lamented with fountains, basins and numerous sculptures. In the shrouded darkness it became a sinister spectre. Its name is derived from the French word *tuilerie* which means *tile,* as the site originated as a large clay quarry in the sixteenth century. It was the most central garden in the whole of Paris, flanked on either side by the Musée du Louvre to the east and the Grand Palais to the west.

The obelisk was basking in a honey-gold hue in the eighth arrondissement. Behind it lay the Church of Marie Madeleine. They huddled together in the cold and examined the granite pillar, which had a distinct red tint to it. James ran his hands up and down the smooth façade and felt the grooves where features had been carved into the stone. 'These images, they look like hieroglyphics! How did the Egyptians get all the way out here?!' he remarked incredulously.

'Oh, you're quite right actually' Tiffanny explained. 'This was a gift from the Egyptian Government in 1833. It depicts an era of peace and prosperity under the rule of Pharaoh Ramses II, which is quite ironic because before it arrived here this site used to house a great guillotine for eliminating thousands of people during the Revolution. In the summer of 1794 one thousand four hundred people were executed alone. The obelisk is more than three thousand years old, it's seventy-five feet tall and weighs over two hundred and fifty metric tonnes. And look at this; see the images on the pedestal? They are instructions!'

James looked on. 'Instructions for what?'

'For moving the obelisk!'

'Moving it? Why on earth would anybody want to move this thing?'

Tiffanny took the question to be rhetorical and monitored the obelisk with greater scrutiny.

'See anything useful?'

'Not yet James. Aren't you going to help me?'

'Of course. It's a beautiful monument.'

'Hmmm. If you like it that much perhaps you should give it a kiss?!'

'I don't really go for fair-featured things' the lawman remarked.

'I guess that confirms one thing; Radka is your ex-wife, emphasis on the prefix.'

Their task was made difficult by the darkness, despite the obelisk's arbitrary illumination. James peered warily into the darkness beyond their position. His role was bodyguard, after all. He could let Tiffanny do the legwork and stick to reconnaissance.

The streetlights provided ample lighting for the nocturnal footman or nightshift employee. His eyes panned the night-time noir. He took deep, reassuring breaths. He tapped his feet against the cold. The Frenchwoman was keeping herself busy studying the obelisk at close range, making note of every detailed inscription.

There was no foot traffic; the street appeared derelict and deserted. Up ahead he could see the Hôtel de Crillon where, as legend would have it, Marie Antoinette relaxed and took piano lessons, and in more recent times served as the headquarters of the German army who occupied the city during World War Two. In the immediate foreground stood two distinct fountains, about three hundred yards away. They were designed by Jacques-Ignace Hittorff and were inspired by the fountains of Rome. Their bodies are laden with maritime themes because of their proximity to the Seine and also the Navy Ministry.

'James, come over here!' His attention was diverted from the beauty of the fountains to the beauty of her. He marched over to the obelisk, where Tiffanny was pointing to a section of the pillar on the south side towards the bottom. 'It's very minute but you can just about make out the words. It's the same lettering.'

James squatted on his haunches and checked the granite. He could feel the warm glow from the Eiffel Tower seeping down into his face. The searchlight was periodically giving him scrutiny. Then he saw what Tiffanny had seen.

Serenade the modern Romans with a heartfelt song.

*

The man in the tanned jacket peered out at them from the relative confines of the west fountain. He was kneeling on the ground with one knee raised, as if to make a proposal. Something in their body language had suggested his targets had discovered something important at the sight of the obelisk. The metallic vibration emanating from his trouser pocket was disengaged after five seconds as he answered the incoming call.

'Chaplin here.'

'Status report?'

'They are flitting from place to place around the city. Very specific landmarks. Each time they appear to make an important discovery and then move on. I have yet to discern what that is, but they haven't left my sight since I picked up their trail. I can only envisage they will eventually lead me to a final location that houses what we are looking for.'

'Fine. There's not much else you can do. Keep on them and keep me posted. Oh, and Chaplin; no more murders please. Keep yourself clean until the time is right. You are not a monster; at least, I did not raise you like one!'

'I understand, Mr Ross.' The line clicked and went dead.

Chapter Eighteen

5:45 p.m.

'So, where to now?' The lawman and the Frenchwoman had left the Place de la Concorde and were heading north on foot.

'Opéra, and the Boulevard des Italiens. It's not far; come on.'

The realisation for James was instantaneous. *Serenade the modern Romans with a heartfelt song.* Opera, song, modern Romans, Italians. Hardly a Mensa-level puzzle. 'There's one thing that concerns me about all of this.'

'What's that James?'

'The calligraphic text is old-fashioned and faded, which means somebody put those words there years, perhaps even decades ago. You can see how the elements have scorched and worn the charcoal lettering into the weathered façade of the monuments.'

'Yes, and your point is?'

'My point is that I've spent the last two days running around Paris trying to protect you; I've made decisions and actions which have led to the death of two innocent natives; my wife, sorry, ex-wife as you so kindly pointed out, has been kidnapped by an entrepreneurial megalomaniac; and there is a covert operation occurring somewhere that involves the secret production of something called B17.

'Whilst my intel is sketchy at best, no thanks to you, it doesn't take a genius to appreciate that something rather serious is happening at the very heart of sub-society. But all of these events are recent; only four days ago I was prowling through student papers looking for ways to keep them above the fail threshold. I was living a normal life. Albeit a lonely one; but normal nonetheless.'

'Hmmm. I'm still waiting for a grand conclusion to this great speech.'

'What I'm trying to say, Tiffanny, is how is it possible that these recent events are connected to cryptic handwritten clues here in Paris from a bygone era? Those messages could be fifty years old.'

'I think you over-think things James. Somebody could have made those messages to look old, only really they were done recently. I imagine common household cleaning products such as a good detergent or bleach could have been applied to give them that eroded effect.'

'Would somebody really go to such pedantic lengths, at the risk of desecrating a national treasure like the monuments we have been to?'

'Take a look around, James. A good look. Take a look at the shutters on that storefront over there, for example. What do you see?'

James squinted in the darkness, squeezing his eyes open as far as they would go without popping out of their sockets. 'All I can see in this light is a load of graffiti, to be honest with you!'

'Exactement! Graffiti! And you will see that everywhere you go around the city. And not just this city. Go to Berlin, or Vienna, or Budapest or Prague. You will see the same thing; graffiti. People desecrate things all the time. So don't be so surprised about an inconspicuous little poem on a piece of granite.'

Point taken, James thought to himself. As a traditional art and architecture historian with a scientific employment background, Tiffanny would no doubt have been proud of the landmarks in her capital city and probably missed the bohemian creativity and expression in the day-to-day graffiti splattered around the tenements. She must have had a deep resentment of street-artist desecration.

Still, James had a sinking feeling they were slowly dredging up the remnants of an old forgotten problem. The writing looked too authentic to have been doctored by modernity. What he could not fathom was how a potentially fifty-year old set of messages related to the production of B17 today; whatever B17 was. And yet whenever he pressed Tiffanny for more information, she was always quick to rebut his frustrations with a teasing jibe or an alternative viewpoint. Perhaps if he kept his focus on Radka, that could be his take in all of this. Regardless of what Casino Collins and even Tiffanny was up to, if he just locked on to the hopeful beacon of Radka's safety, he could stay strong; stick it out, for her.

'I need more information about B17. I must know why Radka has been taken from me.'

'She was taken, granted; but in light of your personal difficulties, was she really taken from you? Had she not already removed herself from your circle?'

'Why do you always do that?'

'Do what?'

'You are so cruel sometimes. You never provide a direct answer. You always have a quick-witted reply, and sometimes they are quite hurtful. I am going through a distressing time, and you are not being very supportive.'

'I'm sorry, James. I didn't mean anything by it. We should hurry along now.'

'So you can't honestly tell me anything more about B17?'

'That depends on your definition of can't. I can tell you more, a great deal more, as in I have the capability to do that. It's the willingness on my part that is lacking.'

'Aha, now we are getting somewhere; you can, but you won't.'

'I suppose you could put it like that, oui.'

'Why do you feel you need to hold back? Have I not been anything other than helpful to you? What about Fabien and Camille – do they not deserve your full honesty and cooperation?'

Tiffanny remained aloof and refused to answer his question, which had not been intended as a rhetorical conclusion to the conversation, and of course he knew as much. He knew it wasn't personal – they were both wired from possibly the most eventful day of their lives. They had eaten little yet had covered miles of the city's landscape; they had burned carbs but not replaced them. And there was more to be done before the day was out. James' primary concern was with the man in the tanned jacket.

'How many of these messages do you envisage finding, Tiffanny?'

'I don't know' she spat testily.

They marched briskly against the cold, heading northwest through the grounds of the Marie Madeleine. They turned east onto Boulevard de la Madeleine, a wide and conifer-lined thoroughfare that eventually became Boulevard des Capucines, and finally Boulevard des Italiens. Up ahead they saw a car park in the distance, and when they reached it they realised that it served the Office du Tourisme, which had closed its business for the day judging by the shutters on the windows and the darkness emanating from within.

James decided to back off and give the Frenchwoman some space, so he set off on his own looking for clues in the immediate vicinity. In doing so he ensured that she remained in his eye line just in case the man in the tanned jacket returned.

In the past, when he had been in Paris, he had not wanted to leave; the post-holiday blues were like coming down from a hallucinogenic substance, not that he'd ever taken any. But that's how junkies always describe the low point of their foray into the world of crazy.

Not this time; this time he wished he had never boarded the plane. If it wasn't for Radka, he wouldn't have. He pictured the relative tranquillity of Albion Place, Chester – home. He thought about his neighbours. The Australian couple's baby would be up walking and speaking her first words by now.

The College would be wondering about his disappearance. He wondered if it might have escalated into police involvement. He pictured a mugshot of himself on the front cover of the tabloids. *Missing tutor*. Then he recalled the mugshot on the sheet of paper in the possession of the man in the tanned jacket and realised it wasn't too far fetched a possibility.

'You know, anyone with an inclination towards suspicion would think this street had something to hide' the Frenchwoman remarked. She was making an effort to be civil.

'Why's that?'

'It's been through more name changes than a stage performer on the run. Boulevard Neuf, Boulevard au Dépôt, Boulevard de la Chaussée d'Antin, Boulevard Cerutti, le petit Coblence, Boulevard de Gand, the list goes on!'

James was fascinated by the history lesson. He nodded thoughtfully as the mademoiselle listed the shadows of the street's former self. He glanced around at the moonlit features; the facades, the canopied bistros, the smooth concrete of well-kept pavements and the impeccable blacktop of the road surface. In fact James caught a whiff of the lingering scent of brand new tarmac as it floated on a zephyr current.

The street was a veteran of Parisian heritage. As Tiffanny explained, the late eighteenth and early nineteenth centuries offered the street as a meeting place for the elite, right up until the outbreak of the Great War in 1914. Some of the old remnants remained, but as James gazed through mediocre night vision at the tenements lining the streets, all he could make out was evidence of twenty-first century modernity; renovated stonework that now housed the headquarters of corporate behemoths such as Credit Lyonnais and BNP-Paribas, and the Palais Berlitz.

'That used to be a restaurant' Tiffanny stated as she pointed to the BNP-Paribas head office. 'La Maison Dorée, it was called. Again, one for the elite, in the 1830's.'

'You really know your stuff! I must say I'm impressed!' Tiffanny pouted at the flattery.

Her mood was slightly uplifted. Her subconscious had momentarily relieved her of her troubles. 'I'm a little concerned about this next clue. Up to now we've had a specific monument to be going at. Here all we have is a street; and a long one at that. Is it just going to be here on the pavement somewhere? That will take us ages to find, especially in this light.'

Tiffanny's reply was drowned out by a sudden rapture of noise. The music was coming from north of their location, and it was growing cumulatively louder as they walked towards it, like a crescendo to their efforts. It was a street musician, they soon realised.

The tramp was dressed in old olive fatigues and wore an unkempt beard that matched the dark blonde in his shoulder length hair. He was playing an acoustic guitar and singing. It sounded like Irish gypsy folk music; some derivation of the twelve bar blues.

He perched on a small wooden stool and held the guitar down at an acute angle – it was the only way he could comfortably play without the aid of a strap. He beamed when the man and woman entered his field of vision. He was clearly a seasoned musician, perhaps a former session player, able to keep his eyes on the objects in front of him whilst his stubby vagrant fingers picked notes and chords off the fretboard.

'Bonne soirée Monsieur et Madame' he uttered pleasantly, as his rolling hillbilly jaunt reached an interlude. He was the type of gentleman that if he had been wearing a hat he would have removed it in recognition of Tiffanny's status as a lady.

James returned the pleasantry and reached into his pocket. He peeled off a five Euro note from the wad of bills and placed it inside the busker's guitar case. The case had an external black veneer and a deep purple inlay made from plush velvet. It looked like a sturdy piece of carpentry. 'Merci beaucoup, vous etez tres gentile!' the tramp exclaimed. *Thank you, you are very kind!* Then he said something altogether unorthodox. 'Lisa complains that the pyramid is wrong.'

'Excuse-moi?' Tiffanny said.

The musician repeated himself, in very broken English. 'Lisa complains that the pyramid is wrong.' Tiffanny took a step closer and James followed suit. There was an odour in the man's immediate vicinity that reeked; a concoction of whiskey and no showers for a good few months. In spite of his apparent frugalities and the harshness of his routine, he appeared to be in jovial spirits, although James suspected it was just the whiskey talking. At least the liquor served a double purpose; he may have kept him merry, but more importantly, in the biting February chill of the Parisian winter, it probably kept him warm. Probably. Tiffanny engaged him in rapid-fire French.

'What does that mean?'

'What does what mean my sweet darling?'

'What you just said?'

'What did I just say?'

'Lisa complains that the pyramid was wrong.'

'What does that mean?'

'I don't know! That is what I am asking you! You just said it!'

As Tiffanny continued in her vain attempt to draw blood from a stone, James glanced around at the sound of an incoming vehicle. Then he saw the wash of headlights. A white Renault careened past them. James could not make out the driver in the darkness; all he caught was a blurring of tanned leather. A tanned leather jacket.

'Tiffanny, what is the registration number of your car? The one we left by the Sacre Coeur this morning?'

As the Frenchwoman turned from the tramp to face him, her eyes locked on to the rear of the vehicle moving south down the boulevard and her expression spoke in advance of her mouth. 'Mon Dieu! That's my car!'

'I didn't make out his face in the dark, but he was wearing a tanned leather jacket. It's the same man I saw when I was waiting for you to come down from the Eiffel Tower. Now do you believe me?'

'Oui.'

Then James turned to the busker and addressed him in English. 'Lisa complains that the pyramid is wrong. Where did you hear that?'

The man appeared confused and in some distress. He appealed to the Frenchwoman for help. She translated the question. He responded in their mutual mother tongue. Tiffanny translated. 'He says he did not hear it. He says he saw it.'

James grew impatient and suddenly grabbed the tramp by the collar. 'Tell me what it means you fool. Tell me now! We need to know where you saw it.' The lawman began to shake him from side to side.

'James, stop it! You're hurting him!' The Frenchwoman intervened and prised James' hands free of the flinching busker, whose body language confirmed his fear and confusion. He lost the grip on his guitar and the acoustic six-string crashed to the ground.

James relented and Tiffanny dragged him away. 'It's not his fault; he doesn't understand you!' She gave him a look of sheer disdain and then looked back to the tramp with sympathy. His right arm was out, his finger pointing to a strip of wall across the street. He was chattering to himself; it sounded like a religious incantation, similar to the apocalyptic warning given by the hobo on the metro. Their eyes followed his gaze. Tiffanny ran across the street to where the man was seemingly directing his finger. James ran after her, checking the streetscape for any sign of the Renault.

Tiffanny approached the stone wall and searched the façade for the calligraphic lettering they had become more than familiar with. It was there.

Lisa complains that the pyramid is wrong.

'I suppose you already know where we have to go now' James muttered dispassionately. Tiffanny was smiling.

'Bien sur! We have to go to the Louvre. More specifically, we have to go to the courtyard beside it.'

Chapter Nineteen

6:30 p.m.

'The Pyramide Inversée is in the courtyard of the Louvre' James stated factually. 'The inverted Pyramid. Is that why Lisa thinks it is wrong?'

'Probably. And we both know that if we are talking about the Louvre, there is only one Lisa that could be referred to.'

'The Mona Lisa. It's in the Salle des États section of the museum. It's encased in a bullet-proof glass case, with a climate control facility to help maintain its integrity.'

'It's in a better position than I am' the mademoiselle reflected sombrely.

'What do you mean by that?' James pressed.

'My role here is integral to the protection of B17, as is yours. I just don't feel like I'm doing a very good job.'

'You are solving the clues. I think you are doing a great job.'

'Thanks for the sentiment, but at what cost? Two people are dead because of me.'

'Not because of you, Tiffanny. Because of the person that killed them. Remember that.'

'I can't help but feel responsible.'

'You need to remove that angle from your mental processing' James spoke tentatively. 'It won't do any good; in fact it will drive you crazy in the long run. The worst kind of guilt is unnecessary guilt. It's a waste of your energy, like the anger emotion. Getting angry over something completely out of your control is a fruitless endeavour. You need to forget about it, and move on. I know it's

171

hard, but it's the only way, if you want to keep your sanity.'

'And how do you keep your sanity, James?'

'I keep myself occupied, mentally. For instance, I think about what possessed somebody to leave us these clues to solve years later. I think about B17, and what it could be. I think about whether or not you're telling me absolutely everything you know. I think about Radka, about the students whose papers are not being marked, but are instead lying by the wayside in a desk drawer in my house.

'I think about the city walls of Chester, and how to get back to them. I think about the man in the tanned jacket, and what I'd like to do to him. I think about the road ahead, not the road behind. I don't even glance in my rear view mirror anymore; I just plough ahead through the darkness like a joyrider on a midnight cruise through the back of beyond. Come; the Louvre's courtyard awaits.'

'It's dark; you won't be able to read the map. I will lead; you follow.' The Frenchwoman was nothing if not assertive. She pushed the wall of doubt to the back of her mind like scrap metal waiting to be incinerated. They were both hungry and tired.

The night was drawing in, bringing the day gone by into its final conclusion. The heavens opened and plumes of fine rain plummeted to the surface from the troposphere. A biting gale drifted in from the west coast; another prodigy of the North Atlantic Drift. James knew they should be fitting in a meal before they bedded down. He could still taste the slow burn of sugar and the flour from the crepe dough from earlier, lingering in the back of his throat, making his stomach rumble like a seismic blip.

He only half-believed in the mantra he had given Tiffanny about looking forward. He was preaching to her resolve to remain steadfast and resolute. Truth was, he had gremlins lingering in the four corners of his psyche. A number of decisions he had made in his recent past had seemingly led to a chain reaction of unfavourable events. Those events were regrets stacked up like dominoes, and all he needed was a fresh start; one new event to knock them all down in one fell swoop.

172

The first domino had been planted the moment he had decided to walk away from Radka, triggering the breakdown of their marriage. The second had sprung up when she had moved out of their beautiful home, taking her spirit and her essence with her, leaving behind a cold house and an empty void. The third offered a layer of foundation to the building blocks of his misfortune when the law firm he was training with had to let him go. The adverse publicity from the Aequitol scandal and the fallout from the politician whose case had sparked the debacle had fused into a dirty bomb of unwanted grief for the equity partners, who wanted the whole thing to just disappear, like a bad smell.

A hellish number of strings had been pulled in order to get him the teaching position – enough strings to keep the entire cast of Thunderbirds in suspended animation for an indeterminable period of time. Truth was, he hated acquisitions. Pushing thirty, what did he have to show for it? His classmates from law school were well on their way; some of them had finished their training and would soon become associates, with a fast track to partnership.

James would probably never again see the inside of a law office. He had fallen by the wayside, and he felt he was being left behind. Granted, he had no mortgage and no additional mouths to feed. He had become an eligible bachelor. There was a trade-off to that situation, between freedom and loneliness. The company of a woman was something unrivalled.

Modern life offers many thrills and vices – extreme sports, jumping out of planes, rollercoasters, the energy from a rock concert, alcohol, food, narcotic substances, escaping a near-death experience. But none of that compares with the rush a man gets when he is gifted the opportunity of loving a woman; holding her, kissing her, feeling her warmth, hearing her heartbeat, falling asleep with her wrapped in his arms. The feeling of togetherness is a feeling of one, of completeness. It was the greatest pleasure, and James had destroyed it. He had walked away from it; abandoned it like an unwanted child in the rain.

The words of Pearl Jam's Nothingman suddenly shot into his ears like a teasing mantra; a soundtrack to his misery. *Once divided, nothing left to subtract. Some words when spoken can't be taken back. Walks on his own, with thoughts he can't help thinking. Future's above, but in the past he's slow and sinking. Caught a bolt of lightning, cursed the day he let it go. Nothingman, Nothingman, isn't it something, Nothingman.* Right there and then, in that moment, James felt like a Nothingman.

They set off due south on foot, walking down Avenue de L'Opera with an urgency that betrayed their purpose. They were heading towards the Palais Royal, a large stately chateau that served as the living quarters for monarchs of the bygone era. Its modern day function remains as the Constitutional Court of France and the Culture Ministry. In the evening twilight it was basking in an ochre wash, and it beckoned them in from eight hundred yards away.

'Will the museum still be open at this time?' James asked incredulously.

'No, but we should still be able to access the courtyard and see the Pyramide Inversée.'

The rain remained a stubborn drizzle, yet the wind blew it in haphazard trajectories, occasionally soaking the street dwellers. It was a miserable evening, compounding their own miseries. A torrential downpour seemed ominously imminent. They passed the Palais Royal and converged onto Rue Rivoli. The Louvre complex was dead ahead.

'So what do you know about Casino Collins?'

'What do you know about him, James?'

'Not a great deal. I know that he has a keen interest in the Space Program. I read an article in a Chester newspaper about him the day before I came to France. He wants to be the first to own lunar real estate.'

'Oh yes, Collins is a big player in that game.'

'Big player? I don't follow?'

'He has a majority shareholding in NASA. You saw that thing he's having the next Apollo crew take up there for him?'

'The American-style letterbox? Yeah, the article mentioned that too.'

'Well, there you go. Imagine the weight he must be able to throw around to have them do that for him? He pours a great deal of private funding into their initiatives, more so than any government grant, that's for sure.'

'Do you think it will happen?'

'Do I think what will happen, James?'

'Do you think in the near future we'll see colonies of our kind up there on the moon, a civilised expansion of our race?'

'Hmmm. Probably not in the near future. And I'm not sure civilised is the right word. If we can't achieve such a thing here on Earth, what makes you think it will be any different up there?'

'No oil up there, Tiffanny. Just dust and rocks! Nothing to exploit!'

'Maybe you're right. But there will be something up there worth destroying. If it's there for the taking, why would the human race break the habit of our lifetime?'

'I didn't put you down as a cynic, Tiff.'

'I'm not; I'm a realist, is all. If you cannot find a happy medium between cynicism and naivety, I would always suggest erring on the side of caution and opting for the former. It's a failsafe defence mechanism.' James wondered what cruel twists of fate Tiffanny had suffered in her short life to date, to make her feel so uptight and cautious. Perhaps she too had gremlins to overcome.

'Are you sure we're going to be able to get inside the courtyard? It's late.'

'Don't worry, James. There are three entrances to the Louvre – the Passage Richelieu to the north, the Porte des Lions from the south, and the Carrousel to the west. As we only intend to see the courtyard, and not the museum itself, we can access through the Carrousel. People like to take a stroll around the courtyard; it's not restricted. There is an open gangway for pedestrians.'

They approached from the west as intended, walking with a quickened pace down the gauntlet of concrete until the alleyway branched out into the courtyard itself. There was a painted sign in red lettering on a white placard that read *Accès général,* reinforcing what Tiffanny had said. General access.

The main pyramid, not inverted, stood proud as the centrepiece. It was flanked on three sides by miniature versions of itself. The courtyard was known as the Cour Napoleon. The main pyramid is constructed of six hundred and seventy three glass panes reinforced by a metal frame; six hundred and three are rhombus-shaped and the remaining seventy are triangular. The tip of its apex stands seventy feet tall.

The Louvre itself stood in the foreground; a monolithic architectural creation that hugs the perimeter of the courtyard on three sides like a giant U shape. The pyramid is connected to an underground chamber that provides direct access to the museum, and serves as one of many entrance points.

'I still think we have a problem' James reiterated as they reached the main pyramid. 'The inverted version, referenced in the last clue, is in an underground shopping mall on the other side of this courtyard, near the Louvre entrance itself. The museum closes at six p.m. It's now approaching seven. We're too late!'

'I have a plan' the Frenchwoman revealed. 'But it involves a degree of thespian trickery on your part.'

'What on earth do you mean?' James asked.

'I know the night watchman here. It's a long story, but if you play the excited tourist in Paris for the first time, desperate to see the site of the conclusion to the Da Vinci Code story before you fly home tomorrow morning, I think he will let us at least have a look at the pyramid. The museum would be aiming too high, but it seems all we need is the area near the pyramid.'

'I'm not in the mood to play games Tiffanny.'

'Well tough luck. If we can't see the pyramid, we don't find the next clue, and that doesn't help Radka or anybody for that matter. The clock is ticking, James.'

James resigned to the inevitable and Tiffanny led him away from the main pyramid to the Passage Richelieu to the north. A man of North African descent, probably Algerian, stood rigid in a navy blue uniform by the entrance. He held a flashlight and shone it towards the two figures approaching him. He smiled when Tiffany reached his field of vision. 'Tiffany, coucou ma cherie! Ca va?'

They spoke in French for five minutes. Occasionally the Frenchwoman pointed in James' direction, at which he would grin at the Algerian like a buffoon, for maximum effect, feigning excitement. The security guy held himself on a stocky frame. His broad shoulders carried a well toned abdomen, and his neck was wide and rigid. His eyes were huge and piercing, his lips full and pronounced. James decided he wouldn't want to be on the wrong side of the man. His demeanour was intimidating, yet in the same vein as the military officers James had seen patrolling the grounds of the Eiffel Tower with M16s, that was kind of the general idea. But as the guard spoke to Tiffany his posture was mellow and friendly. They clearly went back a ways.

What shocked James the most was how jealous he became at the sight of the mademoiselle giving another man all her attention. She was laughing with the guard, using touchy-feely gestures such as the occasional pat on his shoulder, a squeeze of his hand. He did not return the gestures – either he was the kind of guy uncomfortable with too much affection, or he was just being professional.

Jesus! James chastised himself. *Get a grip!* It was a totally irrational reaction. He watched the Frenchwoman pleading with the man but he seemed to be holding his ground. Then he shook his head; not a subtle movement but a firm gesture. The answer was no. No admittance tonight. Come back tomorrow. The stone wall of the façade was too high to breach, and the facilitator of a legitimate passage was stonewalling.

Tiffany bade her farewell and returned to the spot where James had planted himself. He met her gaze as she came within his immediate vicinity. 'No good?'

'Non. It's not happening. Merde! Putain!' The Frenchwoman cussed her way through a number of expletives, and the words echoed their frustrations like a beacon from a watchtower. James remained passive in response to her outburst – he fully appreciated that to swear in French was to wipe one's ass with silk.

'The cluemaker wasn't so clever in regards to predicting our arrival time' the lawman chided. Tiffanny ignored the remark. Instead she walked back towards the main pyramid in the centre of the courtyard. 'What are you doing?' he called after her. She carried on without looking back. He glanced over at the night watchman and gave him a cursory nod in acknowledgment. A *thanks anyway* gesture. The man returned the pleasantry. James took off after the Frenchwoman.

'What are you doing?' he asked for the second time as he caught up with her stride and stepped in line.

'Something you said gave me an idea' Tiffanny replied.

'What did I say?'

'Well, you said the cluemaker didn't predict the time we would get here, that is to say whether the Louvre and the shopping mall housing the Pyramide Inversée would be open or shut. Which makes me wonder if the cluemaker ever wanted us to go inside after all.'

'I don't follow, Tiffanny. The clue clearly stated…'

'I know what the clue stated, James. But think about it; the Pyramide Inversée is such a sacred monument, and in light of the furore surrounding it, in no small part to the Da Vinci Code, it has become a place that is maximum security personified. There is no way the cluemaker could have managed to write any message on the features down in that underground chamber. It's protected from any kind of desecration twenty four seven.'

'I see your point' James mused.

'Of course, this also puts a dampener on your theory about these messages being fifty years old' the Frenchwoman continued.

'Why's that?'

'The Pryamide Inversée was only constructed in nineteen ninety three. It's the first modern structure the clues have directed us to. It's a mere seventeen years old.'

'I see. And you think we have misinterpreted the current message? You think *Lisa complains that the pyramid is wrong* is not a cryptic route to the inverted pyramid?'

178

'James, I think we interpreted the clue correctly. It's the cluemaker who has fooled us. This is another failsafe mechanism; a trick to throw any impostor off the scent. It's a test to see if we are the genuine protectors of the secret. It has been too easy so far – this was bound to happen sooner or later.'

'Ok, so if the real inverted pyramid is not the correct place, then where is? Is there another inverted pyramid I don't know about?'

'Yes, James, and you're staring right at it!'

'Tiffanny, this is the main pyramid in the courtyard, and it also happens to be a standard pyramid shape – not inverted.'

'That depends on your vantage point' the mademoiselle explained.

'I don't...oh. Ah.' The penny had dropped.

Tiffanny moved closer to the glass façade of the pyramid. 'Check it carefully, James. It's likely to be on the metalwork, not the glass pane.'

They moved around the pyramid in opposite directions, aiming to meet back in the centre where they had begun. Six hundred and seventy three panes, some rhombus-shaped, some triangular. Seventy were triangular, which meant they had three sides, which meant that each of those panes had three strips of metal making up the frame.

A total of two hundred and ten possible places to scrawl a discreet message. A rhombus was a quadrilateral shape, giving it four sides. It basically looked like a warped square; compressed and compacted like a diamond. All of its sides were equal in length. There were six hundred and three of these shapes on the pyramid. Another two thousand four hundred and twelve lines of metalwork to check. A grand total of two thousand six hundred and twenty two possibilities.

'This could take all night' James shouted across.

'It will take as long as it takes' Tiffanny evaluated, a response typical of a scientist – factual and straight up; no room for chance or probability or sheer damn luck. A clinical analysis. They shuffled around the circumference, James checking the higher sections leading to the apex and Tiffanny the middle and lower sections, which widened out to the base at the bottom.

They moved awkwardly, trying not to get in each other's way. It must have been an odd sight for the night watchman, who looked on from the comfort of his post by the Richelieu entrance point. The glass panes were impeccably clean; the metalwork polished to a shine.

James remained doubtful. 'If this pyramid is so immaculately kept, surely any message will have been painted over by now? Or bleached out?'

'It's a chance we have to take, but yes it is a possibility.'

After forty minutes of shuffling around in the dark, Tiffanny exhaled a triumphant release of air. 'There is something written here.'

'And is it...'

'Upside down? Yes it is! So I was right. The writing is upside down on a standard pyramid. If I stood on my head and read the message the correct way, I would be looking at an inverted pyramid!'

James smiled. 'An uncanny piece of misdirection. I'm inspired.'

'I'm not prepared to stand on my head. Luckily I won't have to.'

'Oh, why's that?'

'Every woman carries essentials in her handbag, James; surely even you must know that!' She pulled something small out of her bag and placed it on a section of the pyramid near the bottom. She lined the object up with the artificial lamps on the façade and it cast a reflection into James' eye. He placed a hand to his face to shield it. He realised that she had a small mirror and was reading the message the easy way. It said:

Still dying to know the truth? Knowledge is power. At your last stop H is the key.

180

Chapter Twenty

8:05 p.m.

Still dying to know the truth? Knowledge is power. At your last stop, H is the key. The construction of the latest message indicated finality to the proceedings. *Your last stop.* James felt a pang of exhilaration and relief, knowing that the end was in sight. He was tired and hungry and frustrated. Chaperoning the Frenchwoman had become a frivolous pursuit. Solving the clues had done little to console or motivate him.

The more he pressed Tiffanny for their raison d'etre, and the finer details of B17, the more she repelled his efforts. It was the proverbial blood from a stone endeavour. Still, he couldn't go home. He was trapped. He had been lured into something, at the behest of Radka's survival. He had to trundle onwards through the ordeal in order to reach its unequivocal conclusion. He was caught between a rock and a hard place.

'I take it the final destination is a library, considering the fact that knowledge is power, and libraries are widely considered to be the most blatant facilitators of knowledge, barring the internet of course?'

'I think you're right James. And I get the feeling that if the cluemaker has gone to all this trouble so far, he probably isn't the kind of guy to do things by halves, if indeed we are referring to a *he*. So, bearing that in mind, we're heading towards the Bibliothèque Nationale de France.'

'The National Library? That's the biggest and boldest library in the city.'

'Oui.'

181

'Then that's where we need to be. And I would also assume that a national library in a city like Paris will be open twenty four hours?'

'Never assume, James. It makes an *ass* out of *u* and *me*!'

James grunted. 'Where did you pick that one up?'

'In a movie I think. Actually the library is closed to the public from eight in the evening. But as I was a student here I have a special pass. So we're fine.'

'You did your undergraduate studies here in Paris?'

'Oui. French Cultural Studies and Modern History. I spent four years here.'

'Where did you live?'

'I inherited a studio on the outskirts. My aunt passed away; in her will she had left it to me.'

'I'm sorry about your aunt.'

'Thanks, she was effectively my parental guardian since the age of thirteen.'

'What happened when you were thirteen?'

'My parents were flying home from a skiing trip in the Swiss Alps. There was a storm. Their plane was hit by lightning; it disintegrated over the Atlantic Ocean. There was no trace of it; no bodies, no part of the aircraft. Nothing left except tiny particles of vapour.'

'My God that's terrible. I am so very sorry.'

'It was a long time ago.'

'I don't know what to say.'

'There is nothing to say. Remove it from your mind. We have enough to worry about. You will see it later on.'

'I'll see what?'

'The studio. Unless you want to go back to the Hotel Magenta? Perhaps you can make a bed from the police ticker tape?'

'The studio will be fine. Thanks, Tiffanny.'

'De rien.' *It's nothing.*

They jumped on the metro at Place du Châtelet and rode on a south-eastern bearing to the Bibliothèque Nationale, following the snaking path of the Seine. It was a long, sweeping journey that lasted thirty minutes. In the darkness the scenery they shunted past was well concealed. James watched the endless black of the underground

182

tunnels and listened to the relentless double-click as the carriages chugged along the track in conformity with the cab and the motorised engine it carried.

His own motor functions were beginning to gradually shut down, like a slow computer. He felt like an old machine, with insufficient processing memory and a clogged hard disk, struggling to cope with the excess demands of its user. He was burnt out. To say the last two days had been unpredictable was an understatement of the highest order.

'Assuming this is the last stop, what do you expect to find in the library?' he enquired of his Gaelic counterpart.

'Your guess is as good as mine, James.' Tiffanny too was a wreck. Today had been particularly eventful. She looked to be exhausted.

'Hopefully it will provide more information on B17 than you have!'

'We'll see.'

They disembarked from the train at Gare de Lyon in the twelfth arrondissement. Dead ahead to the south, on the opposite bank of the Seine, lay the Palais Omnisports de Paris Bercy, a colossal indoor sports arena that housed a capacity of seventeen thousand. It was shaped like a cake and it was offset on all four sides by a verge of grassland leading up to a serious of horizontal steel girders making up the top frame. Its perimeter was shaded by a cluster of out-of-bloom cedars.

To the west, the Jardin des Plantes housed the Museum National D'Histoire Naturelle, the National Museum of Natural History, and the Grande Galerie de L'Évolution, formerly known as the Jardin du Roi; the Garden of the King. It was a hub of botanical brilliance, basking at that moment in nocturnal indifference.

The drizzling precipitation continued with a steely determination, but the gale calmed to a zephyr. The National Library was due south, beyond the Seine, beyond the stadium. In spite of their deference they huddled together, linking arms, and skipped towards the river. More electricity blitzed through him with the promise of close proximity and physical contact. The curls of Tiffanny's hair brushed against his cheek. Her breath was warm and fragrant on his face. The one benefit of James' volatile situation was that it solidified their interdependency, and he longed for a more sustained intimacy.

It was a twenty minute stroll from the Gare de Lyon to the Bibliothèque Nationale. Vehicle presence on the streets was light, as was foot traffic. It was a little after eight; most Parisians would be contemplating dinner preparations. The French ate late, but they ate well; their cuisine was one of par excellence, far removed from the microwave TV dinner mentality north of the Channel.

For the French, mealtimes were a formal occasion; most French employers granted their workforce a two-hour respite for lunch, and evening meals were a foray into family values. It was about sitting down and having a meaningful conversation; beginning with a nice aperitif; a little wine washed down with the chef's chosen entrée, and concluding with a main meal comprising of a concoction of flavours, some subtle, others gregarious, lasting two or three hours in total. Food was to be enjoyed at a decently relaxed pace in France, as was life itself.

The Pont de Boulevard de Bercy was situated at the intersection of Quai de la Rapée and Boulevard Vincent Auriol, and served as a bridge across the Seine. As they crossed James gazed down at the dark water. It was calm and without foreboding, but if threatened could swallow him up whole. It was an inviting proposition for a moment; but James managed to steer clear of that destructive path and he prised his eyes away from the eerie black bastion below him. Tiffanny permitted herself a cursory glance and suddenly stopped in her tracks, causing James, who was still interlinked through her arm, to be yanked forward awkwardly.

'What's wrong? What have you seen, Tiff?'

The Frenchwoman remained speechless but pointed, her finger angled downward at an awkward trajectory, towards the far side of the river; to where they had just come from. James saw her point of reference and felt a cold chill in his spine.

'Are you sure it's the same one?'

'Definitely.'

'It's dark, plus it's a popular model. There could be many like it in my city.'

'I know my car when I see it, James. It's my Renault.'

'How can you be so sure, from three hundred yards away?'

'You see the shadow between the licence plate and the left corner of the rear bumper? It's not a natural shadow. Somebody shunted me a while back. I never bothered to have it fixed.'

James craned his head and strained his eyes. He saw the shadow. He looked across the street at other parked cars. There weren't many, but the ones that he saw lacked the same shadow. 'Yeah, I see it. But I don't see the tanned jacket.'

'He's probably watching us right now, from a place of hiding. Come on; I want to be inside the library. We will be safe there.'

They huddled closer and continued along the bridge. They descended down a ramp at the other side and hung a left onto Quai de Mauriac. They saw the entrance to the Bibliothèque Nationale immediately. Tiffanny hustled him along and as they reached the foyer she took a pass from her purse and swiped it through the machine in the entrance. The doors opened automatically and they entered the library.

James was instantly reminded by several factors that he was in an academic institution; the pastel-grey paint lick standardised throughout the building; the smell of buffed carpet, the silence except for whirring computers and the thumping of books being placed back on shelves, the swoosh of open pages being turned, the excess warmth from unnecessary heating; the occasional click of high-heeled boots on mezzanine.

He had been in many like it before. Cambridge University had possessed an impressive law library. The law college's own at Chester was modest but more than adequate. The layout inside the Bibliothèque Nationale had the same rugged tenacity; the same uniform repetition, where but for the labelling every aisle appeared identical. *H is the key* he immediately thought to himself. That's what the cluemaker had said.

He glanced around at the headers atop each aisle, but as he expected he found that none were alphabetised. They were the main subject areas; *Histoire, Actualitiés, Arts, Économie et Politique, Langues et Littératures, Sciences humaines, Philosophie et religions, Sciences sociales*. Within each topic area there would be alphabetised collections of books, by author surname. Each book would also be labelled with a three digit numerical code and a string of letters, according to an even more specific subject area within that subject area; a sub-subject.

It was the Dewey Referencing System at work. In addition, there would be a barcode on the inside sleeve of every book, and an electronic tag, which would trigger an alarm at the desk if taken out of the room without authorised permission. Knowledge is power. Information is key. If one wishes to source it, one must use the proper channels.

'How are we supposed to know what we are looking for in here?' James whispered. 'We know H is the right place to be, but in which subject area?'

'Let's start with *Sciences de la matière et de l'univers*. Studies of matter and the universe. Within that department we should find *Chimie*.'

'Chimie? Chemistry? That makes sense, I suppose. B17 is a drug after all; a compound.'

'Exactement. Alors, I will ask at the desk.' She walked to the reception point and began to converse with a young man who looked like he fit the bill of a librarian; large-framed glasses, a beard, dowdy clothes. But he appeared friendly and unthreatening, which was a great comfort compared to seeing Tiffanny's white Renault parked outside across the Seine. The man in the tanned jacket.

As James panned the room like a CCTV camera sweeping, scrutinising every nook and cranny of the building, he began to ponder again who the man could be. He presumed that he had been sent by some rival of Casino Collins to thwart their secret activities. He was unlikely to be a cop, because the various agencies and factions of French law enforcement were pretty thorough in co-ordinating their efforts and communication channels were open and effective. As Lacroix of the Paris Prefecture of Police had already eliminated them from his enquiries, and released them from incarceration, there would be no reason for another officer to be tailing them. So the man in the tanned jacket had to be an outside threat.

Tiffanny came back and directed them towards the southeast corner of the library. James watched as students pored over texts and wrote up their mid-term papers. Some were knee-deep in research, others were looking for specific references for bibliographical purposes, and a few were just typing up their ideas into a coherent essay format. He had been all of those people once. He had written papers and studied and taken exams. He had sat in classes and listened. He had answered questions in front of the others. And then he had changed roles and become the head of the class himself, teaching a subject he knew in great detail but cared little for. That was a dangerous proposition, he appreciated. From a student's point of view, the teacher was the key to passing a course. It was all down to the standard of teaching and personality of the teacher. A student could always tell if his teacher was passionate about the subject matter. On numerous occasions as a student he had complained about his teacher. He wondered if any of his students had complained about him.

They found the *Chimie* section and James went straight to books about Chemistry written by authors whose surname began with H. *H is the key.* H was a big section, taking up two shelves, so Tiffanny started out on one and he took the other. He had no idea what specifically to look for. Did one particular book trigger a secret passageway to open somewhere, if pulled out, like in the movies? James sniggered to himself. Too far-fetched. He glanced back at Tiffanny. She was monitoring each title with due diligence; her eyes displayed a hypnotic intensity. She looked very intelligent, which undoubtedly she was. A woman with beauty and brains; the full package.

They spent an hour in total, and afterwards they had picked up and studied over two hundred books about chemistry. They had flicked through all the pages to see if any note had been left for them, but no sheets of paper fell to the floor. They had studied the author names to see if they triggered any alarm bells or memories, but none did; most were written by Frenchmen unknown to James, some were familiar to Tiffanny but none struck any chords with her. Most of the other patrons had now disbanded. One or two remained, but the library had become derelict and its emptiness stirred their disconcertion. The bearded guy at the desk glanced at them intermittently, probably hoping that the gesture would prompt them to leave so he could call it a night himself.

'I don't understand' James eventually said, resignedly. 'H is the key. It's too vague.'

Tiffanny herself looked despondent. 'We must be looking in the wrong place. And perhaps we are studying the wrong type of information.'

'What do you mean?' James asked.

'Well, as you will be well aware from your law student days, when we conduct research we have access to two categories of data, right?'

'You mean hard copy and electronic resources?'

'Oui. We have spent the last hour looking at hard copy material – books. Perhaps we should log on to a PC and search electronically?'

'Ok. Under H again, in Chemistry? Are you thinking the electronic catalogue will be wider than these two shelves?'

'Definitely.'

'We still have the same problem though; we don't know exactly what to look for.'

'Let's try it anyway.'

They approached the desk together and Tiffanny explained that she wanted to use a computer and she had her student pass, although she was no longer a student. The bearded employee was not impressed. His shoulders sagged and he smiled falsely and pointed to a bank of beige monitors in the corner. He shook his head vehemently. Then he pointed out a lone black machine which sat snug up against the side wall on its own, and nodded. Tiffanny thanked him and they headed for the black computer.

'He said that as I am no longer a student I cannot access the fast machines, but they retained one of the older models for visitors.'

'The black one' James confirmed.

'Oui.'

Tiffany sat on the swivel chair provided and James leaned over her as she logged on. He placed his hand on her shoulder to support himself as he came closer to the screen. She did not protest. The chair was old and worn; the insulated stuffing was bursting out of its plastic seam at the top. The machine was no spring chicken either; it was made by an unknown brand, presumably bought in bulk from a bureaucratic budget. Every expense spared.

Tiffany entered her username and password and the machine chugged and took four minutes to process her details and eventually took them to the main menu interface. It was probably running an old version of Windows. James thought about Moore's Law of Microprocessing; microchips doubled in capacity and halved in cost every eighteen months. Computers had to be updated regularly or they would be soon rendered obsolete. The rate of technological advancement was mind-blowing.

Tiffany double-clicked an icon to launch the library's in-house catalogue software. There were different methods of searching for a book; it appeared complicated. But Tiffany knew how it worked, as did James; they were both graduates and therefore seasoned researchers. The only limitation for James was that everything was in French. The bearded man hovered nearby, busying himself with an imaginary task whilst glaring at them under the bridge of his spectacles.

'Try searching for B17' James suggested.

'Already did. It doesn't exist. I even Googled it, James. Its secret has been well guarded.'

'Try it again, just in case.'

Tiffany sighed but complied. The machine whirred and lights blinked and after two minutes of deliberation it bleeped furiously and brought up a message in a pop-up display box; *No results found, please try again.*

'Excuse-moi.' The staffer had busied himself for long enough and had clearly lost patience. He said something to Tiffany which James was certain translated as a polite way to tell them to get lost. He looked at his watch. Nine thirty. The Frenchwoman spoke calmly and warmly and offered him her best smile and he pursed his lips and retreated back towards the desk.

'Nice charm offensive!' James teased.

'If only I was as good at solving riddles as I was at flirting' she responded.

'Hey, you've got us this far. We're almost there. This is our last stop, remember!'

'Indeed, and H is the key. But the key to what?'

They traded places and James sat in the worn chair. Tiffanny returned his gesture by placing a hand on his shoulder. It was a soft, petite, feminine hand full of warmth and James felt once again recharged. He overworked the software by searching for anything he thought was relevant to a secret drug. He switched the language to English and searched using the terms *Casino, Collins, new drug, B17, secret cure, Czech Republic, Tiffanny Tourneux.* No results found, please try again.

'You searched for me? Aww, that's sweet of you James. But I didn't write any books.'

'You seem like the type'.

James thumped the desk in frustration. The receptionist darted his head towards the noise and glared furiously. Tiffanny gave him another apologetic smile. Then the lawman returned his thoughts to the last cryptic clue. A question had been asked of them, the answer being in the affirmative. *Still dying to know the truth?* He typed out the first section of the message without the question mark into the search box, mirroring his feelings. *Dying to know the truth.* Then he hit enter.

'James? We don't have time for games!'

The machine whirred and the lights blinked and it chugged and deliberated. After forty seconds, the unexpected happened. *1 result showing. Cancer: why we are still dying to know the truth. Author: Pierre Chartier. ISBN: 845784589579. BNF Ref: 301.55CHA.* It was in English, not French. James got up out of his chair.

'James, where are you going now?'

'301.55CHA. That's where I'm headed.'

'Oh James, this is wasting precious time.'

James went back to the two shelves in the *Chimie* aisle. His eyes darted across the numerical and alphabetical spectrums until he found 301.55. CAR. CAS. CAT. CEL. CHA. There were three different authors with the surname *Chartier* on the shelf. None of them were called Pierre, and none had written about cancer. Guillaume Chartier had written about ionic and covalent compound structures. Jean-Baptiste Chartier had produced a thorough analysis of the mechanics of chemical warfare. Michel Chartier's book concerned spectroscopic methods in organic chemistry. 301.55 CHA was missing a book. It wasn't there.

James returned to the reception desk where the agitated guy was drumming his hands on the counter. 'I have a problem' he said in English. 'I need to find a book – it is on your computer catalogue but not on the shelf. I need to know where it is.'

The man sighed; the sound of inevitable resignation, realising that the sooner he co-operated the sooner he could be out of there. 'Give me the title.'

'Cancer: why we are still dying to know the truth, by Pierre Chartier. 301.55CHA.'

The guy ran it through his own machine, and they all waited patiently for two minutes. Then he frowned. 'Oh.'

'What is it?' James pressed.

'James, we are wasting time' Tiffanny reiterated.

'It was taken out in 1996 and never returned.'

'What?'

'It was taken out in...'

'Yes I heard you the first time. How is that possible?'

'I don't know, Monsieur.'

'Well I'd hate to be the guy who took it out; thirteen years of fines will have added up to a princely sum!'

'That's just it, Monsieur; the computer shows no record of the transaction since 1996. There appear to be no fines logged on the system. The book was removed from the library and never came back. No questions appear to have been asked; it just disappeared.'

James pondered the response. 'Could your system have made a mistake? Could it have forgotten to process the transaction or log any fines?'

The bearded man laughed for the first time since they'd been there. 'You're joking, right? This thing? Mon Dieu, have you any idea how many complaints I get from students about overdue fines they get hit with for returning a book seconds, even minutes late? This thing is a corporate monster; it doesn't miss a trick. Trust me, nothing slips through this monster. There is no mistake.'

The guy lost patience and said something to Tiffanny in French. It must have been colloquial because James failed to pick up the meaning in his words. 'What did he say, Tiff?'

'He said he is going to the bathroom, and when he returns he wants to see that we are gone; he wants to see an empty room.'

'Is B17 a cure for cancer?'

'I don't know, James.'

'The missing book does not explain why H is the key; especially considering the author's surname is Chartier. Surely C is the key?'

James sat back on the worn swivel chair and prepared to log off the computer. He glanced down at the keyboard as his thoughts swirled in a cauldron of confusion. *H is the key. H is the key.* He looked at the H key on the cheap desktop keyboard. It was a simple piece of engineering. Inside the keyboard there is a microprocessor and a simple circuit construct called a key matrix. The circuit is broken at a point below each key. When you hold a key down, a tiny switch is activated, completing the circuit, thus allowing that letter to appear on your screen. *H is the key. H is the key.*

A door slammed to their right. The receptionist was in the restroom. 'Tiffanny, find me a screwdriver. A flat-edge, not a Phillips.'

'Why, what on earth are you going to do?'

'Just find me one, quickly, before he comes back!'

The Frenchwoman skipped around the counter and crossed the threshold. She was in the staff domain. She found one on a corresponding shelf behind her in the corner and brought it back for James. She handed it to him.

'Please tell me what you plan to do' she pleaded.

'Something bordering on criminal damage' he replied. 'Just a hunch.'

'A hunch?'

James took a deep breath. 'If he comes out, you have to distract him.' Then he set to work. He dug the screwdriver in at a sharp, forty-five degree angle and prised the H key off the keyboard.

Tiffanny gasped in disbelief. 'You imbecile! You've damaged the National Library's main computer. You'll be thrown into a maximum security penitentiary for this! I'll go down as your accomplice. What reason could you possibly have for such madness?!'

'Calm down! It will click back into place. People remove and replace their keys all the time!' James pulled the H key off and placed it on the desk in front of him. He ignored her protests and scooped out a plastic ringer underneath the board. In the cavity where the key had been was a small spongy circular piece of plastic. He peered into the gap between it and the circuitry. There was a folded sheet of paper inside. He prised it out and put it in his pocket. Then he clicked the H key back in place, as if the keyboard had never been interfered with.

He logged off the computer and grabbed Tiffanny by the hand and they ran out of the room, through the barrier and back to the entrance. They heard a door slam and realised the receptionist was back from the restroom. James imagined the smile on his face at having witnessed the empty room signalling his freedom. Tiffanny swiped her pass through the scanner and the door released. They ran through and out onto the street outside. The air was cold, biting, but ultimately refreshing. The library had been stuffy.

'I'll ask you again Tiffanny; is B17 a cure for cancer?'

'As I already told you James, I don't know.' Her answer was firm and unrelenting.

'I don't believe you.'

'What's on the paper, James?'

He took the sheet from his pocket and unfolded it. The paper was scorched a dull beige. It was old and worn. It had clearly been lodged inside the library's computer for some time. On the sheet of paper there was a diagram and some text.

LAETRILE – VITAMIN B17

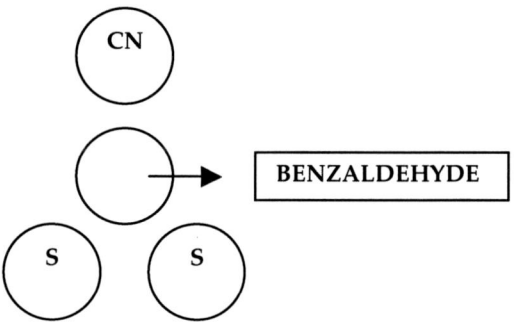

L – MANDELONITRILE – BETA GLUCOSIDE

Pierre Chartier, Rue

Charles de Gaulle, 69510

Soucieu en Jarrest, Lyon.

Chapter Twenty One

9:25 p.m.

'First thing tomorrow morning, we're going to Lyon' James stated authoritatively. 'To this address.' He pointed at the sheet of paper which was violently shaken up in his hand by the wind. 'We are going to talk to this Pierre Chartier, and we're going to get some frigging answers. They are long past due.'

'So let's go to my studio and recharge our batteries' Tiffanny suggested.

'You have food there?'

'Of course! The cupboards are stocked. I'll cook.'

'No' James countered. Tiffanny frowned at his dissidence. 'We'll cook. I'm not one of those types of guys. If you're putting me up for the night, the least I can do is help prepare a meal for the two of us.' Her frown vanished and her lips creased into a smile; the first of the day directed at him.

'Perfect. I graciously accept your offer.' James upturned the collar of his coat to preserve the heat trapped inside it and to keep the offending chill at bay. Once again they huddled together and set off from the pavement outside the national library.

As if the heavens had been testing the water and were now satisfied to move on to the main event, the drizzle advanced into a hard-line downpour. Droplets of rain bounced off the pavements in a ferocious wash. The wind picked up a bar and the enhanced pressure engaged them with its miserable fury. James felt the water beating down into every orifice from above him, dripping into his eyes and ears and seeping into his mouth, impeding his view.

It tasted salty and acidic. It lapped through his hair and down his back. His socks squelched inside his shoes. An umbrella would not have helped much – in fact the gale would have blown it inside out. The Parisian foot traffic wallowed beneath storefront canopies and huddled inside newspaper kiosks. Some stayed in their cars with the heater turned up to maximum and their windscreen wipers on fast mode.

He sensed Tiffanny stopping so he did the same. 'Why aren't we moving?' he shouted over the whirr of the wind and the beat of the lashing rain.

'Because I can see my car, and the man who took it.'

James blinked the rainwater out of his eyes and focused on the road dead ahead. The first time he looked he saw nothing. The second time was a different story. The Renault was idling, its motor ticking over. It was an old car, and the configuration was just out of alignment.

James listened to the hum and thought about it in musical terms. The beats were like triplets. One two three, one two three. Like a waltz. It should have been a 4/4 signature. But the engine kept running nevertheless. The man in the tanned jacket was stood by the bonnet, watching them effortlessly, without any inclination towards espionage or stealth. He was out in the open, in plain view, with his arms crossed, relaxed, watching them. He was maybe eighty yards away. There was no expression on his face; no grimace, no smirk, no look of intention, or satisfaction. His eyes were locked on to them as if a computer inside his head had categorised them as targets.

He pulled away from Tiffanny and took a few steps forward. The rain began to ease off. The man continued to watch but remained perfectly still. James took another few steps forward. The man did not react. James reached into his right trouser pocket and took out the clamshell cell phone Murgatroyd had given him in Chester. He flipped open the shell to reveal the keypad.

The man did not react. James looked at the phone then at the man. The man did not react. James thought about calling the police; his fingers hovered over the numbers on the keypad. 112 was the emergency police number in France if you are dialling from a mobile phone. The phone had been registered in the UK and was now in France, roaming for networks.

It had found Eurotel. The dual-band GSM had sent a message to the nearest control tower. A cell phone is just an improvised radio. When you dial a number, a signal is sent to a control tower to locate and use one of hundreds of possible frequencies, especially in a city, a big city like Paris. A carrier splits up these potential frequencies into cells, each one with a radius of ten square miles and fifty-six voice channels. That means that fifty-six people can be talking at the same time within a single cell. The phone and the base station talk to each other, using a special code transmitted by the phone, which the base station matches with its own code. Of course, all of this happens in a split second, and then the user hears dial tone.

So, all James would have to do is punch three numbers in, hit the call button and wait for the matching code and hey presto, he'd be speaking to a French emergency services operator. He'd need a few more seconds to explain, in a language foreign to him, requiring even more time, the situation. Then, depending on the nearest on-duty police patrol's current location, and traffic, more time would pass before anything could be done, by which time the man would either have killed them or fled and be long gone.

But James wasn't thinking of calling the police. So he relaxed his arm, and let it dangle by his side, his hand still clutching the cell phone, which rested just above his knee. He did this deliberately and slowly, to ensure that the man would notice. The man continued to stare at them intently, but he did not react.

Suddenly James sensed movement to his right and swung out his free right arm. 'Hey!' he cried. 'Not yet. Not now. Wait!'

As he had predicted, Tiffanny landed straight in his grasp. 'But the bastard has my car!'

'Let it go. It could be worse. It could be a lot worse. You want to join Fabien and Camille in the morgue?'

She was silent. The curls of her hair had darkened from chestnut to oak in the soaking wet and were plastered to her cheeks like glue. She wriggled around his arm for a second, furious, and then her anger subsided.

'I didn't think so.' From somewhere close by there was a sound; a clicking resonance, as if the chamber of a gun was being locked. The Frenchwoman flinched at the sound. James remained still, staring back at the man. The man did not react.

'What was that noise, James?'

'I hope he smiled' James remarked. Without moving his arm he clamped the shell of the cell phone shut, and then replaced it back into his trouser pocket. He interlocked his arm around Tiffanny once again, and they started to back away, keeping their eyes on the man in the tanned jacket, sat on the bonnet of the white Renault. The rain died, and the wind subsided. A misty haze was left in its wake, like steam rising from a bowl of soup. The man jumped off the bonnet and waved sardonically. Then he clambered into the idling hatchback and sped away.

'The sooner we get back to your studio, the sooner we will dry out' James explained. Their clothes were sopping and drenched.

'What happened back there?' Tiffanny asked,

'What do you mean?'

'I heard a noise, then you said *I hope he smiled.* What happened?'

'This guy thinks he has the upper hand. That's clear from his body language and his arrogance. Think about it; he wasn't hiding, he was out in the open, watching us, trying to put the fear of God into us. He knew we wouldn't go on the offensive. That's his role. So I thought I'd redress the balance and help Lacroix in his investigation. I was evidence gathering.'

'What did you do?'

'I took his picture.'

'With what?'

'My phone. The cell phone I was given is an old model, with a one eighty degree rotating camera. He was eighty yards away, and sat on your bonnet, which meant he was on higher ground. The angle was tricky.'

'That's why your arm was down at your side?'

'Yes. I had to guess the angle; I couldn't risk looking at the screen without arousing his suspicions. I used maximum zoom.'

'And the noise wasn't a gun, it was the snapshot from the camera-phone' Tiffanny realised.

'Right. I'm going to send this to Lacroix when we get back to your studio. Fingerprints came up without a match – maybe the Police Nationale will have more joy with his photograph.'

'Now I understand why you wanted him to smile. But James, we don't know for sure that this man killed Fabien and Camille.'

'True, but he was been tailing us ever since we started this charade. He's a likely suspect, and at the very least we need him off our backs. He needs to be watched.'

'From where I'm standing, it's him doing the watching. And for the record, this is no charade. I don't think Radka would appreciate you referring to helping safeguard her life as a charade.'

'Why did you react so strongly back there? So, he has your car. Cars are replaceable; people are not. I stand to lose more than you do here.'

'It's not the car itself James; it's the principle of it. He's taken something that's mine. I'll never forgive him for that.'

James thought for a moment. It seemed irrational to be thinking of an old battered Renault in such a way. Wife or ex-wife, Radka was a loved one; a cherished human being, and she had been taken from him. She was no possession, like Tiffanny's car, but she deserved to be free. Right now she wasn't. That was something he'd never forgive the man for. He let the thought pass.

They walked north, back towards Gare de Lyon. They re-crossed the Seine over the same bridge in the opposite direction, passing the Paris Bercy stadium once again, and when they arrived they rode a long lone metro train northwest, crossing the radius of the city; the palm of Paris' outstretched hand, in total silence.

Forty-five minutes later the carriage pulled into the Gare du Nord and Tiffanny indicated with a slight twist of her head that this was their stop. They were back near the Hotel Magenta, where twenty-four hours ago James had been preparing to sleep off their first interaction at Café Kléber.

The Frenchwoman led them in the opposite direction on this occasion, east towards Rue Lafayette. Her studio was situated on a quiet street off Rue Lafayette, called Avenue Secrétan. It was lined with elm trees, their branches ripped bare by the winter solstice and nature's beguiling routine. Nature; the eternal mystic.

Tiffanny retrieved a set of keys from her handbag and unlocked a heavy front door. It had been painted British racing green some time ago, and had faded into a shade reminiscent of evergreen buds. The door creaked under the strain and the Frenchwoman led them into a dark hallway.

The apartment complex was situated on seven storeys, and the hallway floor was lined with other people's mail. A generator was mounted on the wall to his right, humming intermittently. Her studio was on the fourth floor, so they mounted three flights of stairs and came abruptly to a door painted the same colour as the one outside. She grabbed her mail from the top of the banister and plunged three different keys into three respective locks and then they were inside her studio.

She flicked on a light and threw the keys back into her handbag, which she promptly placed on a breakfast bar to her left. The room was full of trapped heat which her boiler had diligently provided since it had clicked into action on a timer hours before their arrival. James shuddered agreeably; then he sized up the place.

Size was the operative word. Her abode was miniscule. There was one single room, about the size of a manager's office, which served as the kitchen, dining room, living room and bedroom simultaneously. A multi-purpose, multi-functioning den. The kitchen area took up about ten feet by five. A tiny stove with two hobs perched in the far corner. The breakfast bar was littered with typical household facets; bills, a diary, address book, jotted notes on post-its and a key.

Five metal-shaped letters were displayed neatly across the marble surface, meticulously in line with one another. They spelt out *A P E R O* and served as tiny containers for random junk, such as paper clips and blu-tack. Directly in front of James was a set of double doors that looked out onto a balcony out back.

To their right was the living area – there was a television mounted on brackets on the wall, a futon for her clothes and a sofa. Next to the sofa there was a small coffee table with a laptop on it. The cable from the portable computer ran out of the back and disappeared behind the futon. The laptop was switched on but in sleep mode – green lights flickered and it whirred in the background.

A panoramic print was mounted on the wall – art nouveau James guessed, although he was no expert. The walls were painted a dull white and the furniture ranged from autumnal browns and reds to vivid spring greens. It gave the room a drabness that was not altogether unpleasant, but in contrast it offered little in the way of light. But it was cosy, James had to admit.

'Nice place' he said. 'Where do you sleep?'

Tiffanny pointed to the sofa. 'It folds out into a bed.'

'Where do I sleep?' he asked.

Tiffanny pointed to the floor beside the sofa. 'I have a sleeping bag, pillows, blankets and a small mattress. Don't worry James; I'm sure you will be more than comfortable.'

'Sounds great, I really appreciate it.'

'Well you hardly have a choice now do you? Where else would you go?'

'True. Can I use your bathroom?'

'Behind you to the left. Take a shower if you want. Put your clothes on the radiator and they'll be dry by the time you're done. Here.' She handed him a towel.

'Thanks.'

'I have plenty of spare toiletries, so if you need a toothbrush or shampoo, just shout. Help yourself to anything you find in there.'

'Thanks' he repeated. He stripped until he was naked. It was a relief to be out of the soaking wet clothes. His body convulsed from the dampness they had created. He was freezing. He turned on the faucet and lifted the lever behind the taps to activate the water through the shower head. He turned up the heat as far as he could stand it, and showered thoroughly. He washed his hear twice with shampoo. The invigorating blend of mint and lime filled his lungs and he began to unwind. He dried off and dressed back in the same clothes, which were now practically bone dry as Tiffanny had preordained.

They switched places and Tiffanny went into the bathroom to shower. James retrieved the cell phone from his trouser pocket and opened up the photo he had taken of the man in the tanned jacket. The phone boasted an eight megapixel camera, and it had a decent zoom. The quality of the photo was more than adequate considering it had been captured on a phone.

He took out his wallet and fished inside for the business card Lacroix had given him upon their release from the police station. He keyed in Lacroix's number and sent the photo as a multimedia message. He included a brief line of text. *Possible suspect for your murders. Seen him tonight. Check him out.* Once the message had sent, he dialled Lacroix's number to confirm receipt and waited.

After seven rings he reached an answering machine. At the tone he left a short message explaining the context of the photo. He was unable to leave a return number because he had no clue what number he was calling from, and he assumed that Collins had set up the account securely to ensure that outbound calls made from the cell were classified to the recipient as *private number* or *caller ID withheld*. He hung up and preyed that Lacroix would act on the message and process the photo through their database. Hopefully the man in the tanned jacket would be ID'd as a known criminal with a record.

He heard the jet stream from the shower continue to run through the closed bathroom door. He heard occasional splashing thuds, which meant that Tiffanny was running her hands through her long hair and sending occasional mini-streams of water off course and onto the shower tray by her feet. She had been in for ten minutes. He recalled from his student days of living with girls that long hair took a while to wash, and the Frenchwoman would probably stay under the jet for another fifteen to twenty minutes.

He intended to live up to his earlier promise, so he began to ransack the kitchen cupboards for ingredients. He found a vegetable rack under the sink and took out a handful of large potatoes and two onions. He also found a whole garlic and ripped off three moderate sized cloves. He looked in the fridge and found the two items he needed; he took out a pack of streaky bacon rashers and a block of brie.

He switched on the antiquated oven underneath the hobs mounted on the stove and turned it up to two hundred degrees centigrade. The contraption was old and therefore not fan assisted, so he needed a good output for preheating. He found salt and pepper in a cupboard above his head and set them down on the counter for later. He sliced the potatoes into thin circles while he boiled a pan of water from a pan already sat on the stove.

He cut the bacon and onion into small cubes and the brie into tiny slices. He found a frying pan and some oil and gently fried up the bacon and onion. The smell was invigorating. The bacon gave off a smoky, meaty pallor and the onion glazed from white to brown, basking in the oil. He turned the heat right down to let the frying ingredients simmer, and he cranked up the boiling potatoes so that in fifteen minutes both would be ready.

He stopped for a moment and listened. The shower was still belting away. He smiled in satisfaction. He wanted to have it nailed before she came out, otherwise the effect would be lost. He found a baking dish in an adjacent cupboard and crushed the garlic cloves and mixed them with a little butter and then rubbed the mixture all over the dish, working in the baste. He used the fifteen minutes and let the food cook.

He set the table and found a bottle of Rioja sat on a rack unopened opposite the counter. He found a corkscrew and popped off the cork and half-filled two glasses with the red wine. He looked at the letters on the breakfast bar. APERO. There would be no time for an aperitif – they were going straight into the main course.

After ten more minutes he poked at the potatoes with a fork and found them suitably soft in the centre. He stirred the bacon and onion in the frying pan and turned off the hob and poured the whole lot into the baking dish. He sprinkled the brie on the top and spread the mixture out to evenly fill the dish. Then he flicked salt and pepper over the dish and shoved it in the oven. Twenty minutes, and it would be ready to serve.

He heard her turn off the faucet and sat on the sofa and waited. He made a mental note of the time; five minutes to eleven. It was late to be eating, although more acceptable in France, and they had endured a long, arduous day. They had survived on reserved energy after they burned out the carbs from the crêpes earlier that afternoon.

The meal he had prepared was loaded with fresh new carbs and protein. He waited ten more minutes and then she emerged from the bathroom, a towel wrapped around her head like a turban. She had changed into a black silk dress that covered the length of her calves and cut off just above her ankles. She walked barefoot across the den. She had painted her toenails in a pale cerise. James watched her feet spring effeminately across the laminate floor and felt a stirring of arousal in his loins. She was a dream to behold.

The concoction of flavours seeped out from the oven and began to waft across the room. 'You really cooked?!'

'Of course I did. A promise is a promise.'

'What are we having?'

'You'll see. It's a warm winter French favourite. Have some wine.'

He pointed to the two glasses sat in unison on the counter and she walked over and picked them up. Then she joined him on the sofa and handed him one. 'Sante.'

'Cheers.' They chinked their glasses together in a toast to something subliminal and unknown. The oven was old, therefore there was no timer setting. James' mental timer silently bleeped from within his psyche and he got up and went to the oven. 'Plates?'

'Cupboard above your head, to the left' she replied.

He took two and microwaved them for two minutes. A hot plate kept hot food hotter for longer. Then he found an oven mitt and opened the door and the blast from the furnace thumped into his face and he staggered backward an inch. He put the baking dish on the hob and dished out two decent portions. He set the plates down on the breakfast bar, and Tiffanny joined him.

'Ah, you made tartiflette! Excellent. Alors, bon appetit!'

'Toi aussi.' *You too.*

The Frenchwoman made clinical incisions with her fork and created tiny feminine portions. She chewed slowly and quietly. James watched as her soft lips delicately handled her food. He was hypnotised by her unrelenting beauty. Her eyes caught him fantasising and he briefly looked away.

'Did you send the photo to Lacroix?'

'Yes. Then I rang him to explain but I got his answering machine. I hope he'll do something about it.'

'He will. He has two unsolved murders in his jurisdiction; he'll do what it takes to catch the person responsible. His neck is on the line.'

'Can you tell me about the diagram we found at the library?' For effect he took the folded paper from his pocket and laid it down in the centre space between them. He brushed the crinkles and creases out of the starched papyrus and waited for her response.

Tiffanny paused at the question, her fork hovering over her mouth. Then she took the bite and chewed thoughtfully. She swallowed and dabbed at her mouth with a napkin. 'Well' she stated cautiously, 'Benzaldehyde is an organic compound. It gives off an almond smell in liquid form. It was used in the Sixties by glaciologists to help the recrystallisation of snow, which prevents avalanches because it hardens the surface of the snow. It is used more commonly today in the dyeing process.'

'Ok. And where is it found?'

'Most abundantly in the seeds of fruit and almond kernels. Apricots and apples are a particularly good source.'

James pondered that. Apricots. He had been nibbling on dried apricots as a healthy snack back in Chester. Tiffanny had more to say.

'On its own benzaldehyde is pretty much redundant. It's used in conjunction with other substances to create its maximum effect.'

'What effect?'

'Well, for example in the oxidation process it is converted into benzoic acid. Other processes produce different results. That's when it starts to get a bit more complicated, and the science is difficult to explain to a...'

'Idiot?'

'I didn't say that, James.'

'What about the other elements on the diagram?'

'L – Mandelonitrile – Beta Glucoside is a little more complex. In 1822 a scientist called Ernst Theodor Krebs Sr discovered it when he boiled and evaporated it in alcohol, which left little white crystals. But you'll notice from the diagram that when everything is combined, it forms something called Laetrile.'

'What's Laetrile?'

'Laetrile, or amygdalin as it is sometimes called, is effectively B17, which is more commonly referred to as Vitamin B17. Krebs pieced it all together. And to answer your earlier question James, yes, it is a cure for cancer.'

'And you knew that all along?'

'Yes.'

'So why didn't you tell me before?'

'It wasn't part of my arrangement with Collins. You are strictly a bodyguard.'

'So how does B17 work? Tell me everything.'

'Krebs spent his entire adult life researching nutrition and health. He studied a category of foodstuff called nitrilosides. They are natural foods rich in vitamin B17, enzymes and minerals. Krebs claimed that there were fourteen different naturally occurring nitrilosides across twelve hundred species of plants. They are also known as cyanogenetic glycosides. Again, they are found in the seeds of apricots amongst other fruit and vegetables.'

'And what's their significance?'

'Well Krebs pointed out that tribal people such as Indians, Aborigines, Eskimos and Kiwis relied historically on a diet of raw fruit and vegetables; a diet that contains about three thousand milligrams of nitrilosides per day. For these people, degenerative diseases such as cancer and heart disease are simply unheard of. They don't exist.

'Compare that with the daily diet of the Western, *civilised* man, who probably consumes about five milligrams of nitrilosides per day. Heart disease and cancer are a Western disease; we've always known that. All that processed food is no good for us.'

'Go on.'

'Krebs actually stole his discovery from two Frenchmen, two Germans and a Russian, but developed the idea further. In 1830, scientists Roubiquet and Bontron-Chariand officially discovered B17 in its natural, untainted form. Then von Liebig and Woehier realised that amygdalin can be split down by a specific enzyme into hydrogen cyanide, benzaldehyde and glucose.

'This was then used in 1845 in Moscow by Inosmetzeff to successfully treat a cancer patient; a man of twenty who received forty six thousand milligrams of amygdalin over a three month course and was still alive three years after diagnosis. After that success a woman of forty eight with a tumour in her ovary was treated in a similar way and survived for at least eleven years.'

'Fascinating. I guess there's more?'

'Yes, there's more, and this next part is truly fascinating. The engineering of the human body never ceases to amaze me. You see, when a cell is still in its embryonic state, before the baby is born, it acts in a way like a cancerous cell; it mutates in order for the baby to grow and develop.

'It's called a trophoblast cell. But, after the fifty-sixth day of pregnancy the baby's new pancreas starts to produce an enzyme called chymotryspin which kills off the trophoblast cell as it is no longer needed.

'The trophoblast cell is formed in a chain reaction by another cell, referred to as a total life cell. When the total life cell comes into contact with oestrogen it creates the trophoblast, and depending on the circumstances that is either wonderful or terrible.'

'Because it means either pregnancy, or cancer.'

'For a woman, exactly that James, yes. For a man, there can be only one outcome.'

'Right. So how does B17 stop the trophoblast cell from wreaking havoc?'

'The ironic thing about cancer is that it occurs because the trophoblast cell is actually trying to do good. It's trying to help growth, but sometimes it carries on even when maximum growth has been achieved.

'It believes it is doing good, but actually too much growth then causes tumours. So, B17 becomes a toxic substance to the trophoblast – it is a poison. This is where hydrogen cyanide and benzaldehyde come in; they are manufactured by beta-glucosidase and together poison the trophoblast cell, thereby killing it.'

'How does this make B17 any better than traditional cancer drugs out on the marketplace right now? Surely they do the same thing.'

'I'm just getting to that. You see, chemotherapy and drugs cause so much pain and damage to patients because they cannot distinguish between cancerous and healthy cells, so they target both. B17 only targets the trophoblast; it doesn't damage healthy cells.'

'Impressive. How does it make the distinction?'

'Healthy cells contain another enzyme, called rhodanese. It acts as a controlling agent and lives inside the body in inverse proportions to beta-glucosidase. Therefore it does not exist at the site of cancerous cells. Rhodanese detoxifies the cyanide and oxidises the benzaldehyde.'

'So let me get this straight. B17 poisons cancerous cells with its toxic compound, but when it comes into contact with healthy cells it detoxifies so that those cells are unaffected?'

'That's a very simplistic explanation, but yes, that's essentially what happens. All those chemicals gear themselves up and work together, like an army, and they declare war on cancer, and they win. They obliterate it from the body. And not only are the non-cancerous cells unharmed, they are actually enhanced; the non-toxicity of B17 nourishes them. There are no negatives.'

James had to admit he was stunned. It sounded too good to be true, but it wasn't. The evidence was right there, existing covertly in underground, clandestine channels. 'That simply blows my mind.'

'I can imagine' the Frenchwoman replied.

'But there is one general theme that I'm not following here.'

'What's that?'

'If a small community of scientists have known this for years, why have we had to solve numerous clues to get to the information?'

'It's a valid point you put on the table, James. It can only mean that there is more to the situation than meets the eye.' She picked up the piece of paper. 'This diagram must hold more than just an incomplete B17 action diagram. It's an incomplete picture, both literally and metaphorically.'

'How do you know it is incomplete literally?'

'Because I understand the full scientific process, and this is not all its constituent parts.'

'You haven't mentioned the two circles with the word sugar written inside them.'

'Well they are just two additional sugar molecules that Krebs added to enhance the effect. Without the sugar molecules, there was amygdalin. With them, there is Laetrile. But the overall result is pretty much the same – B17.'

'If the world knew about this, they would go nuts. Just imagine all the billions of dollars and pounds pumped into cancer research, and all the drugs that are released onto the marketplace that taxpayers make happen. It's all a waste. This is a conclusive, total cure for cancer. It's unfathomable.'

'What's unfathomable is that we have known this for one hundred and eighty years. And nothing has been done about it.'

'Which means that our man in the tanned jacket is trying to thwart our efforts. So there are people out there who want to stop us. People who stand to gain from stopping us. He must be an associate of some pharmaceutical giant.

'Which is why he is watching us and not trying to kill us. He knows that he needs us alive in order to eventually lead him to the secret. Which means he knows what that secret is. We do the dirty work, then they swoop in and destroy us.'

'It's the only logical conclusion' the Frenchwoman offered.

'How did this all start? How did you become involved? What was the spark?'

'I was responsible for an elite team of scientists called Unity-Six. They were based in the mountains of Slovakia. They were manufacturing B17 into a marketable product, and they were succeeding. No, they did succeed. It was done. Then they died.'

'How?'

'Somebody discovered their location, I have no idea how. They were killed. At least that was the official report. Actually, five were killed, and one survived.'

'How could you know such a thing?'

'Because the sixth guy made contact. He explained everything. He should have died – he jumped off a cliff. He was covered in bandages from head to toe.'

Suddenly James had a flashback to Chester train station, when he had cracked the Deep Purple reference and went to the portaloo cabin to get ultraviolet light. There was a man sat at the coffee kiosk, covered in bandages. He had thought nothing of it. Then he smiled.

'What is it James?'

'The guy at the train station in Chester. That was him. That was your guy. Covered in bandages. I saw him three times and thought nothing of it.'

Tiffanny nodded. 'Yes. His name is Stewart Banks. He is an American.'

'What happened after he jumped?'

'Rescue chopper picked him up on a random sweep. Took him back to Bratislava.'

'And then he made contact with you?'

'Yes, he broke radio silence. They had been up in the mountains for months, formulating the perfect recipe for the B17 agent. Casino Collins was funding the research.'

'Where is Banks now?'

'In hiding, somewhere. But he makes contact intermittently. His role in this is done. He just needs to stay out of sight until it's safe to come out of the woodwork.'

'So Collins became a target as the project's main source of finance?'

'Absolutely. If it wasn't for Collins, B17 would have remained in the underground history books.

Without him we wouldn't have been able to get this far. He is a wanted man, by whom we do not know.'

'And Radka was purely the hook to get me involved?'

'Primarily, yes. There may be other reasons, but I am not privy to them.

'This is unbelievable. There are so many unanswered questions.'

'Which is why we have to go to Lyon first thing in the morning. I'm guessing Pierre Chartier exposed all of this in his book and that's why we can't find it in the library. Think about it. The receptionist said it had simply been removed – no fines or anything. That implies a permanence to the decision. I bet every copy has been burned to a cinder.'

'Hopefully this Chartier can fill in all the gaps and give us the full picture, both physically and metaphorically.'

'Indeed. It's after midnight, James. We should sleep. It has been a very eventful day and we will need our energy for the day ahead.'

Tiffanny folded out the sofa and made her bed. Then she took a sleeping bag and blankets from the futon and handed them to James. He arranged the items on the floor and dressed down to his boxers and zipped himself in. Tiffanny went into the bathroom and came back out two minutes later in a black robe. She pranced across the laminate floor and slid into bed. She turned out the light and they said goodnight.

James realised he needed to use the bathroom a final time, so he unzipped the sleeping bag and tiptoed across the hallway. When he came back out she was stood by the breakfast bar holding a glass of water. She drained the contents then put the glass on the counter.

He felt exposed in his boxers, but she didn't seem to care. She smiled at him with large, unflinching eyes that reflected the soft lighting from a lamp adjacent to the futon. He couldn't prevent his erection. He moved to her and held her firmly in an embrace, stroking the curls of her hair and holding her head tight in his chest. The gown was silk and felt soft against her skin. Her skin was even softer.

He had been fighting it ever since their initial encounter at Charles de Gaulle airport two days ago. He waved his white flag in surrender. He felt a shortness of breath. She murmured softly. Then he gently arched her back up so that they were looking at each other, and he lent forward and kissed her long and hard and firm on the lips.

She responded favourably, inching her tongue out to meet his in the middle. They kissed passionately but tenderly for ten minutes without coming up for air. She undid the buttons on her gown very slowly, teasing, and then it cascaded down her body and fell to the floor at her feet. She was wearing nothing except a thong.

He placed both hands on her cheeks and kissed her more and more. Then he moved down to her neck and shoulders. Her skin was heavenly to the touch; olive-brown and blemish-free. He cupped her breasts gently and kissed them. She placed a hand on his penis through his boxers. He moved further south to her flat stomach.

He kissed her belly button. He lowered himself onto his knees and kissed her bare legs. She moved her hands to the top of his head and massaged it lovingly. He lifted up her left foot in the palm of his hand and kissed the top, then the sides, then all her toes. He did the same with her right foot. She pulled off his boxers and he did the same with her thong. He picked her up in his arms and their naked bodies became intermingled. He placed her down on the bed and they made love for thirty minutes. He kissed her while he thrusted, holding the back of her head with one hand and her hand with his other. She moaned quietly. They built up a rhythm. A slow, gentle, persistent movement. They climaxed together and he collapsed onto her and continued to kiss her.

Then they did it again. And after that they were sweaty and exhausted. He rolled over and she snuggled into him and he held her tight and kissed her more and more and more. And then they fell asleep.

Chapter Twenty Two

NASA White Sands Test Facility, Las Cruces, New Mexico, United States. Friday 25th February. 1:05 a.m. (GMT 8:05 a.m.)

An hour after midnight Mountain Standard Time, Las Cruces was still basking in an omnipotent noir that extended beyond the Organ mountain range around Baylor Pass and Pine Tree Trail, stretching to the infinite sky at vertical limits. To the west the Rio Grande valley was in a habitual nocturnal hibernation; in a few hours dawn would peak over the crevasses and its inhabitants would begin their daily routine at the grindstone.

The sun would caress the hills and light up the caves at La Cueva; hollow mounds drilled into the cliff face by eons of natural phenomena, caves that had served as home for Mogollon Indians thousands of years ago. Spanish explorer Francisco Vasquez de Coronado discovered the land in 1540; it later became the state of New Mexico in 1598.

It carries the moniker *The Land of Enchantment.* The US took control of the land in 1848 during the Confederate War. After the Second World War New Mexico developed a reputation as a market leader in energy research and development and Los Alamos built its Scientific Laboratory. The state is mapped south-centrally, bordered with Texas and Arizona, and boasts an abundant supply of minerals, including uranium and potassium salts which are ingredients for nuclear power, along with petroleum, natural gas, copper, gold, silver, zinc, lead and molybdenum.

The White Sands test facility was a military installation, and careful observance of the grounds betrayed the fact; it had US Army written all over it. The entrance was manned by four guards in a shack, beyond an imposing black gate and a barrier where all personnel were diligently scrutinised. Six camo-painted Humvees were parked in a neat row behind the guard shack.

Inside the ninety-two acre compound several men were busy preparing themselves for their mission. They were huddled in a sandy desert enclave at the crossroads of Mars Drive and Orion Avenue. They stood next to a huge gantry; a twisted contortion of reinforced steel painted red and yellow, a mass of engineered scaffolding better known as the LC-32 East Launch Complex.

Placed near the gantry was a cylindrical metal bowl finished with galvanised grey paint. Rectangular slits were cut into the surface around the bottom circumference to form a grille. The bowl served as the launch stand and the grille was crafted for heat displacement. It had been manufactured at the Dryden Flight Research Centre at Edwards Air Force Base in the Mojave Desert, ninety miles north of Los Angeles.

Mounted atop the launch pad was a PA-1 separation ring and stacked on the separation ring was the crew module, a white saucer branded with the NASA logo. It was the size of a typical restroom. Affixed to the crew module, shimmering in a night time ambience, dripping with early morning dew, was a two and a half tonne Ares I rocket standing tall at three hundred and twenty one feet.

The assembly of the component parts had taken place at NASA's Vehicle Assembly Building in Langley, Virginia using seventy-foot trailers and cranes. Then the whole package had been flown out to White Sands on an Air Force C-5 Galaxy – a very large aircraft. The avionics and roll control system had been stacked vertically.

Wearing the trademark orange jumpsuit of the NASA astronaut, the eight-man team finished up final preparations. Their spirits were high; their destination higher. Payload Commander Carlos de Souza was the first of them to break the silence. 'All these years of testing have finally paid off. I can't believe we finally have a privately-funded mission approved by the Board, here at White Sands.'

Flight Engineer Gerry Kaplinski smiled whilst he busied himself checking the payload. 'Why should Cape Canaveral have all the fun?'

'This is a momentous occasion; the first actual launch from this site in years' Mission Specialist Mitchell Downey chirped in. He was holding a laptop in the palm of his hand, scrutinising the interface of an advanced software package that made sophisticated trajectory calculations.

'Guys, keep on schedule and cut the banter. This needs to run like clockwork.' Commander Gabriel Munoz was a short, wiry Mexican who had surpassed his compadres and chicos and risen to dizzy heights in the NASA hierarchy. He had fought racism and won hands down. He spoke with a trace of his never-forgotten Hispanic roots, accented into a short, raspy, near-musical Latino drawl. Vowels were accentuated in particular by a pursing of his lips. He had majored in astrophysics at Harvard. Not bad for a man from Santa Clara, a New Mexican town with a population of less than a thousand.

'Sir, I'm ready to roll.' Commander Munoz acknowledged the voice of Pilot Sam Wexford with a cursory nod and nothing more.

'How did the Board agree to this?' Spaceflight Participant Gregor Medvedev spewed out the question in a harsh Russian monotone to nobody in particular.

'They think this is another reconnaissance mission to map out the lunar surface.' Payload Specialist Roger DeMico explained. 'They think we're up there finding nice flat terrain for future landings.'

'And they've willingly authorised the spending of sixty-nine million dollars with that notion in mind?' Engineer Doug McIntyre countered incredulously.

'Trust me – it's better than if they knew the real purpose of this mission. We wouldn't have a single cent to play with if they did.'

They caught the glaring eyes of Commander Munoz and heeded his earlier order to pipe down and focus on the preliminaries. His head was shaved in a military buzz cut. 'Ground Control is prepped and good to go' he stated tersely. 'Who has the artefact?'

'Here, Sir.' A second Spaceflight Participant walked into view, carrying a small cardboard carton. The box was white and plain; no logo or lettering or barcode or branding of any description. He handed it to Munoz. The Commander opened the carton and peered inside. All he found was all he expected to see; a white American-style letterbox with *Collins* stencilled in black calligraphic lettering. Munoz grunted then resealed the carton. 'The rich are crazy' he said.

'He's a lunar-tic!' Payload Specialist Roger DeMico retorted. 'Get it? Lunar-tic?!' The others burst into laughter.

'Jesus' Munoz cursed. 'It's like working with a bunch of space monkeys.'

His crushing blow silenced their camaraderie. 'But when a man has the means to fund a NASA missile project single-handedly, I guess we gotta hand it to him. You better look after that thing, Murgatroyd.'

'Absolutely, Sir.'

'All personnel please board the craft' Munoz barked. The men packed up their equipment and carried it to the crew module. A code sequence was entered into a panel display mounted on the external casing and an automatic door whirred into action, revealing the entrance to a small cabin. The men clambered up a lone step and filed into the crew module.

The module doubled up as a launch abort system should anything go catastrophically wrong during take-off and ascent, serving as an emergency extraction vehicle for the crew. Inside was a gunmetal chamber filled with an array of electrical equipment and computers. Lights blinked and processors whined. An extractor fan hissed in the background.

Munoz took a walkie talkie from his belt buckle and held down a button to talk. 'Ground Control, we are inside the capsule. Five minutes to initiation, over.' The radio crackled with a garbled reply. *'This is Ground Control, we copy that, over.'*

Pilot Sam Wexford sat at the front of the hub. The other men took their positions. Munoz took the rear. They strapped in and manned their equipment. 'Three minutes, Ground Control' Munoz updated. *'Ground Control copies. Three minutes, over.'*

Levers were flicked, dials were turned, buttons were pressed. The flight would take a little under five minutes all in all; like flying from one side of London to the other in a conventional airliner. Except this was no conventional mode of transport. One day in the future it would no doubt become as much, but for now it remained a bastion of scientific genius, its access limited to the Government and the military. And billionaires like Casino Collins.

'Everybody mark up' Munoz bellowed. 'Tell me you're ready.' One by one the astronauts checked in and reported a *standing by* status. 'Standing by' Munoz declared over the radio.

'Ground Control copies. We are standing by. One minute, over.'

'This is it, people. Let's do this.' Munoz received cheers of positive attitude from his subordinates. 'Stand by for the countdown' he ordered.

Then the radio crackled to life. *'T-ten, nine, eight, seven, six, five, four, three, two, one. Ignition. Liftoff!'* The desert brush was suddenly illuminated in an explosion of heat and fuel and vapour. The Ares I lifted upwards in a sonic roar. It was a formidable sight to behold. It picked up speed and altitude and headed for the atmosphere and beyond.

It reached thirty thousand feet, typical cruising altitude for a commercial airliner, in the blink of an eye. A commercial airliner used a jet engine, fuelled with kerosene, to combust with oxygen. Where the NASA team were headed there was no oxygen. They were travelling into the final frontier; the great cosmological vacuum of space. The Ares I continued on its epic quest towards the heavens.

Inside the capsule the module shook violently. The men braced and buckled against the numerous physical forces around them – mass, gravity, windspeed, air. 'Status report' Munoz barked furiously. Ground Control had a direct videolink to them and they could see and hear everything.

Mission Specialist Mitchell Downey spoke up. 'Altitude now two miles. Chamber pressure now tapering off.' A Russian fighter pilot in a MiG-29

Foxbat could reach eighty thousand feet in his jet-fuelled craft and show you the edge of space for twelve thousand US dollars. But that wasn't good enough for Casino Collins. Instead he had paid close to seventy million to go the extra light year. Two miles up, vertically, is a long way from home.

'Vehicle is aligning itself with the planned trajectory' Pilot Sam Wexford stated. 'We've passed Mach one and we're now passing max Q. We have our max Q system ID manoeuvre PT1 engaged.'

They passed through the atmosphere like a knife through butter. 'Now passing Mach two' Wexford reported. 'Vehicle now ten miles altitude, downrange distance eight miles, velocity of one thousand five hundred and forty miles per hour.' Three times the speed of a cruising commercial airliner, six times the speed of a sports car's maximum acceleration, twelve times the speed of a typical motorway motorist, twenty times the speed of an inner city driver, about a thousand times faster than a pedestrian idling away on foot. But a great deal slower than light or sound.

'Plus 80 seconds. We've started our supersonic large aptitude ID manoeuvre PT1. We see the response. And we've started the last PT1, structural mode ID.' Wexford gazed into outer space. The stars were no longer just holes to heaven, their white contrast against the black backdrop a mesmerising juxtaposition. The swirling blue-green planet they had just left grew smaller in the distance; the Earth they called home.

'And we've passed T plus one hundred and five seconds' the pilot continued. 'Vehicle is now travelling at Mach four, twenty miles altitude, downrange distance thirty-two miles.'

'We are approaching phase two gentlemen' Munoz declared matter-of-factly. 'Prepare for burnout and separation.'

Mission Specialist Mitchell Downey monitored the laptop and checked the trajectory. 'Looks good from here' he reported. 'A steady gradient. All systems normal. Nothing to worry about.'

Suddenly the rocket shook violently for the second time. There was a hissing sound that gradually died out and left the sonic spectrum behind.

'The SRM tailoff is observed' Wexford stated. 'Burnout. Our APUs have shut down. CRDs have shut down. Medium fire. And separation. We show a sep and a tumble motor ignition. And we can also confirm on video we see both parts of the vehicle tumbling. Repeat, the first stage and the upper stage has occurred.'

'Successful separation' Munoz confirmed. 'Good job guys. Good job. How does it sound down there, Ground Control?'

This is ground control. We are receiving you. A good, clean signal all the way.

'WAHOO!' There was a collective cheer from the crew, and the camaraderie was back.

'We're going to the moon baby!' Flight Engineer Gerry Kaplinski exclaimed excitedly.

'Alright, keep it together guys.' Munoz, somewhat ironically, brought them back down to Earth.

This is ground control. Well done crew. Successful mission reported. You're right on track for the lunar surface. Over.

'T plus one hundred and fifty seconds' Wexford reported.

Munoz relaxed and allowed a smile to creep across his lips. He was a hardliner, and a disciplinarian. Furthermore, he resented the pointless circumstances governing the mission. Space exploration was, for him, purely to advance the human race, and therefore it was not to be taken lightly.

Still, he could not help the feeling of exhilaration and joy when his mind processed that he was no longer on the planet he had inhabited for forty-one years. As he gazed out at the beautiful silence of the solar system, and saw the sun and the approaching moon, he felt his face clamming up in a well of tears. It wasn't his first astronomical expedition, but every time he ventured up into the universe he was stabbed with an intense poignancy he could not explain.

He rationalised the inability to comprehend as being a flaw in the human brain, which had a finite capacity. He felt like an ant drowning in a bathtub. If he tried to explain the universe to himself he knew that insanity would be right around the next

219

corner. So instead he stopped trying, wiped the tears from his eyes and looked out at the infinite blackness.

'Collins wants to be the first to live up here, you know that?' he said to DeMico, purely because DeMico was seated adjacent to him and therefore the sound of his voice would travel across the vacuumed chamber and reach him before the others.

'I think we're a long way away from that' Demico responded.

'What makes you say that?'

'Don't you think we should resolve the problems we have on the ground before we make new ones for ourselves up here?'

'What problems?'

'Everything! War, famine, law, crime, the works. Coming up here is just running away from our problems. We can't hear starving Africans scream if we're up here, can we?'

'True, but moving the species onto the moon does alleviate the issue of global overcrowding. The estimated population of the planet by 2100 is ten billion, you know that? Ten billion people on our planet is pretty crowded. Everywhere will be like China is now. If we lived on Jupiter, that wouldn't be a problem. Jupiter is much bigger.'

'It's also swirling with poisonous gases and insufficient oxygen or carbon dioxide' DeMico countered. 'Plus, if we had been living on Jupiter, we'd have been wiped out by now. Remember that meteor a few years back?'

'How could I forget? Jupiter blocked its path to us. We have Jupiter to thank for every new day we live on Earth.'

'Maybe you're right, Sir. Maybe lunar living is the future. There are certainly less resources to exploit on the moon. There's no oil up there for starters.'

'It's not all about oil DeMico. Americans get a bad name for that. But it's exaggerated. We're not all about oil.'

'Our Russian friend over there might have an alternative viewpoint on that' Demico retorted, pointing at Spaceflight Participant Gregor Medvedev.

'Probably. But if we're talking about corruption, I think I'd have some return fire.'

'Return fire? You're using military aggression as an analogy for debating, Sir?'

'Is that another one of your American stereotypes, DeMico?'

'My lips are sealed, Sir. My focus is on the mission. What are you thinking about, Sir?'

Munoz stirred in his seat. 'Just the sheer scale of the environment up here. The never-ending black void. And Casino Collins.'

'What about him, Sir?'

'Well, after we put this letterbox in the lunar greytop, what next?'

'What next, Sir? What next is we take some aerial photographs of nice terrain for future landings, and then we come home, Sir.'

'No, what I meant was, what will he want us to do next? Bring him a house up here? A space-hopper? A nice alien wife?'

DeMico laughed. 'He can't have that much money, surely.'

'He's becoming a pretty powerful shareholder. Along with that other guy I don't like.'

'Which guy, Sir? The pharmaceutical tycoon?'

'Yeah, what's his name? Should have died a long time ago.'

'Paul Ross, Sir.'

'Yeah, that's the guy. Paul Ross. Well, between the respective shares of Paul Ross and Casino Collins, they pretty much own NASA now.'

The Ares I continued onward, moonward bound.

*

Undisclosed location, one hour later

It was eight degrees centigrade inside the cave; a cold underground alcove stretching twenty kilometres in diameter. It had been created in a long forgotten past by the ebbs and flows of a nearby

221

river, and formally discovered four hundred years ago when a local townsman was mapping the landsite in preparation for a visit from the Emperor, and accidentally stumbled upon it.

Today the cave was a home for the endemic olm, the largest troglodytic amphibian in the world. The olm is a slithery creature, similar in appearance to an eel or a salamander, with a pale pink-white outer skin. It feeds from the shallow waters of the cave and nutrients in the limestone rock. The olm is blind because its eyes are undeveloped and relies on its hearing and taste senses to survive. The cave was one of no less than nine thousand others in the region. But this cave had been deemed the most suitable for what needed to be done, in the protective confines of secrecy underground, therefore the other eight thousand nine hundred and ninety nine had been rejected and eliminated.

The operation that had been set up inside the cave was essentially an autonomous factory environment; a batch production process the same as any above ground. And like all batch and mass production processes today, this one had taken its inspiration from the just-in-time and total quality management techniques the Japanese had pioneered in the nineteen seventies, much to the frustration and bewilderment of the Americans, and had become the global norm for maximum output at minimum expenditure – the ultimate trade-off, the perfect opportunity cost.

The majority of the cave served as a tourist hotspot and therefore a constant stream of revenue for the government of the land, throughout the year and all seasons. Ninety minute tours carried camera-slinging culture vultures around the substrata of the cave on a motorised mine cart; a yellow carriage known as the Cave Train. Mock subway stations had even been built to facilitate the entrance and exit to and from the cave back to the outside world.

A portion of the cave the size of a small village had been siphoned off from the prying mantle of the public eye and was being used solely for the operation. It was an isolated section of limestone cut deep into the earth in the far eastern corner of the cave. It had been chosen because it offered the operation's personnel the best conditions for their task. It gave them the best lighting, and the air concentrations were perfect. It was also the least damp; the shallow sludge of river did not extend this far; its best estuaries were trapped further west by granite slabs that ran from floor to ceiling.

Setting up had been their toughest objective. Moving boxes full of equipment from the surface to their makeshift underground dwelling in a clandestine fashion had proved irksome and dangerous. A number of people had been paid to look the other way. Others, they who could not be bought, had been blackmailed. It was a tactic the personnel had not been proud of; they were not terrorists or villains by nature. They were decent people. Their actions had been for the greater good. And they could afford a little collateral damage, in the grand scheme of things to come.

The facility included refrigeration units, portable gas heaters, water filtration tanks and metal food containers. Foldout beds and chairs were stored away in a corner. A complicated array of servers and laptops spanned a wall of the cave thirty metres in diameter.

A bespoke software system handled the scientific analysis; it dovetailed with other programs offering ultimate synergy. It was apparent to even the latent observer that the personnel stayed inside the facility for long periods of time. They actually lived in the cave; had done for months. Lower hierarchy staff were relegated to servant duty and ventured to the surface for supplies, took out the trash and kept the facility in top hygienic condition. It was perversely clean, as if they all suffered from Obsessive Compulsive Disorder. It was a quarantined site.

The formula had been perfected in a Slovakian mountain retreat six months earlier. Unfortunately, all but one of the people responsible for that perfection had been wiped off the face of the Earth; Unity Six. Fortunately, the lone survivor had managed to escape with the formula and deliver it to a covert faction interested in saving the world.

For the last six months that faction had been working diligently inside the facility to produce the ultimate panacea and ready it for the black market. The end product came out in pill form and billions would be manufactured; enough for everybody. The latter phase of the operation would involve packing and storage, in preparation for logistical distribution. In the midst of the operation a conversation was taking place between two key personnel members; a senior pharmacologist and a corporate manager.

'When our operation is fully initiated, what do you think the ramifications will be for them?'

'Them who?'

'You know who.'

'Oh, them. Well, a conflict of interest is inevitable. This is what this whole venture is about, right? A stand-off between the two biggest cheeses in the dairy farm.'

'Don't you think it's an unfair fight?'

'What makes you say that?'

'Well, one is old and frail, the other youthful and strong.'

'Perhaps on an individual level, in the physical sense, but look at the bigger picture, will you? They are both infinitely powerful.'

'Nobody is infinitely powerful.'

'It's a figure of speech; you know what I mean. Both control the greatest space agency in the world. Both have the means to bring about an economic cataclysm.'

'The fallout from their inevitable confrontation could result in the same, or even worse.'

'Yes, that is one of many possibilities. The after-effects are too difficult to predict; there are numerous potential outcomes. But we don't need to worry about that right now.'

'We don't?'

'Of course we don't. We are doing heroic work here. We will be hailed as saviours, regardless of the quarrels of two men.'

'If we succeed. One of those men is our boss. One of those men is accredited with arranging this facility. If it wasn't for one of those men, we'd be out of work.'

'When we succeed. We wouldn't be unemployed; we'd be doing something else; something trivial and unimportant. We'd be testing out new cosmetic products on animals, and we'd be despised for it. So be thankful that instead of that fate we have this benevolent alternative.'

'When will the distribution phase begin?'

'It can only be a matter of days now.'

'I can't wait to see the results.'

'Me too. Although, it's not going to be easy. This is where it gets real complicated; and dangerous.'

Chapter Twenty Three

Paris, France. 9:35 a.m.

Streaks of early dawn light filtered in through the shutters attached to the balcony window. James was the first to wake. Tiffanny's head was mounted on the top of his chest and she rose and fell in syncopation with his slow, deep, peaceful breaths.

She murmured and then opened her eyes. Her brain processed the man she was gazing at and she smiled with renewed audacity. James looked on, stroking the strands of curly hair back against her scalp. He kissed her on the forehead and they said good morning. They hugged and kissed hungrily on the lips. Her tongue was small and soft and she tasted like wild berries. They rolled into the missionary position and made love. Afterwards they lay in a moist hedonistic embrace for fifteen minutes. Then James rolled away and Tiffanny stretched and sat up on her haunches. 'We have a train to catch.'

They showered and dressed and James prepared coffee and croissants with butter and jam. They sat on rustic red stools on the balcony beneath an apricot sky. The yard was dusty and a few weeds penetrated the concrete surface, vying for survival.

The balcony did not offer much of a view. The backsides of neighbouring apartment blocks jutted out and converged in the centre like a haphazard Stonehenge; a collage of granite and sandstone. From somewhere high up a mother chastised her child in angry musical French.

In the opposite direction a radio was playing out Europop. A door was being repeatedly slammed. Tiffanny and James ate silently and pondered the lifestyles of their unseen but well heard neighbours. The coffee was excellent; it was an unusual blend with a soft, buttery scent that glided down the throat with untold pleasure. Not too strong, not too weak. It had been filtered in a home machine.

The caffeine warmed his bones and set his heart in a firm, powerful thudding beat, although the Frenchwoman's presence was going a good enough job of creating that effect on its own. She wore blue jeans and a tight black cardigan over a white blouse. Her feet were clad in pretty white boat shoes, flat with a bow on the front, rounded at the toe. By force of habit she rotated her ankle in a tight concentric circle and flicked her shoe, like women often too when they are either nervous or thinking about something. He dressed in the clothes she had provided for him at the Hotel Magenta.

He had never been to Lyon before and the drifting adventurer in him was relishing the occasion. After the hectic three days he had been in Paris he was ready to leave. The two murders, their incarceration inside a Police Nationale cell and their pursuit by the mysterious man in the tanned jacket had sapped all the romance out of the city's experience like a microwave irradiating nutrients from a vegetable. He hoped Lyon would reinstate his adoration of France and provide the answers they so desperately needed, not least for Radka's sake. The mademoiselle broke the silence.

'Did Lacroix get back to you on the photograph you sent him?'

'No, he didn't' James responded. 'I'll try him again.'

'If you have to leave another message give him my number. He can call back on that when we're in Lyon.'

'Good thinking.'

He went back inside the den and found his cell phone lying dormant on the coffee table next to the sofa-bed he had slept in and the makeshift floor-bed he had abandoned for better things. He smiled to himself pleasantly as he picked up the phone. He could feel the after-sex glow glazing his cheeks red. It was probably the release of the endorphin serotonin that made him feel so content. It was the only action he'd seen since Radka had left him.

He hit redial and the line dialled out and rang seven times and then the same answering machine message played out. The same rapid fire French followed by a bleeping sound. He left another message and gave the police captain Tiffanny's cell number to return the call.

'Any good?' she asked as he came back out onto the balcony.

He shook his head. 'I left another message, gave him your number.'

'He's probably just up to his neck in bureaucracy and paperwork' the Frenchwoman offered in consolation. 'He'll call back.'

'He better do, before I take the law into my own hands with tanned jacket creep.'

He cleared the table from the balcony and pushed the stools to one side and washed up the plates and the cups and cleared away the mess he had made preparing breakfast. A ring tone suddenly belted out from nearby; a ferocious tinny ditty.

'Lacroix.' James said.

'Can't be.' Tiffanny responded. 'It's yours, not mine.'

'Collins' James reiterated. He answered the call and heard a pause followed by a click and then the all-too-familiar voice distortion software kicked in and the robotic voice offered vocals.

'James?'

'T-1000, is that you?'

Another pause. 'Don't get cute, James. Because speaking of cute, Radka is quite a healthy, virile specimen now isn't she?!'

'You touch her, you die.'

The voice roared with laughter. Robotic laughter. Distorted vibrations, like a vacuum cleaner had suddenly been activated. Then it retained its earlier dulcet demeanour. 'You've really gone to town on Paris, haven't you James? I mean, you have been everywhere! Whose studio are you currently stood in? Tiffanny's?'

'I'm not in anybody's house, jerk-off, I'm in a park.'

'No, you are not. You are stood inside a small studio apartment on Avenue Secrétan, a side street running off Rue Lafayette. You have been to the

Sacre Coeur, the Arc du Triomphe, the Eiffel Tower, Place de la Concorde, Opera, The Louvre courtyard and the Bibliothèque Nationale de France. And then you came to that apartment late last night. And that is where you are now. So don't play games with me, and most importantly of all, do not lie.'

James placed a hand over the facia to mask his voice and looked gravely at Tiffanny. 'He knows where we have been. Everywhere!'

'How is that possible?' she asked. She was stood by the counter next to the A P E R O letters. He was perched at the threshold separating the balcony from the den. Then a sudden realisation drowned him in fear. 'It's him. It's the man in the tanned jacket!'

'The man on the phone?'

'It has to be! Who else could know our every movements?'

He went back on the phone. 'So you're the man in the tanned jacket?'

'What on Earth are you talking about?' the robotic voice boomed.

'Come on. You don't want me to lie to you? Well it works both ways. So don't lie to me. You are the man who stole Tiffanny's car and who has been running surveillance on us the last two days. Who are you?'

'I do not own a tanned jacket. And I am not in France. I have no idea what you are talking about.'

'So how is it that you know where we were, and are?'

'The cell phone Murgatroyd gave you is fitted with a very unique and very advanced GPS facility. We pay the US government a great deal of money and in return they provide us with unlimited access to our very own satellite. We've been watching you since Murgatroyd gave you the cell. That's a lovely looking property you have in Chester, by the way. Bird's eye view of the river. Very nice location.'

James removed his ear from the shell and examined the phone. It was a relatively basic design, covered in a cheap silver paint; probably acrylic. It wasn't built for durability, it was built for design and purpose.

'James, what are you doing?' The Frenchwoman was growing restless by the door.

230

'There's a tracking bug in here somewhere. It's been lighting us up like a flare.'

'Not a tracking bug, James. Satellite navigation, similar to the type you would put in a car to help you find a place. It's very sophisticated. And it's our insurance policy. I do hope you have made some progress in Paris.'

'You already have an insurance policy; you have Radka.'

'Ok, so now we have two insurance policies. I'm growing inpatient, James. What did you find?'

James paused. He thought about whether to spill. Tiffanny looked on expectantly.

'I'm waiting, James. Your last location was the library, then you came to the studio. So I guess that means the library was your last stop in Paris. What did you find there?'

James paused.

'James?'

James paused. He looked at Tiffanny. She nodded eagerly, as if to say *just tell him what he wants to hear.*

'There is a book.'

'A book?'

'There is a book that was written by a Frenchman some years ago. It has gone missing from the library. The guy who worked behind the desk was bewildered by it. There was no paperwork. It had just vanished.'

There was an audible robotic sigh on the other end of the line. 'What book? What are you talking about? It sounds like you are wasting my time. It sounds like Radka will have to pay for your ineptitude.'

'NO. WAIT. There's more.'

'Well hurry up and spit it out then.'

'The author of the book left an address. We are going there now to follow up; it's a big lead. A clue.'

'Where is it?'

James paused.

'You might as well tell me now; I am tracking you, remember.'

'Lyon. A man called Pierre Chartier. The book is about a cure for cancer. But then again you probably already know that, as Tiffanny did.'

'Aha, now we are getting somewhere. You see James, all you have to do is co-operate, and give me all of your information. Then nobody gets harmed. It's very easy.'

'Do you know what B17 is?' James suddenly became the interrogator.

The robotic voice grunted. 'It sounds like you really are making progress.'

'Do you know what it is?' James repeated the question.

'I think we both know the answer to that. Hasn't Tiffanny filled you in on the science?'

'What she knows, yes. And I think this Pierre Chartier in Lyon will know the rest. Which is why we're headed there today.'

'Good. I am very pleased with your new attitude. I will be in touch for another update soon.'

'Hang on' James pressed. 'I need another reassurance that Radka is alive and well.'

'Why should you care? I know where you slept last night.'

James felt the onslaught of anger; his cheeks reddened and his temperature rose. His blood reached a higher pressure. Then he took a deep breath and the notion subsided. 'Just put her on the phone.'

'James?'

'Radka? Are you still ok?'

'I'm still ok, James. What did he mean? Where did you sleep last night?'

'So you can confirm that the robot is a he then?'

'You're changing the subject.'

'Er..well..'

'I don't want to know James. Just know that I am alright.' Her voice was strained and without warmth.'

The robot came back on the line. 'There you go, there's your reassurance. She doesn't sound too happy about your new girlfriend does she?'

'What's to stop me from smashing this phone into bits and pulling the plug on your sordid little perversion?' James spat.

'Oh, I wouldn't do that, James. I wouldn't tamper with the cell phone. I've installed a very small C4 charge inside the circuit board. If you try to remove anything from the inside of the device, it will blow up and take your face off with it. So be very careful with that phone. You don't want to drop it!'

'You're joking, right?'

'Try me. Or do you value that set of handsome, rugged features you wear on your head so well?'

'Point taken, asshole.'

'Get yourselves on the next train to Lyon. I'll be in touch.' The line went dead.

James snapped the clamshell phone shut with a greater degree of care than he had previously been bothered to utilise. He placed it delicately inside his trouser pocket and explained the brunt of the conversation to Tiffany. The Frenchwoman appeared momentarily awkward about the love triangle developing with Radka and James. But they were effectively over. So Tiffany had nothing to feel guilty about. Still, James could see it in her eyes; they were suddenly full of doubt. She checked her own cell and then threw it back into her handbag. There was still no word from Lacroix.

'This isn't good, James. I don't like that he's been watching us all the time.'

'Let's get the hell out of Paris' he retorted.

They went to Gare du Nord metro station and Tiffany asked for two adult tickets to Lyon whilst James peeled off notes from the lockup roll amounting to a hundred and five Euros and slipped them through the counter window.

The cashier flicked a polished fingernail quickly over the bills and counted them. She printed off two tickets and placed them through the counter window and into the tray. The Frenchwoman scooped them up and gave one to James. They triggered the barrier release by slipping their tickets into the slots and made it through to the platform.

They waited for their carriage to arrive. They were travelling by TGV – better known as the bullet train. It stood for Train à Grande Vitesse, meaning *high speed train*. Originally intended to be powered by gas turbines, the TGV evolved into an electric vehicle. It typically travels at a hundred and seventy miles per hour. Owned by French rail operator SNCF since the nineteen seventies, the bullet train has revolutionised passenger travel in France and provides fast direct access to Belgium, Germany, Italy, Switzerland, Spain and the Netherlands.

But today they weren't travelling too far. Paris to Lyon would be a routine sojourn taking the TGV a paltry two hours and ten minutes. They were due to arrive at Lyon Saint Exupery around noon.

At ten the train arrived and they boarded. The internal façade of the carriages was a primer of sophistication; you'd expect nothing less from the French. A combination of white and cyan polymers had been coated to the underside of the aluminium. The SNCF logo was displayed on every panel. The seats were plush with steamed fabric painted royal blue, and they were comfortable. The legroom was plentiful and the aisle carpet was immaculately well kept. There were magazines framed in wire baskets attached to the seats in front.

A steward walked the length of the carriage with a snack cart. Tiffanny declined to purchase from it; James ordered a café au lait and a pain au chocolat. They were sat in carriage C, the third of nine. Tiffanny gazed out of the window as the train left the station and picked up speed. James stared into the space directly in front of him. It was mid morning; that time of day when he was still sleepy and had to wait for lunchtime to set him up for the rest of the day.

*

In carriage G the man removed his tanned jacket and sat back in his seat. The woman with the cart came past and he ordered coffee and a ham and cheese sandwich. It was packed with the finest emmental and jambon. He smiled at her and she blushed as she accepted his money. Then she continued down the aisle and disappeared into the next carriage. The call he was waiting for came soon after. He picked up his cell phone and answered.

'Chaplin.'

'It's me. Where are you?'

'I'm on a train bound for Lyon.'

'What? Why?'

'Because that's where the targets are going.'

'How can you be certain?'

'They are on the same train.'

'Jesus, Chaplin. Don't let them see you!'

'I think they already have. One of them took my photograph using his cell phone. It does not matter – I don't exist remember. I won't show up on any computer.'

'Fine, but just be careful.'

'I will.'

'Chaplin, I sense tension in your voice. Is there a problem?'

Chaplin glanced up as two teenage girls boarded and walked past him and followed the cart steward into the next carriage. 'There are too many...temptations' he said edgily.

'Just keep it together! Are you taking your medicine?'

'The pills don't help that much.'

'Then perhaps we need to administer a stronger dose.'

'That's up to you, Sir.'

'Yes, it is' Paul Ross responded. 'Let me know what happens in Lyon.'

'Of course, Sir. Later.'

Chaplin hung up the phone and reached into his pocket and retrieved the box of pills. He popped the lid and slid two into his mouth. He swallowed them down and swilled the coffee, draining the rest of the mud at the bottom of the cup. He wiped his brow with a shirtsleeve and took a deep breath. He had to rid his mind of the poisonous obsession swirling around it like a lacklustre fog.

He passed five women on his way to the restroom. He locked the door and lifted up the seat. A pulsating throb jolted through his neural core. Another bad headache. He spread his legs and unzipped his pants. He flicked out his penis and rubbed his hand along the shaft vigorously for ten minutes. He thought about the cart stewardess and the two teenage girls boarding, and the five women he had walked past on his way to the restroom. He pictured them in short skirts, boob tubes and seven inch hooker heels.

He imagined playing with each one in turn. He visualised stripping them slowly and teasingly. He envisaged their collective gasps and moans as he ran his hands over their breasts and down towards their waiting genitals. He embellished the thought of putting the spikes from their shoes in his mouth, then licking their feet. He imagined their lips around his penis and his hands around their necks.

He imagined the impending orgy and their resulting death as he squeezed and wrenched the last echoes of life out of them. Then the sweet release came and he groaned and then sighed. He wiped himself clean with a tissue and zipped up.

He flushed the toilet, washed his hands and left the restroom, making his way back to his seat. He managed to make eye contact with three of the five women he passed in the opposite direction to his approach. They all smiled warmly at him and he returned the pleasantry. He sat back in his seat and relaxed. It was nothing like the real deal, but it was the next best thing.

Chapter Twenty Four

Lyon, France. Approaching noon.

The route from Paris to Lyon had taken them on a southeasterly bearing, crossing through the city of Troyes which lay along the banks of the Seine on an old Roman route that eventually leads to Milan, and on past Dijon in the Burgundy province, famous for its production of the finest French mustard. The path snaked on through a number of smaller principalities along the eastern borderlands. Switzerland lay a hundred miles to the east. The train shunted due south. James gazed out of the window and saw Lake Geneva shimmering on the horizon. They passed through Annecy and were ten miles from Lyon. The Frenchwoman sliced through the silence like a knife through butter.

'Did you dream last night James?'

'As a matter of fact I did. It was a recurring dream from my childhood. I had not visited that place in years.'

'What place? What was your dream?'

'There isn't much to it, but it's very enchanting. I'm stood high on a cliff top, gazing down into a shimmering blue lake below me. This lake is unlike any lake in real life; the shade of blue is so intense, so vibrant. And then I jump off the cliff and the second I've started my descent, I feel this rush of exhilaration knowing I'm going to land in the lake. The closer I get to the lake, the more excited I become. And then finally I splash through the water and I feel reborn. I'm all alone, in this beautiful lake, with forest and jungle all around me. It could be somewhere like Brazil, but it probably isn't. It's a brand new place that my mind created.'

'That sounds like a beautiful dream James.'

'It is, but it doesn't make sense.'

'Why not?'

'In real life I am terrified of water. I barely learned to swim at school. I mean it was a nightmare for me. The night before our weekly swimming lessons I used to throw up. So my mother had to write me a note and I sat on the bench watching the other children dive in and go underwater and do all these crazy things totally beyond my comprehension.

'I did learn to swim and received a certificate as proof when I was thirteen, but I haven't been in a pool since. And when I'm at the beach I don't go in the sea. The daily shower is my limit. And yet in the dream I can't wait to jump into that lake. I feel so good when I land; exhilarated, refreshed, happy.'

'What else do you dream about?' the mademoiselle enquired.

'Usually my dreams involve a journey. Either I'm sat on a plane, or a train, or a bus. And here's where it gets interesting from a psychoanalytical viewpoint. I'm usually headed homeward. I get off the bus or the train and I realise that I'm still very far away from home, but now I have to walk. So I start walking.

'After half an hour I realise that I have been walking in the wrong direction. So I turn back, but now I have an extra half an hour on my journey. I just can't get home. I never arrive at my destination.'

'What do you think that means?'

'I guess it means that deep down I worry that I'll never get to where I want to be. Not in a geographical context, but in life.'

'Do you worry about that?'

'Don't we all?'

'I guess we do. But you've done ok for yourself. You were a lawyer, now you're a teacher, right?'

'I was a lawyer for a very short amount of time. The Aequitol scandal sealed my fate. And yes I'm a teacher, but I haven't shown up for work in four days now. There's probably a nationwide manhunt scouring the UK for my body. And I guess there's another job I don't have anymore. And I'll expect divorce proceedings from Radka when this is all over. I'm pushing thirty and I have nothing to show for it. '

'I'm sorry James. I feel responsible.'

He ignored her apology because she knew it wasn't her fault and he knew that she knew that. 'Going back to dreams, I do have one strong inclination of belief. You might think it nonsense though.'

'Try me' the Frenchwoman offered.

'Well, I am of the opinion that when we dream we are actually visiting a parallel universe. We exist, but the rules are different. So, in the lake reality I am not hydrophobic. Haven't you ever realised that when you're doing something in a dream, something mundane, something that you would do often in real life, for example going to the cinema, in the dream it feels more exciting?'

'I don't follow.'

'One of my regular dreams is a visit to the cinema. But this particular cinema doesn't exist in real life, as far as I know. At least I have never been there in real life.

'In the dream this cinema, I can visualise now its layout, the popcorn counter, the screen, the upholstery on the seats, it's different somehow to any real-life cinema I know. And when I have that dream, every time feels like I am enjoying the experience of watching a movie at the cinema for the very first time. And when I jump in the lake I feel reborn.

'Real life for me in the twenty-first century has become one of endless routine. I get up, I shower, I brush my teeth, I dress, I have breakfast, I go to work, I come home, I watch the same shows on TV, then I go to bed. When I dream and do those things it feels more fulfilling.

'It could just be the dream-state's effects on the brain. Perhaps when we're asleep our senses are more perceptive of our experiences than when we are awake. One thing's for sure though – being in that dream state is the only way I can feel truly alive anymore.'

Tiffanny looked on thoughtfully. Then she smiled. 'I never really thought about my dreams in that way, but now that you point it out to me, yes I think you are right. There is something magical about the dream world, for sure.'

'So what do you dream about, Tiffanny?'

The Frenchwoman cleared her throat. 'My parents, mainly.' Her words came out stiff and harsh like sandpaper.

'I'm sorry, I shouldn't have...'

'No no no it's ok.' She squeezed his hand and shook her head. 'It's ok' she said again. James felt a pang of awkwardness.

'But unfortunately, back in the mundane real world we have business to attend to. We need a plan for Lyon.'

'Thanks for bringing me back down to Earth, Tiffany. We have a plan – the address. Pierre Chartier's residence.'

'You think it will be that simple? You think that's where he lives today? You think we're just going to walk into his house and shake his hand and he'll give us all the answers and we say thanks very much and shake his hand again and that's it?'

'I suppose you're right. But it's a starting point.'

'Yes James. Just don't hold your breath. I wouldn't expect this Pierre Chartier to be a man easily found. If a book can disappear off the face of the Earth, so can its author.'

'Point taken.'

'How much money do we have left?'

'Enough for accommodation, food and travel costs in Lyon, that's for sure.'

'There is a budget set for our investigations.'

'Collins isn't exactly signing on now is he?' James scoffed. 'I'm sure we're not breaking the bank.'

They were due to arrive in Lyon Saint Exupery any minute. James looked at Tiffanny; she was sat with her shoulder resting on the window grille, twisting the curls of her hair. It was what she did when she was in deep thought. 'Do you want to talk about what happened in the studio?'

Her gaze shifted towards him. 'What do you mean?'

'Do you want to talk about what we did?' he reiterated.

'What we did?'

240

'Ok, let me put it another way. Do you want to talk about what we did four times, in the studio?'

She stopped twisting her curls and smiled. 'So you're keeping count now?'

'I'm a statistician at heart' he said sarcastically.

'Vying for an even five?' she shot back.

'Is that an open invitation for another trial run?'

'Trial run?' she asked, puzzled.

'You know what they say; practice makes perfect!'

'In that case I don't think five times is going to break any records' she responded, demurring.

'You are a mean woman' he told her.

'I can go further. Is there a suggestion box for comments? Or even better, do you have a complaints procedure in place?'

'Hey! You were pretty satisfied.'

'How do you know I wasn't faking it.'

'Your eyes told me otherwise.' She looked away in a moment of coyness. Then she said nothing and returned to busying herself with her curl-twisting.

The train pulled into the station and powered down. The passengers stood and stretched, then retrieved their belongings from the overhead compartments. Tiffanny and James had no such baggage – theirs was purely mental, and it was beginning to weigh them down.

They joined the accumulation of passengers by the exit, waiting for the noise to signal that the doors could be opened. When the sound came one of them pressed a large circular grey button illuminated in red LED graphics and the doors of their carriage whirred open.

They disembarked onto the platform and felt a blast of cold air. The rain from yesterday had subsided and the wind was elsewhere, but the temperature remained a smidgen above freezing. Four carriages further down the platform the man in the tanned jacket descended from the step and took up position on a bench, watching his prey from a distance of a hundred yards. He was adequately camouflaged amongst the throng of other passengers and therefore did not arouse suspicion. Tiffanny and James glanced back out of habitual paranoia but failed to pick him out of the crowd.

They threaded through the crowds and noticed that there were two kinds of passenger movement – the purposeful walk of the city dweller taking a power lunch and the idling slow dawdle of the disoriented tourist. Their tickets were checked at the barrier and James ordered a cappuccino to go from the station vendor. They passed a bookstore on the way towards the exit and James bought a city map from the lone shopkeeper.

Out on the main thoroughfare he unfolded the map and held it out for them to study. They had travelled to the centre of the country, and here the climate was a few degrees above Paris' ground pressure. The sun was shielded by a swirling coat of arms in cloud formation. Thin beams of nectar coloured light pierced through the bloated sky and cast distorted pictures on the skyscrapers and tenements in shadowed reverie.

James retrieved the piece of paper he had prised out from underneath the national library's computer in Paris and looked again at the B17 action diagram and the name and address of Pierre Chartier. 'Ok, so we're looking for a place called Soucieu-en-Jarrest. Downtown Lyon is here.' He jabbed a finger at the centre of the foldout map. 'You take the left side and look in the northwest and southwest. I'll take the right and handle northeast and southeast.'

They studied their respective sectors in silence. The map showed downtown Lyon to be sandwiched by two rivers running parallel along the city's flanks – the Rhône and the Saône. To the south lay the ruins of a giant amphitheatre, impressed on the map by sand coloured concentric circles similar to a cyclone pattern on a TV weather report.

The Saône was more like an estuary of the Rhône, and a few hundred miles south of Lyon they converged upon each other. James followed the path of the Rhône; it snaked and slithered around the valleys and the towns and sliced a trajectory all the way through the country, past Avignon in the far south, and eventually ebbed out into the Mediterranean Sea. The sheer scale of the water colossus was impressive.

Eager to avoid an unnecessary impasse James focused his mind and his eyes back on Lyon and the name of the place that matched that on the printout. Tiffanny spoke up after twenty seconds.

'It's here. I found it. Voila. Soucieu-en-Jarrest.' The Frenchwoman pointed with a perfectly manicured nail towards the southwest quadrant of the map. 'K3. Look.' He followed the trail of her hand and his eyes settled on the terrain. Soucieu-en-Jarrest lay some distance from downtown Lyon. He checked the scale of the map and did the maths and figured it was about thirty miles.

'We'll need to hire a car' he reported. 'It's a good thirty miles from here, and looking at the terrain, it's much higher ground and the gradient is steep. It looks hilly, possibly even mountainous.'

'Do we have enough money to hire a car?' Tiffanny asked.

'Depends on the price I guess. We should be ok. There should be a brochure for some of the rental companies in the station. Maybe we should go back and check.' He drained the coffee and threw the Styrofoam cup into a trash can on the sidewalk.

His instinct had been correct; there was a notice board near the ticket counter and a wooden tray with all kinds of tourist information and museum pamphlets. He found what he was looking for. The rental company was called Europcar; their offices were a few blocks west of downtown. As it turned out they were also near Lyon airport – the prime location for such a service.

Using the map they threaded across the streets as a Boeing 747 roared past them overhead; judging from the low dip and the angled ascent the plane had just taken off. Lyon was serviced by three airports; Grenoble, Garibaldi and St Etienne, and its tourism industry was in a blatant boom cycle.

The men in the rental office were unwilling to speak English so Tiffanny did the talking. Their first offer was fifty euros per day but Tiffanny charmed and sweet-talked and convinced them to lower it to forty. James rolled off the bills whilst the employees at the desk watched in silent scrutiny, casting aspersions on a man who carried around so much cash.

But they were more than happy to take it, and in return they handed over the keys to an Alfa Romeo coupe which Tiffanny duly snatched up. James was

243

happy to let her do the driving; she seemed to enjoy it. For him it was more of a necessary chore than a pleasure. In England there were too many cars on the roads and nobody played by the rules. He just found it stressful. Of course the French weren't exactly known for their cautious use of automobiles either, but they had three times the road infrastructure for the same number of cars per household, giving them much more space to play with.

They also bought a more detailed map from the Europcar people and James spread it out over his knees whilst the Frenchwoman steered them out of the customer car park and onto the smooth downtown blacktop. He stole a glance at the petrol gauge and noted a full tank; the kind people at Europcar had been generous. 'We should stop for lunch first; it's a long journey' James explained.

'It looks like there are some nice cafes here. I'll park and we can find something.' She parked on a quiet side street and they locked up the Alfa Romeo.

'Here looks nice' James proposed, pointing to a modest eatery at the intersection of two busy streets.

*

The old battered sedan didn't put up much of a fight. Besides, it wasn't the first time he had boosted a car. The door gave way after a brief moment of twisting and fiddling with the aerial from the roof which he'd eloquently snapped off for the task. Once inside he bent over and prised the frontal casing off the panelling underneath the steering column. He found the two cables he needed and coiled the metal shafts together to form the circuit. The engine ignited and he revved the accelerator pedal to warm the old junkpile up.

The parking lot was deserted which made for the perfect crime. He took off and drove back towards the station and caught sight of them stood by the sidewalk with their heads in a map. They'd seemed to have made up their minds about something so he just sat and watched them with the engine running.

They suddenly disappeared back into the train station and it made him worry. Were they catching another train? Surely they wouldn't do that if some intelligent investigative work had led them here. He was in two minds whether to get out of the car and run after them. His mind was made up when he saw them re-emerge and he sighed a deep breath of relief.

They had set off on foot so he'd tailed them from a safe distance. He saw them walk into a car rental place with the word Europcar branded all over the premises. He figured if they were getting wheels they weren't staying in the downtown area. They were heading further afield, where public transport became cumbersome and unreliable. They were heading for the countryside; rural terrain could only be crossed in large distances by car.

Business was quiet and the only car that pulled out of the lot was a small, modern, scarlet-red Alfa Romeo. He gazed through the windshield and saw the man and the woman and confirmed his targets. He waited until they were a safe distance away and then he eased out onto the blacktop and headed in their direction. He wondered where they were headed. The thrill of the hunt sent new inklings of pleasure through his central nervous system. This time there was no erection, but the adrenaline was pumping through him as if there was no tomorrow.

Chapter Twenty-Five

Lyon, France. 1:05 p.m.

According to Felix Benoit Lyon is *'a town where one laughs, as one makes love, in private.'* A favoured idiom amongst its bourgeoisie is *'pour vivre heureux, vivons cachés',* which means *'to live happy is to live hidden'.* It seemed therefore like a fitting place for a fugitive author to reside.

The city is symbolised by its grand centrepiece the Fourvière mount, on top of which Julius Caesar and his battalion camped in 58 BC during the Gallic Wars. Back then it was known as Lugdunum and the second most impressive city in the whole of the Roman Empire.

Today it houses a beautiful basilica; an acropolis gazing proudly down on a metropolis. The Rhône and Saóne rivers converge at Perrache but perhaps more interestingly their intertwined passages chose to copulate and have birthed a small stretch of water within their own borders called the *presqu'ile.* When literally translated *presqu'ile* means *'close to an island'* and is more commonly known as a peninsula, although the Lyonnais inhabitants consider it an island in its own right.

Historically the region is famous for its production of silk which is finely weaved in the now classic Croix-Rousse style, and its people have cultivated a penchant for fashioning the finest jewellery, something they are paradoxically reluctant to express to the rest of the world.

Lyon came close to being the French capital in recent times, only to be pepped to the post by Paris at the behest of Francois I in the sixteenth century and Napoleon in the eighteenth. The underground connections once forged here played a monumental part in the Resistance.

James' own resistance was a war raging inside of him, a conflict brewing like a cyclone in his mind, willing him to succumb to the precious beauty of the Frenchwoman sat before him. Yet something did not feel one hundred percent right. Was she using him in order to achieve her endgame? Was it just pure physical attraction, conveniently exacerbated by two consenting adults in the right place at the right time? Or was it more than that? He could not be sure.

Tiffanny's resistance was her reluctance to fully co-operate and answer all of his questions conclusively. She was holding back from painting the complete picture. Her story was an incomplete mural on the façade of his mind.

They were on Rue de Bonnel, in Café Bonaparte, catching up on vital sustenance before the road ahead to Soucieu-en-Jarrest. As with many other aspects of culture, Lyon's reputation for its delectable gastronomy far surpassed all of its contemporary counterparts. It was Maurice Edmond Sailland, adopting the Russian pseudonym Curnonsky, who stated *'Here, cooking reaches the apex of any art, that is to say – simplicity!'*

James and Tiffanny had both elected to eat a *mâchon* dish, a very traditional concoction of pork rinds, sausage, donkey snout, mutton foot, giblets and salad. It was a Lyonnais delicacy and a hearty meal and James thoroughly enjoyed it. At Tiffanny's recommendation they washed it down with a *Monaco;* a strawberry beer containing grenadine. It was a good, satisfying eat, full of protein and carbohydrates.

James picked up the cheque using more bills from the dwindling stack and they went back to the Alfa Romeo and clambered inside. Again Tiffanny drove. The coupe had an in-built GPS facility so James switched it on. He retrieved the sheet of paper he had taken from the library in Paris and rechecked Pierre Chartier's address.

He programmed the 5-digit postcode into the navigation system and it brought up the details. 28 miles to destination, an estimated 31 minutes. His initial guesstimate had been right on the money. Then the unexpected happened. The robotic female GPS voice began to direct them in Italian.

'Oops' James exclaimed. Tiffanny let out a burst of laughter. 'I hadn't put two and two together – it is an Italian car after all.'

'Yeah, I speak a little Italian but she speaks too quickly for me to understand everything. Although I think she wants us to turn left up ahead at some point because I heard the word *sinistra.'*

'Yeah I heard that too. It's where our English word *sinister* derives from.'

'Oh really? I did not know that James. So are things generally associated with the left side considered sinister?'

'In Catholicism, yes. The left side is considered the Devil's side. It is why left-handed people were persecuted in centuries gone by and why still today they are a constant source of mockery.'

'Wow. I had no idea. But I also heard that left handed people are considered more introverted, intelligent, intellectual, something like that? Like they are special?'

'I think that might be an old wives' tale to make left handed people feel better.'

'Are you left handed James?'

'As a matter of fact I am.'

'And do you feel special?'

'Because I'm left handed? Not especially. I don't know any different.'

He turned off the GPS function and went back to the map he had bought in the train station. 'Looks like we'll have to do it the old fashioned way!'

'Fine by me. I hope you are a good map reader James!'

'We'll soon find out. Looking at this map I guess the N roads are your motorways and the D roads are the carriageways through the towns?'

'That's it. Think of the N roads as like your M roads, and the D roads like your A roads.'

'Sure. In that case we first need to get on the N6 and head west out of the city. We are currently in the fourth arrondissement. Let's look for signs.'

They soon found a sign directing them to the highway and they converged onto the N6. It was a fast highway and the lacklustre frivolity of the

French behind the wheel soon became apparent. People rode bumper to bumper at speeds in excess of sixty miles per hour. Tiffanny appeared comfortable with the situation and matched their speeds. It was probably safer to do that than drive too slowly and become a hazard.

James realised that she was a really good driver; certainly more competent than him. She soon got to grips with the Alfa Romeo, which must have been a huge step up from her rickety old Renault that the mysterious man in the tanned jacket had stolen and commandeered in Paris.

He suddenly wondered whether the tanned jacket had followed them into Lyon. He eyed up the rear view mirror for suspicious tails but found nothing except irate Frenchfolk performing dastardly lane changes, zigzagging across the highway like objects in a giant pinball machine.

The afternoon was overcast with a light drizzle. The gradient began to slowly rise as they had envisaged. The landscape either side of the highway was barren save for the odd skyscraper or corporate billboard. One building they passed was finished in jet black marble and appeared hostile and imposing.

Tiffanny had an intense look of concentration on her delicate face as she focused on the road ahead and the other wily road users. A tuft of curly hair fell onto her right cheek. James reached over and tucked it softly under her ear. She smiled and her cheeks made a prominence. She was so beautiful up close; it was like watching a sunrise and a sunset in simultaneous awe. He squeezed her shoulder affectionately then returned his attention to the map.

'We need to come off soon. There should be a sign for the D307, in the direction of Tassin-la-Demi-Lune.' They found it and took it. It subsequently became the D489 and they looped due south on a heading towards Craponne. The city quietly gave way to the suburbs and they entered a sleepy world of hills.

In the distance high rise mountains sprung up from nowhere. Swirls of fog and moisture danced at their apexes like enchanted spirits. Past Craponne they took the D311 towards Brindas. At Brindas they cut onto the D50 which became the D30 and took them through Malataverne and Verchery and eventually they saw signs for Soucieu-en-Jarrest. The gradient became ever more inclined towards verticality. The Italian coupe had no problem with it. Its suspension clung to the road as if there was a maternal bond between the two.

They soon found themselves out in the sticks. The countryside was oddly striking for the time of year. They passed hectares of land where lush greenery would be in its full splendour in the coming months, where vineyards would prosper yielding the perfect batch of vin rouge or vin blanc. Hundreds of species of plant would thrive here when the solstice completed its metamorphosis, giving the surroundings a somewhat didactic character. In the summer the fruit trees would be in full bloom. There would be Virginian tulips, Gingkos, sophoras, limes and Byzantine hazels. February was unable to do the place justice.

James switched the GPS back on. Tiffanny frowned inquisitively. 'We are in the right town but we need to use this to pinpoint Chartier's postcode' he explained. The Frenchwoman nodded her concurrence. He switched off the volume and instead of relying on the Italian baritone voice they followed the arrows on the map to determine the correct route.

The GPS system took them up a winding country road towards the mountains; grey concrete scorched black in parts by nature and man, flanked on either side by loose chippings and gravel. The topography of the valleys below them soon became clear, providing them with aerial views of the soon-to-be-lush landscape.

Natural phenomena from eons past had shaped the land into a giant bell shaped curve, and the Alfa Romeo flew up it with minimal resistance. At its crest the land levelled out into a shallow dip and the summer heat of the coming months would turn the valley into a giant bowl of soup.

They had barely passed any oncoming traffic during the commute, save for the occasional farm vehicle, suggesting that the area had once been a hotbed for the agricultural industry and had witnessed a pivotal but not total decline. After five minutes on a road topped grey with stone chippings the GPS bleeped furiously from the dashboard interface. *You have reached your destination.*

They parked up and clambered out of the coupe. Their gaze swung around in a three-sixty-degree pan but the landscape appeared barren and long forgotten. They exchanged puzzled glances. GPS systems had been known to slip up in the past. They had a track record of sending heavy goods vehicles down dirt tracks too narrow for their carriages. Sometimes postal codes changed and the devices were not updated accordingly.

James could make out something in the far distance; blurs of silver and beige. His vision was not perfect but he could just about make out blurry movements a mile ahead in the distance where the ground lowered, as if someone had sliced down a block of cheese at an acute angle. James figured that's where the village centre of Soucieu-en-Jarrest would be found. Tiffanny gazed northeast and saw the shimmering lights of downtown Lyon twinkling in the distance.

They slipped back into the Alfa and followed the curve of the road towards the compound James thought he had seen. They reached it in ten minutes. He had been right. It was a construction site; a large scale operation from what they now saw. Builders in hard hats worked away on scaffolding as JCBs, cranes and diggers toiled the earth and cement mixers prepared for mortar production. There were tools lying in the dirt and huge pieces of scrap metal were strewn haphazardly across the walkway. Slabs of concrete packed in plastic sheets were stacked up against an oil drum in the far corner. They were looking at hectares of workspace; an area the size of a shopping mall was awaiting its grand rebirth.

Dust crunched into the Alfa's tyres and they pulled up beside a thin sheet of fencing which bordered the entire perimeter. Warning signs were pinned to the mesh at equidistant sections; the construction company heeding to health and safety legislation in the hope of warding off potential personal injury suits being filed against them. *Restricted Zone. Danger.*

One of the labourers noticed the couple approaching. He was probably the site foreman, the gaffer, because he walked with the gait of authority, like he knew he was the boss. Tiffanny beckoned him to the fence line with her hand and as they conversed she translated to James sentence by sentence. The man adjusted his hat several times as he spoke, and occasionally wiped the grease from his toil onto his dirt soaked jeans.

'We are looking for our friend who lives up here' the Frenchwoman explained. 'We have never visited him before. Our GPS pinpointed his place to be about a mile southwest of here, according to his postcode.' She pointed back towards where they had just come from.

'There are no houses back there' the man replied.

'Are you sure?'

'Yes, very sure, I have lived around here all my life, and will probably continue to do so for whatever is left of it! Not many chances for an uneducated man like me, eh?'

'But with construction you'll never be out of work. It's a respectable job. Can you help me with my problem?'

'Can I help you with your problem?' The foreman scoffed. 'Probably not, if you want me to make appear a house that does not exist! I may be a good builder but I'm no magician, Madame.'

Tiffanny winced. *Madame.* She was no age to be referred to as a Madame. She was a Mademoiselle, not a Madame! Her allotted window for small talk was officially slammed shut. 'James, give me the paper.' He handed her the note of Chartier's address alongside the incomplete diagram. She thrust it through the hexagonal gap in the fence and the foreman took it with interest. 'Where is this place?' the Frenchwoman ordered.

The foreman laughed. 'No wonder you cannot find your friend's house. It was very nearby.'

'Was?'

'Yeah, was. In fact, that address belonged to a house that used to stand right about there.' He pointed behind himself to the scaffolding his colleagues were busy working on.'

'You mean it's been pulled down?'

'Exactement. Along with all the others. We're building a big Leclerc and some other retail outlets. Should be completed by this time next year. The community had a big to-do about it but the

253

Government ignored them and signed off the contract anyway.'

'Merde! And what about the inhabitants, what happened to them?'

'Your guess is as good as mine, Madame. They were given some compensation which covered the value of their homes plus a little extra. They probably moved closer to the village.'

Tiffanny pursed her bottom lip. Twice this infuriating man had called her Madame. Three strikes, and he was out. 'I need to find the guy who lived at this address. His name is Pierre Chartier. Do you know him?'

Again the foreman snorted. 'I work here, but I live in Verchery and commute. I don't know people that used to live here, what do you think this is?'

'When was that house in particular pulled down?' Tiffanny pointed to the paper the foreman held dispassionately in his hand.

'Actually that was one of the first ones to go. It went down ten months ago.'

Another employee approached the scene. He spoke to the foreman in a pleading tone; he was no doubt trying to negotiate his next cigarette break. The foreman waved him away with a gesture if resignation and the man smiled; break granted. Then the other man spoke again to the foreman, pointing at Tiffanny and James. The foreman replied and they exchanged words for a few minutes whilst James and the Frenchwoman waited patiently.

The foreman turned back to Tiffanny. 'Marc here says he remembers the initial protests from the residents. He said most of them were old and had lived there all their lives. He says a policeman came by a few times to speak to the residents. He does not know why but he figures it could not have been to do with the demolition because it was state approved. He felt something else was going on. He says you should go into the village and find this policeman. He might know where your missing man is. He goes by the name Didier and he spends every afternoon drinking in a café called Le Bistrot de la Pecherie. It's a small village; you can't miss it.'

'Merci beaucoup.' The Frenchwoman reached through the hexagonal frame and prised the piece of paper out of the foreman's hands. The foreman returned to his supervisory role and the other man lit up a smoke and sat on the oil drum by the concrete slabs. They clambered into the Alfa and reversed out of the complex.

'Let's go, Madame' James chided.

The Frenchwoman indulged him with a look of mock disgust. Then she executed a perfect one-eighty and they took off towards the village of Soucieu-en-Jarrest.

*

The workers of the construction site were interrupted for the second time when a battered orange sedan crunched through the dirt and pulled to a stop in a cloud of dust. A man in a tanned jacket slithered out and marched up to the fence line. The foreman snorted in disdain and powerwalked over to the unannounced visitor. He was a busy man and wondered what this salty looking dude wanted from him. He would have thought that the warning signs would have been enough to keep the prying eyes of the public away from the site altogether.

As the foreman reached the fence line Chaplin pulled the photofit sheets out of his pocket from Paris and pinned them onto the fence with his left hand. The foreman's interest was piqued as he saw the faces of two people he had spoken to less than half an hour before. 'Have you seen them?' Chaplin barked. His headaches were coming back but he had left his pill stash in the car. There was a faint smell of almonds in the air, Chaplin found odd. He looked around at the workplace before him. *Not a woman in sight. Damn.*

'Je ne parle pas Anglais. Je suis desole.' *I don't speak English. I'm sorry.'*

Chaplin stuck his arm through the hexagonal mesh and grabbed the foreman's shirt collar at the scruff of the neck. The foreman was caught off guard and toppled towards the fence. Chaplin maintained a vice-like grip on him as he spoke. 'Listen chico, I don't care what languages you speak. Tell me if you saw these people or so help me God I'm going to cut you wide open.'

255

The foreman did not understand the words but the look in his eyes demonstrated his full comprehension of Chaplin's tone. He gazed down to the hand that held him. Then at the other hand, which was holding up the black and white mugshots of Tiffanny and James. The sun struck Chaplin's belt and the foreman caught sight of a shank pinned beneath the waistline. It looked like a Stanley knife, except the blade was already out in readiness.

With his free hand the foreman pointed frantically southwest, towards the village. 'La ba, la ba, ils allent a la centreville.' *There, there, they are going to the centre of town.*

'Village? Centre?' Chaplin spoke in that slow demeaning manner Englishfolk speak to foreigners as if they are addressing an infant.

'Oui. Ah, yes. Centre of village.' The foreman managed a broken sentence of English but his intended effect had been a success. Chaplin understood and released his grip.

'When did they leave?'

The foreman appeared confused for a moment, and Chaplin bubbled with rage. Then the foreman murmured in triumph and nodded his head. He held out both his palms flat with his fingers and thumbs outstretched. He flashed his hands three times, indicating three counts of ten. 'Trente' he murmured for added emphasis.

Chaplin watched the man's hand signal. 'Thirty? You mean thirty minutes ago? Half an hour ago they left?'

'Trente' he repeated, and grinned a toothy smile of benevolence. He would go home that evening and tell his folks about the strange day he'd had, with the strange Madame asking questions about the project and then the even stranger man, the *etranger,* threatening him with a knife and holding up photos of the former and her friend. It had been a day unlike any other on the construction site.

Chaplin relinquished his grip on the foreman and slithered back towards the stolen sedan. His head was banging like a jackhammer and he could still smell almonds. He popped a pill from his stash and washed it town with a miniature bottle of tequila he kept in his sock. Then he started the rickety old engine and threw the sedan in a lazy turning circle and sped off towards the village.

There would certainly be women there, of some description. Neither his standards nor his tastes were any kind of measured. So long as they had the ability to cleanse him of his wretched urge, then so be it. He didn't even need their consent. He was strong enough to insist.

Chapter Twenty Six

4:00 p.m.

They took the road already travelled, in the opposite direction, and dipped back down into the valley. It took them fifteen minutes to reach the village on the same irrigated greytop until a small rustic sign for the village prompted them to detour from the main thoroughfare onto a bumpy gravel track. Small stones crunched underneath the Italian roadster's tyres until the hamlet appeared on the immediate horizon. 'The name of the café is Le Bistrot de la Pecherie' Tiffanny reiterated.

'I will keep an eye out for it' James replied. The village centre was a juxtaposition of small scale civilisation set against a medieval backdrop of old colonial typography. Most of the residential tenements were recent developments; municipal three-storey units cast in peach stained concrete and housing rotundas and balconies painted a vibrant royal blue. But there were conspicuous Napoleonic remnants too, and state funded social housing projects for the less precocious.

James figured that this outshoot of French suburbia was the kind of place that the elderly retired to, a habitat where children could still ride their bicycles day and night without the threat of hostile abduction. No doubt the schools would offer extracurricular schemes in their plentiful entireties and foreign languages such as English and Spanish would be instilled in pupils from an early onset; they were the languages of the global world of commerce after all. It seemed to be a simple yet prosperous community of farmers and wine merchants.

He spotted Le Bistrot de la Pecherie up ahead on the right, sat between a hair salon and a charcuterie. They parked the Alfa immediately outside the premises and there was a welcoming burst of warm air as they entered the bistro. Edith Piaf's *Je ne regrette rien* played over speakers mounted to the ceiling. Regular patrons conversed using animated gestures and close proximity to one another.

A lone man sat by the counter shouting in an aggressive drunken stupor; he was dressed like a vagrant and unkempt stubble clung forlornly to his face like weeds creeping out of a flagstone. His sultry vocals reverberated around the room and peaked over the conversational tones of the customers, the clash of metal equipment and crockery in the kitchen out back and the wartime waltz playing back through the sound system. The other patrons ignored him with a fine tuned dedication. They were clearly used to his antics.

A waitress dressed in the traditional black and white uniform of a Maitre d's underling brought them to a small table in the far corner of the restaurant and handed them beverage menus. 'Pour manger?' she enquired. *To eat?* They politely declined and the waitress refrained from reeling off the specials of the day, politely excusing herself from their vicinity to bring them coffee only.

'I wonder what his problem is?!' James remarked, nodding towards the counter. The angry vagrant clearly had a lot to say, despite having a disregarding audience. It was an interesting dichotomy.

When the waitress came back to check on their need for a drink refill Tiffanny declined but asked her if she knew of a regular called Didier, a policeman who supposedly drank in the bistro on a regular basis. The waitress laughed in response and pointed towards the counter. She rolled her eyes in frustration as she spoke to the Frenchwoman and then extended her palms outwards in a gesture of *What can you do?!* James followed Tiffanny's glance back towards the counter and then back towards his own glare.

'Don't tell me' he said.

'I'm afraid so' she responded.

'Jesus. Well, shall we introduce ourselves?!'

They drained their coffees, leaving the muddy dregs at the bottom to bask in their own insignificance, and walked towards the counter. James picked up the smell of stale alcohol on the vagrant's breath a good metre away. He was perched on a barstool, bent forward like Quasimodo, with a pint of ale and a glass of what looked like whiskey idling in front of him.

His voice had subsided to a lesser volume but he was still chirping away, apparently aiming his verbal onslaught at nobody in particular. His eyes felt the presence of others nearby and when he turned around and saw the both of them stood there he appeared bemused for a moment, as if their company was an unexpected pleasure.

He stopped mid sentence and gazed at Tiffanny. James smiled, fully embellishing what the vagrant was going through. Tiffanny's beauty was enough to stop any man in his tracks, even a babbling old drunkard. She had done the same thing to James when he had encountered her for the first time at Charles de Gaulle airport in Paris just three days ago. He had to remind himself that he had known her for a little over seventy-two hours, yet so much had happened in that time, on both physical and mental planes. The man made an obvious point of giving her his undivided scrutiny, his eyes roving up and down her body with the patient efficiency of an airport metal detector.

He seemed about ready to return to his grand monologue but Tiffanny jumped in before he had the chance. 'I'm looking for Didier' she stated.

'Oh, you're looking for Didier are you?! I'd say you were rather looking *at* Didier! Unless I am so intoxicated that I have forgotten my own identity. But who truly knows who they really are these days? Hmmm?' He turned around and gulped from the pint glass, draining the ale inside. He swiped the back of his shirt sleeve across his mouth and belched in inebriated satisfaction.

'That's deep' Tiffanny scolded sarcastically. 'Listen, Didier, we need your help with a very serious matter. We are looking for somebody.'

'Yes, you are. You are looking for Didier! And you just found him, but then I just told you that. Are you drunk too?'

'No, we are looking for another person, a missing person. This is my friend James, from England. We need to find a man called Pierre Chartier; a man who wrote a book that is missing from the national library in Paris.'

As Didier prepared to drain his pint down to the halfway line, he suddenly choked and an irrefutable coughing fit proceeded. When he had recovered he stood from his stool and glared sombrely at his two guests. The transition from intoxication to full sobriety appeared instantaneous, like a sudden metamorphosis. More surprisingly, he responded in English.

'Pierre Chartier. Now there is a name I haven't heard in a while. A name that took over my career, a name that took away my wife and caused my daughter to become estranged from me. A name that has the power to destroy a man.

'You want to know why I spend every single day of my miserable life drinking in this hovel, this shithole? Pierre Chartier is the reason. Putain! Pierre Chartier did this to me. Putain!' Didier drove his fist hard into the counter and the Frenchwoman flinched in retaliation. James stepped up in her defence.

'Calm down, Didier. We need to know more about Pierre Chartier. Can we talk?'

Didier drained the last of his pint and looked at the glass of whiskey like it was too much of a guilty pleasure yet too difficult to resist. He eyed up James for the first time in the exchange. 'Yes, we can talk, but not here. I am sick of this miserable place. We go outside, to someplace else, if you want me to talk about Pierre Chartier.'

'Fine' James said.

'You have a car?' Didier asked.

'Right outside.'

'Good. I am too drunk to drive. You can take me downtown, into Lyon centreville. There, we shall talk about Pierre Chartier.'

'After you.'

262

The drive from Soucieu-en-Jarrest into Lyon took twenty minutes and was predominantly downhill all the way. Now the mountains were behind them and the early evening sun was preparing to set in the west. It was a glowing red ball perched low in the sky, a phenomenon James had only witnessed a handful of times in his life to date.

Its mystery provided a jarring sense of foreboding as James pondered why Pierre Chartier, author of a missing book about cancer, had ruined the life of a policeman. They cut onto the highway Tiffanny had taken them on earlier that morning and once again passed the imposing jet-black marble building on the opposite side. Didier explained that it was Interpol's headquarters. His words had become less slurred and his pupils less dilated. He remained sober throughout the journey. His appearance was mismatched with his line of work; naturally they had taken him for a hobo, not a man of the law. He needed a shave and a change of clothes to complete the transition.

As they neared the borders of the old town centre the Fourvière basilica loomed ahead, perched on the crest of a grassland mount. 'I saw that on the way out to Soucieu-en-Jarrest' James explained. 'You can see it from any point in Lyon it would seem. Is it a monument of some importance?' He figured that engaging Didier in pivotal conversation would keep his sobriety reigned in before they reached a place to talk properly about Pierre Chartier. Didier took the bait, hook line and sinker.

'It is the most significant piece of architecture in the whole of Lyon' he explained. 'In 1870 Napoleon was defeated, and the Lyonais people feared an imminent attack from the Prussians. The Virgin Mary has an omnipresence here, so the natives prayed to her for the Prussians not to attack. They promised to erect a sanctuary in her honour if she granted them this blessing. The Prussians never came and the basilica was the ultimate homage to her compassion. It was consecrated in 1896.'

'It is beautiful' James remarked.

Didier smiled. 'Yes, yes it is.' They passed the Rhône once more, a once wild river that had matured into a gentle waterway since its banks were raised in the not too distant past. Its cousin the

Saône is even calmer, made famous by Julius Caesar who threw his coat into the water to check the direction of its flow when he first arrived. Both have become muses for poets and painters alike, offering them discreet inspiration without polluting their egos with delusions of grandeur.

Ahead the Credit Lyonnais headquarters shunted up towards the heavens, a skyscraper built in the shape of a giant crayon. The financial institution seemed at first glance out of place in a city clustered with facets of art and grand design. Its commercial reality stole a small part of the city's bohemian essence.

Tiffanny stopped at a level crossing to allow a white tram to slice across their path. They crossed the vacant tramway in its wake and passed the Cité Internationale in the north end of town, a three-thousand capacity hall and exhibition centre with attached casino. 'All this territory is considered World Heritage' Didier explained. 'UNESCO designated a large chunk of the city in 1998. It is how we preserve the old town. About ten percent of the whole city is on their World Heritage List.' The area had seen two millennia of urban development, and therefore it was a decision befitting UNESCO's respect for human endeavour.

The amphitheatre came into view, and Didier continued his diatribe. 'The amphitheatre was built in 19 AD under instructions from Emperor Claudius. Gladiatorial combat was the most common sport to be found here. It could hold twenty thousand spectators.' It reminded James of the amphitheatre in Chester, a literal stone's throw from his terraced house on Albion Place, where just three days ago he was trudging through the routine chapters of his life as a law tutor and the misery of his recent split from Radka Rosická, the delectable Czech.

They hit downtown soon after and Didier instructed Tiffanny to park across the street in a leafy pavilion overlooking a shopping precinct. The thoroughfare was lined with cafes and boutique shops. Dusk was vast approaching from the west, and the last remnants of light cascaded around the cityscape in a last ditch effort for prominence before its inevitable decline into twilight. 'There is something I have to show you before we lose the light' Didier stated.

They alighted from the Alfa and Didier led them across the pavilion towards a large myriad of closely connected buildings offset against a block of residential apartments behind it. As James neared the façade he became increasingly confused. The wall appeared to be patterned in some way, like graffiti, except it wasn't graffiti. It was as if a traditional painter had used the façade as a blank canvas and produced a watercolour piece on the wall itself. Surely he was hallucinating. Perhaps the din of dusk was playing tricks on his eyes.

They reached the façade and James realised he was not hallucinating. Didier followed his bewildered gaze and huffed. 'It's quite remarkable, isn't it?!'

'Yes, am I seeing a painted wall?' James asked, feeling clumsy at stating the obvious.

'Indeed you are! This is one of Lyon's murals. The city is famous for them.'

'They look so real, so lifelike!' James retorted.

'They are!' Didier proclaimed. 'It started in the nineteenth century. The Lyon School of Painting funded many of the projects. A painter called Thomas Blanchet covered the façades of the municipal buildings with mythological allegories. This was the pre-Raphaelite era, you understand. Today there are hundreds of painted murals here in Lyon.'

'So why bring us to this one in particular? This one your favourite?' James admired the detail up close. Every inch of the external wall had been covered in art; not an inch of blank canvas remained. It looked like a giant still from a cartoon. The people were drawn like caricatures and appeared wacky and disjointed. Windows were painted on to give the effect of a block of flats. Painted steps led to a painted dry stone wall in the background. Painted storefront windows offered painted goods.

Yet from a distance it all appeared real; it was only when James came within a few hundred yards of the mural that its artistic deception became clear. One particular detail stood out for James; it was a lone man dressed in black motorcycle leathers, stood by a café veranda whose sign read *Aix en Provence*. The man held out his thumb in the upward position denoting approval, and he was producing a zany smile. He showed it to Tiffanny and she smiled.

'No, that is not the reason why I brought you to this mural' Didier said.

'Then why?' James pressed.

Didier cleared his throat. 'This mural is the last known location of Pierre Chartier before he disappeared. It was here where he was last seen alive.'

'When was that?' Tiffanny enquired.

'2004. Six years ago. Back then I was a highly respected officer here in downtown Lyon. I've handled missing persons cases before, don't get me wrong. But never one this strange.'

'Strange in what way?' James urged.

'Strange in so many ways' Didier offered. 'He did not leave many clues behind. He was some kind of recluse; lived alone, no friends no family. Nobody in Soucieu-en-Jarrest knew who he was. His background was science and medicine - that we could determine. We found no record of anything else he had written and published.'

'Just the book about cancer' James interrupted.

'Precisely. And there is no single record of that book's existence either. You search on any bookstore website online, or check into any library, you will not find that book. I spent months scouring the stores for it; it drove my wife crazy, and eventually it drove her to leave. I stopped coming home, I stopped sleeping altogether. I told myself I'd sleep for an eternity once I solved the case. But I never did.'

'So we have a missing book and a missing author' Tiffanny evaluated.

'Indeed' Didier confirmed. 'And in the last six years I have been unable to determine if those two facts are linked, or just a coincidence.'

'I'm not sure I believe in coincidences' James said.

'So you're of the fate and everything happens for a reason persuasion?' Didier asked.

'Yes.'

'Don't you think that makes life a little dull, if everything is already mapped out for us? Don't you want to believe that our decisions affect our lives? We only have one life and it is short; we should have the power to tailor it to our own choices and their subsequent outcomes.'

'That is the ideology of a control freak' James responded. 'I don't want to be in control of every decision in my life. I don't need that much responsibility. Some things are easier to understand if you just accept that it happened just like that and that is the way it goes.'

'And that is the ideology of somebody who feels his life lacks purpose' Didier shot back. 'I am an investigator; it is my job to question everything. I need a reason for everything. I need to know why. Why is the sky blue, why is the grass green, why did Pierre Chartier disappear from the face of this Earth? This is something my wife could not comprehend.'

'I'm sorry about your familial situation' James offered. 'Is there anything more we need to know about Pierre Chartier?'

'He came from a long line of silk weavers. His ancestors practically invented the industry. He paid his taxes, behaved himself, never had so much as a parking ticket. Judging by state registries he voted regularly, he attended school and university here in Lyon. He graduated with an honours degree in medical science. He worked in a local pharmacy for some time then suddenly quit, presumably to start writing his book about cancer.

'I went through his house over and over again before they tore it down last year. I collected belongings and paperwork I thought could potentially be important evidentiary items and filed them away at the station. There appeared to be no next of kin to collect anything, at first. He was all alone in this world. It's all been archived now. I haven't touched the file in two years.'

'What happened two years ago?' Tiffanny asked.

'I lost my job' Didier explained. 'They were pulling the plug on the Chartier case. They said it was due to finite resources and the fact that the case was unsolved after four years. It was like they had their own statute of limitations for solving crimes. I was so angry; I lost it. There was a heated argument between myself and the Chief of the Lyon Prefecture of Police.'

'What was the conclusion of that argument?' James pressed.

'I hit him' Didier exclaimed. 'I had dedicated four years of my life to the case. I'd driven my wife and daughter away, and become a narcissistic alcoholic insomniac. I was a mess; in a real heap of shit. They took my badge and my gun and told me to clear off. It was like a dishonourable discharge. I was shamed and ridiculed. It was very humiliating. I was the mighty and I had fallen flat on my ass. It was like the demise of Caesar himself.'

'You hit the Chief of the Prefecture?' Tiffanny remarked, astonished. 'I'm surprised you didn't have to serve time for that.'

'Strings were pulled and I was spared that disparagement' Didier said. 'But I will never again be an officer of the law, at least in the official sense, and Pierre Chartier's case remains unsolved. Not a happy ending.'

'Perhaps we can help you on that front' James offered.

'Why would you do such a thing? What's in it for you?' Didier's eyebrow arched upward in intrigue, as if he had stumbled on some glorious conspiracy.

'Well, if we don't find Chartier, the people who have my wife might not return her to me in one piece' James explained. He then filled the Frenchman in on everything that had transpired in the last three days, from the cryptic messages in Chester to meet Joel Murgatroyd, the ultraviolet clue which had taken him to Paris where he had met Tiffanny, the traipse around the French capital solving clues, culminating in finding the piece of paper inside the computer in the national library containing a scientific diagram and Chartier's address. As James recounted the events he began to feel like he was reading the script to a Hollywood blockbuster. It beggared belief.

Didier listened intently and expressed conflicting emotions of disbelief and excitement. 'A fascinating turn of events. Do you think the diagram you saw was Chartier's own? He was a pharmacist after all.'

'We think he found a cure' James stated.

'For cancer?' Didier remarked incredulously.

'We think so, although the diagram we found in Paris is incomplete and we need Chartier to fill in the gaps and complete the picture. Our dear friend Tiffanny here is also in the pharmaceutical game and she is holding back from telling me everything she knows.' The Frenchwoman shot him a disparaging glare.

'Why would you do such a thing?' Didier asked of her. 'Why would you withhold information from your friend?'

'It is complicated' Tiffanny stated tersely.

'You are protecting somebody?' Didier may no longer have been a police officer, but old habits die hard, and his inquisitive instinct remained fully intact; it was burnt onto his soul.

Tiffanny refrained from further comment, as James predicted she would. He turned back to Didier. 'Can we see the case documents from your station archive?'

'I would gladly provide you with this information' Didier intoned. 'However, as I am no longer an employee, that would be easier said than done.'

'Damn.'

'But fear not' Didier chimed in. 'I have a friend who still works there. He told me the alarm codes for the doors. I can get in; I just can't get spotted.'

'Unless I go in?' James offered. 'You still have your uniform?'

Didier frowned at the thought. 'You are suggesting an illegal break and enter of a police station? What if you were caught?'

James scoffed. 'Just tell me where the British Embassy is and I'll make sure I get out of the building. Once I'm in the embassy the French have no jurisdiction.'

'It's very risky' Didier predicted. 'But I appreciate your spirit. This whole town thinks I have gone mad. They consider me a raging lunatic. But you want to solve this case too. We should go to my apartment and you can change into my uniform. We appear to be roughly the same size and build.'

'What do you think about this, Tiffanny?' James asked.

'I think we have no other choice' the Frenchwoman replied tacitly. They clambered back into the Alfa and Didier directed them through cross-town traffic to a modest bed-sit near St Paul's church. Inside, the Frenchman showered, shaved and changed into fresh casuals. He took on the appearance of a respectable member of society once again.

Darkness encroached and the temperature dropped to a biting sub-zero chill. Didier cooked a hearty meal for the three of them. Aside from cultural differences in the décor and architecture, Didier's house resembled James' place on Albion Place in one fundamental way – both had once contained the signs of a female inhabitant; the lingering scents of perfume and shampoo, clothes strewn on the floor in a prior heated moment of passion, a magazine about the life of celebrities on the kitchen table.

Now all of that was ancient history. James immediately felt a bond towards this French policeman-cum-roustabout, for they had both lost their wives. The framed photographs on the mantelpiece confirmed that Didier had also lost a daughter in the process, making his situation a great deal more upsetting.

After the meal James changed into Didier's old police uniform. Didier gave him the codes to the various doors in the building, and also provided a set of blueprints for the layout of the premises. The archive room was a small cubbyhole located in the upper east corner of the third floor. Didier debriefed James on police etiquette, told him to keep his head down and be in and out as quick as possible. James hoped his basic French vocabulary and conversational acumen would be enough to blag his way through any unavoidable interaction with the staff inside the police station.

They would have to wait until late evening when the night shifts kicked in and the station was manned by a skeleton workforce. They watched old French movies with subtitles and drank wine until midnight. Then they were ready for a most dangerous mission.

Chapter Twenty Seven

Saturday 26th February. 12:15 a.m.

The Commissariat de Lyon was located ten miles north of downtown, in the fourth arrondissement. It was the centrepiece of Rue de la Terrasse, a leafy suburb on the edge of the city, offset from a wide thoroughfare that connected it to the Boulevard de la Croix Rousse. The building itself was a boxy peach-stained concrete structure that stretched the length of two blocks. Its aesthetics were totally unpleasing, although localised municipalities were rarely splendorous. The streets were deserted through the influx of the nocturnal solstice. They parked the Alfa on the opposite side of the road, across the boulevard, and disembarked.

Didier's uniform was stiff with starch, and James wriggled inside of it. It had been pressed with steam from an iron two years ago and left hanging in a cupboard ever since. It was a different shade of blue to that which the Paris officers had worn. It made him feel like a figure of high society, like his Pierre Cardin suits used to do when he practised law. A good suit or uniform conveys a shroud of power upon the wearer; an instant confidence booster. The shirt collar was perhaps half an inch too tight, pinching at his neck like a small piranha. The hem of the trousers would have benefited from being let down an inch or two, but there was no time to be fashionable. He just had to look the part. He would endeavour to be in and out in five minutes tops. He wore his own tanned loafers.

271

They were parked in the Alfa across the street. Didier described the layout of the interior in great detail, mapping out mental blueprints for James to memorise. After he finished for the first time he made James reiterate it back to him. He made a few mistakes, so Didier recited his descriptions once more.

Tiffanny waited patiently whilst they went back over it again and again until James had memorised the layout. Then he crossed the street and found the side entrance; the one for employees, not perpetrators. The code for the front door was 438510, which he punched into a panel encased in the stone façade. A small red LED blinked and turned green. He pushed the heavy door ajar and warily stepped inside.

As soon as he had crossed the threshold a pang of fear pierced him like a lance blade. *What if I am caught?! I'd be stuck inside, and the embassy could do nothing. It would be outside of their jurisdiction.* He let the door click shut behind him, sealing him inside the tomb of the law. He found himself inside a dimly lit hallway.

As he eyes panned his surroundings he heard Didier's account of the ground floor pulsing through his mind, and he verbally checked off each feature as he heard it. *Straight in front of you there should be a flight of stairs. To their right there will be an elevator. To your immediate right is a set of double doors that lead into the post room. Diagonally to the right, between the post room and the elevator, is a single door with an opaque window; this takes you to a locker room. Check.*

James flanked the left wall and listened for signs of life. The lights inside the post room were switched off. He walked over to the double doors and peered in through the frame. He made out franking machines and bench boards containing logbooks and delivery notes. He saw large stacks of paper, envelopes, staplers, hole punchers, staple removers, plastic sleeves, binders and boxes of pens and pencils; the bureaucracy of police work laid bare. Endless reports had to be filed with the courts and the councils, letters sent out to the public, and everything had to be meticulously logged.

He dismissed the elevator and headed for the staircase; he figured an incident inside a metal box would immediately seal his fate, whereas an open stairway gave him the option of running; a slightly lesser of two evils.

He slipped up the staircase, his ears pricked to detect the sounds of others. Again he allowed Didier to direct him from the inner recesses of his subconscious. *There are two flights of six stairs. At their apex you will be on the first floor. You will see an alarm panel on the wall directly in front of you. To your left is a door that leads into the cell block. Further left, parallel to your position, are a set of toilets. You need to continue around to your right and mount the next staircase to the second floor.*

James mounted the staircase and rounded the corner just as an officer was preparing to descend. They slammed into each other awkwardly and the officer winced. He had been holding a scolding cup of vending machine coffee, most of which ended up all over James upon impact, covering Didier's uniform. He was bent double. James went to his aid.

'Je suis très désolé' he muttered awkwardly. *I am very sorry.* This was the type of encounter he had hoped to avoid. He had blundered into it; it could have been avoided. Now he was forced to interact. The more he said the deeper he could end up digging his own grave. The officer initially blanched but then evaluated the situation without losing his cool.

He picked up the papers he had dropped and threw the now empty Styrofoam cup into a trash receptacle behind him. He muttered something in staccato French which James failed to grasp in the intensity of the situation.

James thought about the science of conversation. If two people are making small talk in the same tongue, then often if one mishears what the other said he lacks the patience to get clarification. Instead he will respond with either a question or a statement on the next topic, and the conversation continues unbroken. James hoped that what the officer had asked him did not warrant an urgent response.

He knew it had been a question because of the rising intonation towards the end of the sentence. Of course it could have been a sarcastic or rhetorical question, like *What the hell are you doing?!* James dived past his miscomprehension and responded by asking the officer if he could buy him another cup of coffee to make amends.

The officer smiled and shook his head emphatically. Then he made a remark and James picked out the words he recognised, translating them as *nothing, this, drink* and *shit.* He took the officer's response to be something like, *It's nothing, this coffee is like drinking shit anyway!* It had come from a vending machine after all. Then the officer bade him a good evening and took off down the stairs. James sighed in relief. He had to wipe a small fountain of sweat beads from his brow. His heart was pounding like a jackhammer. He cursed himself for being so lackadaisical.

As the officer's voice trailed out of his vocal boundary Didier's returned to the forefront of his inner recesses. James regained his composure and soldiered on to the third floor. The staircase's apex brought him to an identically bland corridor which dead-ended a hundred metres to the right by a seemingly abandoned swivel chair and an elevator. James dismissed it and instead looked to the left.

Again, Didier provided the running commentary as the soundtrack to his escapade. *To your left there is a single brown door. It leads to the main office. You will need to enter and without drawing attention to yourself walk the full diameter of the room and exit through the adjacent door. Be as casual as you possibly can.*

James paused to compose himself. Out of habit he adjusted Didier's cap on his head and then he opened the door with the confidence and natural inclination of a man who did not expect it to be locked; a man who entered through that door at that particular time on a frequent shift rotation, a man who knew the employees inside the room by first name, a man who walked with a purpose and who knew his reason for entering the room and that it was not the end of his journey but a stopgap.

The room was a cauldron of everyday smells; stale eau de toilette, the lingering aroma of coffee, sandalwood varnish and the faint waft of incense. Shabby would have passed for a generic description of the place. Spatial management had not been considered. Desks and paperwork were haphazardly strewn in whatever inch of space was available. Walls and notice boards were littered with wanted posters and police psychology. A promotional recruitment poster was splashed with the strapline *Etez-vous le flic gentil ou le flic mauvais?* James appreciated the humour and acknowledged it silently. It translated as: *Are you the good cop or the bad cop?*

Skeleton staff was no misconception; James pinpointed two officers at opposing sides of the room and acknowledged both with the obligatory custom they deserved. 'Bonne soire.' *Good evening.* They paid him only a moment of scrutiny before returning to their duties. One punched furiously on a desktop keyboard, the other photocopied documents from ring binders.

James walked straight through and paused at the door to the next room. He waited for any sign of resistance from the officers behind him. He heard nothing except the furious clicking of fingers on keys and the churning audacity from the photocopier.

Didier's dictation ebbed back into his mind. *Go through and head left. Head down the small staircase and take the third door on your right.* James obeyed his mind's eye and found the third door on the right after descending the steps. The corridor was dark and seemingly shut off at this hour. A chill hung in the air. Clearly the station ran on stretched resources during the night.

He slipped on a pair of latex gloves and punched in 342006 on the wall panel. Then he opened the door and flicked on the light. It took a few seconds to trigger the halogen beam above his head, but when it did it illuminated what James could immediately deduce was the archive room.

The police had a habit of being straightforward – simple but thorough procedures were applied to all processes. James started opening filing cabinets and the alphabetised files made for a pleasant discovery. It did not take him long to find Pierre Chartier's file. It was in a place it was expected to be – placed neatly in the centre of the C's.

It was a large file, but then that was to be expected too. Several years of investigative work had been applied and everything was meticulously catalogued and reproduced for the paper file. The A4 binder was heavy and some of the sheets were tattered and straying out of their original positions, the result of everyday wear and tear.

He wondered how many people had studied the file. Most of Didier's co-workers seemed to think of him as a crackpot. Perhaps it was he alone who had turned the papers into crisp parchment – by reading the same information over and over again, hoping for new answers to reveal themselves from old facts.

James figured that the easy part was done. He had entered, successfully maintained his disguise and acquired the target item. But now he had to leave with it; he had to walk out of the police station with a case file under his arm like it was the most natural thing in the world. The officers would track his movements and put the obvious together; he had gone down to the archives, and now he was leaving with a file from said place.

Didier had confirmed that it was not standard practice to just leave with files. They had to be signed for and marked in a log book. There were issues of confidentiality and professional embarrassment to consider. Taking the files without authorisation would be a serious breach of privacy laws. It would land James in a whole heap of trouble. It was also apparent that the Chartier file would spark particular scrutiny from the officers, considering it cost Didier his job and ultimately his life. It was hot property.

In the silence of the archive room during the early hours of the morning, James carefully removed the documents from the binder, lifting the hole-punched sheets out of the clasp without damaging them. It was a time consuming task with the latex gloves on, limiting his sense of touch and making his nimble fingers clumsy. He attempted to reshuffle the papers to keep them in a neat pile.

He took a jiffy bag provided by Didier out of the jacket pocket of his uniform, which was already franked up and marked with a would-be client's address. He unfolded the jiffy bag and carefully placed the papers inside. He sealed up the package and placed the empty binder back inside the filing cabinet. He flicked off the light and closed the door.

He held the package under his arm with one hand to again convey the image of a casual, recurring act, and slipped back up the staircase. He walked back into the office and acknowledged the same two officers who had now changed positions. The keyboard batterer was in the kitchen area brewing a fresh pot of coffee; the copy guy was back in his desk speaking on the telephone. The copy guy waved him away with a hand gesture and sputtered machinegun French over the wire. The keyboard batterer poured boiling water into a mug and whistled Edith Piaf's *Je ne regrette rien.*

James ignored the men and walked steadily towards the door that would take him back into the corridor where three flights of stairs would take him down to his extraction point. 'Oi! Qu-est que c'est mon ami, eh?!' *Hey, what is that you have there, my friend?*

James winced before he composed himself and turned around. Staying in character, he walked up to the kitchen area to address the keyboard batterer. He took a swig of fresh coffee and gesticulated with the mug in the general direction of the package under James' arm.

'Je peux t'expliquer' he began. *I can explain.* James explained in French that the package was a gift he had wrapped for his wife for their anniversary; he had left it in the archive room the previous day by mistake and had gone to retrieve it. He had intended to post them to her work address, which he had written on a jiffy bag.

The keyboard batterer glared at the package under James' arm for a few moments. James hoped he would be able to appeal to the fellow man's sense of romance in buying his woman a nice gift for a special occasion. Eventually the man cracked and beamed in approval. He blurted something which James failed to catch; no doubt some form of bravado or chauvinism, judging from the childlike grin on the officer's lineaments.

James chortled a fake laugh in response and bade his farewell. For added effect he yawned and looked at his watch before leaving the office. He figured that if he appeared not to be in a hurry, he would not arouse suspicion.

Once the door had clicked shut he bolted down the stairs flight by flight and made his way back to the exit. He ran the risk of running into someone again by being so boisterous, however he encountered nobody until he emerged on the street and handed the package to Didier whilst Tiffanny gave him a victorious hug.

'Mon Dieu, you have it!' Didier remarked.

'You look good in a uniform' the Frenchwoman chided.

'Thanks to the both of you' James confirmed wearily. 'Now can we make like the wind before they cotton on to what I just did?!' They hurried along the Rue de la Terrasse and clambered back inside the Alfa. Didier navigated them back towards his apartment.

It was approaching two a.m. and yet they could not entertain the prospect of sleep. James and the Frenchwoman were enthralled by the potential information in the file. Didier had of course seen it before; he had put it all together over years of solid police work. But the fact that two new pairs of eyes would be glossing over the material gave him a new sense of hope. He brewed some coffee and they went to work.

Out on the street a cell phone was vibrating until the call was successfully placed.

'What's going on?'

'They drove to a police station. The male target was dressed in a police uniform. The female and the driver stayed in the car. The target came out about half an hour later carrying a package. Then they drove back to the home of the other man. There's a light on, so they're not sleeping.'

'You will need to find out what was in the package.'

'How do you propose I do that?'

'You'll have to work that out for yourself. You're the field operative. I'm not there. Just get it done, and stay on them. They're obviously working on something. There must be important findings to be had in seizing that package. Keep me posted, Chaplin.'

'Sir.'

*

Unknown Location. 3:05 a.m.

The man entered the cave under the cover of darkness. He was alone yet he walked with the hurried anxiety of an accidental hero; a leader who had been bestowed with a responsibility undesired. A responsibility undesired, but an inevitable responsibility nonetheless. His words. His text. His research, his imagination, his bold fortitude.

He munched on an apple as he clambered into the cave train and habitually tapped the button underneath the seat with his foot. The electricity whirred and burst into life. He rested his arms on the metal girders that were painted yellow decades ago to accommodate the birth of the tourist trade after the collapse of Yugoslavia and the new freedom the territory had laid testament to. He was known to his associates simply as Guignol.

The cave train plummeted on its track, sweeping and gesticulating around the curves of the cave, taking him past scores of calcite formations, stalactites and stalagmites and deeper into the core. The speleothems were breathtakingly beautiful but the man dismissed them as inconsequential white noise in the background of his world. He bit through the apple with haste, devouring the fleshy outer layer until he reached the core. Somewhere a clock was ticking; ticking down to a full-circle conclusion. He disembarked at the end of his journey fifteen minutes later and entered the facility.

The cartons of stock were beginning to stack up; cardboard boxes stamped only with a mysterious logo; a crab being pierced by a blade. As the man lifted up one of the boxes his shirt sleeve slid partway up his arm, revealing a tanned brown under-layer of skin and a clump of black hairs protruding outwards, and he gave an approving nod to nobody in particular.

A lone beam from the lantern above his head was suddenly struck by a straying bat, causing the man to jump in shock. As he did the light hit his arm and showcased the tattoo inked onto his forearm just below the funny bone; the tattoo matched the logo on the carton to the nth degree; a crab pierced by a sword.

He swallowed the pips and then started in on the core itself. Once he had finished eating the apple all that remained of it was the stalk. He caressed his tattoo with an inkling of affection and smiled to himself.

Chapter Twenty Eight

Saturday. 8:40 a.m.

After bunking down for the few hours that could be afforded, they used Didier's apartment on Rue Charles de Gaulle as a base of operations. The file on Pierre Chartier contained a hefty bundle of paperwork, bound, paginated and indexed for easier consumption. A4 dividers categorised the sections.

The initial report of Chartier's disappearance had been submitted by his estranged sister Laure, Didier explained, whom he had stumbled upon by chance when he found a letter to her from her brother amongst his effects. She had since started a new life in Papua New Guinea. The first section of the report contained her address and contact details; information that was now defunct and useless. It stated her relationship to the missing person – sibling. Pierre had no nicknames or shortened versions of his name that other people may have known him by.

In the next section of the report Laure had described Pierre's physical appearance at the time of his disappearance. Laure had estimated his height to have been one hundred and sixty five centimetres, and his weight to have been a hundred and forty five pounds. Therefore he had to have been a slight man. The former would have been unlikely to have changed, assuming of course that Chartier was still alive. For the latter anything was possible depending on diet, exercise, genetics and again whether or not he was still a living breathing person. Chartier had short wiry black hair and brown eyes. According to his sister, who could be considered an expert on the subject, he had no distinguishing marks or features such as tattoos, scars, afflictions or wounds.

Chartier had been out on his motorbike on the day that he was last seen, and the report detailed Laure's recollection of him wearing black motorbike leathers and a black helmet with a white insignia on the side, although she was not au fait with the branding of motorcycle paraphernalia and therefore could not remember the company name.

No items of jewellery or other accessories were referred to in the report. The motorbike itself was found parked outside the home that had now been demolished; a red and white Kawasaki Z1000 which boasted a 1043cc engine, the same size as Tiffanny's Renault, and produced 136 break horse power. It weighed 218 kilograms and a full tank could accommodate 15 litres of petrol. It had a street value of eight thousand Euros. It was a beast, and an expensive beast to boot.

It had been found in seemingly innocent circumstances, parked inside Chartier's garage with half a tank of fuel contained therein, and there was no evidence of vandalism or any other damage. It had not been involved in a road traffic accident, and it had not been abandoned. And yet its rider had vanished, in clothes that were intended for the machine.

The report contained a copy of the bike's licence plate number and Chartier's insurance documents, which were all in order and above board at the time he went missing, but which had now expired. Laure had explained that he was an avid motorbike enthusiast and had spent a long hot summer eight years ago travelling around India on his beloved Kawasaki. There were photographs from his expedition, which included Delhi, Bangalore, Chennai, Bhopal, Calcutta and Mumbai.

Laure's report then detailed that at approximately 3:30pm on Tuesday 23rd May 2005 Pierre and his sister were dining at the Café Chez Thibault opposite the painted mural on the façade of the Conseil Général building. He explained that he was travelling to Paris the next day on urgent business. What urgent business a pharmacologist could have, Laure did not know. But she did not press the issue; they were not terribly close, and

Pierre's business was his own. They dabbled in small talk for an hour or two, Laure recalled, then Chartier kissed his sister on the cheek, paid the bill and left. He was never seen again.

It was a mysterious affair, and the only aspect that stood out on her report was that she remembered seeing a fire in her brother's eyes that she had never seen before. She guessed that his urgent business was something he had been proud of; perhaps it was a scientific breakthrough, a great achievement. He was agitated and had itchy feet. He seemed desperate to get to Paris. But again, Laure had not coerced her brother into elaborating, for as long as he was safe and happy she cared not for the finer facets of his life.

The next section of the report was a chronology of events in the twenty four hours leading up to Chartier's eventual departure. Laure had paid him a special visit and had been staying with him for a few days. She was taking a career break and had managed to find a job teaching English to children in an impoverished province of Papua New Guinea. She was going out on a one year contract but would possibly be disappearing into the wilderness.

The previous twenty-four hours had been uneventful. Laure had come to tie up some loose ends before her expedition; their father Francoise Chartier had recently passed away and they were the joint administrators of his estate. Francoise had not left them a great deal of assets; a modest duplex in downtown Lyon, and some government bonds that had yielded in the dot.com boom five years prior.

Chartier had confirmed that he was happy for Laure to go ahead and administer the estate just as she had outlined to her brother. His business in Paris could not be interrupted, so it was up to Laure to manage the transactions and transfers of legal ownership.

Mundane details about Pierre's work, sleep, exercise and eating patterns were added to the report, although Laure herself was the first to express her doubt as to the integrity of this information, as her brother lived alone and his then current habits were largely unknown to her. The information was intended to assist the police investigators eliminate risk factors for possible abductions. But this did not feel like an abduction – first of all there was no ransom demanded. Pierre had simply blended into the landscape.

The next section of the report contained a medical history for Pierre Chartier from his general practitioner. There was a comprehensive list of all his past medications, conditions and any psychological issues, the latter of which there were none. Pierre Chartier had no special needs. The worst case on the medical chronology was a bout of severe pharyngitis in 2001, a throat condition which Laure recalled he had made a full recovery from after taking a course of antibiotics. Certainly nothing as terminal or malevolent as cancer, Chartier's chosen specialist subject for his book which had vanished from the Bibliothèque Nationale in Paris.

Attached to the report was an extended history of Chartier's personality. Laure had set out in as much detail as she could her brother's employment problems, bad habits and personal relationships. He had partaken in the odd joint at college just like the next person, but considered himself a social smoker only, enjoying the water pipe which he passed between his friends on long hot summer days in the privacy of his garden.

He'd had a total of five girlfriends, in relationships that ranged from one month to three years, the latter of which had been the most serious, a seemingly committed monogamous affair that was building up to wedding chimes but which was suddenly cut short a year before his disappearance by reasons unknown to Laure. He had remained single ever since.

He had graduated from the Université Claude Bernard with a first in Chemistry. He had practiced the art of pharmacology for three years before quitting his job to become a full-time writer. Laure recalled her surprise at the time of this revelation. She felt that he was too young and too talented to be throwing in the towel at that pivotal point in his career. He had a superior mind and would have gone far. But he seemed adamant on finishing his first novel, which he would only accomplish once his business in Paris was complete, Laure recollected.

There was another pharmacologist involved, a girl from Strasbourg, but Laure could not remember her name. Laure suggested that she was courting her brother and that they were shacking up together, but she had never been able to confirm her suspicions.

What concluded in the file were Didier's own investigations. He had started with the obligatory door-to-door missing posters, which had yielded no joy. He had then relentlessly interviewed every citizen of Lyon within a reasonable proximity of Pierre Chartier's inner circles. Didier had started out by interviewing his neighbours. He had sat down with Laure herself and she had produced a personal statement which did little more than cover already annexed territory.

Pierre's mother was still alive; a ninety-two year old frail lady withering away in a suburban retirement home. There were no other family members to speak of. Didier had interviewed his work colleagues, who all reported the same findings; Chartier was a man of great intelligence worthy of the Nobel Peace Prize. He adored his work and it was as much of a shock to them as it was to Laure when he had chosen to give it up in the name of penning his manuscript. They had been even more astonished at his apparent disappearance. They ruled out suicide as Chartier wasn't the sort – his business in Paris seemed so pivotal and fundamental that he would have taken any step necessary to see out its conclusion.

What was remarkable, James decided, was that upon hearing of the proposed construction works to the site of Chartier's residence, which included demolishing the properties and rebuilding new luxury apartments, Didier had campaigned vigorously to put a dampener on those proceedings. It was a crime scene, he had protested.

It had been a crime scene until the Department had thrown the case on the unsolved heap, abandoning it like an unwanted child on Lyon's doorstep. Didier's obstruction was short-lived. His wife was a municipal administrator for the Ministry for the Environment. The houses were being torn down due to the area containing remnants of dust from a long forgotten industrial effort, which was causing problems such as asbestosis.

The properties were discovered to be a health risk and were to be pulled down so that the problem could be alleviated and the neighbourhood cleaned up. It was the ultimate rift to tear apart man and wife. Although not explicitly stated in black and white, James read through the political and domestic undertones and concluded for himself that this was the final straw which must have pushed Didier's family away from him.

Judging from Didier's continued notes, he had hit rock bottom after all leads had dead-ended or dried up, and he had then engaged in a random interrogation of the whole city, desperate for any scent of the man that was Pierre Chartier. Local newsagents, Pierre's general practitioner, friends, friends of friends, the local punters and proprietors of various eateries known to have seen Chartier's custom at some point in the not-too-distant past, the lecturers at his university and other alumni, he'd even stopped joggers passing him by and interrogated them. There were personal statements from one hundred and seventy eight people filed. James found it hard to fathom Didier's sheer tenacity and his attention to detail; his will not to give up should have rewarded him with some result. It had not.

And then there were the silk weavers, who were gifted a whole section to themselves in the report. Chartier came from a long line of them, a lineage that stretched back towards the Middle Ages. James read the history lesson with enthrallment. In 1466 King Louis decided to create a factory where silk and gold could be manufactured on a grand scale. Before then, France would have to import the fabrics from Italy, and this was proving to be economically unsound. But it never got off the ground. Later, in 1515, Francis I placed an embargo on foreign silk and decreed that foreign silk weavers settling in Lyon would be exempt from paying taxes. The new king had put out all the stops to maintain a monopoly over the silk trade.

By 1554 there were 12,000 silk weavers in Lyon, so many that their very own Trade Union was established. But France's silk was considered inferior to Italian silk. So in 1606 Claude Dangon perfected a brand new loom which would rival the Italian production process. Pierre's ancestors were the Canuts, a thoroughbred of silk weaving genius. They peaked throughout the eighteenth century until the French Revolution saw their pivotal decline. Six thousand of Chartier's forefathers campaigned for a minimum wage in 1831. They brandished black flags and uttered their motto: *vivre en travaillant ou mourrir en combatant – we'll earn a living or fight to the death.*

In 1855 a silkworm infestation practically wiped out the industry, destroying looms left right and centre. It meant that the silk had to be imported again, despite Louis Pasteur's best efforts to preserve the integrity of Lyon silk. In 1930 a new printing technique called *à la Lyonnaise* and silkscreen printing replaced block printing. In 2010 looms were computerised and air-jet run. Only 350 tonnes of silk were still produced in Lyon. A niche group of historical preservers keep the sentiments of the Canuts alive by producing fine fabrics for Haute Couture designers.

The history lesson on the silk weavers concluded the report. Tiffany had been hunched over James' shoulder for the duration. James turned the pages back to the beginning and placed the binder down on Didier's coffee table.

'It makes for interesting reading, non?' Didier remarked.

'Interesting is definitely true' James evaluated. 'But it doesn't really bring us any closer to unravelling Chartier's mystique. He could be alive, or dead, here, or there. Is this everything we have?'

'There's just one more thing' Didier said. He walked through the foyer of his den and James heard a rustling sound. The Frenchman returned with a slip of paper. 'I found this too, but I could never make any sense of it. It looks like some kind of scientific diagram.'

Tiffany snatched it out of Didier's hand before James had chance to process what he had seen. She placed the paper on the coffee table for all of them to see. It was a diagram:

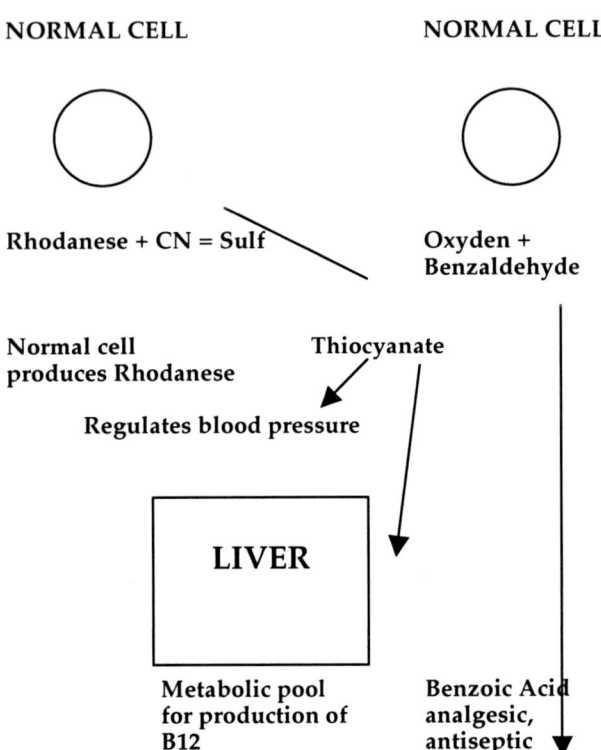

NORMAL CELL   NORMAL CELL

Rhodanese + CN = Sulf   Oxyden +
                               Benzaldehyde

Normal cell   Thiocyanate
produces Rhodanese

      Regulates blood pressure

LIVER

Metabolic pool   Benzoic Acid
for production of   analgesic,
B12   antiseptic

'Where did you find this?' Tiffanny gasped in awe. James revelled in seeing another piece of the puzzle before his very eyes. But James was more disturbed by another thought; an inkling nagging away at the far recesses of his memory, a smidgen of familiarity.

'It was mailed to me' Didier remarked wanly.

'By whom?' James enquired.

'Je ne sais pas. *I don't know.* I could not trace it. I just found it on my doormat about three months into the investigation. Hand delivered, no post mark.'

'Jesus' Tiffanny remarked. 'Mon Dieu'.

'Why didn't you file it with the rest of the report?' James asked.

'Well to be honest I really don't know' the Frenchman declared. 'I just had a feeling that it would be important somehow, and I was failing to catch the scent of any leads, so I kept it for myself as a personal trophy, so that the investigation wouldn't be a total dead loss. You know what it is?'

Tiffanny and James stole themselves a curious glance at each other. Didier spotted the gesture. 'Eh? Come on, out with it. What is it? S'il vous plait?'

James retrieved the piece of paper from the Bibliotheque Nationale which he had stowed away in the inside pocket of his parka and placed it on the coffee table next to the one Didier had just shown them. James glanced at Tiffanny and saw her brain working overtime. She reached forward and reordered the sheets.

'Are we looking at the complete diagram now, Tiff?' James asked.

The Frenchwoman shook her head despondently. 'There's one more piece of this puzzle missing.'

'Can you explain what this new section means?' James posed the question.

Tiffanny studied the diagram for some time before elaborating. As she spoke she let out a sigh that epitomised her sombre mood. 'This doesn't make sense.'

'Really?' James made no effort to hide his astonishment. 'The first part of the diagram made perfect sense to you. And now you're saying that you don't understand this?'

Tiffanny shook her head nonchalantly. 'That's not what I meant. I mean literally, yes, it does make sense, I understand it. But that's just the thing; the whole situation doesn't make sense. I have seen this diagram before a million times. It is not new information; it has been common knowledge for one hundred and eighty years.'

James pondered the implication. As he did the nagging sensation of familiarity came back to haunt him. What was it he had seen in the missing persons report that he thought he had seen before? 'So what you're saying Tiff is that there's no new science in this section of the diagram to explain?'

Again, Tiffanny wagged her head sideways. 'No, what I explained to you before was effectively the whole diagram, the whole process. What I was expecting to see was something more; a greater explanation.'

James processed the revelation. 'Can you explain again how the process works, for Didier's benefit and for mine?' Didier grunted his appreciation in advance.

Tiffanny explained again about the nitrilosides Krebs discovered in the seeds of apricots and other fruits, about the discovery of B17 by two French scientists in 1830. She demonstrated how amygdalin can be split down by a specific enzyme into hydrogen cyanide, benzaldehyde and glucose. Tiffanny went on to inform Didier that when a cell is still in its embryonic state, before the baby is born, it acts in a way like a cancerous cell; it mutates in order for the baby to grow and develop.

That it is called a trophoblast cell, but after the fifty-sixth day of pregnancy the baby's new pancreas starts to produce an enzyme called chymotryspin which kills off the trophoblast cell as it is no longer needed. The trophoblast cell is formed in a chain reaction by another cell, referred to as a total life cell. When the total life cell comes into contact with oestrogen it creates the trophoblast, and depending on the circumstances that is either wonderful or terrible because it means either pregnancy or cancer for a woman, or in the case of a man, only cancer.

Tiffany explained that cancer occurs because the trophoblast cell is actually trying to do good. It's trying to help growth, but sometimes it carries on even when maximum growth has been achieved. It believes it is going good, but actually too much growth then causes tumours. B17 becomes a toxic substance to the trophoblast. Hydrogen cyanide and benzaldehyde are then manufactured by beta-glucosidase and together poison the trophoblast cell, thereby killing it. She informed him that healthy cells contain another enzyme, rhodanese, which acts as a controlling agent and lives inside the body in inverse proportions to beta-glucosidase. Therefore it does not exist at the site of cancerous cells. Rhodanese detoxifies the cyanide and oxidises the benzaldehyde. B17 poisons cancerous cells with its toxic compound, but when it comes into contact with healthy cells it detoxifies so that those cells are unaffected.

For Didier, and for James, both of whom were not scientifically trained nor gifted, the explanation was fascinating, even for James who had heard it once already, and especially for Didier, who was hearing it for the first time. The Frenchman broke the silence that had ensued after Tiffany's science lecture had concluded. 'This is turning out to be something quite more than a missing persons case.'

James built on Didier's deductions. 'Chartier's book must have exposed all of this in glorious Technicolor. He must have become a target for some high maintenance pharmaceutical giant who foresaw this as their inevitable downfall. Who would need a veritable smorgasbord of drugs to fight cancer if a simple natural remedy was out there, a vitamin found in abundance in certain fruits? The ultimate panacea. Pierre's cause was a cause for concern to these people.'

Tiffany and Didier acknowledged their agreement. And then James' cognition struck gold. 'Of course!'

The Frenchwoman caught James' mental revelation with a raised expression of her brow. 'What is it?'

'Didier, hand me that report again would you?' Didier duly complied, reaching over the coffee table.

291

'What is it, James?' Tiffanny pressed for the second time. James flicked to the beginning and found Laure's description of Chartier's last known twenty-four hours on the planet. He removed the photograph of the missing author dressed head to toe in black motorcycle leathers, grinning at the camera lens. 'I know why you're smiling!' James remarked. 'It's because you're always one step ahead of us!'

Didier scorned. 'James, tell us what you're seeing.'

'I've seen this picture before.'

'Are you sure?' Tiffanny asked. 'He loved his motorbike. He was dressed like that in many photographs.'

'Yes, you're right, he was. But this is a very striking pose. The position of his body, in this photo, I recognise. I have seen this exact same picture replicated, but not in a photograph.'

Tiffanny frowned. 'Then where have you seen it?'

'On the mural. The painted wall in downtown Lyon.'

'So let's go there' Didier exclaimed. 'We can pick up a petit-dejeuner on the way.'

It wasn't that they did not believe James, but they had to see it for themselves. So, armed with a copy of the photograph taken from Didier's report, the threesome took a ride in the Alfa Romeo. The late morning sun was watery in the pale cyan sky. As they zipped through the lazy streets back towards the centre of downtown, guarded from above by the Fourvière basilica, its twin minarets shunting into the clouds, James knew deep down in his heart of hearts that they would be leaving the city and heading south to the Mediterranean coastline.

They returned to the Conseil Général building and James took the photograph of Pierre Chartier out of his pocket. He quickly found the section of the mural that displayed the same image. There was no mistaking it. Black motorcycle leathers, the same position of the body, same demeanour. It was a self-portrait, and it was uncanny. Tiffanny and Didier simply nodded their approval. And then James pointed his finger to the text above the image; the three words written on the relief above the painted man's head.

'I guess we know where we have to go next' Tiffanny remarked sardonically.

'You mean, where Pierre Chartier can no doubt be found?!' Didier added.

'Absolutely' James concluded. Breakfast had been taken over by events. He pointed at the three words etched onto the façade. 'We're getting on the first bus to Aix en Provence.'

Chapter Twenty Nine

10:03 a.m. Brno, Czech Republic

The house in which she found herself residing under duress was a wooden clapboard structure detached from its neighbours and perched on a plot of prime suburban grassland. At the cornerstone of urban bohemia, it was the product of a fruitful alliance between artistic vision and inspired functionality. It was entered at the rear side from the main thoroughfare, through the garage and into the small patio courtyard, which then led inside the kitchen.

The décor inside was distinctly Moravian – understated chic. The kitchen was finished in walnut and as you progressed east through the porch and into the living and sleeping quarters the veneer became mahogany and maple, a stark dark contrast. It was a one-storey bungalow. No stairs. It opened out at the front into a spectacular garden, where wild berries grew on the trees; loganberry, gooseberry and whitecurrant.

The west bedroom was where Radka had been holed up for six days. She had been well looked after for a captive. She had enjoyed the best gastronomy, presumably cooked by Collins himself. He had not laid a finger on her. Her bed was springy and firm. No torture, only treats. It made her feel more perturbed than if she had been starved and beaten. For that latter scenario carried with it a well-established modus operandi – either Collins in that scenario was a woman-hater, a jealous ex-lover or otherwise a general psychopath. But this princess treatment and a total lack of explanations on Collins' part for her comfortable incarceration drove her to despair.

Collins was a known entrepreneur with many links to the national community, so any malevolence on his part would be ill-conceived and not in keeping with his public image. He appeared smug and satisfied during their brief exchanges, and she'd heard how he played it up when he called James. But Radka sensed that this was a save-face measure. Beneath his façade she sensed a forlorn sentient being struggling with his inclinations.

She was beginning to miss her new life in Prague. She still missed James terribly, although she had started seeing a photographer and their dates were shaping up into something fruitful. She had found work in a small research laboratory, and she had written a paper on the media's influence on global panic at a pandemic's fever pitch. She had referred to foot in mouth disease, avian flu, and the most recent swine flu outbreak in Mexico which was, predictably, short-lived.

The thesis had been published as a serial feature in New Scientist magazine and had earned her instant reputation in the niche field of pharmacological journalism. She was renting a minimalist apartment in the capital's cosmopolitan downtown.

And then in an apparent mugging on a tram by two men who resembled Romany gypsies and brandished shanks, a not uncommon occurrence in Czechia, she had been dumped in a transit van and taken to Casino Collins. There had been very little she could have done. She never saw her two attackers again; they never came to the house or showed up around Collins.

From there on in it had just been the two of them. She had thought of Petr and the build up to something promising, but her frame of reference in her mind's eye kept flitting back to James Loxbridge. She remembered standing in the doorway of their Chester through-terrace, watching the silhouette of his head disappear as the taxi eased down Albion Place and then disappear, out of her life forever.

His last words to her had been the three that are said too much but are not enough. *I love you.* She had repeated the gesture, fully meaning the sentiment behind the phrase. She could not believe that their marriage had disintegrated so quickly. She blamed herself for the most part. She knew that she had pushed it too far. She knew that he hadn't been ready. His career was just getting kick-started, and she was trying to get herself knocked up. She refused to admit to herself that her motivation for trying to become pregnant lay in her fear that if she did not hold on to him he would get bored and disappear from her life forever. As it transpired, that's just how it had panned out, save for the embryo.

She had not seen or been near a computer terminal in all the six days she had been a hostage. She felt herself becoming stir crazy as she stared out the window in her bedroom at the garden and the thoroughfare beyond. Every time the neighbours struck up a greeting outside, or a passer-by's dog yelped, she would run to the window in a vain effort to attract their attention, so that they could contact the police and get her out of there. But it was futile. They were all preoccupied; too caught up in their own business to care about hers. That's how it was in the suburbs – ignorance is bliss. NIMBY – Not In My Back Yard.

James' persistent rejection of her had left her cold and empty. Her friends had told her that her green eyes were without their usual omnipotence. They had faded to a passive grey; the sepia tone of the neutral fence sitter, lacking passion or panache. Life was unfair at times. Their time together had been utter bliss. Her feelings and her love for him had never wavered, yet the burning fire of reciprocity rarely kept the candle lit at both ends.

He had seemingly, to put it bluntly, gone off her. At least that was how she felt. She knew she could be demanding. Their marriage had come about as a result of an argument, which had culminated in a heated bout of lovemaking before James had popped the question. Perhaps he had sealed their fate with that ill-advised sentiment. A marriage should not be borne out of anger.

She also knew that parenthood wasn't a race, although it was beginning to feel like it. With most of Radka's über-catholic friends already married and beginning to sprout offspring, she had felt she was lagging behind. And now she was well aware that whatever Casino Collins was up to, he had dragged her ex-hubbie into it. She preyed to God that he would find and rescue her, especially in light of the cryptic clue she had given him during their last telephone exchange. *Say hi to Charlie for me, if you're downtown.*

She knew that James would remember the Charlie Centrum in Brno's Lišeň district. Once, years ago, they had walked down the main thoroughfare towards the tramvaj and a large terracotta tray full of bulbous plants had suddenly fallen from a third storey balcony and smashed on the sidewalk a mere two feet from them. They had escaped serious injury, possibly even death, by a split second of good fortune.

Yet in spite of that she knew, deep down in her heart of hearts, that she would have to start the ball rolling with divorce papers, and try to move on with her life. Perhaps Petr would give her the closure she needed. A new man, a new start.

Her downward spiral into depression was crudely interrupted when the lock was released on the bedroom door and Casino Collins walked in. He was alone, as per the usual protocol. He was holding a small object in his right hand which dangled loosely about his thigh. He suddenly threw the object at Radka, who instinctively reached out and caught it. It was a blindfold.

For a moment Radka's heart sank, fearing the worst. She had just been musing over Collins' apparent lack of hostility towards her. Had he suddenly become bored and irritable? Was this part of a sordid fetish? Was she about to be abused in what for a woman was undoubtedly the worst possible way.

Collins read her thoughts and interjected. 'Don't worry. We're leaving. I've packed a bag for you, with clean clothes and toiletries. Please put that on. We're to leave immediately.'

Radka gave the entrepreneur a puzzled expression. 'Where are we going?'

Collins shook his head in frustration. 'No questions, just put it on. The time has come and we need to act fast. The plan has changed. I've just been provided with the salient piece of information I asked James to find.'

Radka shoved herself up off the bed and lifted the elasticated strap around her head. It was a tight fit and she had to adjust her hair. There were two crude eyehole slits that had been ripped through the patent material. It probably had been used in the pursuit of sadomasochistic pleasures in its past role. Radka shuddered at the thought of such a thing being on her face. Collins took her gently by the arm and directed her outside. She willed her senses to feel and stay familiar with the terrain. She knew that she was walking through the kitchen because the clink of her heels cascaded on the tile floor.

'If that's the case, why do you still need James? Or me, for that matter? Surely you can let me go, tell James to stop looking for whatever you have just found, and everybody's a winner?' Collins ignored her.

Once they were outside on the patio she was navigated back through the garage and onto the sidewalk by the main thoroughfare out back. 'Car' Collins stated. He then lowered her into the back seat of a vehicle and the door slammed. Radka felt debilitated but strangely at peace with what was happening. She was far from succumbing to Stockholm Syndrome, and yet she sensed that wherever Collins was taking her, it would not result in any harm or pain being sent her way. He had been gentle so far, why would he suddenly turn on her at their new destination? Plus, with this new revelation, her usefulness as an insurance policy had just expired.

Radka counted the seconds once the engine had started and she lurched forward as the gear was thrown into first and the car embraced the power of forward movement. She figured she could find a way to convert the seconds into kilometres later; distance into time, through speed – the three elements that many laws of physics are based on.

They drove for twenty minutes before Collins answered his cell phone. 'Collins. Yes. Ok. Fine. We're coming as quick as we can. Yes. We'll be boarding the plane in a little over an hour. We should be with you in about two. She's fine. I'm sure she will do a great job for us. We're nearly there, Guignol. See you on the other side. Yes. Bye.'

Radka stopped counting as Collins ended his call. He had mentioned boarding a plane, so there was only one place they could be taking her. After another twenty minutes the car stopped and Radka was helped out. She figured they must be at Brno-Tuřany Airport, Brno's only international. Radka was led on a walk that lasted five minutes, presumably to a private hangar. 'Wait here' Collins ordered. He placed a firm hand on her shoulder. Radka shrugged it away. Where on Earth was she going to go with a blindfold on?

After a few more minutes she made out a low humming sound. It grew louder and closer and became a fierce roar. Radka guessed it was a light aircraft coming in to land. It hit the tarmac, looping around the runway and following the full concourse, eventually turning and coming back towards them. It lurched to a stop, its twin propellers cranking out to eventual stillness. Again Radka was shunted forward and gently guided into the aircraft. She was pushed down onto a seat where they waited for several more minutes. She heard Collins panting next to her, the stink of his cologne trapped inside the small cabin.

They waited for what felt like an eternity. 'What's going on?' Radka enquired.

'Refuelling' Collins muttered in a lacklustre fashion. He seemed distracted by his thoughts, if his tone of voice was anything to go by, and that was all Radka, sat in her blindfold, could go by.

Then the engine cranked back up and dials were heard being flicked in the cockpit, separated from the cabin by a mere partition. The craft gathered speed and the thrusters were applied and the bird was airborne. 'Flight time is one hour. Weather conditions are good. We're due to arrive at 12:50 a.m.' Words spoken through the intercom by an unseen pilot.

'Arrive where?' Radka asked.

'You'll find out when you get there' Collins remarked, remaining stoic.

Radka figured she should save her energy. Collins was seriously playing hard to get. The bastard wouldn't give up a pickle. Silence ensued for an hour until the pilot's voice cracked on the intercom again. 'Landing sequence commenced.'

Radka remembered Collins' telephone conversation in the car ride to the airport. He had said that she would do a good job for them. What the hell did that mean? She wondered if that was why they had taken her – for her abilities as a pharmacologist?

Or possibly her other abilities, the abilities few knew about. She was known in the underground school of hackers and crackers as Eva, international information thief and global problem for the authorities and cross-national security. Whatever the case, her abduction was becoming more unorthodox by the minute.

The wheels hit the tarmac with relative fluidity and reverse thrusters immediately slowed the bird down to an eventual halt. They disembarked with Collins' help and Radka stepped out onto gravel that crunched beneath her feet. Her boots had thin heels on them, and occasionally she slipped on the gravel as stones left them lodged in small trenches. Collins had a strong arm that lifted her periodically out of trouble and then she was bundled into another car.

She felt no need to count this time – she had absolutely no clue where she was. A one hour flight from Brno could have landed her in a plethora of countries, depending on the direction they had taken. Due east would have taken them over Slovakia and into Ukraine. West would have landed them in Germany, near the border with Holland and Belgium. North would have taken them over the Baltic Sea and into Southern Sweden, perhaps landing in Malmo or Göteborg. South and they'd now be in Croatia. And they were due directions. Any alternative bearings and she could have been in Slovenia, Poland, Romania, Italy or Hungary.

They drove for half an hour and then Radka was asked for the second time to exit the car. She tried to feel the outside temperature in order to make sense of where they were. If it had been significantly colder then she would have surmised that they had headed north or east, which would have put them in Scandinavia or Ukraine, possibly even Russia. Milder and she would have put money on the journey having taken them on a south or westerly bearing, probably to Italy or Croatia – the Dalmatian

Coast. But she felt no distinct change in the climate. She was left totally clueless.

Collins grabbed her arm for the umpteenth time and they walked for what seemed like miles. Radka became breathless and clammy. They stopped and she heard Collins rustling. 'Water' he uttered, and then she felt the cool touch of plastic at her mouth. She gulped down healthy portions of mineral water and swabbed her lips with her sleeve. 'Thanks' she offered meekly.

She held the bottle outwards and it was snatched from her. They walked on. Radka felt the gradient begin to shift towards a vertical incline. They took sharp steps and her breathing became laboured and raspy. Again she was offered water and again she gulped down as much as she could. 'Mind your head here' Collins warned. Radka ducked instinctively and walked awkwardly, bent forward at the waist, towards an unknown place – her oblivion, or a narrow passageway, she had no idea, but hoped for the latter.

Suddenly she did feel the temperature drop. She shivered and Collins signalled for her to stop. 'You can take off the blindfold now.' Radka prised the mask from her face and staggered back on her haunches as her eyes adjusted to her new surroundings. It was very dark. Collins handed her a waterproof cagoule. She gazed around the narrow entryway. She blinked ferociously. Then she made out shapes, silhouettes, intricate silver shadows that when her eyes focused became intricate patterns.

Radka realised that she was looking at stalagmites and stalactites. There were speleothems everywhere. That's when she realised – she was in a cave. She heard footsteps approach her from behind a large crystallized formation that had no doubt been there for thousands of years, growing at a rate of a centimetre per year. A small, wiry man appeared with a torch. Its beam danced all around them. 'Collins?' he suddenly bellowed, ensuring that he had encountered friend and not foe. He spoke in a musical accent. French, Radka decided.

Collins extended his own hand and they shook. 'Guignol? Nice to meet you.' Radka watched as the other man's shirt sleeve slid up his arm to reveal a tattoo. A crab pierced with a sword.

'I'm glad you're here' the man called Guignol uttered. 'Both of you' he added, turning his attention to Radka. He offered his hand to the Czech, who reluctantly returned the gesture. 'You are our knight in shining armour' he said. 'Or the female equivalent of a knight, if you catch my drift. What would that be? A chevalière? Yes, you are our chevalière!' Then he laughed to himself. Radka was slightly creeped out by the display, but chose to bide her time.

'What is it you want me to do?'

Guignol cleared his throat. 'Help us to save the world. Rid it of an evil. We're almost there, but we need your finishing touch.'

Radka nodded blankly. 'What did you say your name was again?'

The man laughed again. 'Guignol. But that's just a nickname. You may call me Pierre. Pierre Chartier.'

Chapter Thirty

12:50 p.m.

It was a mutual decision to take the bus to Aix en Provence. They figured that if they were still being watched by the mysterious man in the tanned jacket, which they did not doubt for a moment, then a change of transportation would help to throw him off their trail.

They ate croque-monsieurs at a downtown eatery and then Didier drove them back up to his apartment on the outskirts on Soucieu-en-Jarrest in the Alfa Romeo. They left the Italian hatchback there and took a cab back to the bus station in the city centre. The watery sun had been lost in a complex myriad of cumulus cloud cover. It was to be another overcast February day. Some of the cloud may have been ash from a recently erupted Icelandic volcano.

They waited at the bus station for forty minutes. They bought one-way tickets to Aix en Provence for thirty Euros a piece. James' stash from the Charles de Gaulle airport locker was beginning to dwindle. He showed Tiffanny the paltry wad as he took it out of his pocket to count off thirty. The Frenchwoman patted him on the back in reassurance, as if to say *don't worry, we'll manage..* Whilst they waited James allowed Didier to recount the tale of how the missing person case tore his life apart.

As the Frenchman spoke, James had to remind himself that his first encounter with the man in a Lyon bistro had seen him heavily intoxicated. Didier had been cold turkey for at least twenty four hours. Speaking in a state of sobriety, he came across as intelligent and articulate. He, like many other men, had lived for his family. They were his everything. His wife and daughter were the two most important women in his world. As such, he had constantly doted on them.

He had spent his formative years walking the beat after graduating from the Police Academy. He had not been a particularly ambitious man. But one day during a routine call out to a disturbance, what had appeared at first glance to have been a simple burglary had turned into Didier capturing an Algerian man who was on Interpol's most wanted list.

The arrest had landed him an instant promotion to detective. From that moment on, his wife had felt that he changed overnight. His new role demanded longer hours. He began to neglect his domestic responsibilities as he took it upon himself to solve Lyon's most unsolved and inexplicable crimes.

Things went from bad to worse when his beloved teenage daughter started to mix with the wrong crowd. She was thrown out of school for abuse of narcotics. Didier hadn't taken it very well. He'd come home from a shitty day at work and heard the news from his wife Élodie. He'd reacted in a moment by taking the back of his hand to young Monique's face. Élodie had been appalled; she had wept and wailed all night. It was the first time, and consequently the last time, he'd laid a finger on either of them.

Didier explained that he'd always experienced difficult cases, and some went unsolved for so many years that eventually they were written off and shelved in some precinct's archive room where the dust could lay down roots.

But there was something about the Pierre Chartier case that had nagged at him from day one. He couldn't explain why, but he felt somehow connected to it, in a personal way. He felt vibes when he picked up the documents. Every time he had interviewed somebody who might have seen or known Chartier, and every time the interviewee had answered in the negative, Didier felt like he had been stabbed in the heart.

He was desperate to solve the mystery of his disappearance. And ultimately Élodie had concluded that he suddenly loved the job more than her. So they had duly separated and Elodie and taken Monique with her. Apparently Monique was doing better; a reformed character in a new school in Lille, with new friends and a totally fresh outlook.

James explained to Didier his own situation with Radka. They both found solace in each other's company, batting viewpoints off each other in a round of psychiatric tennis. Tiffanny sat away from them as if not to be interested; a look of deep musing on her lineaments. But it was of course a charade. She was soaking up every word as a plant takes in water via osmosis.

She eventually tired of the act and spoke up. 'I hate to interrupt your premature midlife crises, but we are about to catch a bus to Aix en Provence with no idea as to what we will do or where we will go when we arrive. How are we to find one man in a city of thousands?'

Didier grinned. 'The lady is right, of course. We detract from the task at hand. How the hell do we find Chartier?'

James pondered. 'I don't think it will be as difficult as we think.'

Tiffanny frowned. 'What makes you say that?'

'Well, if you leave such an obvious clue as the photograph on the mural, then it tends to suggest that subliminally you want to be found. Otherwise, why leave a clue in the first place?'

'So obvious, yet it escaped Didier' Tiffanny countered.

Didier blanched. 'Thanks for the vote of confidence my dear.'

Tiffanny waved his platitude aside. 'I didn't mean it in that way. I'm just saying, maybe this time it's not quite so clear cut.'

'But I fear James may have a point' the old timer stated. 'After all, I missed the mural clue. It needed a fresh pair of eyes on it, which is just what James provided. I've sat and stared at that report over countless sleepless nights, only to come up with zip. James had been on the case two seconds before he spotted the resemblance.'

'So let's go over the motions again' James decided. 'Tiff, hand me the report.'

'Hang on, our bus is here.' Tiffany pointed as a white coach came into the station. It pulled into a designated bay and the driver hopped out to release the luggage bay on the side of the vehicle. A bunch of people disembarked and stretched their legs. They appeared weary and were grateful for the fresh air. They had probably ridden for several hours, perhaps from the North, somewhere like Lille or Normandy. They located their baggage as the driver lifted each item from the bay and sat it down on the causeway. He started out patient and gentle, but by the last few he was tossing them out like garbage bags.

The small entourage of passengers threaded through the forecourt and out towards their own destinies. The small troupe of new commuters that had waited in line with James, Didier and Tiffany threw their own suitcases and holdalls onto the bay and formed a queue by the staircase to the cabin.

The driver had disappeared, presumably to indulge in a cigarette and visit the local facilities before the next leg of his journey. He reappeared several minutes later and began to check their tickets, tearing off a stub each time at the behest of his superiors. They boarded and chose adjacent seats at the rear, with James and Tiffany sitting together and Didier planting himself down opposite. The bus was warm and cosy.

Tiffany handed James the report just as the driver started up the engine and they eased out of the forecourt and onwards to Aix en Provence. The journey would take an hour and a half, traffic permitting.

Didier gazed out the window in solitude, watching the facets of his township begin to whiz by as the bus picked up speed and rocked up a steady pace. Tiffany tossed her hair, demonstrating the volume in her curls. James wondered if it was a natural phenomenon or whether a degree of hair product was applied to maximise the effect. He didn't care either way. The pale afternoon sunlight rays found themselves caressing her face, accentuating her subtle beauty.

He distracted himself from temptation by reading Didier's report again form cover to cover. Nothing triggered a new direction of thought or jumped off the page as a clue so obvious that he would have kicked himself for missing it the first time.

He fought to control his urges, and yet the Frenchwoman was sat within arms length. He gazed over at her. She had closed her eyes and the gentle rocking motion of the bus had sent her into a doze. She looked tired yet peaceful. James imagined that the events of the last four days could only have taken it out of her. He studied her facial features as one might admire a Van Gogh painting.

As he gazed longingly at her, he drifted from the world and into a daydream trance. He thought about the various forks in a road spanning nearly thirty years, forks that had led him to this current point in his life. There were a million and one things he would have done differently.

An unseen force suddenly yanked him back into the realm of the living, as he realised that Tiffanny's eyes were now wide open and staring back at him with a curious yet unblinkered coyness. He'd been caught in the act, red handed.

He smiled fervently then returned his gaze to the report. The Frenchwoman adjusted her position so that she had her back to him and her face to the window. James glanced to his right, where Didier was watching them with a laconic smirk. He had been young once. He had felt the surging passion and desire that women like Tiffanny provoked.

'You look like you should get some rest too' he said.

James closed the report and left it on his lap. 'Rest. I haven't had any of that in a long time.'

Didier nodded in mutual comprehension. 'Me neither, James. Me neither. We all have our demons. You should get some downtime before we get to Aix.'

The coach lumbered south, following the path of the Rhône towards Avignon. To the East the Italian borderlands loomed. The landscape branched out as they neared the Mediterranean coastline, and the lush alpine basin of rural middle-France gave way to quaint coastal villages, where valleys cut into the vast towering mountains in a funnel shape.

The romantic eddies of Monte Carlo, Nice, Cannes and Saint Tropez lay in waiting east of the

Gulf of Lion. James drifted between blissful ignorance of his surroundings and a dream where the events of the last days were nuanced into a short still. He remembered meeting Tiffanny Tourneux in the Charles de Gaulle airport and falling head over heels. The Hotel Magenta in Paris, and their dash around the city limits solving riddles inscribed decades ago by someone who was becoming more likely to be Pierre Chartier by the growing minute, and finally pulling a sheet of paper from the National Library's main computer terminal.

He dreamt of Fabien the waiter in Café Kléber, murdered, and Camille, Magenta's receptionist, murdered. He dreamt of the man in the tanned jacket, watching their every move, commandeering Tiffanny's white Renault and running reconnaissance detail. He dreamt of their arrival in Lyon, the construction site, being pointed in the direction of a drunken Didier, slurring his words and playing spitting games. He dreamt about a cure for cancer. The ultimate panacea.

He thought about Radka, Chester, being a law tutor, his students, marking assignments, Albion Place, a former life now ancient history, a chapter in a closed book, the credits of a film, over and done with, dissolved into time's mysteriously elusive ether, fin. He dreamt about Casino Collins, and he pondered why he had kidnapped his ex-wife.

He prayed that she was still being treated well in Brno. *Say hi to Charlie for me, if you're downtown.* The Lišen district. Another remnant of a past life in which the Czech Republic had been his second home. How he longed to be sat in the Air Café sipping a cocktail and studying the photographs on the walls of the Czech pilots who fought the Germans in the Second World War.

His past haunted him, and his future terrified him. That only left the present for him to dwell on these matters. The coach hit a pothole in the road and James bolted upright. He gazed over at Tiffanny. It was her turn to be caught gazing at him. He smiled and squeezed her shoulder. Her head came to rest on his.

He soaked up the smell of her shampoo and listened to her heartbeat. He kissed her on the forehead and held her close to him. She relented and he kissed her hard on the lips, feeding his hungry need. She was so beautiful, he felt breathless and his spine tingled with pleasant shivers. He gently slid part of his tongue into hers and she returned the action. They held each other in a unified embrace for fifteen listless minutes.

The coach rumbled on, caressing the southern blacktop until it rolled into the main Aix en Provence bus terminal at a little after three. The passengers disembarked from the front and out the cabin. The driver was out first, opening the baggage bay around the side of the bus and lifting out the luggage one by one, just as he had done in Lyon. As before, the baggage carried by James, Tiffany, and Didier, was purely emotional. It had been nice to recharge on the bus, with the dizzy motion and the drowsy notion, but now they were out sucking in fresh air and stretching their legs.

'Time to begin our proverbial needle in a haystack quest' Tiffany balked.

James thought back to his dream from the bus. 'I have a proposition for a starting point.'

'We're all ears' Didier confirmed.

'Well, we went hunting for Chartier's book in Paris' national library. It wasn't there, but it was supposed to be – it had been there at some point. Chartier must have faced all kinds of heat from the pharmaceutical companies. Somehow one of them went and had that book removed. Perhaps they sabotaged the print run, or went fishing and had all copies in circulation burned. We're clearly not dealing with amateurs here.'

Tiffany nodded but appeared perplexed. 'Get to the point, James.'

'Assuming Chartier is actually here in Aix en Provence, what do you think was the first thing he did when he arrived here?'

Didier frowned. 'He would have found a library here, and asked them to stock his book. A reincarnation, a new home for the work in Aix.'

James smiled. 'Precisely. So we need to find out where the main library is in this town.'

*

311

His cell phone vibrated again. He was quick to flip the clamshell to reveal the display. It was not necessary to check the display of course – only one person could be calling, for only one person had his number.

'Chaplin.'

'Chaplin, update me.' Paul Ross' raspy and withered voice croaked at him.

'Sir, they took a bus to Aix en Provence. I drove down to intercept. I've just arrived. They just got off the bus. The other man is with them. He moves like a cop.'

'That will add an extra dimension of complexity to your mission.'

'Don't sweat it, Sir. I can take care of them all.'

'You're not to do anything until you have confirmation of the target's location. They must be getting close.'

'Agreed, Sir. I'll continue to follow from the shadows. Once we have determined the target's location, what then?'

Ross paused. Chaplin heard the laboured breathing down the line. The old timer was struggling. All it would take is a bad winter, and he'd succumb to influenza or pneumonia and he'd be shuffling off this mortal coil in time for the summer. Chaplin preyed the ageing relic would muster on through the difficult times ahead.

Ross finally broke the awkward silence. 'There's a couple of Lebanese men. We've used them before. They have the equipment needed to destroy the target. All they need is the target's location and a few days to prepare.'

'Understood, Sir. I'll keep you posted on future developments.'

'You be sure to do that, Chaplin. Now get off the line and find me our target.'

'Sir.' The line clicked dead.

Chaplin snapped the clamshell shut and pocketed the device. He eased out of the bus station in the sedan he had boosted in Lyon, taking care not to attract any unwarranted attention to himself. He had flipped the lid on the glove box on the ride down from Lyon, and had found what he had expected to find – registration and insurance

312

documents for a Gerard Chevalier – valid documents, but for a person whose photograph carried mismatched aesthetics to his own. Gerard Chevalier was thirty years Chaplin's senior, and so the documents would not stand up to police scrutiny. He had to be scrupulous.

He kept the trio in plain sight as he navigated the sedan through cross-town traffic. The women of Aix en Provence looked ripe for the picking – forbidden fruit. Guilty pleasures. He was hungry for meat. He would have to get his fill. But which one to choose? The mere thought had his erection aching in arousal.

He drove one-handed and used his free hand to reach deep into his jeans and pleasure himself. He never took his eyes off his targets. They were on foot and appeared disorientated. It was the classic look of tourists in a new town. They were glancing around in all directions, gathering their bearings, pinpointing significant monuments, their spatial awareness kicking in.

Gripping his shaft, he watched the sole female target of the three. She had brown skin and curly hair and her figure was sublime. He began to reach the critical climactic moment when a sudden rush of pain in his neural cortex stopped him short. Another headache. It was a splitting migraine. He took both hands in his head and groaned in pain.

He reached for his pills and popped two, swallowing them dry. He slammed his hand on the steering wheel in frustration. The headaches were becoming more painful each time. The pills usually kicked in after ten minutes. He zipped up his jeans and focused on the stationary targets a mere five hundred yards across the other side of the thoroughfare. His urge had not been fulfilled. He looked on at the female target and grimaced. *I'm going to enjoy her* he thought to himself.

Chapter Thirty One

As the bus bellowed away into smoke dust, James soaked up the ambience of downtown Aix en Provence. He picked up a laid back vibe in syncopation with the Mediterranean stereotype. The main industry here was the tourist trade, despite it being just out of season. It would peak in the summer months when the Earth's axis pointed the continent towards the full brunt of the sun. They found a restaurant called Les Deux Frères and ate grilled sea bass and salad.

'If Pierre's alive, how has he managed to exist this long?' James suddenly pondered out loud.

Tiffanny's fork twisted around a portion of lettuce. 'What do you mean?' They'd ordered ice tea and were alarmed when Didier asked for a beer. He'd been cold turkey since their first encounter with him in a Lyon bistro the previous day. *Just one for the road,* he'd said. Maybe the situation was getting to him.

'Well', James continued, 'If he is still alive, then he still needs the blueprints that society demands of us all. A social security number, bank accounts, credit cards, a passport, driving licence, a permanent address. He's been gone six years. Does he live like a Neanderthal in the wilderness?'

'I doubt it' the Frenchwoman mused. 'Hey Didier, can't we corroborate with the police down here, show them our missing persons report? Ask for their full co-operation?'

Didier frowned as he chewed on his calamari. 'Only with something infinitely more serious, such as a major crime. If it was domestic then we could

315

engage the local foot soldiers. Anything transcending national boundaries and it would fall to the jurisdiction of Interpol. But with a missing persons case, the force is inundated. Too much bureaucracy. They won't push more pens just for our friend Chartier. I think James' idea of hitting the library is one borne of logic and rational thinking.'

James raised his fork in gratitude for the compliment. 'What we need is a map of this town. We need to find Tourist Information.'

They found it in thirty minutes, after traipsing through the central thoroughfare. They followed the largest throngs of people, who appeared to be heading towards the same central hub, the beating heart of Aix. The initial streets they encountered on the outskirts, as they headed south from the bus station, were residential and housed studios and apartments. Eventually they gave way to commercial fronts, narrow and lined with trattorias and cafés.

James glimpsed a street sign which told them that they were on Rue Marie et Pierre Curie. Eventually it broadened out and became Rue Matheron. Boutique shops appeared and designer labels clung to facades as they threaded further southward. There was a lazy air to the surroundings. The natives did not rush, as they would have done in Paris or London or New York, rather they jostled gingerly down the sidewalks, enjoying a steadily paced life that James envied. He wondered if the College had found his replacement yet. They probably had. A quick turnaround was needed as each student was shelling out £15,000 in fees for the course; there had to be a quality service for such princely sums. James had been a quality service briefly. But now he was disconnected from that life. He was a wraith in no mans land, drifting through on a plane all of his own.

They reached Place des Prêcheurs and encountered a myriad of restaurants at intersecting streets. The French were very proud of their own gastronomy, and so they should be. They weaved around the menu boards and tables clad in upholstered cloths and bored waiters with patient smiles and emerged on Rue de Monclar. They snuck through a stone arch and ended up in a large courtyard square flanked by the gilded walls of a grand architectural design. It must have been the town hall, or some other municipal effort. The grandeur was not delusional. A French flag emblazoned on a pole flapped in the breeze from the east side.

In the square itself a band of musicians were setting up on a wooden stage. A sign mounted on a placard read: *MUSIQUE DANS LA RUE. Music in the street.* As they neared the stage, James discovered that a full orchestra was in preparation. There were brass, woodwind, percussion and stringed instruments being fine tuned by their handlers.

James embellished the culture. Music in the street in England comprised of some young jock in a souped-up hatchback blurting out rap music from a boom-box packed into the boot along with subwoofers. Ice, they called it. France was a world apart. No ice here, not even the literal kind, despite the winter solstice. Here, near the Mediterranean coastline, there was a mildness to the temperate outdoors and an unfettered respect for society.

They passed through the courtyard, not waiting to hear the band play, and made out onto Rue Marius Reynaud, heading southwest. They passed the Museum d'Histoire Naturelle de Aix-en-Provence and headed down Rue Espariat, another commercial artery of the town containing delis, bistros, high-street retailers and the Hotel de France.

Rue Espariat concluded at the foot of a large roundabout, a glorious fountain planted in the centre. Car horns bellowed. A sign bore the name *Place de la Rotonde,* the rotund being the fountain. To the west Avenue Napoléon Bonaparte pincered out of downtown on D17. To the east ran Cours Mirabeau, which Tiffanny explained was the Champs Élysées of Aix en Provence. More boutiques, more designer labels. High-end green exchanged hands. It was a haven for the affluent.

And straight ahead, the opposite side of the roundabout and the fountain, was the Office Municipal de Tourisme. *Tourist Information.* They traversed across the busy roundabout using the numerous pedestrian crossings and James went inside. Tiffanny and Didier found a bench near a small park and waited.

James emerged after five minutes clutching an orange sheet of printed 250gsm paper stock. He held out the map. 'They spoke perfect English. The nice lady said there are two libraries in the city. The first is Bibliothèque Méjanes, which is here.' James placed a finger on the map where the lady inside the tourist office had ringed a small beige icon with her biro. 'The second is Ludothèque Cerf Volant, which is not on his map and is miles away to the North. It's not really in Aix en Provence centre per se.'

Tiffanny's piercing eyes pored over the map. Then she nodded in concurrence. 'Then it has to be Méjanes. It doesn't look to be too far from here.'

'It's on Rue des Allumettes' Didier observed. A mile further southwest of their current location. They set off down Avenue des Belges, leaving the fountain behind. A disturbing thought occurred to James. 'You think the man in the tanned jacket followed us here?'

Didier did not appear flummoxed by James' concerns – the sign of a cop who hoped for the best but planned for the worst; a cop who had seen his fair share of human hostility, and, upon the departure of his family, a cop who probably no longer gave a rat's. 'I don't see how, but it's possible. If he's a pro then we'll have been monitored all the way, even at the bus stop back in Lyon.'

'Surely he wasn't on our bus?' Tiffanny appeared appalled at her own thought. 'We'd have noticed that, right?'

James frowned. 'We'd have noticed that – it was just a coach, and we sat at the back. We saw everyone get on, and subsequently alight. No way we could have missed him.'

Didier was two moves ahead, like a chess champion. 'He could of course, in theory, have watched us ride the bus out of Lyon and then driven down here. All he had to do was check the bus' destination with a clerk at the customer information point inside the depot. He or she would have only been too happy to supply our man with the details. Service with a smile, et cetera.' That would have made Chaplin the chess grandmaster, for he was always a few steps ahead.

'So we need to be vigilant, as always' James reminded them. Avenue des Belges gave way to Avenue de l'Europe. They hooked right onto Rue des Allumettes and searched for the library. The street was lined with sycamores. They passed a pharmacy on the corner and threaded up towards a shallow stone building opposite a block of high rise flats. The building had a sloping tiled roof painted terracotta and spanned the entire length of Rue des Allumettes.

They found a revolving door on the west side to be the entrance. Inside, the library was not terribly different to the interior of the Bibliothèque Nationale in Paris. It was used predominantly by the student populace, which became apparent when James glanced around and saw scores of young learners with books under their arms or seated at plush pine tables with a pencil gripped in their hands, highlighting texts, finding citations, backing up their research with the appropriate authority on the subject matter.

It made him think of his own students in Chester. Or ex-students, just as Radka was no doubt his ex-wife. It then hit him that 16 Albion Place, Chester would have to become his ex-abode. He was losing everything, like a snake shedding its skin, severing ties like an umbilical cord. He was losing his identity.

'How do we play this one out?' he whispered to Tiffanny. 'Same as in Paris? Do we take up an enquiry at the counter or hit the computer?'

Tiffanny pointed towards a free terminal in the far corner. 'The computer.'

They took up seats on swivel chairs and James refreshed the monitor with a wave of the mouse. It soon came to life and displayed the library's internal catalogue software. James typed in the same key terms he had used back in Paris. *Dying to know the truth.* He hit the search box, feeling hopeful. The message he saw once the page loaded was not what he had hoped for. *I'm sorry, no documents match your enquiry. Please try again.* Even though it was written in French, he understood it perfectly.

'Now what?' He was downhearted. Tiffanny pursed her lips, a habit he had noticed her partake in whenever she was deep in thought. 'Try similar search terms. Here, let me try.' One by one she entered search terms and hit enter. *Cancer. Pierre Chartier, why we're still dying to know the truth, B17.* All drew blanks. *I'm sorry, no documents match your enquiry. Please try again.*

A thought suddenly perturbed James. 'What if we're looking in completely the wrong place? What if we misinterpreted the mural painting. It could have been a coincidence. He might not be here. He might never have come here.'

Didier spoke up. 'I don't believe in coincidences, James. It was a replica of the photograph. It has to be here.'

'What about the other library, the one that's miles further north?'

'Ludothèque Cerf Volant?' Tiffanny mused. 'No, it's off the beaten track. I think Chartier would have made the answer more obvious. Not too obvious, but enough to guide the right people in the right direction.'

James felt a vibration. He flipped open the cell phone that the robotic voice had been calling him on. One of two students glanced at him and then back to their books. It was on silent mode so it had not really disturbed them. He had a new text message. *From: Private. Message: You already have the code, James.*

James showed the message to Tiffanny and Didier. They expressed a look of bewilderment in synchronised unison. 'He usually calls on this phone' James explained. 'I've never had a text message before.' They pondered in silence what code they could already have.

James clicked off the catalogue software and launched an internet browser. He went to Google and searched for the library they were currently inhabiting. Two words – *Bibliothèque Méjanes.* Twenty six thousand two hundred results. Still no Googlewhack. He made a full note of the address. *8-10 Rue des Allumettes, 13100, Aix en Provence, France. 04 42 91 35 53.*

He took a notepad and a pencil from the desk and wrote down the postcode and the telephone number on two separate lines.

13400

0442913553

'Ok, we already have two codes here. A postcode, and an area code. But which one did Chartier mean?' James chewed on the pencil.

'That's a stab way out of leftfield, James!' Didier remarked.

'But like he said' Tiffanny observed, 'It's the only code we already have.'

James got up and started to look at random shelves. 'They're not using Dewey here. The system is different.' The books were organised according to their subject matters, as logic would have dictated. But the numbering was different. There were sets of five digit numbers. *18465, 17996, 13502.* 'Find *13400*' James ordered.

The three set about searching for category 13400 amongst the interspersed shelves of the open-plan library. The university lay further to the south, beyond the fountain. The library must have served all faculties; every subject was accounted for. It took forty minutes of careful searching across three floors of shelves, acres of space and tens of thousands of books, before the Frenchwoman found a small specialist section tucked away towards the west corner on the second floor. *13400: Miscellaneous Science.*

Tiffanny called over the two men with a wave of her arm, maintaining the quiet sanctity of the learning environment that was the library. Didier spotted it before James; the Frenchman grabbed a book from the third shelf, at his waist level, and held it up. *Cancer: Why we're still dying to know the truth. By Pierre Chartier.* There was just one copy. Didier turned over the first place and they studied the photograph inset in the inlay. It was a picture they had seen before; Pierre Chartier in his black motorcycle leathers, with that curious pose. The same picture, last seen on a painted mural in Lyon, had led them to this juncture.

They flipped to the index and picked out the B17 Action Diagram on page eighty-six. The diagram was what they had already seen, plus a missing piece that they had not been provided with.

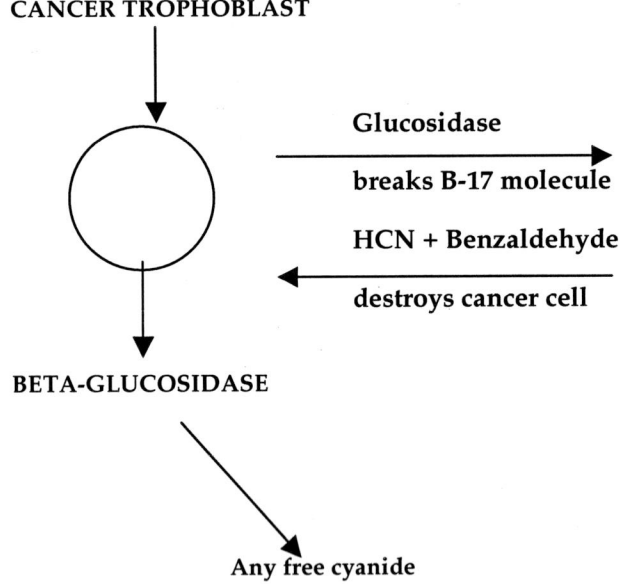

CANCER TROPHOBLAST

Glucosidase

breaks B-17 molecule

HCN + Benzaldehyde

destroys cancer cell

BETA-GLUCOSIDASE

Any free cyanide

When combined with the other two sections, it illustrated the full scientific process that Tiffanny had explained earlier; pioneered by Ernst Theodor Krebs Sr in the first instance, and perfected by two Frenchmen; Roubiquet and Bontron-Chariand. B17, a vitamin abundant in apricots, cured all forms of cancer. But there was one thing the diagram, or the book in its entirety for that matter, failed to explain; the whereabouts of Pierre Chartier.

They skimmed through the book, wondering if a sheet of piece of paper would drop out and reveal a final clue. No such luck. Didier was animated in his method of shaking the book furiously. 'Be careful Didier' Tiffanny counselled. 'That appears to be the only copy.'

James took the book from Didier's weathered hand. 'Follow me.' He led them back down to the first floor. He approached the reception desk. Tiffanny translated as James spoke to an African girl behind the counter, who was busy twiddling her dreadlocks. She had bleached them a dark blonde. She wore jeans and a jersey depicting the team emblems of some sport James did not recognise. She appeared to be a student herself. She was friendly and came across intelligent when engaged in conversation.

'What can you tell me about this book?' James asked. Tiffanny translated. The girl appeared nonchalant and appeared not to understand the question, despite the translation. After all, her job was to scan the barcodes and process the loan transactions, sort through returned books and levy fines on late returns. She was not expected to know the intricate details of every book that the institutions stocked. That would be utterly irrational.

The girl, who bore the name tag Mimmi, picked up the book as if it were a precious gem to behold, scanned the pages, checked for a barcode, checked the quality of the book to ensure it had not been mistreated, skimmed the pages, scanned the blurb on the back and placed it back down on the countertop. She appeared satisfied. She shrugged her shoulders at Tiffanny.

James was undeterred. 'Is there anything special about this particular book? How often is it taken out? When was it last taken out?' Tiffanny rephrased the questions in their mutual tongue. Mimmi must have felt like this was the second reckoning of the Spanish Inquisition. She responded helpfully, answering all the questions in the correct order, like an efficient machine. Tiffanny translated back. There was nothing particularly special, as far as Mimmi knew, about this particular book. It had been taken out once in its history. Six years ago. About the time Chartier disappeared from Lyon, Didier figured.

James bit his tongue in fury. Radka's life depended on this. The lives of millions of cancer sufferers worldwide hinged on this. 'One more question, Mimmi. Because I like you, and my father loved Mimmi Rogers.' He gave the girl the most genuine smile he could muster under the terse circumstances. 'Can you scan the book in and tell me if your computer flags up any additional information that might be useful.'

Mimmi complied with Tiffanny's guiding translation and she nodded triumphantly when the task was completed. She spoke in rapid fire to Tiffanny and the Frenchwoman's face lit up like a Christmas tree.

'James, she says there is an additional journal in the short-term loan section that corresponds to this book. It has the ISBN 0442913553. That's the same number as the telephone number for the library. You Googled it.'

James smiled in recognition. 'So Chartier used both the post code and the telephone number to guide us. He was a clever fellow.'

Didier noted the use of the past tense. 'Don't be so sure that he isn't still alive. He's pulling some serious strings here.'

James nodded his agreement. Mimmi excused herself and walked around the countertop. She came back a moment later with an A4 sheet of paper encased in a plastic document wallet. Eagerly the trio took it from her and read with bated breath. It was a thesis that somebody had written on the molecular properties of basalt. Their shoulders sagged. This would make for dull reading. They thanked Mimmi, found an empty table bereft of hardworking students and took the sheet out of the plastic wallet. The thesis was thirty pages long, bound, stapled and laminated at the front.

Applying great care, and so as not to attract undue attention, they turned each page methodically. They hit gold at the centrefold. Somebody had stuffed a folded sheet of paper in the centre pages as a makeshift bookmark. Perhaps fifteen pages of analysis about basalt was all anybody could stomach, so the one reader who had taken this out six years ago had given up halfway through. They'd probably gone home and picked up a Dan Brown novel to make up for the mind numbing they'd endured at school.

James unfolded the sheet of paper. Tiffanny and Didier gathered around. There was a message written on the paper:

AT LAST YOU HAVE THE FULL PICTURE,
MINUS A LITTLE CHARACTER!
FRET NOT, NOT LONG TO GO NOW, JUST A
FINAL BIT OF LAT. THINKING TO DO AND
YOU'LL KNOW WHERE WE ARE.

45　46　36　N　　　　14　13　0　E

'We can't take this out' Tiffanny scorned. 'We're not members.'

James took out his cell phone. 'Fear not, my dearest.' He quickly typed the contents of the note into a new text message and saved it in the drafts folder. Then he refolded the paper and placed it back inside the thesis just as he had found it. He shuffled the thesis back into the plastic document wallet. Didier returned Chartier's book to the second floor shelf. Tiffanny returned the journal to Mimmi at the desk. She thanked the girl for a final time and they took off towards the exit.

Twilight had arrived as they stepped out onto Rue des Allumettes. The temperature had dropped to a chill. They hustled on the street corner. 'One final puzzle' James remarked. 'And then it's all over.' He took off and crossed the street, setting up on the opposite sidewalk to collect his thoughts. Tiffanny and Didier stood together in a huddle fifty yards from him.

Didier paced towards a litter bin, creating a gap of about ten yards between himself and Tiffanny. He emptied something from his pockets into the trash and stepped out onto the road. James breathed out and began to walk back across the road towards them. As he stepped off the pavement something caught his eye. It was an involuntary, automotive reflex. First the sound, then the sight.

A dusty orange-brown sedan screeched down the street from the north at breakneck speed. It took an extra second for James' cognition to sense danger. Didier was whistling, some old Revolutionary song, and Tiffanny was frozen to the spot, her eyes fixated on the sudden intrusion. James was forty yards away now. He picked up pace, walking directly towards the car. His eyes squinted in the dim light and he pinpointed the driver of the sedan; male, about his age, wearing a tanned leather jacket. *Him.*

Another second passed. His cognition reached another gear. He began to wave frantically with his arm. Didier was still whistling. He glanced towards the car as it accelerated even more. The driver swung the sedan in a direct path with the Frenchman. Time retreated back into a painful slow motion. Didier's shape blended into the scenery as the sedan swerved around Tiffanny and ploughed straight into the uncomprehending Didier. He was hit at approximately sixty miles per hour. His body twisted and convulsed, and the force of the vehicle bent him back into the front windscreen. Then he rolled off the bonnet and shattered onto the concrete road.

James was thirty yards away and closing. He was running like the whole world depended on it. It was a clear cut hit and run, except there was an extra twist to the run element. Instead of speeding away, the driver slammed on the brakes and the sedan came to rest beside a stunned Tiffanny, who was pointing at Didier's corpse in the road and screaming like a lost kestrel.

James was fifteen yards way. It was too far. The tanned jacket burst out of the car, grabbed Tiffanny by her arm and yanked her through the open window of the rear passenger side door. James was ten yards away. He began to scream himself. *No! God no!*

Then the sedan lurched forward and screeched, as rubber scorched the tarmac. The man in the tanned jacket stole away in a heartbeat, as James was five yards away and sprinting like an Olympic athlete. He reached Didier as the car turned a corner and disappeared.

He reached down and checked Didier for a pulse. There wasn't one. He shook the Frenchman wildly. 'Didier. Didier! Wake the hell up! Now! Didier! Come on!' It was hopeless, and James knew it. He collapsed in the road. There were no witnesses in this sycamore-lined street. He was alone in a dark street in the south of France. Tiffanny was gone. And Didier...Didier was dead.

Chapter Thirty-Two

6:58 p.m.

Numb with fear and paralysed by pain, James tugged on the lead weight his arm had become and forcefully reached into his trouser pocket, as saltwater tears trickled down his face, seeping across his lips. His legs were like jelly. He collapsed in the road.

Didier remained still as rigor mortis began to set in. Unbelieving of what maddening happenstance had manifested, James drifted into a dizzy realm where the demons were waiting to swallow him whole. The sky darkened to black, matching the void inside his head and his heart. As black as Didier's lifeless eyes, staring out onto the blacktop.

He pulled the cell phone out of his pocket without taking his eyes off an unseen fixation. Without looking at the phone he keyed 118 for emergency services by feeling the keypad positions. Instead of dialling out the phone produced an intermittent bleep. Low battery? No. He checked the phone's display. There was a message scrawled across the interface. *Nice try James. No authorities.* Collins had rigged the phone so that James was unable to alert the authorities to Radka's kidnapping. A clever ploy by the entrepreneur. James grimaced at the realisation, almost in admiration.

Ironically James had not even contemplated that course of action. He had figured that alerting the authorities would have been a dumb thing to do from the outset. And now, when he needed those authorities for an altogether unconnected purpose, to save Didier, he had been denied. Of course the endeavour would have been fruitless. There was no doubt that Didier had crawled off this mortal coil. He wasn't coming back. Not now. Not ever.

Alone in the dark, kneeling on the harsh concrete of Rue des Allumettes, on a spot five yards from where Tiffanny Tourneux had been snatched away from him, James somehow managed to force his cognition to return to the land of the living. It struck him that Radka had been kidnapped as an insurance policy, to ensure that James completed the task Collins had given him, and that Tiffanny had been kidnapped to prevent him from completing his mission. Therefore the two acts were polar opposites. One was instigated by a friend, the other a foe.

It confirmed that the man in the tanned jacket did not work for Collins, but for his enemy. No doubt a corporate pharmaceutical entity bent on preventing the B17 cancer cure from ever seeing the light. An entity who'd profit largely from the mass production of drugs in a billion dollar industry. An entity who would stand to lose everything if B17 hit the shelves.

And then another thought hit him like a bolt of lightning. He cursed himself for not seeing it earlier. An obvious implication. B17 was a wonder-drug. Tiffanny was a pharmacologist. But she wasn't the only. Radka was a pharmacologist too. Radka Rosická. That was the real reason for her kidnapping. It was the only reason that made sense. Not as some insurance policy, to coax him into complying with Collins' whim. Her role was much more involved than that. Radka must have been headhunted for the scientific process itself. She was going to take B17 through the chemical processes and into a marketable product. It was what she did best.

And it would be the perfect atonement for Radka. Three years ago she had inadvertently created Aequitol – a drug designed to kill. B17 was the polar opposite – the nemesis of Aequitol – it was designed to preserve the anamorphic beauty that is human life. She'd probably volunteer for the post once Collins explained what needed to be done. A perfect case for Stockholm Syndrome. Radka no doubt saw Collins as an accidental hero. She was going to save the world. His ex-wife was going to be

330

responsible firsthand for curing cancer. For a moment his heart filled up with pride like a hot air balloon taking to the azure skies.

James summoned the strength to stand up. He wiped away the tears with his shirt sleeve. He clocked a payphone at the end of the street, its metal glinting in the darkness like a tormentor. He felt bitter about abandoning Didier in the middle of the deserted street. He hoped the Frenchman's soul had transcended into eternal peace. It had been such a sudden impact, and an instantaneous death. Being hit by several tonnes of steel travelling at sixty miles per hour and packing over a hundred break horse power is too much a calamity for the internal organs of the human body, which haemorrhage internally, causing a total systems failure.

His legs remained like sponges but he limped to the payphone and dialled 118, knowing he did not need to insert money for an emergency call. He explained in broken French what had transpired on the usually blissful streets of Aix en Provence. It took five minutes for an ambulance and a squad car to tear around the corner of Rue des Allumettes much like the tanned jacket had.

Two paramedics launched themselves out of the still moving ambulance, carrying a stretcher which they quickly folded out like a gurney. Didier's pulse was checked, both at his wrist and at his neck. The lead paramedic placed his ear to the Frenchman's chest, then looked to his assistant and simply shook his head. The assistant nodded in comprehension and Didier was placed in a body bag. It was zipped to the clasp and then lifted onto the stretcher. The stretcher was loaded into the ambulance bay.

Two men clambered out of a cruiser whose stickers contained printed letters that read *Police Municipale d'Aix en Provence.* The officers were in full regalia. One hung back and observed the paramedics clear away Didier's body, ensuring that the crime scene was preserved. He was an Algerian with a military buzz cut. His partner, a robust looking local Gaul, approached James, who was stood off the kerb rooted to the spot, gazing into a vast expanse of nothingness.

Extending a hand, he said 'Patrice Antoine.'
James remained statuesque, ignoring the man.
Patrice withdrew and waved his partner over. The
Algerian loitered behind him. They conversed with
one another in rapid-fire French. Finally the penny
dropped and in broken English Patrice said to
James, 'You talk English? You know what happen
'ere? You make a call from the box 'ere?' He pointed
towards the booth on the corner.

James did not react. All the lifeblood had been
drained from him. He stared on through his field of
vision at something unseen. Patrice waved his hand
in front of James' face. Nothing. He placed a hand of
comfort across James' shoulder. No result. He
looked to the Algerian, who shrugged an *it's your
call* gesture back at his partner.

Another squad car turned the corner and pulled
into Rue des Allumettes. Men in suits wearing white
gloves disembarked. The forensics team. Patrice
acknowledged them and pulled James across the
street and bundled him into the back seat of the
BMW he had screeched up the street in. James
stared on through the front windshield,
expressionless, devoid, numb and hateful.

James was chauffeured to Commissariat d'Aix en
Provence on Avenue de l'Europe, the provincial
police station for the downtown jurisdiction,
planted nefariously on the city limits. Avenue de
l'Europe was lined with silver birch trees. A central
reservation spruced with lavatera flowers ran the
full diameter. The station itself was a stilted boxy
concrete structure housed on the ground floor
below residential high-rise apartments.

The officers led him through the entrance and
into an interview room. He was invited to take a
seat. There was only one other feature in the room
besides the chair – a battered wooden table. They
left him alone, staring into space, and exited the
room. Five minutes later another officer entered and
walked over to the table. He perched on the edge
like a schoolteacher. He wore trendy narrow-
rimmed glasses on a bracelet around his neck.

He extended a hand and spoke to James in
English. 'My name is Nicolas. I am your equivalent

of a superintendent. The reason why you are here, and not the hospital, is that you did not witness an accident. By your own account, you witnessed a murder. You are the only witness.'

No, I am not. Tiffanny witnessed it too. But now she's gone. Nicolas continued. 'I want to make it clear that you have not been arrested – you are not a suspect. But we would greatly appreciate your voluntary assistance with this matter. Killing a citizen, any citizen, is a heinous act. But to mow down a police officer in broad daylight. Well, that just cannot be forgiven.'

James stared on, dead ahead, fixated on the peeling neglect of the inner wall. It was coated in that industry-standard institutional grey paint lick seen the world over. Nicolas appeared to be a patient man. He watched his prey sat in the chair like a predator waiting for the mother to flee the nest.

Nicolas leaned back, then he stood. 'Could you please do me a favour? Could you empty your pockets and place the contents on the table? I will reiterate, you are not a suspect, but in line with standard procedure we have to make a full inventory. I'm sure you understand.'

James understood. Nicolas had clearly plumped for the good cop routine, all the way. Like Nicolas was his best friend. *Co-operate, and we'll play nice.* James was willing to bet that Nicolas was a man who could turn into an angry *bad cop* son of a bitch in a heartbeat, if the occasion called for it. But he saw no need to cause unnecessary problems for himself. So he calmly complied with Nicolas' request.

On the table he placed his wallet, a small wad of bills, the dwindling remnants of the airport locker in Paris and the cell phone Murgatroyd had given him. He did so without giving Nicolas eye contact.

'Thanks. I appreciate that. Good, no deadly weapons. Not that I thought you would have had. But protocols are protocols, n'est pas? Young man, you appear to be experiencing post traumatic stress disorder. It is not something to be taken lightly. I think you'll need to be referred to a specialist. But just for the next few minutes, can you bring yourself to indulge me as to exactly what happened on Rue des Allumettes?'

James said nothing. His eyes were pools of dark matter, the antithesis of willingness to cooperate. Nicolas reached across the table and picked up his wallet. He removed the pink driving licence card. 'Your name is James Loxbridge. Nice to meet you, James. You are twenty nine years of age. Man what I would give to be that age again. You married? Kids?'

James looked on, devoid of life and warmth and everything that's good and holy. Nicolas frowned. His patience and his austere façade were beginning to crack. He placed the wallet back on the table and picked up the cell phone. A Nokia clamshell. He flicked it open. The device was switched on and had roamed to the local Eurotel network. 'I have a wife and three children, James. They are my everything. A loving wife. Great kids who do well in school.'

Good for you. My reward for solving this mystery and freeing my wife is a nice fat divorce. James remained stoic, steadfast and resolute. But something freed him from his impromptu trepidation. Nicolas was fumbling with the back of the cell phone, trying to prise off the rear shell. A cell phone Collins had rigged with C4, an explosive charge that would be detonated if tampered with.

'DON'T!' Nicolas jumped at the sudden interjection.

'Put the phone down Nicolas, please!'

Nicolas, maintaining the role of good cop, duly complied. For the first time James made eye contact with the superintendent. He studied the facial features of the man who had shared the interview room with him for the past twenty minutes. A small fire had been reignited in James, like he had come back from the brink of the dead. Something had resuscitated him. Nicolas frowned.

James recomposed himself. He placed his hands on the table. 'It's a long story. But please be careful how you handle that phone.'

Nicolas sensed he had suddenly made progress with the inquisition. He had reached out and connected with James, albeit through unintentional provocation. He suddenly produced an evidence bag from underneath the table. Inside the transparent plastic was a sheet of paper. Nicolas placed it on the table in front of James.

'We found this in the deceased's right trouser pocket' the superintendent said. 'Do you know what it is?'

James leaned forward. 'The deceased? His name is Didier.'

'I meant no disrespect, James. Didier was a fellow officer after all. I want to catch the bastard who did this as much as you do. What can you tell me about this?' He jabbed dramatically at the evidence bag with his index finger.

James breathed out a sigh of consternation. 'That is the reason for me being in Aix en Provence, as a matter of fact. It's why I've been gallivanting all around your country this week, from Paris, to Lyon, to here.'

Nicolas repositioned himself on the table and leaned in. He was all ears. 'What is it?'

James snorted. 'You wouldn't believe me, trust me. It sounds like the script to an elaborate movie. Except it's a low budget affair, as the main character is yours truly. Hardly Brad Pitt, right?!'

Nicolas smiled triumphantly. He was getting through. He had broken down all barriers. His patience and his good nature had paid off. He knew it would. He had never been one for the hot-headed approach, shaking suspects to within an inch of their lives before they spilled all their beans.

'Try me' Nicolas prompted. 'It looks like some kind of diagram to me, or part of one.'

James leaned forward in a gesture of compliance. He gave Nicolas the full picture, just as Tiffanny and himself had done with Didier earlier that day. Back when the man was breathing air.

It took him fifteen minutes to recount the entire tale. Nicolas nodded thoughtfully throughout the exchange. At the end he raised up off the table and paced across the room.

'A cure for cancer? Really? Mon Dieu, that's incredible. And you do not know who this man in the tanned jacket is?'

James pointed to the cell phone which Nicolas had placed back on the table. 'No, but I took his picture. It's not great quality, but you might be able to do something with it. My man in Paris, name of Lacroix, never responded.'

Nicolas nodded and picked up the cell phone once again, only this time James could see the effort he was making to handle it with care.

'It's in the images folder' James explained. Nicolas found the photo and stared at it. It was grainy on the cell phone's two megapixel camera. He shrugged thoughtfully. 'I'll give it to the techs. I'm sure with the software we have they can do something with it. It might be high-res enough to blow up somewhat. The tanned jacket is distinctive. I'll see what I can do.'

'So what happens now?' James asked.

Nicolas opened out his palms in a gesture of *it's your call*. 'As I said, you're not under arrest. You're free to go at any time. But you might want to stick around a while longer. We need to get your girlfriend back.'

'She's not my...never mind. What do you propose?'

Nicolas motioned for James to stand. 'Come on, we need to work up a game plan. First thing to do is get a mugshot out on the tanned jacket. Work up a police photofit. We'll use the picture on your cell phone. He has an hour head start and he's vehicle bound. Who knows where he's headed with...what's her name?'

'Tiffanny Tourneux. Two n's.'

'In Tourneux?'

'No, in Tiffanny. Usually there's just one n in Tiffany. But Tiffanny spells her name with one extra.'

Nicolas frowned. 'Interesting. It's not a quintessentially French name.'

James nodded. 'She was named after an Olympic swimmer called Tiffany Lisa Cohen. An American. She won double gold in 1984, the year Tiffanny was born. Her father was a big fan, but to retain some individuality he added one extra n.'

'Well, one n or two, the girl's in danger James. Is there anything else you can tell me about this creep?'

James pondered. 'He's followed us all over France. He boosted Tiffanny's car in Paris. There was a brief stand-off in Lyon; that's when I took that picture of him. He was just stood there staring at us like it was the most casual thing in the world. I think he's been monitoring our every move somehow. He must have been. When he…when he hit Didier it was the first time he had, you know…?'

'Not stood back on the sidelines and watched, but rather acted on some instruction or impulse.'

James nodded. 'Precisely. He seems to work alone. We've never seen him with anybody. But he must answer to some higher authority. My guess is someone in a high place within the pharmaceutical industry.'

'You think he knew about B17?' Nicolas mused.

'I think he had to have done. We've been traipsing around France working the clues. We had nothing concrete to go on, until we found that in the library.' James pointed to the final section of the B17 diagram housed inside the evidence bag. 'He must have known that we'd finally solved something. Except we hadn't. That appears to be the final clue, but we'd no sooner exited the library than…Didier.' James looked down at his loafers in diffidence.

Nicolas processed James' analysis of the happenstance to date. 'He must have thought you had the answers right there. Which means…'

James looked up. 'Which means what?'

Nicolas breathed out. 'Which means that the moment you solve all the clues, you become surplus to requirements. Collateral damage. Expendable.'

James nodded in realisation. 'Didier was technically a third party in all of this. He had tagged along back in Lyon.'

'Investigating the disappearance of one Pierre Chartier, author of a book about a cure for cancer.'

'Right. So tanned jacket man figures he needs the cop out of the way. So he takes his chance. One out of three. And then he takes Tiffanny hostage and drives off. Where were you?'

'I told you, I was pacing the other side of the street. No reason for it. I was stretching my legs and thinking. I'd left them for thirty seconds. I couldn't run back quick enough. Lord knows I tried.' James shook away tears.

'James, don't beat yourself up. You are not responsible. Trust me. Sit tight.'

'Where are you going?'

'To give this to our techs. They'll arrange for a photofit to be made up. If tanned jacket slips up, shows up on CCTV, commits another crime, whatever, we'll have eyeball witnesses.'

James shook his head. 'He won't slip up. I just don't understand why he took Tiffanny prisoner. What value is she to him alive?'

Nicolas shrugged. 'That, we do not know. C'est une mystoire, vraiment.' *It's a mystery, really.* They left the interview room after James had placed his valuables back in his pockets, and Nicolas took him through into an open plan office. Deskbound cops were working the clues, faxing documents and speaking to their sources and snitches on the phone. 'Welcome to our homicide department' Nicolas said proudly.

James glanced around the room. 'We need to solve this last clue.' He pointed to the evidence bag that Nicolas was now carrying.

Nicolas nodded. 'We'll work at my desk. If it's the final clue, what could it be a final clue of?'

James pondered. It was the ultimate question. 'We already know the diagram explains the cure for cancer. So I can only assume that there is a manufacturing process in place. Probably somewhere off limits. The people the tanned jacket works for no doubt want to sabotage it.

'So they want to know where this supposed manufacturing plant is. It must be somewhere out of sight. Underground perhaps. The last clue must explain where the plant is. The tanned jacket no doubt assumed we'd already found it.'

Nicolas frowned. 'Come. We'll get started immediately. The clock is ticking, James.'

The minute he had set foot on French soil James had been pursued by the man in the tanned jacket. For the first time their roles had been reversed. Defensive play had not worked out for team Loxbridge. So the tables were going to have to be turned. He would have to find out exactly where he had taken Tiffanny. And once their location had been confirmed, he was going, with Nicolas' help, to find the bastard. And when he did, he wasn't planning on holding back. Full offensive. There was no doubt in James' mind. Whoever the man in the tanned jacket was, he was going to pay. Big time.

Chapter Thirty-Three

9:45 p.m.

There had been no initial chance to escape. The moment she was bundled into the car she had felt a sharp force shunt her into submission. The man in the tanned jacket had slapped her hard across the face and she had fallen back against the rear upholstery in a daze. She tried the doors but she knew it was a futile act – they had been locked electronically from the front console controlled by him. She tasted blood on her lip. She dabbed it away with the back of her hand. There was a stinging sensation where she had endured the blow.

He drove so fast that it made her want to vomit. She lay prone on the back seat, taking slow, deep breaths, trying to compose herself, biding her time, thinking up a plan. She noticed that his seatbelt was in the idle position, dangling near her face. It meant that he wasn't wearing it. She buckled up. His seat and the headrest were the only objects separating her from him. At this vantage point she could not see him, nor him her. She was too scared to bring herself to look at his face.

She glanced at the rear passenger window over by her feet at the other side. She was wearing low-heeled boots. She wondered if she had the strength to kick out and break the window. Or was there some other way to sabotage the ride? Something that would have him hurtling through the windshield, and her protected by the secured seatbelt.

It was pitch black outside. She saw reflections from the occasional streetlight cast themselves over the roof of the car. She heard the man's laboured breathing. He seemed to be panting, as if out of breath. Wheezing, almost. Was he asthmatic? Or was it the adrenaline that kicks in when you've just murdered someone and kidnapped another? Tiffanny did not know because she had never been in such a situation.

Just as she was preparing to put her plan to fruition, the car screeched to a halt and her seatbelt bit into her. Her foot slid off the adjacent door. She had missed her opportunity. She would have to wait for another. She heard him open the door and clamber out. She heard him step around to her side. She unbuckled the seatbelt and held the metal clasp in her hand like a slingshot.

He opened the door to grab her and she swung out and the clasp hit him on the temple and he staggered backward. Tiffanny dived out of the car and made a run but he caught her with a clothes line and she fell to the floor. The blow had only stunned him for a second. 'Nice try, bitch.' He heaved her back up off the ground by her shoulder and they walked away from the car.

She gazed around but it was too dark to make out where she was. The drive had only been about fifteen minutes, unless the blow to her face had stunned her into a state where time and space were blurred and as such her perceptions were distorted. They had to still be in downtown Aix.

All that she remembered from the movements in the car was that the man had swerved several times and then suddenly corrected himself. *Had he been dodging traffic?* There was no traffic at this time. *Or had they been on a main thoroughfare lined with mini roundabouts?* That would have made more sense. *But which direction had they travelled?*

'Where are we going?' she suddenly asked of her oppressor.

'You'll see' Chaplin balked.

There was a cold breeze in the night air. Chaplin appeared not to feel it. Tiffanny was cold with fear more than the temperature. They appeared to be in a light industrial area. They passed warehouses with sloping tin roofs and nailed up clapboard structures. There was little greenery. They had entered a realm of concrete and mortar.

Up ahead Tiffanny saw the twinkling of lights from a storefront façade, dancing in the pale moonlight. As they neared she realised it was a pharmacy that operated late night hours. 'What's your name?' Tiffanny asked.

Chaplin remained silent. Then he said 'Shut up and act normal.'

Tiffanny's fear peaked. 'Act normal for what?'

Chaplin pointed at the pharmacy and they went inside. The store was empty save for the proprietor, a small Indian man. Chaplin grabbed a box of Ibuprofen and placed it on the counter.

The man, whose nametag read Prabhaker Patel, studied his customers warily from behind his reading glasses. Chaplin paid cash for the pills and they left.

They walked for five more minutes until they reached a sandpit in the middle of a seemingly abandoned estate. They stepped through the sand and emerged on the south side in a loading bay. There was a warehouse in the corner. Chaplin dragged the Frenchwoman inside and flicked on a light.

The warehouse was threadbare. The place, no doubt a once-prosperous manufacturing operation, had been left to rot. Dust three inches thick lingered in every square foot of space. Scrap metal was strewn haphazardly across the floor and on workbenches. There were no windows and the floor was littered with plasterboard. Work tools sat abandoned on roof rafters. A rat scurried away when Chaplin disturbed its current habitat, making Tiffanny shiver.

'What the hell are we doing here?' she asked.

Chaplin placed a finger to his mouth. 'Sssshhhhh. You speak only when spoken to. There's a good little girl.'

Tiffanny gave him a satanic glare. His face wore a blank expression in response. 'Lie on that workbench.' He pointed to a battered wooden bench in the far corner, near where the rat had been.

'Go fuck yourself' she spat.

He swiped the back of his hand across her face for the second time and she stumbled to the floor.

Again she felt the dizzy sense of blood flow. Chaplin grabbed her and threw her over his shoulder. He carried her, kicking and screaming, over to the workbench. He laid her down on her back and kept her there with the strength of his right arm. With his left he produced a roll of green garden rope wire from a pocket and bound her hands together behind her back. Then he tied her feet together in a crisscross. 'I'll give you a treat and not cover your mouth. Nobody can hear you scream in here anyway, so I'd save your breath if I was you.'

He checked that the knots he had tied were sufficiently tight to hold her in place but not too tight that they would cut off her circulation. He grunted in satisfaction. 'That white Renault of yours was a raggedy piece of shit. I wonder if you'll be a better ride. I'm looking forward to finding out.'

Tiffanny winced. 'What do you want?'

Chaplin leaned over her. 'I want you to tell me what you found inside the library. I want you to tell me what the final message was, and what it means.'

Tiffanny breathed in and breathed out, slow and deep, trying to compose herself, attempting to save her energy for the next opportunity, if one came along. 'I don't have it. The paper was in Didier's pocket.'

Chaplin frowned. 'The cop? Hmmm. Something tells me he might not be in a position to give me that information anymore. I don't think he's particularly vocal these days.'

Tiffanny clenched in frustration. She ached to be free of the rope wire, ached to get up and kill him.

Chaplin said, 'Well, all I can say is, you'd best start remembering it. Because I'm not going back to the scene, and you're not going anywhere little girl.'

'I'm not a little girl, you pig.'

'No, you're not, you're a fine specimen of a woman. I'm going to enjoy you, that much is certain.'

Suddenly Chaplin winced. He reached for the Ibuprofen and tore open the cardboard container. He squeezed two pills from the foil and popped them. He swallowed them without water.

'Something wrong with your head?' the Frenchwoman enquired.

342

Chaplin grunted. 'I get such bad headaches.' Then he leaned in close to her again. 'You're stalling. Remember that message and translate it for me. It should be a location. I need to know what that location is.'

Tiffanny had remembered the message. She had thought of little else during the car journey and the walk through town to the warehouse.

AT LAST YOU HAVE THE FULL PICTURE,
MINUS A LITTLE CHARACTER!
FRET NOT, NOT LONG TO GO NOW, JUST A
FINAL BIT OF LAT. THINKING TO DO AND
YOU'LL KNOW WHERE WE ARE.

45 46 36 N   14 13 0 E

In fact, Tiffanny had already solved the last riddle. It had taken her five minutes, because it was a really simple puzzle. Simple but effective, as most codes are. She knew the answer now. But she still needed a computer to point her in the exact place. It was her last and only bargaining chip, so she wasn't intending to throw it on the table in a hurry. She needed options. She needed James. When Chaplin turned his back momentarily, she desperately looked around for anything that might help her. She saw no useful objects nearby.

Chaplin returned his attention to her. 'Here's what I'm going to do. I'm going to make it fun. I'm going to sit here and wait for you to provide me with the information I have asked for. After every half hour I'm going to remove one item of your clothes. If you do not give me what I need by the time you have no clothes left, then, well, let's just say you're going to give me another thing that I need.'

Tiffanny shuddered at the thought. It was any woman's worst nightmare. Forced intercourse was worse than anything. It was worse than if he were to kill her. At least then she'd be spared a lifetime of humiliation, a lifetime without trust of any man ever again. A lifetime of living with the thought of not being pure. The prospect of damaging her uterus to the point of not being able to conceive.

'I'll come back in half an hour.' Chaplin got up and walked out of her field of vision. Tiffanny began to slither from side to side, as if scratching her back. The bench was hard, cold and uncomfortable. Her lower back began to ache. She continued to sway a few centimetres here and there; the only give she had. Chaplin had tied her up good and proper. But there was just that chance of a wriggle. The only give she had. Tiffanny continued her movement, knowing that she only had half an hour before the vile man would return.

*

James was a couple of hours behind Tiffanny in his progress. But when it all slipped into place, he felt a surge of relief. Nicolas had gone on a coffee run. He had promised to bring back the unhealthiest junk food he could find, at James' request. He figured he was owed a small treat.

And when the hunger pangs had gathered uncontrollably, it had hit him. *At last you have the full picture, minus a little character.* He'd taken that little character from *At last,* a *t* in fact. At last minus t = Atlas. *Atlas. The B17 action diagram was actually an atlas.*

The next piece of the puzzle came to James almost instantaneously. It was those two words in the next sentence that he had picked out, as the messenger had intended. *Fret not, not long to go now, just a bit of lat. thinking to do and you'll know where we are.*

The two key words were *long and lat.* And lat was not shorthand for lateral, as in lateral thinking. No, that was the way in which the message had been hidden – behind alternative semantics. Long and lat. Longitude and latitude. Which naturally meant that the numbers were co-ordinates to one location easily pinpointed by a satellite, by triangulation or trilateration. The numbers. *45   46 36   N   14   13   0   E. Forty five degrees, forty six degrees, thirty six degrees north, fourteen degrees, thirteen degrees, zero degrees east.* Co-ordinates, to one location.

Nicolas had been gone longer than he should have been. *Where was he with the coffee and food?* James had predicted that the superintendent wouldn't have too many qualms with him using his computer, under the circumstances.

So James entered the numbers into Google and the Street Maps utility showed him an aerial map of the territory with those points of longitude and latitude. The map showed terrain which was brown, not green. He clicked the mouse to zoom into the location at street level. There were no streets. It was a cave, in Slovenia. A place called Postojna. He Googled the place and found that Postojna boasted over nine thousand caves. And somewhere deep inside one of those nine thousand was where the final scenario played out.

James' cell phone rang. It made him jump. He flipped the clamshell and answered. 'Yes?'

The robotic voice. 'Why are you in a police station?'

James breathed out a deep sigh of relief. 'Long story. But I've found it for you. The place where B17 is being prepped for distribution. It's a cave in Slovenia, a place called Postojna. It looks like quite a tourist trap, according to Google.'

There was an audible murmur on the other end of the line. 'Well done, James. Well done. But I must confess, I have known this myself for twenty-four hours.'

James frowned. 'What?'

'I'm sorry James. I was tipped off yesterday. We were picked up and flown to Slovenia last night. We're here at the cave now.'

James blanched. 'Is Radka ok?'

'Yes James, she's fine. She has begun her important work for us. The whole team are very proud of her, especially the team leader. I believe you know of him.'

'Who?'

'You'll see when you get here. You might want to hurry, James. We're nearly finished here. Soon our product will be sent out to distributors.'

James exhaled rapid bursts of air. He felt like he was having palpitations. 'Tiffanny's in trouble. And Didier's dead. I'm going to need your help.'

The robotic voice breathed erratically. 'What happened?' James explained.

'So that's why you're in the police station. You'd better find her and bring her back here, James. She's integral to the process too.'

'How do you suppose I find my way to Slovenia at such short notice?'

'You'll both need to get to Marseille airport. I'll have a private jet waiting for you first thing tomorrow morning. I'll call first thing with the details.'

'Wait. If you're deep underground in a cave right now, how come this call has such a clear signal?'

'I'm not inside the cave right now; I'm on the surface. Radka is, though, so I'm afraid you won't be able to talk to her this time. But you have my assurances that she is fine. Find Tiffanny and bring her to me in one piece, James.'

'But…'

Click. The robot had signed off.

James looked at his cell phone in despair. The door burst open and Nicolas threw himself inside. James launched up off his chair.

'James.'

'What took you so long, Nicolas?'

'We've had a tip-off. An Indian chemist ID'd our man buying headache pills in his store about an hour ago. He just phoned it in now. He was with a woman that matches Tiffanny's description. The place is about twenty minutes from here. My Mercedes is parked out back. Come on!

Chapter Thirty-Four

11:03 p.m.

He had lived up to his promise. He had returned every half an hour. The first time he did, she refused to comply, so he took her boots and her socks off. The second time he came back, she again refused to comply, so he pulled down her jeans, exposing her thong. The third time he came back, her resolve remained non-conformist, so he ripped her top right off her. He would have had difficulty shrugging it over her head, being that her wrists were bound behind it. Her bra matched the thong – lace black.

The fourth time he came back she had an unexpected convulsion. He had upped the ante. He had removed his own clothes, save for boxers. But she had a slight upper hand too. Her right wrist was free – her gentle rubbing against a loose nail on the workbench had serrated into the garden wire. She held her right arm in place as if still shackled.

She twisted and contorted her body at the sight of him approaching her. He placed a hand over her mouth and with his free hand unclasped her bra. He slid it off to reveal her breasts. He kept the bra as a keepsake and said, 'Half an hour more, and that thong is coming off, as are these boxers. And you know what happens next.'

She began work on her left wrist, which was awkward because the loose nail was on the right hand side of the workbench, so she had to lean in an awkward position which hurt her back. It was useless. She gave up.

Instead, she placed her free hand on the ground and scrabbled around for anything of use. Her hand brushed past a heavy object. Suddenly there was hope. *What was that?* She tried to find it again, but her hand brushed past it. The clock was ticking down to her inevitable rape. She had twenty-eight minutes.

*

Nicolas and James tore through the midnight streets of Aix en Provence in a Mercedes SLK roadster. They were on Avenue de l'Europe, a wide thoroughfare that sliced through the city and stretched for miles to the west. The car had a compressor and the ride was smooth.

They headed west on the boulevard, cutting through mini roundabouts which split the road into dissecting avenues at one hundred yard intervals. The pharmacy was located on Avenue Saint John Perse. They saw its twinkling lights as they crossed the bridge over a highway called L'Autoroute du Val de Durance. The neon first aid sign, the industry-standard white cross on a green background, glared at them nonchalantly.

They pulled up right outside the storefront and alighted from the Merc. The franchisor had closed up for the evening. The internal lights were shut off. The Indian man must have gone home to his family. They wouldn't be able to grill him on the tanned jacket and Tiffanny.

Nicolas peered into the glass but saw nothing untoward. All he could make out were shelves loaded with drugs, and a counter in the far corner. There was a CCTV camera mounted on a spring bracket in the corner by the eastern wall.

James glanced around in the darkness. Everywhere was black. His eyes tried to adjust. Patches of noir enveloped his immediate surroundings and beyond like a cloak of mystery.

They appeared to be in a modest financial district. He made out ugly office blocks and dilapidated clapboard housing. Black, black, black, wait. *What was that?'* A lighter shade of darkness. James pinpointed a patch of land fifty yards beyond to the north. It was definitely lighter. He walked

348

over to it. As he neared he realised what he was seeing – sand.

He walked closer and saw the full dimensions of the sandpit. It was about the size of a back garden swimming pool. It appeared to have no purpose, stuck in the centre of this downtrodden sub-metropolis of the Provence. 'Nicolas. Come over here.'

The superintendent turned at the sound. He ran to the voice calling him. 'What is it, James?'

James was pointing to the sandpit. Then he was pointing to a spot on the blacktop past the sandpit. Nicolas followed the curve of his hand and stepped around the sandpit to the other side. Then he saw what James had seen. A trail of sand extending further north, away from the pit. Footprints. Two distinct sets, one pair with a shorter radius than the other. Shorter steps. A woman's compared to a man's, perhaps.

Nicolas withdrew a handgun from a shoulder holster and motioned for James to follow.

'Do I get one of those?' he asked, pointing at the Colt 45 clasped in the palm of Nicolas' right hand. Nicolas gave him a disapproving glare. *No James, you don't.*

*

He would be back in thirteen minutes. She knew because she had counted the seconds the moment he had left her peripheral vision. She glanced up at the rotting wooden rafters thirty feet above her head. She shuddered from the cold. She continued to struggle, her right hand firmly secured to the workbench with the garden wire.

She swept her left hand over the grimy floor once more. *Where is it?* She was looking for the heavy object she had dislodged earlier. *There it was!* She caressed its surface, like a blind person feeling Braille to determine the letters.

It was pointed at the tip, and its metal was cold to the touch, but it wasn't smooth, or straight. The metal curled around like a spindle. A spiral. It must have been six inches long. Tiffanny continued to feel further down the object's shaft. It suddenly branched out and she felt a warmer coating. Plastic. A handle. A large button. An L-shaped trigger. She realised what it was.

There were nine minutes left before he would return. She now realised exactly what she was gripping. *My God, this might even work.* But it would need juice. Batteries. And it had been abandoned a long time ago, seemingly. *Would there be any juice left now?*

She dared not test the power button in case he heard the machine whirr to life. It would ruin the element of surprise. It would spell certain trouble for her. She would have to trust purely to luck. Probabilities. There was a fifty per cent chance it would work, and a fifty per cent chance it would not. Simple maths. It would be like playing Russian Roulette. Either it would work, and work well, or it would be totally useless.

She preyed and continued to count. Seven minutes, and he would be back to take all her innocence and purity and benevolence away from her.

*

The sandy footprints led them across a vacant lot and into a courtyard area. Up ahead was a giant warehouse with a sloping tin roof. A battered wooden door lay ajar.

Nicolas motioned for James to halt with a sharp hand signal. He jogged ahead and reached the warehouse door. He planted his back firmly against the wall. He strafed and peered through a one-inch crack between the door's mounted joint and the end of the wall, created by the door being slightly ajar. Apparently seeing nothing untoward, he flicked his wrist and signalled for James to join him.

James jogged to the warehouse and planted himself on the adjacent wall next to Nicolas. The two men flanked the door. Nicolas pointed in the direction of the open door and mouthed an *all clear* appraisal. He then mouthed a *stay quiet* monotribe by placing a finger to his lips.

Nicolas pressed his ear to the wall and waited. He shook his head. No sound coming from inside.

James shrugged a *now what do we do?* motion. Nicolas raised a hand. *We wait.*

*

He was three minutes early. She knew he had returned because she heard the same desperate panting she had heard when in the backseat of his car. Then it dawned on her. Not wheezing. Not asthma or adrenaline from being on the run after committing a murder. They were the grunts of a sex-crazed psychopath. He must have been planning it from the moment he threw her into the sedan. His anticipation had peaked.

She screamed blue murder when he removed her thong by sliding it delicately down her legs and flicked it over her feet. She was lying there, naked, exposed, vulnerable, an animal on the abattoir table waiting for the final act. He removed his boxers and jabbed a finger towards her face. 'Shut your mouth, bitch.'

His penis was fully erect. It was the moment he had been waiting for. 'I usually go for a younger breed, you know. But you'll do. No, you'll do just fine'.

He tried to climb onto the workbench but she kicked out in desperation, trying to ward him off. He grabbed her ankles and her efforts became futile. He held her still. He clambered onto the workbench and lent over her. His penis was hovering half a foot from her zone of intimacy.

It was now or never. Tears rolled down her cheeks. She was losing her composure, breathing haphazardly, going into cardiac arrest. She screamed. She had to summon all her strength to lift the power drill from off the floor. As she did it wavered in her hand, sending dull aches down her arm. It weighed a tonne in her delicate embrace.

She brought it up towards the startled Chaplin and clicked the red power button. Nothing happened. She clicked again. Nothing happened. He grinned at her devilishly. In the same instant he had processed an unforeseen complication only to see it diminish prematurely.

He began to laugh as he looked deep into her eyes. 'Put that down. This might hurt, sweetheart.'

Tiffany clicked the power drill a third time. It whirred to life. The drill bit began oscillating forcefully, making several hundred revolutions per second.

'So might this, you sick fuck' she screamed.

Time stood still for Chaplin. He saw the drill coming towards him, yet he could do nothing to stop it. All his strength was suddenly locked, frozen in a moment of disbelief. It was the realisation of certain defeat that made him catatonic. He had not factored that eventuality in as a mere possibility. It was his undoing.

Tiffany heaved the drill and screamed a battle cry. The drill bit fired into Chaplin's chest with unrepentant fury. A nanosecond passed, and when it had there was blood and tissue flying into the air. Her battle cry was soon drowned out by Chaplin's piercing pain. His scream punctured the sound spectrum, sending pigeons scurrying off the tin roof outside.

She did not stop there. She moved the drill upwards, carving into his neck and face. The metal and the raw power ripped and crunched through skin, ligaments, tissue and vital organ. Blood sprayed everywhere. The pink mist. Tiffany was still screaming, like a tribal warrior leading into a history-making battle, but her efforts were still overtaken by Chaplin's own life-defying resonance.

Her strength ebbed away and she dropped the power drill. It clattered off the workbench and smashed onto the floor. The power faded out, a crescendo in reverse, the noise cutting back down the spectrum to blissful quiet.

Tiffany sobbed bitterly as James and Nicolas burst through the door and ran to her aid. They had reacted when the drill had first started up. They had made it in time. In fact, Tiffany had saved herself. Chaplin lay sprawled on the floor, his eyes lolled skyward in the glazed look of death. Half his internal organs poured out onto the warehouse floor, producing a foul odour.

The sick bastard had folded her clothes up neatly and placed them on a chair in an adjacent room. James found them and quickly helped Tiffanny get dressed. Her dignity had been restored. Nicolas looked away in quiet respect.

When she was fully clothed she fell into James' arms and he gave her a bear hug. He held her tight against his chest for what seemed like a small eternity. He stroked her hair to reassure her. It was over. She was safe. She had avoided the fate of coerced intercourse by a whisker.

She sobbed uncontrollably and James found himself drenched from her tears. He kept it a secret that some of those salty droplets were his own. Finally he looked to Nicolas, who was pacing the warehouse. 'What do we do with his body?'

'Leave it to rot' the superintendent replied. 'The vultures will have a field day with this. It's no less than he deserves.' He picked up the now infamous tanned leather jacket that had been the source of their constant fear. He checked the pockets. Nothing. 'Just what I expected. No ID. He's not a French citizen as far as we know. Interpol would want to know how he entered our country.'

'I guess Lacroix never got back to me because he did not show up on their records. He was a ghost' James prophesised, thinking back to their encounter with the Paris Prefecture of Police Captain, who had initially suspected them of murdering Fabien, until Camille had succumbed during their incarceration, thereby invalidating their guilt.

James looked at the beautiful Frenchwoman, Tiffanny Tourneux, who at this moment he thought he loved more dearly than anything else in the whole world. All he wanted to do was love her, hold her, protect her from evil, keep her safe, preserve her unabridged perfection. 'Hey, you'.

Tiffanny produced a weak smile. 'Hey, you.'

'Did you crack it? The final code?'

Tiffanny thought for a moment. Then she remembered. 'Ah yes, co-ordinates, right? 45, 46, 36, N, 14, 13, 0, E. But I don't know where. No computer.' She was too drained to speak in sophisticated sentences. She had been through the ordeal of her life.

'It's a cave in Slovenia. A place called Postojna. Only thing is, there are nine thousand of them, and we need to find the right one!'

'So what happens now?' Nicolas interjected.

James smiled. 'We're getting a private jet out of Marseille, tomorrow morning. We're going to get a call with the details.'

'You need to rest up, both of you' the superintendent counselled. 'Come back to the station. We'll put you up and feed you.'

James frowned. 'Surely you don't mean...?'

Nicolas laughed as he read James' mind. 'In a cell? Mais non, c'est folle! Don't be crazy! Officer's quarters. Cheapest motel in town!'

James smiled at Nicolas. 'Lead on, MacDuff.'

'Who's MacDuff?'

James shook his head and kissed Tiffanny on the forehead. 'Never mind.'

*

Chaplin was only ninety five per cent dead. There was a pulse, albeit a weak one. He summoned the last remnants of lifeblood and reached for his cell phone, which he had left on the floor by the workbench. He found one last vestige of energy and hit speed dial two.

'Yes?'

Chaplin choked out his last words through the final breaths his lungs would produce. 'Slovenia. Postojna. Cave. Satellite. 45, 46, 36, N, 14, 13, 0, E.' A final thought struck him – Paul Ross, at ninety two years of age, had outlived him. The bastard. Then he signed off – from the call, and from life itself.

Chapter Thirty-Five

Sunday. 3:56 a.m.

Grigor Lipansky and Majid Boughhera were Lebanese. The former was a Jew, the latter a Muslim. Both were in the business of terrorism. Both had hailed out of a long-troubled Beirut.

Their grandfathers had witnessed Lebanon's independence from the Ottoman Empire and later the French Mandate in 1943. Their fathers had witnessed an era of relative prosperity between 1943 and 1975, when Beirut became a centre for finance and culture in Arabia.

At the time of Lipansky and Boughhera's birth, a civil war broke out in their country, dividing the landscape up into a Muslim West and a Christian East. Whilst many citizens at the time flocked to the neutral centre of the country, the no man's land known as the Green Line, Lipansky's father and his people fought bitterly against Boughhera's father and his. Islam versus Christianity. Once again, mankind's history was following the same pattern; the use of religious sovereignty as a pretext for land acquisition.

In 1982, when Lipansky and Boughhera had reached their infantile peak, the Israelis joined the incursion and their troops annexed the West of the capital. By 1990 Lipansky and Boughhera reached teenhood. They had become battle-hardened from childhood skirmishes against the French and US embassies. But the war was on its way out. They were too late, and would not get to fight.

Being secret childhood friends, they had made a pact not to let their conflicting religions disrupt their friendship. So after the war they formed a strategic allegiance and joined forces, entering the illegal arms trade, running smuggling operations and playing spy games with the CIA and MI5.

Their business grew steadily over the Nineties. Saddam needed armaments and accessories for his Gulf War against the Americans. Slobodan Milosevic became a majority client during the tremulous times of Yugoslavia. Whether it was Serbs being slaughtered or Croats, the damage was in all probability caused by a Lipansky or Boughhera product.

When Bush came to power at the turn of the twentieth century, they knew they'd be turning over a tidy profit. That infidel would be causing trouble in the Middle East for sure, they had prophesised. And when the Twin Towers collapsed on 9/11 they couldn't process their orders fast enough. Terrorism was the new fad for their clientele.

And their product was top class. Most of their gear was stolen from defecting Russians or bought on the cheap from Chechnya. Some of it was home made from scrap materials shipped from Syria and Jordan.

They began to feel disillusioned with the politic their country was subrogating, so they joined the Cedar Revolution. When Prime Minister Rafik Hariri came to the Saint George Bay in 2005, Lipansky and Boughhera helped to plot his assassination, which for them was a triumphant success. They orchestrated the opposition rally and in 2006 they successfully drove Syrian troops out of their beloved homeland.

In 2006 the Israelis returned to cause trouble. Lipansky and Boughhera fought diligently to protect Hezbollah targets from the Jews, to moderate success. Their greatest failures were to the south, a Shiite territory controlled by Hezbollah.

The Lebanese Army eventually took over, which was great for Lipansky and Boughhera, because the army were short on munitions. But they were getting too old for this shit. War and terror had taken its toll on them. They'd survived assassination attempts from an incalculable number of interested parties; rival dealers, Jewish gangs, western governments, confused infidels.

But they had always remained the best of companions. The only difference between them was that Boughhera wore a burqa and believed that the Prophet Mohammed had designated the holy land to the Muslims, won fair and square in the Crusades a thousand years before, whereas Lipansky was adamant that Abraham bequeathed it to the Jews when he sacrificed his first son Isaac and donated Jerusalem to his second son Ishmael.

For them, ideology was a preternatural conflict of the mind that bore no fruit. For them religion interfered with business and profit, unless it served that very end. Lipansky and Boughhera represented the 0.01% of the members of organised religions who twisted the essence of their meaning and created a faction of fundamentalism.

It was sad, but that 0.01% gave these religions a bad name. Exacerbated by the media and by public ignorance, they led to irrational judgment of orthodox religious followers, who used their Bibles as benevolent codes for a prosperous lifestyle, taking heed of the preaching for respect of one's fellow man, and how to live one's own life peacefully. In the Koran the Prophet Mohammed states that killing one human being by murder is as if you have killed the whole of mankind. Al-Qaeda have clearly not read their bible lately.

Their latest client was an oddity; an anomaly. He didn't fit the profile. But he paid handsomely; astronomically even. So naturally they were placated from asking too many questions.

Their C-130 cargo plane dotted through the twinkling indigo sky, its twin propeller and single engine maintaining its trajectory eighteen thousand feet above ground level.

Their mission had come at short notice. It was not how they usually operated – diligent planning was essential. But again, their pockets had been stuffed with enough green to enable them to disappear forever. They'd never have to work again, not in their illegal trade or any other.

It had come with a mysterious phone call, which had been routed through their various intermediaries until it was passed up the chain of command. Their organisation was diverse, like intricate branches of a deep-rooted tree. They'd been given the co-ordinates to a target northwest of their homeland. A target deep underground, hidden inside the recess of a thousand year old cave, where the stalagmites grew one centimetre every year, and where the speleothems were beautiful and sacred.

The client had sounded old. Ancient even. His raspy voice scratched out the orders they were in the process of carrying out, as the C-130 carried them over a shimmering Black Sea and across rural Bulgaria.

Inside the cabin the pilot pinpointed the co-ordinates the client had provided. 45, 46, 36, N, 14, 13, 0, E. They soon crossed Serbia and Bosnia-Herzegovina. They arced due northward over Croatian soil and then due west into Slovenia.

The cargo plane dropped in altitude and cruised at ten thousand feet. Fuel was running short, but they'd soon be at the landing strip. They glided over Novo Mesto and the capital Ljubljana. Before they hit the Julian Alps mountain range the plane took a southward trajectory and began to lose more altitude.

They landed at a small abandoned airstrip five miles from Postojna. They were met by associates in a Jeep Cherokee. The plane was refuelled and the pilot returned to Lebanon. The cargo was removed from the plane and carefully stored in the Jeep's load bed. A black tarpaulin kept curiosity's prying eye away from the contents. They were under the cover of darkness, but they were taking no chances. Spy planes could take infra red hi-definition photographs of the landscape from miles skyward, boasting optical zoom magnifications of up to one hundred and twenty times magnification. Not to mention satellites.

They rode with their associates for five miles until the Jeep entered a dirt track on a narrow enclosure and shimmied down it, the vehicle and its passengers bouncing up and down as the suspension was put through its paces.

They saw a sign for Planinska Cave as their headlights caught it in their beams. Lipansky gazed out of the window and saw Predjama Castle perched high on a rock like a tamed kestrel. The GPS bleeped triumphantly when they reached their destination.

The men with the Jeep had brought with them a device for storing the cargo. It was a metal contraption and when Lipansky stole a proximal look he noticed that it was a series of steel girders welded together to form a makeshift gurney.

Boughhera made himself useful by assembling the gurney whilst the other three men, including Lipansky, mounted the cargo onto the gurney. The cargo was heavy and it required all of their strength. They heaved and grunted and eventually the cargo slotted into place on the gurney.

The entrance to the cave was sealed shut. A board had been erected in multiple languages, explaining that this particular cave was currently unavailable to the public. It did not explain why. The men read the signs in English; they had learned their lingual skills from the American agents who came to Beirut in the Eighties and Nineties to play spy games with them.

Lipansky glared at the cave. He had been provided with mission parameters from the mysterious client. Background checks had been run on him, as per standard protocols. He wasn't a spy, or other government personnel, he wasn't police, a rival arms dealer. It appeared not to be a trap, ambush or set-up. He was the magnate of a long-established global pharmaceutical conglomerate. His attributed wealth was the vast majority of the billion dollar medicine market. And he had deep ties to the American space agency NASA.

Lipansky figured whatever was in the cave was a threat to Paul Ross, therefore it had to go. Well, the cargo would take care of that. It would be a shame to destroy the cave – one of a network of seven and a half thousand Karst caves. They were wonders of Eastern Europe, and carried with them a hallowed chapter of natural history.

It was the same old story. Man builds and creates, then man destroys what they have built and created. Mother nature was beautiful but also destructive at times, spewing forth molten lava from rock and slicing through tectonic plates, or driving metre-high waves of water into civilisation. But man was no different. Man was beautiful, but man was destructive.

More tools were taken from the Jeep. One of the men lifted a pneumatic drill from under the tarpaulin and took it over to the sealed entrance. He had studied geology and had told riggers in Dubai where to drill for oil. Now he was using his skills for a less productive purpose.

With the help of the other men, he drilled through the rock. The eeriness of the silent predawn landscape was cruelly cut short by their disturbances. Nocturnal creatures scurried and scampered away in a frantic bid for survival.

The men wore goggles to protect their eyes from the flying debris and linen masks to prevent them from succumbing to asbestosis. The limestone crumbled like plaster and after ten minutes they had made a crater wide enough to fit the cargo through.

The gurney was wheeled through the cave and the men took out flashlights from the Jeep and entered the cave.

Lipansky had studied the map he had been provided diligently. He had assumed that Ross must have pulled some strings to acquire the internal blueprints, but in fact they were selling the maps in the gift shop. Lipansky had grunted in satisfaction at the realisation. How easy.

With Lipansky's help the gurney was manoeuvred through the tunnels and crevasses of Planinska Cave. They slowly descended several hundred metres. It was a tricky proposition, frustratingly awkward. Movement was constricted inside the narrow passageways.

They were following a path paved by Unity Six, the scientific group that Ross thought had been wiped out by his Chaplin. But Ross had since discovered that one of the six had survived in Slovakia, by jumping into the abyss and miraculously surviving the sheer drop to oblivion. Ross had been unable to punish Chaplin for his misdemeanour, because Chaplin was already dead. This had all been relayed to Lipansky.

Eventually the men heard hushed voices; muffled mumblings of resonance through the thick turgid walls. It meant that they had reached the lair that Ross had suspected existed.

The cargo was unloaded and positioned in a small pit in front of a cluster of intricate stalactites.

360

It had been specifically chosen as one of few locations within the cave that possessed small cracks in the rock; airways that carried light and air back to the surface several hundred feet above. And, more importantly, a signal.

The men spent half an hour preparing the cargo. First of all it had to be assembled. Then it had to be wired up. Then it had to be rigged. Finally, it had to be armed. It was a mission Lipansky and Boughhera couldn't have accomplished on their own. Their experience with this specific type of device was limited. They were used to handling munitions with less destructive capabilities. Rocket launchers, mortar grenades, automatic fire rifles and machineguns.

But this was a different kettle of fish altogether. This was nuclear. A dirty bomb, crafted from scrap metal, nails, plutonium, bullets and spent shell casings. The men flicked dials and wired fuses and, once satisfied, they left the device on its own in the darkness of the cave and made their way back up to the surface, the same way they had come.

Their ascent and subsequent extraction was more accommodating without having to heave their cargo on the gurney. They were soon back in the Jeep, retracing their carbon footprints back to the airfield. There was no detonator – the device was on a timer and totally self-serving.

Another C-130 with a different pilot collected them and transported them back east to their homeland.

Inside the cave, the bomb's digitally displayed timer began to count down.

11 : 59: 21

In less than twelve hours, it would be show time.

Chapter Thirty Six

7:43 a.m.

8 : 22: 45

Radka Rosická was flummoxed. The cave was cold, but they had provided her with waterproofs; a cagoule and matching trousers. They were hardly a fashion statement. They were, however, necessary.

Pierre Chartier had introduced her to the whole team. For once, Casino Collins took a step back, allowing Chartier to take the limelight. He was a curious man with an odd gait and a plethora of eccentric mannerisms, such as flicking the side of his head whenever he was illustrating an important piece of information, and pouting his lips whenever posed with a question that required a moment of quiet reflection.

Radka was curious about his tattoo. 'It's a crab being pierced by a sword' he explained. That much Radka had been able to determine for herself. Pierre had explained further. 'In astrology the crab represents the star sign of cancer. Our cause is to eradicate that evil from our world; in fact it has been for hundreds of years.'

'Hence the sword' Radka inferred.

'Precisement' Chartier clapped his hands in celebration. Then he told the Czech everything, from the beginning. He told her about Ernst Theodor Krebs Sr, and about Roubiquet and Bontron-Chariand, about von Liebig and Woehier and amygdalin, about hydrogen cyanide, benzaldehyde and glucose. The cancer patient who Inosmetzeff successfully treated with forty six thousand milligrams of amygdalin who was still alive three years after diagnosis.

Chartier gave Radka a copy of the B17 action diagram and told her all about trophoblasts. He told her about Unity Six, the off-radar unit assigned to the Slovakian mountain retreat six months ago to find a way of chemicalising the process. He told her that five of the six had been murdered because somebody had cottoned on to their intentions.

Then he introduced her to a man covered from head to toe in bandages. He looked like he'd been in a terrible wreck, or a mummy from a thousand years past. He revealed himself to be Stewart Banks. He explained his dice with death after plummeting down into Žiarska valley. Into the abyss. Radka knew the territory well – her parents owned a cottage in Liptovský Mikuláš, and she had spent many summers there on the bike trails.

Banks explained that he had been pursued by the killer of his five associates, a man whom he would never forget. He had a scar on his right cheek and a look in his eye of pure evil. He'd called himself Alpha One and referred to his fellow hostiles as concurrent Alphas. He had spoken on a radio to an unseen boss whom he had simply referred to as Sir. No doubt some pharmaceutical bigwig, directing the upper echelons and deciding the fate of mankind from some sanctimonious throne in a corporate office suite.

Chartier then explained that his father had pioneered their movement in the nineteen seventies. He'd received death threats and became the subject of menacing acts of nuisance, such as having the heads of dead cats placed through his letterbox.

Then he had befallen to an act of arson. The authorities ruled it out; they claimed a cigarette butt found inside a wastebasket has caused the fire. But nobody in the Chartier household had ever smoked. And Chartier's mother was clear about visitors smoking outside. It was a cover-up. Somebody had bribed the firefighters.

Chartier Senior had found a way to chemicalise the process, but the arson destroyed his research; years and years of research. He had been so close to perfection, and it was taken away from him in a moment of smoke and flame. He committed suicide one year later. Chartier, an aspiring novelist and wax weaver, picked up his father's work in his late teens when he became jaded from the way the world had taken a turn for the worst.

Chartier told Radka how he'd picked up radio chatter on the internet that someone in Lyon was meddling in the wares of the pharmaceutical giants once again. Someone was onto him. Faking death or disappearing appeared to be the only way to preserve his mortality.

He showed Radka a copy of the book he had written: *Cancer: Why We're Still Dying To Know The Truth*. His father's work remastered. He moved to Paris to complete the manuscript, blindsided by hatred of the arsonists and spurred on by the promise of honouring his father's memory.

He made important contacts in the French capital. His work was finished. He found representation by a small literary agency who sought controversial material to stir the public's fire for conspiracy. They were so liberal and left wing they were off the scale. The national library snapped it up.

It soon received adverse publicity. The pharmaceutical industry suddenly found itself in a shitstorm. Pierre was informed by a mutual friend of one of his contacts that his book, his hard work, had disappeared from the Bibliothèque Nationale in Paris. Nobody knew how it had happened. There had been no break-in. Books could not be removed without authorisation; attempts to do so would trigger alarms and the thief would be caught red handed.

So Chartier had fled to Aix en Provence, where he tried to clear his head and figure out what he needed to do. By sheer chance and grandiose opportunity he met some biochemistry students at a pharmacology conference. He took them under his wing and created Unity Six.

He had the talent, but not the green. Casino Collins had his fingers in so many pies he must have been looking for more hands. Chartier set up a meeting with the philanthropist and revealed his requirements. Collins was flabbergasted by the Frenchman's revelations, and jumped at the chance to be the majority financier. This was the biggest and best pie of all. He'd be named Time Man of the Year for this. He'd be a hero. Chartier had created the ultimate panacea. But they had to act fast. For the arsonists, the thieves of his book, and the scarred murderer of Unity Six, their cause was clearly one of great concern.

'So where do I fit into all of this?' Radka begged the ultimate question. 'Why was I kidnapped? And what's James' role in all of this?'

Chartier smiled. 'We learned of your underhanded computer skills. Plus you're a pharmacologist. That, to us, is the perfect combination, and to our enemies a lethal one. B17 is, as you now see, a natural phenomenon. But we have found a way to chemicalise the process, thereby making it a thousand times more effective.'

Radka nodded. 'But you still didn't answer my question. Why me?'

Chartier squeezed her shoulder affectionately. 'You're quite right. We found a way to manufacture this product, using the B17 action diagram and all the insights Krebs et al supplied to us.

'But we need you to write a computer program that allows us to calculate the correct proportions of all the ingredients for mass production.

'That way we can get millions of B17 remedies out onto the market; we plan to flood it before the pharmaceutical conglomerates even know what's hit them.

'We thought about putting it in the water supply, but it's proving too difficult. Every country has their own filtration procedures and most are too heavily guarded by personnel.'

Radka pondered Chartier's proposition. Two years ago she had inadvertently created a drug that was designed to kill. Aequitol, it had been called. Now she was being offered a chance to redeem herself, by producing the polar opposite – a drug of sorts, designed to preserve human life.

'I'd better get started then. I assume you have the equipment I require?'

Chartier beamed, as did Casino Collins from the sidelines. 'Atta girl. Come. I will show you your office. It has the best technology money can currently buy.' Collins threw the Frenchman a petulant grin. 'Correction, the best technology Mr

Collins' money can buy.' Casino nodded his appreciation of acknowledgment.

The Frenchman led the Czech to a man-made chamber several feet further below ground. Radka could not believe what she was seeing. It looked like a Bond villain's secret lair. Radka thought it had been lifted straight from the set of Moonraker.

'How much have you already produced and readied for distribution?' Radka asked.

'Just one single batch, actually' Chartier confirmed.

'Is it here in the cave so I can have a look at it?'

'No, I'm afraid it isn't. We had to put it in a safe place. A very safe place, out of harm's reach.'

Radka nodded to herself. Paranoid and scared, they were. And understandably so. This was colossal.

'How much time do we have?'

Chartier looked to Collins, who shrugged his shoulders in nonchalance. 'Well, there is no set time limit really. But we should act fast, lest our oppressors catch a tip-off to our location.'

'How could they?'

'I don't know, Radka, but it happened to my father's garage, and to my book, and to Unity Six in Slovakia. We can never seem to remain under the radar for long. I blame the modern world – satellites, cell phones, trackers, spy agencies, the list is endless.'

Radka smiled. 'We shouldn't hold modernity to account for our own misgivings. Human nature will always be what it is.'

'A wise statement, Mrs Rosická-Loxbridge.'

Radka shook her head. 'It's just Rosická now. Miss Rosická.'

'Going back to your questions Miss Rosická, time is of the essence. We would like to initiate the operation within the next months, preferably even weeks.'

'And James?'

'Well' Chartier explained, 'We needed you for this task, but we needed James on board so that he wouldn't do anything foolish and alert the authorities.

'Then we came to realise his usefulness as a chaperone and bodyguard for another one of our associates. A woman who is integral to this too, just like you are, but for different reasons.'

'Oh?'

'Oui, her parents are here with us now. You met them earlier. The elderly couple, Gertrude and Vincent? Their daughter is also a pharmacologist, just like you. When my father killed himself several years ago, I knew I would need a failsafe, a plan B. So I left clues around my homeland that would eventually lead her to this cave.'

Radka was confused. 'Who is she? And what's so special about this particular cave?'

Chartier beamed. 'There is nothing special about this particular cave, except for its more than adequate conditions for this operation, and its privacy. It's currently closed off to the public. Others have tour guides toing and froing. Her name is Tiffanny. And she is going to be demonstrating our product.'

'I don't follow'.

'When Tiffanny was fourteen she contracted cancer in her throat. Her parents, who knew about B17, fed her dried apricots and apple seeds rich in nitrilosides. She went into remission and the cancer was destroyed.

'Then when she was nineteen she found a lump on her breast. Getting cancer once is unlucky enough. Getting it twice is plain demoralising. Again, we used B17 and we killed it. No chemotherapy, no hair loss, no pain. And, as you will see, she has the most beautiful head of curly hair you will ever see!'

Radka was speechless. *My God, it really does work.* 'But how could her parents have known about B17?'

Again, Chartier smiled. He had anticipated her every question like a chess grandmaster. 'Because Tiffanny, and her parents, and her parents' parents, are direct descendants of Roubiquet. Her family have kept his legacy a secret since the nineteenth century.'

Radka whistled. 'That makes sense. It seems you have an answer to all my questions!'

Chartier curtsied in a mock gesture of appreciation. 'Perhaps you should get started, Radka.'

'Where is James now?'

Chartier looked to Collins and the entrepreneur spoke for the first time since they had arrived. 'South France. Aix en Provence, to be precise. Radka, I have arranged for a private jet to bring him here. You'll see him very soon. He's coming with Tiffanny.'

Radka thought about that. *With* Tiffanny???

'Am I still a hostage? What about him?' She pointed to Casino Collins.

'Well, not strictly no, but I imagine you'll want to stick around and atone for your sins? We know about Aequitol.'

Radka blanched. *What didn't they know about her? Her computer skills, Aequitol. All her secrets were being exposed. Maybe Chartier was right about the modern world ruining the sanctity of privacy. I need to find some new secrets about myself.*

Chapter Thirty Seven

10:01 a.m.

5 : 49: 26

The helicopter was a Bell 206B3 Jetranger III. It had collected Ross and his men in Prague and taken flight on a path towards the co-ordinates that Chaplin had murmured to him in his dying breaths.

The old timer was buckled into his seat. He glanced at his watch and knew he'd only have five or six hours to say his piece and then make a vitally speedy exit. Lipansky had called in and confirmed that everything was in place. He may have been ancient, but he wasn't stupid. He was worldly wise, and he was going to win.

Even in death he would be victorious, because once again the natural lobbyists would be up in arms to no avail. Their natural answer would be eradicated, just like their forefathers' efforts had been.

Hopefully this time the message would be crystal clear. He'd paid Lipansky a great deal of money. He preyed that the Jew had not held out on him, or made any elementary mistakes.

Ross knew he was fading out. We wondered if he would reach his ninety-third birthday. It was eighty six days away. He was living on borrowed time, of that he was well aware.

He wanted to make them see the error of their ways. He wanted them to admit that their efforts were futile and foolish. And he also saw this fleeing visit as a last ditch attempt at salvation. The greater good. He needed to be able to pass on his legacy at the pinnacle of its success.

He had originally planned to pass on this legacy to Chaplin, a man he had looked upon as his own son. But now that man was gone. He was supposed to have taken care of the Frenchwoman – their test case specimen. But somehow she had eluded him and turned the tables on him in the most finite of manners. She had killed him. *How on Earth had she accomplished such a thing?*

Paul Ross rode with six of his Alpha contingent. They were private mercenaries who had returned from the Blackwater operations in Iraq, now forced to earn their keep in domestic skirmishes. They all carried Heckler & Koch MP5 submachine guns with silver tipped bullets.

Killing them would probably be the last thing on Earth he would do. His heart and his brain and his bones were growing weary and weak. The years had been fortuitous to him.

The helicopter touched down in Postojna two hours after it had set off from Prague. Ross unbuckled and prepped the fragile fibres of his mind for the final confrontation.

*

12:15 p.m.

3 : 04: 11

James and Tiffanny had slept well in Nicolas' police quarters. He had been good to the both of them. He had fed them and given them shelter. And, in breach of a million regulations, he had given them each a Glock 12 six shooter and explained how to use them.

Collins had called James on the cell phone but there was no longer a robotic voice distortion program installed on the line. Collins proceeded to update him on Radka and her important work inside the cave.

Now James understood; she was not merely an insurance policy, she possessed the requisite skills.

Unique talent. And James was her hubbie, so he'd been roped into it to avoid asking the right questions in the wrong places.

A Lear jet had met them at Marseille airport and transported them to Postojna in little over an hour. Tiffanny had cast herself in a remote shell ever since her ordeal with Chaplin in the warehouse. Her eyes were glazed and distant, her stare glassy and cold. She had not uttered a word since leaving France.

James had tried to comfort her but she had viciously punched and kicked his healing hands away from her. It would seem for some time that any touch from a man would incite hatred and bitterness. James empathised.

When they disembarked from the Lear, James saw Slovenia for the first time. He immediately processed a smorgasbord of natural beauty. Huge mountains clung to the sky in the distant foreground like limpets to a deity's back. Lush forestry loomed and flanked them on all sides.

Everything looked brand spanking new. The road irrigation was immaculate. Fresh tarmac clung to the blacktop. Slovenia was perhaps the wealthiest of all former Soviet Bloc nations. It appeared that they had applied funds from the municipal pot to efficient ends.

There was no wind – the environment was breathtakingly tranquil. A Toyota Landcruiser broke the silence and veered up the steep path towards them.

A lone figure emerged and approached them on foot. Tiffanny recognised him because she had dealt with him before. James recognised him from the newspaper article he had read in a Chester newspaper less than a week ago. *Space-ious accommodation you can't afford.*

The man was Casino Collins. 'Where's Radka?' James called out, avoiding any initial pleasantries. Tiffanny remained inert.

'She's busy working' Collins replied. 'But she'll happily take a break when she sees that you have finally arrived.'

'Why did you have us on a wild goose chase around Paris, Lyon and Aix en Provence when you already knew the location of this cave?'

'James, I only became informed of this location about twenty four hours ago. I was given instructions to deliver Radka here. It was no wild goose chase. It took them a while to trust us enough to come out of the woodwork. Decades in fact. All's well that ends well.'

James kicked at a pebble with his loafer. 'You think this is going to end well?'

'It has to. The world depends on it.'

They clambered inside the Landcruiser with Collins at the helm and he drove them the short distance to the entrance to Planinska Cave. James pondered removing the Glock hidden in his waistband and holding Collins hostage, just like he had done to his wife. See how he liked it.

But James sensed that Collins wasn't the real bad guy in all of this mess. There were a reluctance and a pleasant quiet about his demeanour.

'Thanks for following my clues, James. Every step of the way. You did remarkably well. And apologies for the nature of our telephone conversations.

'I thought my attitude would spur you on. A little immature perhaps, but a great deal was riding on your full co-operation.' Collins grunted as he caressed the steering wheel in one hand and downshifted the gears with his other.

'I was reluctant to send Murgatroyd, to be honest. I doubted his ability to convince you.'

James gazed out the window at the slow moving wilderness. 'You kidnapped my wife. What did you expect me to do?'

Collins shrugged. 'Granted, you followed the pattern of behaviour we determined. We'll do anything for our beloved women.'

James looked at Tiffanny in the backseat next to him. She appeared to be in a trance; a state of trepidation smeared across her lineaments. He had to find a way to penetrate her shell. Chaplin had tried to penetrate her; literally. And now she was irreparably damaged. She had killed in self defence; the defence of provocation. She would need time to heal, and possibly psychiatric counselling. No, she was tougher than that. But even tough cookies can crumble when the push comes to shove.

Collins pulled the Landcruiser to a halt and they alighted. The cave entrance awaited. The entrepreneur handed them torches and a set of waterproofs identical to those which he had given Radka. 'Put these on – it's cold down there' he said.

They clambered into a waiting cave train and admired the speleothems as it powered to life. Collins sat up front, Tiffanny perched in the centre and James rode the back. He placed his arms around her waist to support her. For the first time she did not refuse the physical contact.

The train picked up speed and the track broadened out and branched off into its predetermined route. James instinctively ducked when they rounded a corner and a low rock formation seemed bent on taking his head clean off. He noticed that Collins remained perfectly still.

'This was a tourist hotspot until they shut it down a few years ago' the entrepreneur shouted back. 'So it's designed along health and safety parameters. None of the rock formations will hit your head, trust me.'

Trust him? Trust the man who had kidnapped his wife and dragged them into this mess? Why? Tiffanny's hair was brushing against his cheek. It was a very pleasant feeling. He looked at her and she at him. She gave him a look, as if to say *Hey, if it wasn't for this mess you wouldn't have met me, right?* James had to agree that it was a monumental consolation prize.

*

2:02 p.m.

1 : 13: 07

Paul Ross was agitated when he and his men entered the cave and found no train. 'You're gonna make an old man like me walk all the way down

375

this shithole?' He glared at his men who provided embarrassed looks.

Two of the men went to grab Ross as if to help carry him through the descent. He gave them a *Don't even think about it* sneer and then took off on his own. The unit followed suit, MP5s cocked and locked for the massacre they'd been instructed to instigate at the bottom of the cave.

*

2:23 p.m.

0: 52: 48

The stalagmites and stalactites became more intricate and beautiful the further the depth they reached. Tiffanny continued to elude all lucidity. The cave train pulled to a stop once the track had channelled out into a concave platformed area the size of a small subway station.

Collins and James both disembarked. Tiffanny remained seated, staring into space. James reached out with his hand and absentmindedly she took it and he pulled her up onto the platform.

They flicked on their flashlights and Collins led them through a series of narrow passageways into a small antechamber. The air was cool and damp. The light beams bounced off the limestone and cast bizarre shadows across the rock formations and speleothems.

Suddenly they heard muffled resonance. Voices, James soon realised. Collins led them into a man-made den cut from the rock and James stopped in his tracks. Several people, men and women, milled about in white coats, carrying beakers and Petri dishes and syringes and other equipment. Scientists.

The men he did not recognise. There were just two women. The elder he did not recognise. The other he instantly recognised as his wife. Radka Rosická.

They hugged awkwardly. 'Are you ok?' They both said it in unison. A mutual gesture of goodwill.

It was a hug of friendship, not borne of romance. James introduced her to Tiffanny, and vice versa. He advised Radka that the Frenchwoman had been through a traumatic experience and as such she should not expect much cognition from her at that current moment.

'My dear, thank God you are here.' A man approached Tiffanny and placed a hand on her shoulder. He was holding an apple in his other hand. James watched him warily. He instinctively found his left hand reaching subconsciously for the Glock underneath his shirt. But then the man extended his hand. As he did, his own shirt sleeve slid up his arm and James noticed a curious tattoo – a crab pierced by a sword.

'I believe you have been looking for me. You must be James Loxbridge. I am Pierre.'

James took the hand. 'Chartier?'

The man nodded briskly. 'The very same.'

'You are a very hard man to find, Mr Chartier.'

'Indeed. I am sorry for all your troubles. It had to be this way, I am afraid. Otherwise this cave would be serving as my tomb right now, not my office.' With that he grinned and bit into the apple.

James nodded, releasing his hand on the Glock and moving it back to his side. He watched as the Frenchman began to eat the seeds and the core of the apple. 'You're not supposed to eat that part' he declared matter-of-factly.

Chartier beamed. 'On the contrary, Mr Loxbridge. The seeds and the core are the best part of the apple. They are rich in nitrilosides.'

'Nitrilosides?'

'Yep. Part of the B17 process.'

'So you're saying that eating apple cores and seeds can help to prevent cancer?'

'I'm saying that it would be a sound preventative measure, although to be entirely truthful the highest concentration of nitrilosides can be found in apricots.'

James thought back to the dried apricots he had habitually been nibbling on in Chester. *No shit.*

James' attention was suddenly drawn to Tiffanny, who suddenly appeared terrified of something.

The elderly couple had emerged from their corner of the den and were now under the direct beam of their flashlights, as if this were a theatre production and the limelight was suddenly on their act.

Tiffanny's knees appeared to buckle as the couple approached. James had to catch her. He held her up for a moment; then she regained her composure and her posture. The couple were smiling. The elderly woman had tears in her eyes.

'No' Tiffanny said. 'No. It's not possible. Putain. Merde. Non. Mon Dieu. Ce n'est pas possible! Ce n'est pas possible!' Then she began to shed tears of her own.

'Mere? Pere? Mon Dieu. J'ai pensé que vous etes mortes! *Mum? Dad? I thought that you were dead!*

James was gobsmacked. The Frenchwoman had told him that her parents had died in a plane crash. A lightning storm had disintegrated the aircraft they were travelling on. No survivors, just a black box floating in the ocean.

The couple embraced Tiffanny and the three of them sobbed uncontrollably. As they made their overdue reconciliations in rapid fire French, Pierre explained to James that every member of their covert faction were believed to have shuffled off the mortal coil by the outside world. It was the only way they could preserve their sanctity and keep their plight alive; keep B17 alive. It was either that or disappearance, and as James already knew, it was the latter misdirection that Pierre had opted for.

The moment was interrupted by a stern looking scientist; a woman in her thirties. 'Pierre! Pierre! Nous avons un problème!' *Pierre, we have a problem!*

She spoke in French and Tiffanny's heart sank, as did her parents. Everybody produced a panicked expression. James glanced to Chartier for a translation.

Pierre's own lineaments appeared grim. 'James, Monique has found a bomb in the cave. It has a timer on it. Monique thinks it's a big one.'

'How does Monique know what it is?'

Pierre pointed at Monique. 'Because Monique here is considered somewhat of an expert in nuclear fission. And as part of her dissertation she developed a research project on this type of power in warfare.'

'Are you saying what I think you're saying, Pierre?'

'I'm afraid so, James. It's a nuclear device. We've been discovered...again. We need to get out of here! Monique says the timer is currently on forty five minutes and counting down.'

'How will you get all the equipment out in that time?'

Radka interjected. 'We can't, James. Impossible. We'd need at least twenty four hours' notice to move everything.'

'Shit. Well, in any case we all need to get the hell out of this cave.'

'Not so fast, you don't.' Everybody's heads turned. An elderly man suddenly appeared out of the darkness. He was carrying a cane in one hand and a torch in the other. He was panting breathlessly. He sounded like a myocardial infarction waiting to happen.

'Who the hell are you?' James bellowed.

The man patiently caught his breath. He looked up at the gathered crowd of onlookers staring at him from within the cave den. 'I am Paul Ross, and your little charade is over. You're all going to die.'

Then six men stepped forth and burst into view from behind him. They were dressed in black fatigues and held submachine guns out in front of them.

'It's over' he repeated. 'Make your farewells. You, and your pathetic little cure, are done.'

*

One of the men stepped forth in front of Ross. 'First thing's first. Who's packing?'

James and Tiffanny involuntarily glanced at each other. The gesture caught the eye of the man and it was enough to give their game way. He waved them forward. 'On the floor, nice and slow. Kick them over.'

The pair reluctantly obliged and the Glocks skitted across the granite floor towards the men.

Another man retrieved them and threw them away out of sight.

'Is this all of you?' Ross demanded.

Nobody spoke. Ross jabbed his cane in the air and one of the men stepped through to the den. He checked every corner of the den and rounded up a few scientists who had cowered away in the corner. Some of them were visibly shaking. They knew they were about to die and had resigned to their inevitable fate.

'Up against that wall, in a line. Now. Come on, we don't have much time. The clock is ticking.'

People began to sob as they shuffled into a line as instructed. The men reloaded their MP5s and clicked off their safeties. One flick of a button and the guns were set for automatic fire – three round bursts. At this close range of several feet, one trigger pull would spell certain instant death for each recipient.

'That your nuke in there?' James asked of Ross.

The old timer stepped forward and waved his cane again. 'It could never be traced back to me.'

'So that's a yes then?' Chartier chided.

Ross took another step forward. He kept his eyes on James, although he appeared to be addressing the group as a whole. 'You know, I used to be like you at your age. So full of balls and panache. Desperate to save the world, and terrified of my own mortality.

'A man in his twenties is in his prime. He has everything to look forward to. Every minute of every day counts, so that he may prove himself. A man in his thirties has calmed somewhat, and his paternal clock has begun ticking. He wants to produce good offspring so that he can carry on the family line. So he marries and has children.

'A man in his forties approaches middle age. He has seen his children grow into men. A man in his fifties loses his appetite for love and sex and war. He feels himself becoming surplus to requirements.

'A man in his sixties has seen and done it all. He has laboured for the best part of forty years. Now he retires and takes what he has learned into a heightened state of moral indifference. He has accepted his fate and becomes disturbingly pacifistic towards his own mortality.

'A man in his seventies begins to feel like he is living on borrowed time. Things start to go wrong anatomically. Systems shut down or fail. Living deteriorates and is demoted to existing.

'A man in his eighties is grateful for every gasp of air his lungs can enjoy. Life is a gift now. A treat. A bonus. Well, I have lived through all of these milestones, believe me, I know. I know what you all feel. You're all desperate to feel important in this diverse world of six billion souls. You want to make a difference. But trust me folks – you can't.

'My industry turns over billions of dollars every year. What do you think would happen if suddenly that money wasn't invested in my drugs? I'll tell you what – there'd be a serious economic deficit, and that money would have to come from somewhere else. And you know exactly where it would have to come from. The taxpayers.

'Prices would increase tenfold in the blink of an eye. Petrol, cigarettes, alcohol, anything that carries value added tax. The global economy would collapse. Anarchy would ensue. Terrorists would be laughing the world over. The Earth would be theirs for the taking. So spare me your sanctimonious horseshit. I told the stem cell nutjobs the same thing.'

'Thanks for the speech' James spat. 'But we can make a difference. You know why? Because lives mean more than pennies or pounds. And with this, with B17, we can save billions of lives as well as pounds. This will be nothing less than a revolution.'

Paul Ross laughed. It seemed to sap a great deal of his strength and for a minute he seemed to buckle under the effort. But he soon composed himself.

Addressing James directly, he said 'When a man is young he is usually a revolutionary of some kind, so here I am speaking of my revolution. You know who said that, James? Wyndham Lewis.

'James, you think of yourself as a revolutionary. But really you're just a lawyer who was in the wrong place at the wrong time. You're quite pathetic really.

'A man of your age should be in his prime. You're facing divorce and unemployment. And now death. What will read on your epithet? Here lies

James Loxbridge. That's it! What's more to say?! Another nobody soon to be long forgotten.'

'What about the two people you murdered in Paris? What will read on their epithets?'

Ross grunted. 'They weren't as innocent as you have been made to believe. They worked for me. But they were bent. They were believers in your pathetic little cure too. So I had to clean up.'

'The man in the tanned jacket? He killed them, right?'

'Yes, James. His name was Chaplin and he was like a son to me. But you took him away from me. Which is why I'm here now. If Chaplin were here, I wouldn't have even dignified you with my presence. I'd have let the nuke do the talking, and you wouldn't have had any explanations. But you went and made it very personal when you killed my boy.'

'Your boy was a psychopathic killer who tried to rape me' Tiffanny spat. 'I want you to know that I really enjoyed putting that animal out of his misery.'

*

2:52 p.m.

0: 36: 16

James stared at their oppressors. Paul Ross was looking tired. 'Let's get this over with. My men and I need to be back on a chopper before that nuke blows.' He waved his cane a third time and the men cocked their weapons. Tiffanny embedded her head in her mother's arms. Radka backed to the wall and paced frantically. Everybody was terrified.

'Wait' James said. 'I need to make one last phone call.'

Paul Ross frowned. 'What? Whatever the hell for? What difference does it make?'

'That's personal. But you owe me that much.'

Ross looked at his men, who waited for his command, their fingers easing around their trigger cages.

'Fine' he said. 'But be quick. Thirty minutes and this cave is history.'

James reached slowly into his trouser pocket. All flashlights were on him. He plucked the cell phone out between his index and forefingers and flicked open the clamshell. With his thumb he slid off the back panel to reveal the battery and the SIM card. Nothing happened.

It was now or never. Do or die. There was nobody James could call, or wanted to call, because everybody that he had ever cared about was already by his side. Radka. Tiffanny.

It had to be quick and it had to be accurate. Collins has warned him not to tamper with the phone, for it was rigged with a small charge of C4 which would render the user without a head if the internal mechanism was sabotaged.

James had to believe that Collins had told him the truth. He had to believe that it had not been a crude mistruth in order to dissuade James from alerting the authorities when Radka had first been kidnapped. An *all talk and no action* altercation.

Time slowed down to a painful slow motion. It merged with space and produced a haphazard blur.

He suddenly threw the cell phone at the rock where Ross and his men were stationed. It shattered and exploded. The scientists hit the deck instinctively. James propelled himself forward towards the blast, as shards of rock and dust flew in a lacklustre myriad of directions.

The blast had killed Ross and most of his men, severely wounding the rest. But one of them managed to squeeze off a three-round burst of fire, and the bullets ricocheted off the internal façade like pinballs.

'Stay down!' James bellowed. He found one of the Glocks on the floor and emptied the chamber into Ross' men. The C4 blast had disturbed the solitude of Planinska Cave.

'James' a woman's voice called out. 'Get over here. It's Casino.'

James followed the sound of Radka's voice. Collins was lying on the floor. His whole abdomen was covered in deep crimson. 'The shots. They all hit him!' Tiffanny cried.

Collins was gazing up at the roof with preternatural defeat written across his brow. He was mumbling to himself.

James bent over him. 'Casino. It's over. We have to get out. The bomb...'

Collins was still mumbling. James lent closer and put his ear to the entrepreneur's mouth. 'The...cure...the...cure' he was saying, over and over, like a stuck music record.

'I know Casino, but it's too late. It's over. The pharmaceutical upper echelons won, again. We can't take this with us. We'll have to start again from scratch. We can do that if we all manage to get out. We have the world's best scientists and pharmacologists here. We can make a difference again, another day.'

Collins was shaking his head. He was still mumbling. But now he was trying to say something different. It was incoherent and James couldn't quite make it out. It sounded like...*letterbox. In my letterbox.* What the hell?

Then the mumbling ceased. James tried to revive Collins, but it was too late. He was littered with lead and mercury. His heart had stopped. He was dead.

Radka prised James away and they followed Monique through an archway where Ross had come from, clambering over his dead body and those of his men.

Monique led them to the base of a beautiful stalagmite. 'Look' she said. 'Here.'

They pinpointed their flashlights at where Monique was pointing. There was a large device on a metal gurney with a digital LED counting down a timer.

0: 27: 01

'Is there any way to disarm it?' one of the scientists asked näively.

His colleague duly responded. 'Don't be absurd, Frederick. We are scientists, not bomb disposal technicians.'

'No' James said. 'Leave it. We need to get to safety.' They ran through the narrow passageways back to the makeshift subway station. Once through the antechamber they found the cave train waiting to take them to their extraction point on the surface.

They dived into the train and James hit a button on the head carriage and the train whirred to life. The ride lasted several minutes and they ascended several hundred feet back to the surface.

Pierre gazed upwards at the rock formations. 'I was so caught up in our mission, I never stopped to seriously consider how beautiful this place really is. And now it's all been for nothing. I faked my own disappearance, cut my sister out of my life, and what for? For nothing, all for nothing.'

'When that nuke goes off, this place will be ruined' Radka curtly observed. 'Thousands of years of natural history, destroyed. Man at it again. Typical.'

James thought about Chartier's assessment. What he didn't know was how it had inadvertently ruined Didier's life too. And now Didier was gone. James paused for thought and took a moment to remember all the people who had fallen for this cause. There was Fabien, the waiter at Café Kléber in Paris. And Camille, the receptionist at Hotel Magenta. Then Didier. Now Casino Collins. And who else that he didn't know about? Were there other casualties and fatalities of this war on cancer?

When they reached the surface they burst out of the cave. The afternoon sunlight burned their retinas and scorched their skins. It was a welcome relief from the darkness and the death.

They clambered inside Collins' Landcruiser. Some of the scientists sat on the loadbed at the rear. The Toyota opened out at the back like a pickup truck, accommodating the entire group. The scientists appeared to be terminally despondent. They had dedicated a secret second life to a cause that now appeared in tatters.

James commandeered the Japanese offroader back towards the airfield where Collins had met them. When they arrived, there was no Lear jet. But there was a hulking black helicopter – Ross' Bell.

'And who knows how to pilot that thing?' one of the scientists barked sardonically.

James already knew the answer to that question. Radka had taken flying lessons before they had met.

'I flew light aircraft, James. I've never touched a helicopter before.'

'The principle is the same' he remarked. 'You can do it.'

They piled into the chopper. The cabin was small and they were forced to sit on each other like frightened sardines in a tin can. Radka found a pilot's manual inside a box below the dashboard and read frantically.

'Come on, Radka! We don't have much time. That thing is primed to blow any minute now!'

'I know, I know! I'm trying.'

The Czech flicked dials and lifted levers, checking off everything she did against the instructions in the flight manual.

The rotor blades whirred to life and picked up oscillation speed. She lifted the throttle and the bird hovered a few metres off the ground. The cabin shook and the passengers held on for dear life.

Radka pulled back on the throttle ever more and the Bell took to the Slovene skies.

James was studying maps to find a direction and a destination when the ground shook violently beneath them.

'There it goes' he said. They had an aerial bird's eye view of the cave as it suddenly collapsed in on itself. A small mushroom cloud rose up from the apex and hissed up towards the chopper. Dust and debris sprayed into the air as if a volcano had been triggered.

Radka steered them clear of harm's way as the Bell punctured the afternoon azure sky and pincered away from Postojna. Tiffanny glanced down at the landscape. A flock of birds darted towards them, disturbed by the sudden explosion.

'I can't believe we failed' she said. 'I really thought this was our turn. Our time.'

The scientists stared down as if looking into the abyss. Some of them cried. Most were relieved to be alive. Technically they were dead, or missing. They were now absolved of their responsibilities and were free to begin new lives. They could be anything they wanted, although for most science was all that they knew.

But it wasn't meant to be. The Frenchwoman was right. They had failed. The pharmaceutical giants had won favour, again. The cards had been dealt, and the hands won. Unity Six had folded. Ross' legacy had trumped everything.

James returned to the maps and helped Radka plot a course for the Czech Republic. It was, after all, his second home. Tiffanny collapsed into his arms, numb with exhaustion and relief, and went to sleep. And the world turned. Just like it had before. Just like it would continue to do. And for the lucky ones, life would go on unabated.

Epilogue

Chester, England. Three months later.

The man moved like he had never moved before. Puddles of sweat dripped down his face. His eyes were wide in concentration, and determination. He was bent forward, his triceps bulging with the effort. He was running out of time. The digital readout in front of him counted down; red glowing numbers glaring back at him. Reminding him.

He had to beat it. He couldn't fail. His pride was too strong. Twenty seconds. The other man was stood next to him. He shouted. 'Come on! You're not going to make it at this rate!' He smiled devilishly, as if he was enjoying watching the other man strain his entire body in effort.

Fifteen seconds. It was going to be a close call. Both men felt the adrenaline and the testosterone fuel their eagerness. Ten seconds, then five. The final countdown. Three. Two. One. Both men braced. Then there was a bleeping sound. It was over.

'Damnit!' James Loxbridge stopped pedalling and recaptured his breath. He gulped from a water bottle.

'You're out of shape, James. I'll have to move you back down the board with that time, buddy.'

James climbed off the exercise bike. 'Don't sweat it, Matt. I'll get it back.'

Matt the personal trainer grunted. 'I don't doubt it. That's enough for today. Take a shower.'

James took an ice cold shower. Summer had arrived in England, and it was a hot, humid day full of promise.

James dressed in jeans and a t-shirt and headed home. 16 Albion Place was home. But it wouldn't be for much longer. The tenancy agreement would expire in three weeks, and he wasn't renewing his contract.

His divorce from Radka Rosická had been finalised. She had returned to Brno. Upon his return from Slovenia he had been flooded with emails from the Law College. He'd missed his students' revision tutorship for their midterm exams. The college had been left with no option but to dismiss him for incapability – a potentially fair reason for dismissal under the Employment Rights Act 1996. They had acted reasonably and followed fair procedures, so there was nothing to be gained in appealing against their decision.

Besides, James needed a change of pace, and a change of scenery. Pushing thirty, what did he have to show for it? Paul Ross had been right about him – he was divorced, single, unemployed, and soon to be homeless.

Tiffanny had returned to Strasbourg to get to know her parents – the parents whom she believed had died in a plane crash fifteen years ago. She had left James her number, but begged him not to use it right away, at least not for the next few months. She had been through a terrifying ordeal at the hands of the man in the tanned jacket, the man known as Chaplin, and she needed to distance herself. With Collins dead, she had confirmed that no inquiry would be made into the Aequitol scandal. It had been an empty threat in any case, she revealed.

Tiffanny also explained that she had at one point in Paris seriously doubted his ability to keep it together. Collins had been worried that he would put two and two together and realise that her passion for the cause was borne from her own dice with the disease. She told James that when she had been on the Eiffel Tower she had contacted him to confirm that he was none the wiser.

A French pathologist had told James that Chaplin had an inoperable brain tumour and would have died soon after the events of that winter regardless. James did not pass this information on to Tiffanny – it would have been no consolation to her, as the tumour would not have prevented him from raping her.

His house on Albion Place was threadbare. All his possessions were piled up in cardboard boxes. Three weeks, and he was out of there. He would miss his Chester life; he'd miss the memories of his time with Radka the most. Strangely enough he'd also miss the daily walks down the canal in peaceful solitude after she had left him, as he passed the drawbridge and greeted the peacock and the donkeys which belonged to the adjacent farm.

Many of his belongings would be donated to charity; his old clothes and the books he had read as a child; the Enid Blytons and the Roald Dahls, Franklin W Dixon's The Hardy Boys. The rest would be stored away in his mother's loft in Ashby de la Zouch, Leicestershire.

It was time to take a career break. He had decided to go backpacking. He had bought a round the world plane ticket for two thousand pounds. Eleven countries in four months. He had some soul searching to do. He had loved Radka dearly, but it had fizzled out like a firework dying in the night sky. He had fallen for Tiffanny, but that had never taken off the ground for reasons understandable.

He had read about the TEFL course – Teach English as a Foreign Language. He wanted to disappear into the wilderness and then do something rewarding and fulfilling. He had heard of a sudden demand for English teachers in South Korea and Japan.

The events of the previous winter had become all but a blur to him. Only one aspect remained – when Casino Collins lay dying inside Planinska Cave, as blood bubbles formed around his lips, he had mumbled his final revelation to James. *It's…in…my…letterbox* he had said.

James called up Radka to explain.

'I'm trying to put it behind me, James. Why are you dredging up that mess again? Leave it be.'

'But Radka, you told me that when Chartier explained Unity Six's legacy to you, he said that they had already made up one single batch, and it was in a very safe place. Your job was to turn it into a mass output endeavour.'

Radka sighed down the line. 'So?'

'So, Collins' last words to me were: *It's in my letterbox*. What the hell does that mean?'

'I have no idea, James.'

'Do you think he meant it literally? Meaning, he kept it at his residential abode?'

'James, for Christ's sake, just put it to bed.'

'Radka, I know I have been unkind to you. I do. But I need your help with one last thing. One final favour. I know you don't owe it to me; you don't owe me a God damn thing, but I'm begging you.'

Again, the Czech sighed vehemently. 'And if I do this, then you will leave me alone? I don't want to ever hear from you again. You understand? No contact, whatsoever. You disappear from my world, just like Chartier and my parents did. Deal?'

James nodded, even though the gesture was meaningless for a telephone call. 'Deal.' Then he told her what he wanted her to do.

She called him back two hours later. 'It wasn't easy. I had to hack into all kinds of confidential places.'

'How did you find him?'

'I'm not telling. Trade secrets.'

'Fair enough, I don't deserve that information anyway.

'No James, you don't.'

'So?'

Radka gave him the address. Collins had lived in North London, between Uxbridge and West Drayton.

James took a train down to Victoria and then found a bus that would take him where he needed to be.

He arrived at a Victorian house in a sleepy suburb and checked the address against the one Radka had given. It was the right place. But James hadn't really thought through his plan. What was he supposed to do, break in?'

It's in my letterbox. A very safe place. James checked the gold brass letterbox. The front door was painted black and the awning white. It was a billionaire's home, for sure.

There was nothing wedged inside the letterbox, unsurprisingly. James disagreed with the now deceased Collins – this wasn't a very safe place at all. If not a thief, then his family members or the executors of his vast estate would inevitably be searching the house in order to divvy up his belongings in line with vested interests in his trust assets. A billionaire's assets – the vultures would soon be circling for their pickings.

A neighbour saw him stood on the step and came outside. 'Hello there' he shouted from his porch step.

James turned around. 'Hello there' he responded.

'You want to look inside?' the elderly man asked. He was a sprightly fellow clad in tweed and his puppy fat paunched out of his trousers as he waddled over.

'You want to take a peek at a billionaire's home?' he said again. 'I have a spare key. He used to let me feed his cat when he was away. He was always away. Billionaire's lifestyle being what it is. Conferences, public events, charity balls. He was seldom here.'

The man extended his hand and James shook it. The man introduced himself as Gregory. Gregory was a retiree.

James entered the house at Gregory's behest and the old man told him to holler when he was done. Gregory then returned to his own home.

James searched every room from end to end, top to bottom. He used gloves so as not to leave fingerprints and he diligently placed everything back where it belonged.

He didn't know precisely what he was looking for, but he guessed he would know once he found it. Would it be in tablet form? Or a liquid? Something to be injected? Would it be pre-packaged? Would there be a brand name for B17? A logo? Perhaps the tattoo that Chartier had worn on his arm was the logo – a crab pierced by a sword – cancer being eradicated, once and for all. The ultimate panacea. If only.

He knew that if Collins was right, and there was one single batch made up, then Unity Six's legacy would not have been in vain. They would be halfway there. Any pharmacologist worth his salt could use a ready made sample, break it down into its constituent components, and replicate the product on a grander scale.

But James found nothing. He spent two hours there, and yet all he found were the innocent everyday items kept in living rooms, dining rooms, kitchens and studies.

Utterly dismayed, he rode the train back to Chester. He thought about telling Radka that he had failed. But she had been quite adamant on their last telephone call – no contact, whatsoever. So he called it quits and respected her wishes.

In three weeks he was flying out to Dubai, and then onto Singapore. From there he would visit Thailand, Cambodia, Vietnam and Laos, along the Indo-China loop. Then he'd go Oriental and see South Korea and Japan. His next destination would be Australia, and New Zealand. The world was there, waiting for him, turning on its axis as it had done before and as it always would do.

Three days before his flight to Dubai from Heathrow, he was sat in the small den at 16 Albion Place, soaking up the last remnants of its memories and his. He thought back over the week that had shook the fibre of his very being, beginning with Radka's kidnapping, continuing with a wild goose chase across the hinterlands of France, and concluding in a Slovene cave. It beggared belief.

And the remaining clue remained unsolved. *It's in my letterbox.* What the devil had Collins meant?

And then it dawned on him. *A very safe place.* He collapsed on the settee, flabbergasted. *Of course. The perfect place to hide it. A very safe place. My letterbox.*

James went to the stack of boxes and began frantically unloading them. *Where was it? Did I keep it or throw it out?* He rifled through his belongings in a haphazard manner. Everything would need to be repacked now. A van had been hired and was coming tomorrow to transport his things to Leicestershire.

He found it in a pile underneath the kitchen table. He counted back the weeks in his head and calculated the day it had all kicked off. Monday 20 February. He found the issue of the Chester

Chronicle from that day and scoured the pages for the article he had read that day three months ago.

He did not have to look far – it had made the front page and continued on page twelve. The article about billionaire entrepreneur and philanthropist Casino Collins. He had donated another hefty wad to NASA for their next mission. He had wanted to leave a keepsake up there. He wanted first dibs on real estate up there. He had certainly had the green to make it happen. The headline, 'Space-ious Accommodation You Can't Afford!', like a mockery of an estate agent's ad. James read for the second time the article in full. NASA had teamed up with construction giant Caterpillar to set in motion the idea of creating civilised communities, kick starting Neil Armstrong's legacy forty years after his giant leap for mankind and his first steps into a brave new world.

The clever people at NASA had figured it all out, right down to the infrastructure, down to the launch and landing pads required, to the irrigation of roads, to water and sanitation systems. It was the next giant leap for mankind. Armstrong would have been proud.

And then James rediscovered the paragraph that explained the entrepreneur's final legacy. Collins' keepsake was to be an suburban-American style mailbox stuck in the grey sand like the US flagpole already erected, labelled *Collins*, marking his territory, establishing him as the very first citizen. James had sniggered the first time he had read the article. It had all seemed so bold and far-fetched. But he wasn't laughing now.

My letterbox. A very safe place. Collins had been right – it was a very safe place. A place known to everyone, but one only a handful of people could ever reach. Collins had left the last batch of B17, cancer cure, in the one place where it could only ever be truly safe.

On the moon.

Author's Note

The book *Cancer: Why We're Still Dying To Know The Truth* is real, and was written by Phillip Day, first published in 1999, not Pierre Chartier, whose character is fictional.

Day's book has received cult status in recent years, and is well worth a read. Concurrently it was the main source of inspiration for this story. Everything contained in this story about vitamin B17 is accurate, and in fact the B17 action diagram appears indiscriminately across the passages of cyberspace. So if you do search for it, you'll have as much luck getting a Googlewhack as James Loxbridge did!

I have been lucky enough to step foot in all cities and countries referred to in the story, and as such these places were described from my own memories. I have stayed at the Hotel Magenta in Paris – it is fantastic. The caves of Postojna, Slovenia are incredibly beautiful and well worth a visit.

James Loxbridge's love for Pearl Jam's music mirrors my own. There was once a Radka Rosická in my life, and for a very brief time it seemed that there might have been a Tiffanny Tourneux. So aside from the plot, this book was a way for me to chronicle my own experiences between 2005-2009.

My thanks to Karl Bowers for a superbly designed front cover.

Michael Hollin.

Lightning Source UK Ltd.
Milton Keynes UK
UKOW04f1933241114

242094UK00001BA/4/P